"We need to set so...

"So you're sitting next to me?" Zach asked.

"I am," Paige confirmed.

"Worried I'm going to go for a replay of last night in the bar?"

A tremor of that incident rumbled through her body. "Zach. Come on. Please stop messing with me."

"I'm not. No matter what happened last night or this morning, I'm determined that you and I will be friends. I'll respect your boundaries. You said you don't want anything to do with me and that's fine."

"I don't think I put it that way. Did I?"

"You said it was just sex. And I said that I didn't understand what the problem was with just sex. That was the beginning of the end."

"You want to be friends?"

"I do."

"Okay. Then let's be friends. Just friends. That's it."

"I can live with that. For now."

An excerpt from *One Wild Wedding Weekend* by Janice Maynard

"Let's get one thing straight. You and I are *not* going to be family.

"John and I? Yes. You and Tabby? Yes. But not you and me," Daley said.

Tristan studied her. "You have something against family?"

"Of course not. But you and I are..."

"Are what?"

Before she was forced to answer, the server appeared and they ordered.

"Let's get back to you, Daley. I think you were saying you and I are...?"

"Strangers," she said firmly. "Only tangentially related by marriage. There's no connection at all."

"Liar. We've had a connection since day one. Surely you can't deny that."

"We don't get along. We're oil and water. I wouldn't define that as a *connection*."

His thumb settled on her pulse at the back of her wrist. "Maybe you and I see things differently then."

"Maybe." When he released her, she told herself she wasn't disappointed.

KAREN BOOTH

&

USA TODAY BESTSELLING AUTHOR

JANICE MAYNARD

———

THEIR AFTER HOURS PLAYBOOK
&
ONE WILD WEDDING WEEKEND

HARLEQUIN

DESIRE

Recycling programs for this product may not exist in your area.

ISBN-13: 978-1-335-45783-7

Their After Hours Playbook & One Wild Wedding Weekend

Copyright © 2023 by Harlequin Enterprises ULC

Their After Hours Playbook
Copyright © 2023 by Karen Booth

One Wild Wedding Weekend
Copyright © 2023 by Janice Maynard

For questions and comments about the quality of this book, please contact us at CustomerService@Harlequin.com.

Harlequin Enterprises ULC
22 Adelaide St. West, 41st Floor
Toronto, Ontario M5H 4E3, Canada
www.Harlequin.com

Printed in U.S.A.

CONTENTS

Karen Booth is a Midwestern girl transplanted in the South, raised on '80s music and repeated readings of *Forever...* by Judy Blume. When she takes a break from the art of romance, she's listening to music with her grown-up kids or sweet-talking her husband into making her a cocktail. Learn more about Karen at karenbooth.net.

Books by Karen Booth

Harlequin Desire

Their After Hours Playbook

Little Black Book of Secrets

The Problem with Playboys
Black Tie Bachelor Bid
How to Fake a Wedding Date

The Sterling Wives

Once Forbidden, Twice Tempted
High Society Secrets
All He Wants for Christmas

Visit the Author Profile page
at Harlequin.com for more titles.

You can also find Karen Booth on Facebook,
along with other Harlequin Desire authors,
at Facebook.com/HarlequinDesireAuthors!

Dear Reader,

I can hardly believe it, but this is my final book for Harlequin Desire. I'm a bit of an emotional wreck thinking about this incredible journey! It started when editor Patience Bloom asked if I might be interested in submitting to Harlequin. Two years later, in 2015, *That Night with the CEO* came out. It was such an amazing moment. I went on to write twenty-seven more books for Desire. There have been plucky heroines, secret babies, surprise pregnancies and more CEOs than I can count! Along the way, I had so much support. The entire editorial staff at Harlequin has been magnificent. My agent, Melissa Jeglinski, has always had my back. And my fellow Desire authors have been my rocks. I'm so grateful.

I hope you enjoy *Their After Hours Playbook*. It's a fun and emotional story of two people who fit together perfectly, even if their worlds don't. It's got a great happy ending. As it should.

Drop me a line at karen@karenbooth.net and let me know if you enjoyed *Their After Hours Playbook*. I've got more books to come, and I love hearing from readers!

Karen

THEIR AFTER HOURS
PLAYBOOK

Karen Booth

For Stacy Boyd.
Through secret babies, surprise pregnancies and CEOs, thank you for letting me be part of Harlequin Desire. It has meant the world to me.

One

Zach Armstrong's manifesto was nearly complete. Fifty-seven tightly written pages, along with twenty-four supplemental graphs and diagrams. It was a road map to push Armstrong Sports into the twenty-first century and catapult them past the competition. Implementing this wasn't going to be easy, but he was the CEO now. The boss. He'd been waiting his entire life for a chance like this.

With more than eighty employees, including thirty agents, several hundred athlete clients and a luxe, sprawling office in Midtown Manhattan, it was a massive responsibility. *Everyone* was counting on him for their livelihood. It wasn't bravado, but he welcomed the challenge. He thrived on pressure, long hours and hard work. And the fact that his job brought together the three things he loved most in the world—sports, being an agent and his family—was all the inspiration and encouragement he would ever need.

Zach's admin, Teri, stepped into the doorway of his office. Tall and trim, she wore her brown hair in a chin-length bob and seemed to always dress in gray. Zach had worked with her from his first days in the marketing department, when Teri showed him the ropes for a few years until he transitioned to being an agent. It was only right that Zach brought her along when he moved into the executive offices. "Is there anything else I can do for you before you head over to the draft?" Teri leaned against the doorjamb and crossed her arms over her chest.

He glanced at the time on his computer screen. The Women's Professional Basketball Association, or WPBA, draft was set to happen in a little over an hour. "The day flew by. I've got to get going soon." His vision swiftly returned to his work. He felt a tug deep in the center of his chest. He could hone this document for hours. That's how strongly he believed in his mission, but also how much he knew it had to be perfect.

"I still can't believe you're doing this, but I'm glad you are. I'm glad you're dragging this agency out of the Stone Age." Teri had worked for Armstrong for nearly twenty years. She started a good decade before Zach arrived. She was well aware of how things around there never seemed to change. Case in point—in the entire history of the firm, less than one percent of their clients had been female athletes.

"Growth requires progress and change, and I'm determined to grow our agency. The way I see it, I owe it to my dad." Zach's father was actually his stepdad, Tom Armstrong, who, until three weeks ago, had been the CEO of the company.

Teri walked into Zach's office and nodded at one of the chairs in front of his desk. "May I?"

"Of course."

She took a seat and crossed her legs. "Is that how you plan to sell all of this to Tom? As a growth strategy?" She cocked an eyebrow.

"The fact that I'm going to the draft?"

"No one from our agency has ever attended the event. Tom doesn't know you're going, does he?"

Zach shook his head and shut down his computer, then organized some folders on his desk. "No. He does not."

"Zach, this thing is nationally televised. What if a camera catches you? Then everyone will know what you're up to."

It was ridiculous that this part of Zach's plan might be deemed in any way controversial, but this was where he found himself. Zach's stepdad, Tom, had always professed that it only made "smart fiscal sense" to focus on male athletes since they historically made more money in sports. Tom wasn't wrong about that, but times were changing, and Zach was intent on creating a far more diverse client roster. This was about building resiliency within their company. If they didn't, Armstrong might be left behind like the dinosaur it was quickly becoming.

"Hopefully no one will spot me on TV. And if they do, then I'll deal with it. I'm having dinner with my mom and Tom tomorrow night. I'm presenting my plan to him then."

"How do you think he's going to take it?"

Despite Zach's rules-be-damned approach, he was still unsure how this would all go. Certainly Tom would pick apart the economics of Zach's idea to go outside their current business model. Plus, Zach was under strict orders not to upset Tom, lest his blood pressure get out of whack. "I'm going in armed with numbers. Lots and lots of numbers. With the amount of dollar signs attached, he'll listen."

"Good. He'll like that aspect of things, I'm sure. Are you also going to tell him that you want to hire more women agents, too?"

"Absolutely. Of course, it'll be a lot easier if you tell me that I can mention you as one of our new agents."

"Oh, no. I'm happy being support staff in the executive offices. I'm not a shark like you."

"I'm not a shark, Teri. I'm more of a honey badger."

"Cute and fuzzy on the outside, but will do anything and everything to get what you want?"

He laughed quietly. "Precisely. I do not care what stands in my way."

"I'm sure that's what Tom loves most about you being in charge," Teri said.

Zach hoped that proved to be true. Although Tom

wasn't his biological dad, Zach thought of him that way. He was the only father Zach had ever known. And he'd also been an incredible husband to Zach's mom, who'd married Tom when Zach was only two years old. "I guess we'll see, huh?"

"We sure will." Teri straightened in her seat. "I'd wish you good luck, but something tells me you'll do just fine in a room full of women."

Zach laughed as he wrote himself a few notes in his planner for tomorrow. He did have a reputation for turning on the charm, but it was never anything intentional. It was just the way he was. It wasn't his fault that women were drawn to him. Nor was it his fault that he often used that to his advantage. "A few women might not be super happy to see me there."

"Let me guess. Paige Moss?"

"Tom never liked her. And apparently the feeling was mutual." Tom's advice rang loudly in his head. *Watch out for Paige Moss. She's a pit viper.* Zach had never understood why Tom disliked Paige or her agency so much, but Tom had a poor opinion of other agents. They were *all* the enemy. Zach didn't see it that way. Yes, they were competition, but Zach felt it was best practice to know everyone and play nice when possible. You never knew when a sliver of kindness might pay a dividend. And if you eventually had to screw someone over, hopefully they'd remember that you weren't *all* bad. "I should probably get out of here." He got up from his desk.

"Good luck. I expect a full report tomorrow." Teri rose from her chair, then led them out into the hall.

Zach splintered off from Teri and strode down the corridor, nodding and waving to his employees in their individual offices. A few people offered thin smiles, although their newest agent, Derek James, grinned from ear to ear as he paced his office, talking on the phone. Derek was hungry. He was eager to learn and climb the ladder of success. Zach liked Derek. Even if he could be a bit much sometimes. Some people in the office delivered an expression closer to a sneer. Not everyone was excited about Zach's promotion. Some people resented him. After all, Zach was only thirty years old and there were some agents who'd worked at Armstrong for nearly as long as Zach had been alive. But Zach couldn't let the chilly reception of a few dissuade him. He'd win them all over eventually.

He took the elevator down to the ground floor of their building and started the fifteen- or twenty-minute walk to the hotel where the draft was taking place. It was a beautiful April day, and Zach appreciated the chance to get outside for a few minutes, even though the sidewalk on 45th Street was jam-packed with people. He'd been cooped up in the office all day, and even he could admit that he'd been working too hard. He navigated the pedestrian congestion of Times Square and crossed Broadway to reach the hotel. As he looked up at the tower of glass and steel above him, he took a deep breath and reminded himself that he was on the precipice of making change, and that was a good thing.

Inside, Zach rode the escalator up to the third

floor, then looped the all-access pass he'd obtained through a friend in the WPBA league offices around his neck. He ventured into the ballroom where the draft was taking place and began winding his way under rows of balloon arches while masses of people filtered inside. Dance music thumped through speakers and a festive feeling was in the air. It was like arriving at a New Year's Eve party. Not a work event. At one end of the space was a large stage adorned with a WPBA backdrop and podium. Before it were dozens of round tables for the top projected picks, as well as their families and agents. The perimeter of the room was ringed with bleachers brimming with fans, while reporters milled about, talking to draft prospects as they waited for the proceedings to begin.

Zach's plan was simple—work the room, talk to as many players as he could, and congratulate them and their families. He would acknowledge their hard work and dedication. He'd make sure they knew his name and that Armstrong Sports was ready to jump with both feet into women's sports. He was about to get started when he spotted Paige Moss chatting with her star client, Alexis Simmons, who was projected to go number one in the draft. He knew he was supposed to fear Paige, but he didn't have it in him, mostly because her dangerous curves, which were all wrapped up in a sinful black dress, were impossible to ignore. Her glossy blond locks were pulled up in a high ponytail that wagged back and forth as she talked, like she was brandishing a whip.

They'd never met, but he'd seen her in lots of photos. She was even more beautiful in person. Sexy. Tempting. A lesser man might avoid her, but not Zach. As soon as he made his way through the rest of the room, he was going to face the opposition head-on. And he sure as hell was going to enjoy the view while he did.

Paige Moss had every reason to be on top of the world tonight. Her client Alexis Simmons, one of the most talented point guards to ever bring a basketball up the court, was likely going to go number one in the WPBA draft. But it was the *likely* part that put her on edge. A lot of things hadn't gone well for Paige in the last few years, personally and professionally— her divorce, her feud with Tom Armstrong and, most recently, the passing of Paige's inspiration: her mom. Paige really wished she could have a guarantee tonight. Unfortunately, there were none of those in the world of professional sports agenting.

"Why do you seem so nervous? I should be the one who's nervous." Alexis tapped away at her phone with her acrylic nails. She didn't wear them during basketball season because she was too much of a battler, but she embraced them when it was time to dress up. Paige could hardly blame her. Alexis looked like a model—tall and trim, with long black braids, high cheekbones and a flawless warm brown complexion. Her nails were simply the perfect touch.

Paige put her arm around her client's shoulders and gave them a quick squeeze. "I'm not nervous.

I'm just excited for you. This is all of your hard work coming to fruition. I hope you can appreciate that although this is a big moment in the spotlight, it's only the first of many."

Alexis smiled. "Thank you, Paige. Thank you for being there for me. I will never forget it."

"No need to thank me. Just doing my job." Of course, to Paige, being a sports agent was so much more than that. It was an all-consuming career, and she couldn't imagine ever doing anything else. She loved sports, but more importantly, she loved women in sports. And she owed all of that to her mom.

Paige turned to survey the room and that was when she spotted a man who made her do a double take, and not just because he was unreasonably handsome. Either her eyes were deceiving her or that was Zach Armstrong. "What the hell is he doing here?" He had zero reason to be at this event.

Alexis looked up from her phone. "What? Who?"

Paige shook her head. Logic said that she should look away. Ignore Zach. But she couldn't peel her eyes off him. It was partly because he was *so* nice to look at, but mostly, she was so damn confused. Zach's agency didn't sign female athletes. "Just an agent who has no reason to be here."

"Who?"

Paige couldn't turn away. "Zach Armstrong. He's running Armstrong Sports, the most notoriously misogynistic agency in the history of sports."

"Hold up. I know that name. He sent me flowers."

That made Paige whip around to focus on Alexis. "Excuse me? He did what?"

Alexis shrugged. "He sent me flowers. The card said congratulations and wished me well for the future. But lots of people sent me flowers."

"Other agents?"

She tilted her head to the side, thinking about it. "No."

"Exactly." Paige felt frozen, while her blood was at a boil so fast it made her dizzy. *Take a breath, Paige. Take a damn breath.* "I'll be right back."

"I'm going to find my mom, then go sit at our table. Don't take too long. We've both worked too hard for you to miss my pick."

Paige grasped Alexis's arm. "I promise you. I will not miss it. I'll be back in five minutes." Paige turned on her heel and marched across the room. All she could think about were the insulting things Zach's stepdad, Tom, had said to her over the years. Now that Tom had been sidelined, did Zach think he could poach Alexis? Show up at the draft, tall and handsome and dressed in a suit that was tailored within an inch of his life, wearing a smug grin that said he was the crown prince of Armstrong Sports? What in the hell was he up to?

She came to a halt at a respectable distance, or more specifically, when she got a whiff of him that was so heavenly it made it hard to walk in heels. "You're Zach Armstrong." It wasn't a question.

"I am." His voice was rich with firm but warm tones.

"I'd be lying if I said I wasn't shocked to see you here."

"And you're Paige Moss. I'd be lying if I said I wasn't absolutely delighted to see you." He took a step closer. Between his shoulders and his considerable height, if felt like he blocked out all light in the room, but she caught the moment when his eyes were drawn to her neckline and he couldn't help but peer right down the front of her dress. So let him look. He wouldn't be the first man who'd become enamored by her breasts.

"Don't give me that. You're not delighted to see me."

The corner of his mouth quirked up in a wry half-smile. "Actually, I am. But okay."

"Why are you here? Are things so bad at Armstrong that you had to come for the open bar?"

He laughed and shook his head, which only drew attention to his alarmingly square jaw and the way his dark hair perfectly peppered it. When he focused on her again, it felt as though his steely blue-gray eyes were staring straight into her soul. Funny, but she'd felt a lot less exposed when he was staring at her chest. "I'm here because I'm changing the Armstrong playbook."

"Changing? In what way, exactly?"

"I'm taking us in new directions. Expanding our purview."

"You are aware that the athletes here tonight are women, right? Your agency doesn't venture into those waters. Your stepfather made sure of that."

"I'm in charge now."

"And you decided to start by stealing one of my clients?"

"I don't know what you're talking about."

She took a deep breath and inched closer to him, raising her chin and facing him head-on. "Do *not* send flowers to my client and think that I won't say anything. I have been building my relationship with Alexis and her family since she was in high school. I went to her games. I made sure her family knew who I was. I know her grandparents. I know her siblings. And I was there in college, keeping a respectful distance until she was ready to go pro."

"I sent her congratulatory flowers. Read the note. It doesn't say anything other than my name on it. I just want important women in sports knowing who I am. It's PR. Nothing sinister about it."

"If your agency was serious about this, you would have been courting the women in this room years ago. You would have been there for them from the very beginning." Paige hoped she didn't sound like she was on a soapbox, but she got fired up about this topic. She often put years into a client before taking them on.

"Paige, I know you don't appreciate my father's stance on women in sports or the shortsighted attitude that goes with it. So why be mad because I'm trying to change that?"

She *was* mad, but mostly because she felt so much resentment toward Tom. He'd sabotaged her in more ways than one over the years. "This whole thing just seems completely out of the blue."

"If I were you, I wouldn't worry about the timing. I'd worry about what another competitor will do to your business. Do you think you're up to the task? Can you take us on?"

Paige could not believe this was happening. She'd deplored Tom Armstrong's take on women in athletics, but she couldn't deny that not having to compete with him had only helped her. So much for that. "Take you on? I will smother you." For an instant, she wondered if he might enjoy being deprived of air by burying his face in her cleavage. But no. She had to not think things like that.

"Good to know I've got my work cut out for me."

"Speaking of work, I need to go. I need to sit with Alexis. The draft is going to start soon." She turned away, but didn't get far. Zach's hand grasped the bare skin of her forearm. Her eyes were instantly drawn to the sight of his strong fingers wrapped around her. Why did she have goose bumps? Why did his skin feel so good against hers?

"Paige. Hold on. Will I see you in Vegas?"

"Vegas?" She looked up, again vexed by his eyes.

"The Las Vegas Sports Expo? The biggest event of the year for agents? It's the best possible chance to land your clients those big endorsement deals and sponsorships everyone is chasing these days."

It was utterly humiliating that she hadn't realized what he was referring to, but she also felt as though she shouldn't be expected to know superfluous things like facts right now. Zach's touch was doing something to her. The thought was bothersome at best. Not only was Zach the enemy, he was a good decade younger than her. "Of course I'm going to Vegas."

"Great. Maybe we can grab a drink or dinner or something."

Paige felt a disconcerting wave of warmth between her legs. She needed to get away from Zach, ASAP. "I'm always very busy in Vegas," she lied. Often, Vegas was a disaster.

"Good for you."

The lights in the room darkened. Paige looked up. "I need to go. The draft is about to start."

He dropped her hand, which left behind a lasting tingle. "Good luck to your client, Paige. I'll see you in Vegas."

Lord, help me. "Yeah. Maybe." She rushed away from Zach and over to Alexis's table, taking the seat right next to her. "I told you I'd be here in time." Paige couldn't help but notice the way her words came out in a choppy fashion. She was struggling for breath. That was all Zach's fault.

"You know, I looked up Zach Armstrong on my phone while I was sitting here. His agency gets their athletes tons of endorsement deals," Alexis said. "Why have we never talked about that?"

"Because we've been so focused on getting this far. The last few years have all been about tonight."

"It seems like I should be able to get in on some of that. Especially if I end up getting drafted first."

Paige swallowed hard. Endorsements had never been her strong suit. But she was prepared to go the extra mile for Alexis. She was *that* special an athlete. She was that important as a client. "I couldn't agree more. That'll be my top priority at the Vegas Sports Expo. It's in two weeks."

"Perfect. I can't wait to find out what you can negotiate for me."

A spotlight appeared on the stage and the WPBA commissioner walked out onto the stage. Paige's heart felt as though it was about to pound its way out of her chest. Between handsome Zach Armstrong encroaching on her territory while simultaneously turning her on, and Alexis deserving the world, the pressure was absolutely on.

Two

Apparently, Zach Armstrong was big on sending flowers. Sitting in her office, bleary-eyed from last night's post-draft party, Paige admired the stunning white phalaenopsis orchids that had come from the luxury flower shop, Flora, here in Manhattan. Flora was owned and operated by socialite Alexandra Gold, who not only had an unrivaled flair for floral design, but also had impeccable taste. Everything that came from her shop was of the finest quality, including the linen-like paper of the enclosure card. Zach's message was simple. Direct. To the point. *Congratulations. Wishing you many more number one draft picks. Zach.*

Paige grumbled under her breath and took a much-needed sip of her latte. *He's up to something.* Zach had spared no expense, sending five tall stems, all of which arched from the weight of luscious tropical blooms. The orchids were elegantly nestled in a white ceramic vessel with pale gray polished stones and bright green moss accenting the base of the plant. Paige couldn't take her eyes off it. It was more than the fact that the plant was beautiful. This was *exactly* the sort of thing she would have chosen for herself. It coordinated perfectly with her office, which was decorated in a calming color scheme of white and ivory with matte gold accents. Had Zach managed to figure her out from one conversation? Flowers or not, Paige was deeply suspicious of Zach and his motives. And that made her feel like she should probably call him and say thank-you. Just to gather a little more intel.

"Henry?" Paige called for her assistant. "Do you have a sec?"

Henry ducked into her office and beelined for her desk while he pushed his black-framed glasses up his nose. Henry was young—only twenty-six—and eager to make his mark, which was great for Paige. Henry got things done. "Of course. Anything you need."

"Can you hunt down a number for Zach Armstrong? I'd do it myself but I have a wretched headache." She kneaded her forehead. She should've known better than to do shots with Alexis and her friends last night.

"No problem. Staring at a screen is not good for a headache. Too much strain on your eyes." He pulled his phone out of his pocket, mumbling to himself while tapping and swiping. "Got it. Hand me your cell."

The second she had it in her hand, the device rang. Despite Henry's warning about eye strain and her phone, she looked at it. Her best friend April Chapman's name popped up on the caller ID. "I should take this. I'll call Zach later."

"I'll text you his info." Henry walked out and quietly closed the office door behind him.

"Hey," Paige said when she answered the call. "What's up?"

"Who's the most badass sports agent in the land?" April's voice sang. "You are!"

Paige laughed. "I don't know about that, but thanks."

"I'm sorry I couldn't be there last night. I tried hard to get the assignment, but they sent me to San Diego for baseball instead. The Padres started the season with a nine-game winning streak." April was on-camera talent for one of the biggest cable sports networks.

"So I saw. That's not a bad gig. I love that city." Paige took another sip of her coffee and sat back in her chair.

"Well? How was last night?"

"It was a ton of fun. We all started crying when Alexis's name was called. You should have seen us. Her parents, her grandparents, her brother and sister. We were all bawling our eyes out." Paige was getting choked up just thinking about it. Everything she'd said to Zach had been absolutely true—years and years had gone into making last night happen. "Alexis has worked her butt off, and she's had a lot of ups and downs. I'm just so proud of her."

"Of course you are. But don't forget to give yourself some credit, too. You spotted her talent before anyone else did."

"Not before her parents. Or Alexis herself. Or her high school coach." Paige stopped herself. She had a bad habit of minimizing her accomplishments. "But you're right. I was there from the beginning. I was there when no one else was."

"That's no small thing."

Paige smiled to herself. "I owe a lot of that to my mom. She taught me what good basketball looks like."

"Aw. That's sweet. I know you miss her, but she would've been super proud of you last night."

Missing her mom was an understatement. She and Paige had been so close. Growing up, Paige idolized her. Later in life, they were best friends. "I like to think that she's somewhere looking down on me and giving me a high five."

"I'm sure she is."

Paige sighed and turned in her chair to look out the window. Her office was on the thirty-seventh floor of a high-rise office building on 46th Street, only two city blocks from Armstrong Sports. "Can I tell you the weirdest thing about last night?"

"Are you kidding? Of course. I'm always here for weird."

"Zach Armstrong was at the draft, schmoozing the

players and making the rounds. And get this. He sent congratulatory flowers to Alexis earlier in the day."

"No way."

"Yes way."

"Is Tom Armstrong aware of this? The man turned misogyny into an art form. Remember when he said all women's sports other than golf and tennis were pointless?"

"I think he said they were boring, but yeah. I remember." Paige cleared her throat and turned back to her desk, putting the orchids in her line of sight. "I don't think Tom knows. But Zach says he's trying to change things at the agency. I suppose he should be applauded for his efforts. Not that I said that to his face."

"I'm not sure he should get any credit for doing what they should've been doing all along. Are you worried that they're going to try to move on any of your clients? Armstrong is known for some pretty underhanded behavior. At least behind the scenes."

"I told him that I wasn't worried. But of course that's a lie. I've worked too hard to lose any of my business to someone else. Plus, the few times I've lost a client, it stung like hell."

"I'm sure. So if Tom doesn't know, I wonder how Zach is going to sell it."

"No clue, but something tells me he'll manage to do it. I got the sense that he could sell a brick to a drowning man. He seems super slick."

"He's not hard on the eyes, either."

"No, he is not." That was the understatement of

the century. Paige was still appalled by how distracted she'd been by his looks. She wasn't the sort to get distracted by a pretty face. Or spectacular shoulders. Or a strong jaw.

"I do have one bit of good news," April said.

"Ooh. I love good news. What is it?"

"I talked the powers that be into letting me go to Vegas. So we can hang out a little. I mean, I'll be working and so will you, but we'll at least get to see each other."

A ribbon of pure elation worked through Paige. "That is so amazing. I can't wait to see you." Time with April would make this trip so much more palatable.

"I can't wait to see you, too. Let's text and make a plan to at least have dinner or go to the pool one afternoon."

"It's a deal. Can't wait."

"Perfect. I should go, but I'll catch up with you later."

"Sounds good. Thanks for calling."

"Congratulations, Paige. I'm proud of you."

Paige and April said their goodbyes and Paige ended the call. That left her with her previous task ahead—thanking Zach for the flowers. Paige opened the text from Henry, then tapped on Zach's contact info.

"Zach Armstrong," he answered.

A tidal wave of warmth washed over her as her brain instantly constructed a vision of Zach. Why did it have to torture her like that? It was entirely unfair.

"Zach, hi. It's Paige Moss. I wanted to call and thank you for the orchids. It really wasn't necessary, but I appreciate it. Thank you."

"I wanted to show you that I'm not the enemy, Paige."

"That remains to be seen."

"So flowers aren't enough to convince you? What else do you want? Candy? Jewelry? A car?"

Paige laughed quietly. He was so effortlessly charming.

"Name your price," he added.

"I don't have a price. Or at least not one that I'm willing to share. But the flowers were a nice gesture. Let's put it that way."

"They're meant to be more than that. Think of them as an olive branch from my agency to yours. I'm sure I could learn a lot from you. If you care to teach me."

Paige cleared her throat as all sorts of ideas for lessons she could teach Zach flew through her head. None of them had to do with sports, but there might be sweating and heavy breathing. "We'll see, Zach. I'm not ready to call you my BFF or anything."

Zach laughed, reminding her of the moment when he'd done that last night. He had an amazing voice. It was so rich and throaty. "Not ready to put me on your Christmas card list?"

"I'll think about it." She took a deep breath and decided this was as good a time as any to probe for more information. "Have you run your plans by Tom yet?"

"Tonight."

"Interesting. How long before he shoots you down?"

"Honestly, I'm guessing he'll be enthusiastic once I make my case. I think his ego wouldn't let him back down from his previous stance on the genders in sports, but mostly because he'd gone and made it so widely known for years. So he's got me to play it off on. He can chalk up the change to there being a new sheriff in town."

She nodded and gnawed on her finger. She was definitely conflicted about this. She didn't want more competition, but there was a shortage of high quality agents willing to go beyond the big moneymaking sports—professional football, men's basketball and baseball. There were women athletes who would benefit from this. She certainly couldn't represent everyone. "Well, I wish you luck."

"So the flowers did work."

She grinned to herself. "You're quick, Zach. I'll give you that much."

"Thanks, Paige. I'll see you in Vegas."

Vegas. Funnily enough, she was looking forward to this year's expo, even if it was going to be a lot of work. "Yep. See you there." Paige hung up the phone. As much fun as she'd had talking to April and Zach, it was time to dig into her workday. "Henry? I'm off my call. Do you have a sec?"

Henry popped into the doorway with a notepad and pen in hand. "Of course."

"Let's sit down and brainstorm some corporate

sponsorship ideas for Alexis. I feel like we need to strike while the iron is hot."

Henry closed the door, bustled over and plopped down in the chair in front of Paige's desk. "I so agree. Alexis is drop-dead gorgeous and she's going to kick ass her rookie season. I'm positive we can come up with a ton of great ideas."

"Perfect. Then I can try to set up some meetings ahead of the Vegas trip."

Henry raised his pen in the air. "Excellent idea."

"I'm glad you think so. I've got my work cut out for me in Vegas. Alexis is expecting a lot. And if I was her, I'd be expecting a lot, too."

Zach had spent far too much of his afternoon ruminating about Paige Moss. She was a lethal combination of qualities he admired—smart, sexy and fiery. That was probably why it stung so much to feel dismissed by her. It was as if she thought he didn't know what he was doing. Or that he was too young. He hadn't done himself any favors by suggesting that she could teach him a few things. Why on earth had he done that? Flatter someone at his own expense? It had made him seem inexperienced, and that wasn't the way he wanted Paige to see him. If he was going to last in this business, he had to focus on getting her and everyone else to take him seriously. But that might require casting aside his tactic of playing nice, all so he could prove a point.

He needed tonight's meeting with Tom to be a step forward in that direction, and the prospect held so much uncertainty that it was souring his stomach. The traffic on his way out to his family's compound on Long Island wasn't helping. He'd been at the wheel of his Aston Martin DBS for more than an hour, frustrated by the congestion, merely to get out and away from Manhattan. Still, it felt good when the roads became less busy and he could roll into the town of Brookville, where Zach was lucky enough to have grown up. The trees were already lush with spring green and he took in the view as he drove off from the main road to the quieter street where his parents lived. As he turned onto the private drive that led through the family's fourteen acre wooded parcel, he finally felt his anxiety recede. As nervous as he was about what Tom would think when he made his proposal, Zach was home, and that was such a comfort.

Zach was only two years old when he first came to live at this house—a stunning white stucco mansion that was updated but still spoke of the elegance of a time gone by, with manicured grounds and formal architecture. As the story went, he and his mother, Angie, had lived in a small apartment nearby before his mom met Tom. Angie and Zach's biological dad had only dated briefly, and he took off the instant he learned she was pregnant. It was a tough road for Angie, doing everything on her own, but she made it work. Then one miraculous day, Tom walked into the restaurant where Angie was a hostess and everything changed. Tom was instantly charmed by her wit and smile, and she was enamored by his good looks and kind nature. Tom had been widowed before he turned thirty and he'd never had children. Tom had always hoped to fall in love again. He'd always wanted to be a dad. It was like a fairy tale that the three of them found each other.

Zach pulled into the circular drive in front of the house. The entrance had staunch pillars and wide front steps, welcoming in visitors while also whispering that this was a home built for making a fantastic first impression. Zach parked his car just a few yards beyond the front door and grabbed the pitch materials for his talk with Tom. The instant he looked up, he was greeted by his mother, who was standing on the landing with a warm smile on her face. "Zachary." She held her arms open wide, and her voice was soft and yielding, as if she'd been waiting years for him to return. In reality, it had only been a few weeks since he'd last been home, but they were close and he appreciated how much she enjoyed his visits. Her reddish brown hair was pulled back in a ponytail. "It's always good to see you."

Zach followed her into the foyer, which had oak floors in a herringbone pattern and long antique tables flanking either side of the main hall. He gave his mom as tight an embrace as he could while having his arms full.

"What are those?" She stepped back and pointed to the binders in Zach's hands.

"These are for my chat with Tom. I'm just going to duck into his office and stow them away."

"I'll let him know you're here and then I'll check on dinner. We'll eat in about forty-five minutes."

Zach parted ways with his mother, started down one of the four halls that branched off from the foyer and arrived at Tom's office. When Zach was a kid, this room had held so much mystery. It was like something out of a movie, with rich brown leather club chairs, a fireplace and a grand mahogany desk, which had been owned by Tom's father, the man who'd started Armstrong Sports in the 1970s. Dozens of framed photos adorned the walls, mostly of Tom with notable figures in sports, some of which amazed Zach as much today as they had years ago. Tom was a legend, beloved not only by his clients, but by athletes around the world. He was especially known for his philanthropic work, raising millions of dollars over the years for various charities. Some of the photos even included Zach and Angie. The one that held the greatest memory for Zach was from the first time he got to go to the Super Bowl. Zach was seven at the time, and he'd met so many of his idols that day. It still made him smile just to think about it.

"There he is." Tom's voice came from behind Zach, startling him.

"Tom. I figured you were somewhere else in the house." Zach gave Tom a hug, then stood back. "How are you feeling?"

Tom ambled back behind his desk, taking his time. He was getting stronger every day since the heart attack that had forced him to step back from Armstrong Sports, but he was still very much in recovery mode. He had a ways to go. He eased slowly into his chair, and as Zach studied his cautious movements and the way his face had gone a bit gaunt, the younger was struck with the same realization he'd had when Tom ended up in the hospital. Tom wouldn't be around forever, and it would be a sad day when Zach lost him. He adored him so.

"Please. Sit." Tom sat back in his tall-backed leather office chair.

"Yes. Of course." He took a spot in one of the club chairs opposite Tom's desk. "So, first thing, I have big news." Zach took a pause for effect. "I'm about to sign Ryan Wilson as a client."

Tom arched his eyebrows, laced his fingers and rested them on his belly. "How did you manage to pull that off?"

He trusts me. I built a relationship with him. Zach had to stop himself from sharing the answer that came to him first. He knew that wasn't what Tom would want to hear. "I saw an opportunity and I took it. I heard he was unhappy with his agent and I made my move."

A wide grin bloomed on Tom's face. "That's my boy. That's how you do it." He sat up and softly pounded his fist on the desk, then cleared his throat. Apparently even that much enthusiasm had taken some serious energy to express. "That's the kind of cutthroat move you need to be making. Every day. That's how you take what my dad built, and what I built on top of that, and turn it into something even bigger."

Zach couldn't help but think about his conversation with Teri the other day. *Cutthroat* was not a word he would use to describe himself. He wasn't a shark, despite what people might think. He simply enjoyed his job and let his genuine love of sports guide him when making moves and decisions. Agenting was a game of chess that just so happened to revolve around things that he was extremely passionate about, like football, baseball and golf. But he'd indulge Tom's perception of the situation, if only to get him to take the next subject seriously. "Thanks. I'm glad that makes you happy."

"Excellent. Absolutely excellent."

"Are you okay to talk about business now? Or would you prefer we do it after dinner? I don't want to put you under any undue stress."

"Are you kidding? I've been waiting all day for you to get here. I can't wait to talk shop."

"Well, good. Because there's something I want to discuss with you." This time, Zach's pause was not for effect. He was genuinely nervous about sharing his idea, but he'd put so much time and effort into this endeavor, he couldn't back down now. "I've taken a long hard look at the numbers over these first few weeks. Looking for areas of growth. We need to start signing women athletes."

Tom laughed. "Oh, boy. Here we go."

Zach couldn't help but be a little miffed. "Don't say it like that. This is a solid idea."

Tom blew out a frustrated breath. "Do you have any idea how many times someone has tried to get me to do this? It's not about sexism, Zach. The money's not there. Female athletes simply don't make as much money as male athletes do. It's a numbers game."

"If you want to talk numbers, I have a lot of them. And I think there are reasons to make this move." Zach got up from his seat and grabbed the two binders, then placed one on the desk in front of Tom. "Here. This is my proposal."

Tom peered up at Zach, skepticism painted across his face while he grumbled under his breath. "It's not our job to fix society's ills."

"Tom. Come on. I'm not asking you to fix anything. All I'm asking is that you look at the numbers."

Tom nodded. "Okay. You're right. Let's see what you've got." He grabbed a pair of reading glasses, opened the binder and began reading.

Meanwhile, Zach did the same, revisiting the words he'd so carefully crafted and the numbers he'd so patiently honed. His plan was simple—endorsements. Female athletes might not make as much money on the field as men did, but they were often far better brand ambassadors than men were. Sponsorships had gone through the roof in the last two years, especially as social media became a viable means of spreading an advertiser's product in a more organic fashion. "Well?"

Tom's lips spread into a thin line. "I'm an old man, aren't I?"

Zach's shoulders dropped. "No. You are not. The business has changed. Or more specifically, the landscape has changed. There are opportunities now that weren't there even five years ago. And honestly, I think a lot of other agencies are asleep at the wheel when it comes to this. Let's beat them."

"Well, you know that's always going to appeal to me."

"Is that a yes? Are you good with me moving forward with this plan?"

"Hold on one minute. Who are you looking at to sign?"

"Turn to page twenty-one. There's a list of possible targets there." Zach flipped through the binder at the same time Tom did.

"Alexis Simmons isn't on this list. If anyone's marketable for the sort of things you're looking at, she is."

"And she's already represented by Paige Moss. That's a no-go."

"There are ways out of any agency contract, Zach. You know that."

Zach felt uneasy. He knew what Tom was getting at and he didn't like it. "Our agencies have had an adversarial relationship. Do we really need to continue with that?"

"Every other agency is our adversary. That's the first rule in our world."

Maybe Tom was right. Maybe Zach needed to toughen up a bit. But if he wanted Paige to take him seriously, that was not the move that would do it. No, that would simply make Paige despise him and he couldn't fathom that as a good idea. "Paige will be in Vegas. I'll get a better sense of their working relationship then. Okay?"

"Okay."

Zach felt as though he could breathe a little easier. "Good."

"Damn. I wish I could go to Vegas. I love the expo. So many deals to cut. So much amazing food."

Zach could hear the wanderlust in Tom's voice and it killed him a little bit. Tom missed the business. Zach couldn't help but feel sorry for him. "I promise to keep you fully apprised of everything."

Zach's mother appeared at the door. "Alright you two. Let's wrap this up. Dinner is ready, and we're having Zach's favorite pot roast, so we don't want to let it get cold."

Zach's heart—and stomach—leaped at the thought. It really was his favorite. "Yum. I'm starving."

"We can finish talking about this while we eat," Tom said, pushing himself out of his chair.

"Oh, no you won't. Meal time is family time." Zach's mom shook her head.

Tom looked at her, and Zach witnessed the moment when they both softened their expression and gave in to their true love for each other. "You're right," Tom said. "And family is the most important thing."

Three

Paige enjoyed Las Vegas, but only in small doses. It was an incredibly fun and exciting place to visit, with its bright lights, near-constant hustle and bustle, and what felt like permission to let loose. After all, what happened there, stayed there. Right? It had been an eon since she'd done anything wild. Although she had zero plans to do a single thing that was out of character, it was nice to know it was an option in this city. Even if she'd never act on it.

In truth, Paige couldn't take Vegas for more than seventy-two hours, but that made the sports expo a little more palatable since it only lasted forty-eight. Of course, some years, even that had been too much. Too often this event became an exercise in humiliation, with the sponsorship offers for her clients being of a much smaller caliber than what male athletes were garnering. Most of the big fish like carmakers, luxury brands and major clothing designers would completely dismiss professional female athletes. There was always an excuse—the demographics were off, or the market research wasn't pointing them in that direction—but Paige knew it was only because those corporate entities were unwilling to change. Hopefully, this year would be different. Alexis had not only gone number one in the WPBA draft, but she was an immensely exciting player and looked like a supermodel. Grabbing her a few lucrative endorsements should be no trouble at all. Or at least that was the plan.

Paige strolled into the expo hotel, which was right on the Las Vegas strip, where the biggest resorts and casinos were. The lobby was a flurry of activity, with agents, sponsors and exhibitors milling about, while the ceaseless music and clanging of slot machines played in the background. Paige strode straight to the front desk and checked in, then headed to the elevator with her room key.

She wound her way through the sea of people with her suitcase at her side, across plush white-and-gold carpet, past even more slot machines. She smiled and waved at a few people she recognized, but she also glanced in the opposite direction when she spotted some she didn't care to see. She was about fifty feet from her destination, when she felt a hand at her waist.

"Paige. Wait," a familiar man's voice said.

She jumped and whipped around.

"Hello, beautiful," he said.

Paige took a beat and caught her breath as she peered into the chocolaty brown eyes of her ex-husband. Andre. He'd once been an agent for Moss Sports, but now worked in the front office for Los Angeles's pro football team. She grasped his arm and lightly pecked him on the cheek. Although their split had been messy, they'd since made amends. And he lived on the other side of the country, so they didn't see each other very often, which made it much easier to be nice. "Don't sneak up on me. You know I don't like it."

"Oh, come on. You like surprises. At least a little." He flashed a grin. "I had to say hi and wish you congratulations on Alexis. Well done."

"Thank you. It was a big night."

"A big night that you put an awful lot of work into."

This was the good side of her relationship with Andre—he understood how hard she worked. "Thank you. I appreciate it."

"So? How are you doing?"

She shrugged. "Same old, same old. Alexis has definitely been the highlight of my year so far. How about you?"

His smile grew. "I need to tell you something before you hear it from anyone else." His grin changed into an expression far more serious. "But I don't want it to upset you."

Great. The stark contrast of his words and facial

expression left her feeling uneasy. She could only imagine what he was about to say. "It won't upset me. Just tell me."

"I'm getting married."

Okay, then. No, she was not in love with Andre, but this still hurt. Surprisingly so. It felt as though the proverbial rug had been pulled out from under her, leaving her fumbling for a way to right herself. Or at least hold on to her dignity. Perhaps she felt this way because he'd moved on effortlessly after her, slipping into a new life with a new job in a new city, seemingly with ease. "Wow. Congratulations."

"You're not upset? Annoyed?"

"Of course not," she said with as much sincerity as she could muster. "Who's the lucky woman?"

"Her name is Casey. She's a cheerleader for the team. Incredibly smart. She's actually in med school. She was just doing the cheerleader gig to pay her tuition."

So she has a smoking-hot bod, is smart enough to be a doctor and is probably in her twenties. Fantastic. "I'm sure she's amazing."

"I think you'd love her."

Paige doubted that. Why did men think things like that? "Are you happy?"

"Very much so."

She forced a smile. She *did* want Andre to be happy and move forward in his life, even if she sometimes felt like she was treading water simply to survive. "Congratulations. I'm really, really happy for you."

"You got a guy in your life?"

"Not at the moment." She said that as if she regularly dated and was merely taking a brief hiatus, which wasn't close to the truth. She'd been on *one* date since their divorce that had gone tragically bad, and she hadn't tried since then. Finding the right guy required work and time, and she didn't have the energy or bandwidth. If love found her, she'd consider it. If sex found her, well, she'd be foolish to turn that down. Especially if he was hot and could make her laugh.

"That won't last. You're too gorgeous to stay single." He eyed her up and down, making her feel on edge. There had been a time when she'd loved it when he did that, but the betrayal that came in their marriage made it seem quite different now. "You look amazing in that dress, by the way."

"Thanks." Paige glanced over Andre's shoulder, and Zach popped into view. He was headed in their direction, but was stopping every few feet to talk to someone.

Andre turned and followed Paige's line of sight. "Oh. Hey. There's the boy wonder."

"Zach Armstrong?" Paige wondered if word had gotten out about Zach expanding the purview of Armstrong Sports. "Seems like a pretty generous nickname. Not sure he's a wonder yet." *Although he is wonder-ful to look at.*

"Are you kidding? He just signed Ryan Wilson. Very big deal." Andre turned back to her. "And of course, more than a little controversial, since Ryan was still represented by Epic Sports. No matter what, it was a baller move."

Paige grumbled under her breath, studying Zach as he continued to chitchat with people. Good god, he was a vision, but her suspicions of him seemed to be proving true. He'd stolen someone's client? Not cool. "That's Tom Armstrong's influence."

"You would say that," Andre quipped.

Paige was not going to walk down that particular path. Discussing Tom Armstrong with Andre would only make her angry. "I'm not wrong."

"Regardless of whose influence it is, the kid has game."

Kid. Paige didn't know Zach very well, but was certain he would dislike that particular nickname.

Andre glanced at his phone. "Oh. Hey. I need to go. But hopefully I'll see you around?" He leaned closer and kissed her on the cheek.

Paige managed a grin. She was glad Andre had found someone. Really, she was. But if he was moving on, did that mean she should be doing the same? "Sure thing."

She grabbed the handle of her suitcase and took the few strides required to reach the elevator, then pressed the button to call for it. She was painfully aware that Zach was nearby, but she wasn't ready to talk to him yet, so she kept her eyes trained on the numbers above the doors. It was taking forever. Absentmindedly, she looked to her left and spotted Zach just as he turned in her direction. Their gazes connected and he flashed a grin. Her head swam. It felt like a bolt of lightning had cracked open the hotel's ceiling, struck her in the chest and all that electricity headed straight between her legs. She quickly looked away and jammed the call button repeatedly. "Come on," she muttered, then pulled out her phone to check the time. Her first sponsor meeting wasn't for another hour. Needing something to do or a lifeline of some sort, she sent April a text. Tell me again when you get here? There was no response.

She looked up from her phone, only to see Zach was right there. Mere feet away. With his eyes trained on her. "Going up?"

"I think it only goes up from here." She hoped the same could be said for her day.

"Right. Which floor are you on?" He punched the button several times and shook his head. "The elevators in this hotel take forever."

"I'm on eight."

He turned to her with a look of utter surprise and, oddly enough, a bit of delight. "Funny. Me, too."

So much for her day improving. *Of course* Zach was on the same floor she was. Fate just had to play that little trick on her. The elevator dinged and Paige jumped. The doors parted and let off an entire carload of people. Zach held the door for her as soon as the coast was clear. She stepped on board and he was right behind her, along with at least another dozen people, including a family with so many roller bags that it was a miracle there was room for any passengers at all. Everyone had to jockey for position and crowd together. That left Zach and Paige penned in the corner by suitcases.

"I saw you talking to Andre Held," Zach muttered quietly. He lowered his chin to his chest to speak to her. "You don't represent any of his players, do you?"

She peered up at him, uncomfortably aware of how hard it was to breathe in his presence while trying not to stare at his mouth. If he was half as good at kissing as he was at making her feel unsettled, making out with him would be all kinds of fun. "He's my ex."

His eyebrows popped up in surprise. "Ex-boyfriend?"

"Husband."

"Oh. I guess I didn't know that."

"Yeah." Of course, Paige wasn't about to tell Zach that his beloved stepdad, Tom, had played a role in the demise of her marriage. That wasn't a subject for light conversation, especially with so many strangers within earshot. The elevator dinged. They were on the eighth floor.

Zach valiantly marshaled everyone out of the way so they could get off the elevator.

Paige consulted the sign directing guests to their room. "I'm this way," she said, pointing to the right.

"Me, too. Room 860."

This day could *not* get any more ridiculous. "I'm in 858."

He laughed. "Seriously?"

"Seriously."

"What are the odds?" He reached for the handle of her suitcase. "May I?"

She held up her hands in surrender. "Knock yourself out."

With Zach pulling her bag, they started down the long corridor. The walls were bathed in gold-and-black wallpaper with a beautiful scrolled pattern, dramatically lit by elegant wall sconces that made it feel more like midnight than morning. The carpet underfoot was impossibly soft. Everything in Vegas was about seduction. It was one long tease designed to make you feel loose and uninhibited. To make you feel good about making poor choices. It was the worst possible place for her to be with Zach Armstrong.

"I heard that you signed Ryan Wilson. Congrats. That's a big deal." Paige was eager to figure out whether Zach planned to make a habit of poaching clients from other agents.

"Thanks. It seemed rude to just come out with it. You and I barely know each other."

Something about "barely know each other" excited Paige. It was the "barely" part. Even though she didn't trust Zach at all. "I had no idea Ryan was looking for new representation." They slowed as they reached Paige's door, and the air hung heavy with the implication she'd made.

"He was, but only behind the scenes. He kept it quiet. He's not the kind of guy who tells a sports reporter that he's not happy. But he did tell his friends."

Paige pulled out her room key card and waved it in front of the sensor on her door. When the light turned green, she turned the handle and stuck out her hip to keep the door ajar. "I didn't know you and Ryan were friends."

"We are. I'm such a football nerd that I blathered on and on about how great he is the day we first met. The friendship grew from there." He looked into her room. "Let me take your bag inside."

"Oh. Great." She took a step and held the door open as Zach wheeled the suitcase into her room and parked it at the end of her bed. She trailed him inside and let the door shut behind her. Paige couldn't help but admire two things about Zach—his genuine love of sports and his gentlemanly ways. "Well, congratulations are definitely in order with Ryan."

"Thanks. I'm excited." He wandered over to the floor-to-ceiling window, which spanned nearly the entire width of her room. "The view on this side of the hotel is amazing."

Paige joined him to take it all in. They were on the back side of the building, with a stunning view of the pool area down below. Far off in the distance was the craggy outline of the sandy brown mountains surrounding the valley in which Las Vegas was so carefully nestled. It was a gorgeous day with bright blue skies and only the most delicate of white, wispy clouds. She didn't love everything about Vegas, but she was indeed in awe of this view.

"It's beautiful in the most unusual way," she said.

"It's nice to get away from New York every now and then."

Paige drew in a deep breath, eyeing Zach as subtly as she could. He was awfully nice to look at and being all alone with him, talking about something other than business, did something to her. It made her feel like it might be okay to let her guard down. It made her wonder what it would be like to kiss him. "It is nice."

Just then, Zach's phone buzzed with a text, snapping Paige back to reality. He pulled his cell out of his pocket. "Dammit. I need to go." He quickly tapped out a response to the text. "One of our new agents, Derek, is downstairs. I promised I'd walk the exhibition hall with him and introduce him to people."

This was for the best. She couldn't stay in her room all day, fantasizing about Zach, or worse—acting on the thoughts in her head. "Time to go be the boss, huh?"

"You probably have a full day, too."

"I do. Too many meetings."

He started toward the door, then turned back to her. "I'd love it if we could find a way to grab a drink or a meal together. Maybe dinner? Tonight?"

Paige would've loved that, too, if she had the courage to be entirely honest. But she still wasn't convinced it was a good idea. "Maybe we'll run into each other? My schedule is packed and my best friend, April, is here. I rarely get to see her."

"April Chapman?"

"Do you know her?"

"I don't. But I'm a great admirer of her work."

Paige wasn't surprised. Not only was April a super talented sports reporter, she was so beautiful it was hard to take your eyes off her. All sports-oriented men seemed to be great admirers of April's, and she had no doubt that Zach was, too. "I'll be sure to tell her."

"Or maybe I'll run into you two?"

"Maybe."

Zach resumed his short trip to the door, Paige following behind. "I'll see you later," he said as he opened the door.

"I'm sure you will." Paige let the door close behind him, then stood there frozen for a moment. She still wasn't sure what to make of Zach, but in many ways, that made him all the more dangerous. She was glad she'd had the courage *not* to make a plan with him. It was better to simply stay away.

Paige strode over to her suitcase and went straight to work, unpacking her clothes, shoes and toiletries and getting it all nice and organized. Then she grabbed a small cross-body bag that she used for the essentials while at a conference and headed downstairs. Her first stop was to get her conference badge, then she ducked into the exhibition hall. There was no sign of Zach and his new agent, Derek. It was probably for the best.

She next made her way to the lobby, where she met up with her first appointment of the day—a rep from a luxury watch brand. After that was a lunch with a rental car company, an early afternoon meeting with a worldwide fast-food chain and her three o'clock with a video game developer. By the time that meeting was concluded, Paige was already exhausted. Giving the same spiel about her star athletes over and over again was so draining, and it only made it worse to either be met with blank stares, meaningless nods or balks at the money she wanted for her clients, especially Alexis.

So she was in many ways thrilled when she got a text saying that her four o'clock appointment needed to back out. She quickly called April. "Hey. Where are you? Do you have any time?" she asked.

"I'm up in my room. I just finished writing a post for our website. And I do have time. Do you want to grab something to eat?"

Paige felt so cooped up. She'd been in the hotel all day long. "Let's kill two birds with one stone and go to the pool. They have a full menu down there. The front desk pitched it pretty hard when I checked in."

"Perfect. I'll meet you there in fifteen?"

"I can't wait."

Four

Zach prided himself on being a pretty energetic guy, but five solid hours of meetings left him dragging. Even though things had gone incredibly well. A few of his appointments had been downright exhilarating, where he effortlessly reached his stride, pitching projects and partnerships with ease, then just as easily asking for the money he wanted for his client and receiving remarkably little pushback. Even after all of that, he needed a break.

He also needed time off from his most junior agent, Derek. He'd shadowed Zach for most of his meetings and had held his own, but mentoring was exhausting. "Hey. Derek. I'm going to splinter off for a bit if that's okay with you. I need to make a few calls," Zach said as they stood outside the exhibition hall.

"Sounds good," Derek said, a bit distracted by all of the hubbub around them. "I was hoping we could grab dinner tonight if that's okay."

Zach was still holding out hope that he'd run into Paige and convince her to have a meal with him, but maybe he needed to stop holding out hope. She kept saying no. "I have one person I'm waiting to hear from."

"Another potential sponsor?"

"No. Another agent."

"Great," Derek said with entirely too much enthusiasm. "I'd love to come. I won't talk. I'll just listen. I learn so much when I'm around you."

Guilt was bearing down on Zach. This was a work trip and Derek needed his guidance. Plus, Zach was not about to invite Derek along if he and Paige got to have dinner. "Maybe you and I should just go out on our own. Grab a burger. Play some blackjack?"

Derek's face lit up. "Yes. That sounds amazing. Seven? Meet in the lobby?"

Zach clapped Derek on the shoulder. "You got it. I'll catch you later."

Zach parted ways from Derek and wandered past the bar. He stepped inside the dark and moody space, made quick survey of the room and came to the conclusion that Paige wasn't there. He would've been lying if he said that he wasn't more than a little disappointed. Running into her would certainly put the spring back in his step, but that wasn't meant to be. For now.

So he returned to his original plan and headed

up to the eighth floor to put up his feet. He strolled down the hall and hesitated for a moment at the door to Paige's room. He raised his hand and left his fist hovering in midair. Was she in there? Would she invite him in? He had to find out. *No rewards for the timid.* He knocked twice, then waited, the anticipation making his pulse race. "Dammit," he muttered to himself when it was clear that no one would be answering, then continued on to his room.

He dropped his key card on top of the dresser and sat at the desk before opening his laptop. After a few quick e-mail responses, he closed it up, then kicked off his shoes and sat on the bed. He leaned against the headboard and put up his feet. The bed was so soft and sumptuous. It would've been so easy to flip on the TV and catch a game, or maybe even fall asleep for a quick fifteen-minute nap, but Zach had to be responsible and give Tom a quick call and an update. He'd promised to deliver at least one while he was away.

"Zach, my boy. How's Sin City?" Tom said when he answered the phone.

"No sins for me," Zach countered. "Just lots of incredible meetings."

"Big deals?"

Zach sat back a little more and ran his hand through his hair. "Everything I could have hoped for. And more."

"Tell me, then. Everything."

Zach gave a quick rundown of the details he knew Tom would care about most—the players, the partnerships and the payday. "The three Ps," as Tom called them. As Zach rattled it all off, he knew he'd done a fantastic job thus far. He knew Tom would be proud. He'd have to be. "So those are the highlights from today."

"Well done. If the rest of your meetings go that well, you'll be able to call the expo a rousing success."

That was exactly what Zach was shooting for. After all, Tom had exceptionally high expectations. Meeting those was one thing. Zach was going to have to keep kicking ass if he wanted to exceed them. "Thanks."

"Where are you at with Paige Moss and assessing her hold on Alexis Simmons? Assuming you're still wanting to pursue the plan to bring on female athletes."

"Of course I'm still pursuing my plan. And Paige and I are getting to know each other." Zach's throat went dry. "I've talked to her some and I'm hoping we can have a meal together or maybe a drink. Just so I can find out how things are going with Alexis."

"I hope you aren't cozying up to Ms. Moss, Zach. I've told you how she can be. She's no friend of Armstrong Sports, that's for sure."

Zach had been struggling with his stepdad's opinion of Paige from the moment he met her. Every additional minute he spent in her company made it seem all the more ludicrous. "Dad, I like Paige. She's smart and she knows her stuff. I really don't think she's the enemy. And honestly, I don't think going after another firm's client is going to make us any friends in the sports world." The other end of the line went dead quiet. "Are you there?"

"I am."

"Are you okay?" Zach worried he might have given him another heart attack.

"I am. I'm fine. I'm just struggling a bit with letting you have full run of the business, okay? It's not that I don't trust you. I do. And I think you're doing an amazing job. I just need you to make smart decisions. I want you to consider the long-term implications of the moves you choose to make. Think about the big picture."

Zach got the message loud and clear, but the only problem was that *his* big picture was quite different from Tom's. "I won't disappoint you. I will hit every projection I've made. And then some."

"I trust you'll do everything you've told me you will. That's all I ever ask."

"Thank you."

"Oh. How's the new agent panning out?" Tom asked.

"Derek? He's learning the ropes. He sat in on a few of my meetings today. Listened. Took a lot of notes. I think he'll do well once he has a few more clients."

"Excellent. Glad to hear it."

"Well, I'd better get back to it," Zach said.

"More meetings?"

"I have some phone calls to make. A few of my meetings for tomorrow aren't set in stone."

"Don't work too hard, Zach. You are in Vegas. I'd expect you to have a little fun."

"Really?" Tom had always spent so much time stressing the importance of working as hard as possible.

"Yes. Of course. No man can be all work and no play. You can't be good all the time. It's not sustainable."

Zach's mind immediately flew to Paige. It was nearly impossible to shake the thought free. If he was going to play or be bad, he wouldn't mind doing it with her. She was tempting like nothing else. "I'll see what I can do about that."

"That's my boy. Take care, son."

"Bye." Zach ended the call and set his phone down on the bed, then got up to walk over to the window and look out over the pool area. It was crowded with people, but that blue water was calling to him. A few laps would do him good. Then maybe a search for Paige and another invitation—perhaps for a drink— if he could work it into the conversation. That was all he needed. Especially if he could get her to say yes.

He quickly changed into his swim trunks and a T-shirt, then made his way downstairs. He grabbed a towel when he arrived, then strode out into the grand pool area. Like so much at a high-end Vegas hotel, every detail was perfect—the water was a stunning shade of aqua, the umbrellas were a crisp white and there were plenty of chairs. Waiters bustled from person to person, taking orders and delivering food on trays and cocktails with elaborate garnishes of fresh fruit. Sun beamed across the pool deck. The air was warm. Zach felt his shoulders loosen. This had been the right call.

He found an open chair and dropped his towel onto it, then pulled his T-shirt over his head and tossed that aside as well. As he took the few necessary steps to the edge of the deep end, he couldn't help but scan the crowd of people gathered. That was when he saw her. *Paige.*

She was sitting on the edge of the pool, at the opposite end, dangling her feet in the water while talking to April Chapman. Paige was wearing the most mind-blowing bathing suit he could imagine. It was a simple black one-piece, but it had a plunging neckline and was cut high up on her hips, leaving very little to the imagination. Not that Zach wasn't trying like hell to imagine all of her, brewing up visions of what was under that stretch of fabric. How was she so effortlessly sexy, so breathtakingly beautiful, all while being calm and cool and collected on the outside? She boggled the mind. His, in particular.

It wasn't only his brain that reacted to the sight of Paige. His body responded, too. His stomach clenched. His face felt flush. Everything below his waist drew tight. Paige did something to him. He'd had instant attraction to a few women in his life, but nothing quite like this. It was like he'd found a whole new level of chemistry with Paige, and it was getting stronger every time he saw her. How could he possibly ignore it? He couldn't, could he? It would be foolish. He might go the entirety of his life and never experience this again. And he knew there was only one thing to do—dive in and swim the length of that pool. It would accomplish a whole bunch of things at one time. He'd be able to cool off, calm down and ultimately end up right next to the woman he could not get out of his thoughts, no matter how hard he tried.

Going to the pool had been a brilliant idea. This was so much better than being in meetings.

"Another mojito?" April asked, already flagging down the waiter.

Paige slurped what was left in her plastic glass. "Sure." She set it down on the side of the pool and swirled her feet and calves in the warm water. Raising her face, she caught some of the day's fading rays. Even though the pool was heated, it wouldn't be long before the sun would dip below the horizon and it would get entirely too cold to be out there in a bathing suit. For now, she would soak up all she could.

"Two more, please," April said, presumably to the waiter.

Paige opened her eyes and returned her attention to her friend as the waiter walked away. "I wish we could do this more often. Every day, maybe?"

"I will gladly take a break from work and hang out at the pool, drinking cocktails with you, anytime."

"We should retire together," Paige offered.

"If that means it could be like this, I'm in," April said.

On the surface, it was a nice idea, but Paige did sometimes wonder how she was going to spend her time later in life. Her business was the center of her existence, but what happened when the time came to set it aside? Sure, it was twenty years away, but time had a way of sneaking up on a person. How would she ever learn to live without that as the center of her universe? "So, I ran into Andre this morning." Paige kicked her legs in the water. "He's getting married."

"Oh, wow. I'm sorry. Are you okay?"

"Yes. I'm fine." Paige waved it off. "I mean, I'd be a little more fine if he wasn't marrying a team cheerleader who also happens to be in med school."

"You can't be serious."

"I am."

"The man can really be a cliché when he wants to be."

"That's not a cliché. That's winning the lottery of love." Paige thought about it, but not too hard. She didn't want to picture Andre and what she imagined his fiancée looked like. "I'm glad that he's happy. That he found someone and figured out how to move on. It at least proves the theory that it's possible."

"Of course it's possible. I just wish you'd been able to do it first. There's no shame if it stings a little. He hurt you. Deeply."

Paige didn't like to think about it very often. It brought up so many unpleasant feelings—betrayal being the worst, and the one that was the slowest to go away. "Anyway. Now you know what's up with Andre."

April clutched Paige's forearm. "Forget your ex. I see a far more stunning prospect."

"What? Who?"

"Opposite end of the pool. Ridiculously tall and hot? It's your friend from the draft. Zach, right?"

Paige looked up, confronted with the vision of Zach as he pulled his T-shirt up over his head. It was like it all happened in slow motion. He was all legs and abs and strong shoulders. The thoughts that flew into her head were not good. They were decidedly naughty. They involved her mouth exploring every contour of his stomach. And other places. "Oh, god. I can't get away from him."

"Why would you want to get away from that?" April playfully batted Paige's shoulder with the back of her hand.

"Because I don't trust him. He's up to something." Saying it out loud made Paige question the idea. Funny, but it had seemed perfectly logical when it was on a perpetual loop in her head.

"You don't need to trust him. Just look at him."

"Did I tell you he's in the room next to mine?"

"No. You did not."

Just then, Zach dove in, hardly making a splash at all. He gracefully slipped through the water, not coming up for air until he'd traversed nearly half the length of the pool. He swam the rest of the way, looking as though he was trying out for the Olympics. His stroke was perfect. Because of course it was.

He reached the stairs at the shallow end, where Paige and April were seated, then stood with his feet on the bottom of the pool, which left him naked and dotted with water drops from his shoulders to his ribs. He swept back his hair in one swift motion with his hand. "Paige. Funny running into you here."

She tried very hard to hide her smile, but it was a pointless effort. Why did he have that effect on her? "Hey, Zach. This is April Chapman."

April held out her hand as he approached. "Zach Armstrong, nice to meet you. Ryan Wilson was quite a signing."

"Oh, hi. Thanks. Ryan is awesome. I'm excited to work with him."

Paige waited for Zach to start fawning over April. She had that effect on men. But to her great surprise, he turned his attention to Paige, stepping closer and putting his hand on the side of the pool, not far from her hip.

"Taking a quick dip?" she asked. Yes, it was more than obvious that he was doing exactly that. She couldn't help her lack of conversational skills at the moment. Seeing so much of his bare skin had her flustered.

"Yeah. I needed to take a break. How'd your meetings go today?"

Paige didn't want to tell him the truth—that they'd largely been unproductive and she was wondering on some level why she'd even bothered coming to the expo. "Oh, you know. Same old, same old. They were fine." She'd leave it at that. No point in embellishing.

He nodded slowly as his eyes fixed on hers. They were the softest blue in this light. His cheeks were flush with color. Water rested in the hollows of his collarbone. Why was he so mesmerizing? Was it simply his youthful exuberance, all wrapped up in a perfect package?

"I'd hope they were better than fine, but maybe you can fill me in later. We still haven't nailed down a time for dinner or a drink. The clock is ticking."

"We live in the same city, Zach. We don't have to get together while we're here."

"Oh, Paige," April interjected. "We should just cancel our dinner reservation tonight. Or you could take Zach instead of me. I've got stuff I need to do."

Paige's vision flew to April. "But, April, it's our one night to see each other." *And I already told you that I'm worried he's up to something.*

"Actually, I have plans. Tonight," Zach said.

Disappointment registered square in the center of Paige's chest, but she tried desperately to ignore it. "Of course you do. You've got a ton of stuff going on, I'm sure."

"With Derek. My newest agent. Trust me. It's not going to be fun or exciting. At least not as fun as it would be with you."

Goose bumps raced up Paige's arms, and the residual energy zapped her chest and face. Her nipples drew tight. "Maybe we'll run into each other tomorrow."

"Are you offering to make an actual plan?" Zach held up both hands in mock surrender, then turned to April. "You heard her. She can't back out now."

"Don't worry. I won't let her," April said.

Paige turned back to April and bugged her eyes. The things she wanted to say to her friend were too numerous to count, but they started with a frantic plea for April to stop encouraging him. She turned back to Zach and sighed. Maybe it was time to simply give in to a sliver of time with him. No harm in that. Hopefully. "Fine. Drinks. Tomorrow night?"

"Perfect. Seven o'clock?" His eyes were wide with expectation.

"That works." Whether or not this was a good idea was up for debate, but she could only say no to him so many times. The fact that he wasn't wearing a shirt made it highly improbable that she'd be able to keep it up.

"I'll see you then. I'm really looking forward to it." He took a step away, then glanced at April. "It was great to meet you. Thanks for being my wingman."

"Anytime," April quipped.

With that, Zach turned and ducked under the water before gliding away effortlessly.

All Paige could do was watch and wonder what he meant by what he'd just said. "Wingman? He's joking, right?"

The waiter arrived with their drinks and April signed for them. "No. The way he looked at you, he's not joking. And it's not about work, either, even if you've convinced yourself that it is." She quickly peered back over her shoulder as the waiter left, then returned her attention to Paige. "He wants you. Big time."

"No. That's not what's going on." Even though the evidence all pointed to that, Paige couldn't help but feel that she was missing something. It didn't make sense. Men didn't fawn over her, especially when April was in the vicinity. She was the woman who turned heads. Not Paige.

"I'm telling you. You're wrong. And what would be so terrible if you were?"

"Not sure I understand the question."

"Would it be bad if you found out that he wanted you? And then you took advantage of that?"

"He's twelve years younger than me."

"So? There are benefits to a younger man, you know." April sucked on the straw in her drink. "Stamina, for one."

Paige nearly choked on her own drink. "Don't get ahead of yourself, okay?"

"All I'm saying is that you are a grown woman and, regardless of the age difference, he is a grown man. You have a very stressful job and you just found out that your ex-husband is getting remarried. If ever there was a time for a woman to let loose and enjoy herself, now is that time."

"Okay…" Paige wasn't fully convinced, but she was getting closer.

"And you're the woman. In case that wasn't clear."

"I gathered as much." She pressed her lips together tightly. "I still worry about the business situation between our two agencies. Whether he might be spying on me or trying to get info out of me."

"You're a smart cookie. You can find out tomorrow night, can't you?"

Paige drew in a deep breath, warring with the feelings and thoughts swirling up inside her. Confusion and excitement were having the biggest battle. What in the world was going to happen? She had absolutely zero clue. "I guess you're right. All will be revealed tomorrow night."

help wear down his ragged edges. He ambled up to the bar and ordered a shot of Buffalo Trace's small batch bourbon. Some people might say it was silly to spend more than one hundred dollars on a drink. But Zach had earned it. And then some. He scouted out the perfect spot to spend time with Paige, and he chose a corner booth in a softly lit corner. If there was a place for quiet and private conversation, that was it. He sat and enjoyed his first heavenly sip. It was smooth and rich. Like velvet. He couldn't imagine anything better right now. That was until the most stunning vision came into view. Paige was walking into the bar, pure poetry in motion. She was there to meet him. And she was even a few minutes early.

He stood and raised his hand to catch her eye. In short order, she looked at him and came to a stop as a hesitant and guarded expression bloomed on her face. She might have shown up, but she still wasn't convinced this was a good idea. "What the hell, Paige?" he muttered under his breath. He was so tired of her not taking him seriously. He drew in a deep breath, resolving to not give up. He was simply going to have to try harder. And he decided that meant trying less. So he sat down and waited for her to come to him.

He glanced at her again and smiled, then took another sip of his bourbon. Her expression softened and she shook her head, then finally started in his direction. His heart began to pound fiercely. Every step she took brought her a little closer, and that made the blood course through his veins even faster. She was an absolute vision in a snug-fitting black dress.

It so closely walked the line between professional and sexy that it left him wondering if he was going to be able to have a conversation with her without falling at her feet and declaring she could have him for absolutely anything she wanted.

"I would like the record to reflect that I'm only early because the person I had a meeting with cut things short." She eased into the booth next to him, clouding his judgment with the lethal combination of her perfume and curves.

"His or her loss if you ask me. What do you want to drink?"

She reached over and raised his glass to her nose to take a sniff. "Mmm. Smells good. I'll have one of these."

Zach flagged the bartender, then pointed at his glass. "Should be over in a minute."

"Great. Thank you. I need it."

"Busy day?"

"Busy, yes. But not…" She hesitated.

"Fruitful?"

"Yes. It's a lot of the same old bullshit I've experienced in other years. People say they want to support women athletes, but they don't really want to. Or if they do, they don't want to pay what they should. I had too many meetings that went nowhere."

Zach hated hearing that things hadn't gone the way she'd hoped they would. "You must've landed a lot for Alexis, right?"

A waiter dropped off Paige's drink. She took a long sip. "Wow. This is delicious. What am I drinking?"

"Buffalo Trace. The fifteen year."

"Whoa. Not the cheap stuff. That's for sure."

"Definitely not the cheap stuff."

She took another sip, this one quicker, then set down her glass and sat back in the booth. "Well, thank you. I appreciate it." Her gaze connected with his, momentarily distracting him from the seeming weight of their conversation. "And to answer your question, I got some leads for Alexis. But as far as actual deals, nothing concrete. The minute I put a price on anything, they back down. They want to see how her season goes. They want to wait to see if she's going to be an all-star. And it's not like I'm asking for the world. She's the top female basketball player in the world. She's stunning. Absolutely gorgeous. She should earn what she deserves. But these companies still can't bring themselves to pay for it."

Zach felt more than a little guilty. He'd hardly exerted himself at all over the last two days. Meanwhile, Paige was putting herself through the wringer and getting less than stellar results. "Alexis is lucky to have you as her agent. Clearly you're fighting for her."

She shrugged. "Thanks. I appreciate that. It's just disappointing. I know exactly how these things go, too. I'll get back to the city and people won't call me back or they'll have some lame excuse as to why they can't do the deal."

"I can't imagine that will happen with Alexis. She's so marketable. It's a no-brainer. Or at least it should be."

"You see that because you're an agent. You've trained yourself to see that. But these brands… I swear it's like they need you to draw them a picture of what your client can do for them. They have no imagination." Paige traced the rim of her glass with the tip of her finger, giving Zach all sorts of sexy things to imagine.

Just then, Enzo Bartolli, a man Zach had already cut one deal with during the expo, walked into the bar. "Have you ever done any work with Maverick Motors?"

"European sports cars? No. I haven't."

Zach scooted across the seat and stood, waving to Enzo, who changed course and headed right over. "Enzo, I'd like you to meet Paige Moss with Moss Sports. She represents Alexis Simmons. I have to think she would be perfect for an ad campaign for Maverick."

Enzo smiled and reached out to shake Paige's hand. "Hello, Ms. Moss. It's nice to meet you. We've never done a campaign with a woman who wasn't a model. I'm intrigued."

Paige sat a little straighter. Her face lit up, and all Zach could think was that he wanted to do anything necessary to put that expression on her face as much as possible. "Well, that's the thing about Alexis. She's a killer basketball player, but she could also be on the cover of any fashion magazine. I'm sure she'd look super sexy sitting behind the wheel of one of your cars. If you want beauty and appeal, she's got it."

Zach realized then that Paige's trouble had nothing to do with a lack of salesmanship. She could sell her clients effortlessly. It was these dim-witted sponsors who needed to wake up. "I have to say I agree. I've met Alexis in person and she's incredibly beautiful."

Enzo nodded, then reached into his pocket and handed over his business card. "Ms. Moss, why don't you call me next week? I fly back to Italy later tonight, but I'll be in the office on Monday. Perhaps we can work together."

Paige took his card and tucked it into her bag. "Thank you. I will definitely give you a call on Monday. I appreciate it."

"No problem. You two enjoy your night." With that, Enzo walked away.

Zach sat back down next to Paige. "Maybe that could end up being something."

"Maybe. We'll see. I'm not going to hold my breath."

"Enzo is a pretty straight shooter. I don't think he would've asked you to call him if he wasn't seriously interested."

Paige took another drink. "Like I said, we'll see. But thank you for making the introduction. You really didn't need to do that."

"I wanted to do it."

"Zach. We're competitors. That's definitely not something your stepdad would've done. In fact, if Tom witnessed that, or even found out about it, I'm guessing he'd hit the roof."

"I want to prove to you that I'm not the enemy, Paige. Neither is my company."

"I know *you're* not the enemy, Zach. I know that. It's just that we're talking about well-tested reflexes. I've spent a lot of years butting heads with your step-dad. That doesn't just go away overnight."

"I still don't really understand the bad blood."

She hesitated and cleared her throat. "Well, some-day I'll tell you the story. Not tonight. I'd prefer to have a nice conversation." She turned and offered a soft smile. "I'm sorry if I didn't sound enthusiastic about meeting Enzo. I am. And as I said, I appreciate the introduction. It was really nice of you to do that."

"I just want you to know how much I admire everything you've accomplished in such a male-dominated industry. I know things are changing, but I'm sure it's not anywhere close to being fast enough for you."

"It will never be fast enough. Maybe because I already had to endure the slow parts."

Zach inched closer to her. "I really do admire you, Paige. A lot."

She turned her head and eyed him. As their gazes connected, he felt a jolt of electricity run right through him. "You don't have to flatter me, Zach."

"It's not flattery. It's the truth. You are the most brilliant, strong and compelling woman I have ever met."

She laughed quietly. "Maybe you need to get out more."

He tilted his head to the side, hoping to get her to look into his eyes. "Don't downplay your assets, Paige. Don't deflect. You are everything. You're smart. Capable." He swallowed hard, his throat dry and rough as he wondered if he really had the guts to take this leap. Getting rejected by Paige would be so painful. "And you're so damn beautiful it's hard for me to think straight when I'm around you."

"You are way too young and handsome to be spending your time flirting with me. Isn't there a twenty-five year old you can hit on?"

He shook his head. "You're the only one I want to hit on."

She laughed again, but then she turned toward him and lowered her head slightly. It was the most imperceptible movement, but it meant the world to Zach. "Is that what all of those invitations to dinner were?"

"Was that not apparent?"

"Not entirely."

"Interesting. I was so sure that I was being ridiculously obvious."

She focused on his face, seeming quite serious. "What exactly were you hoping to get out of dinner or drinks together?"

"I was hoping we could get to know each other better." He glanced down and saw that her hand was in her lap. He reached over and wrapped his fingers around hers, soaking up the sheer pleasure of having his fingertips that close to the tops of her thighs. That close to her center. There was only a thin layer of fabric between his hand and the luscious curves that he longed to touch. Everything below his waist drew tight. He wanted her so bad he could hardly see.

She leaned closer yet. A few more inches erased.

He was so glad. So relieved. "I feel like we've talked a lot, Zach." She looked into his eyes and then ran her tongue along her lower lip. "What other ways were you hoping to know me?"

He let go of her hand and started moving toward her knee, his fingertips barely skimming her dress. With every inch, he felt a little more brave. With every millimeter, he became more self-assured. When he reached her bare knee, his fingers made contact, then he curled them ever so slightly under the hem of her dress. "Like this?"

Her eyelids got heavy and she hummed quietly. "Hmm."

"Nice?"

"So far, yes. Now what?"

He moved his hand beneath her dress, slipping it under the fabric and palming her velvety thigh. "I think you already know."

Her spine softened as she scooted closer to the edge of the seat, granting him easier access. "Zach. What if someone sees us?"

He smiled. "It's so damn dark in here." His words sounded calm and self-assured, but meanwhile, his heart was beating so fiercely he could hear his pulse in his ears. He couldn't believe he was doing this, but even so, he couldn't stop himself. He moved his hand farther up her thigh with his fingers riding the valley between her legs, amazed by how hot things had gotten between Paige and him, so quickly.

A near-silent groan escaped her lips. "I suppose everyone is pretty drunk."

"Exactly." Finally, he realized that he'd reached his destination when his finger brushed a silky bit of fabric.

Paige sucked in a breath and her gaze connected with his. Her eyes were wild with passion, even when they were questioning. "So you're…"

"I am." He pulled the fabric aside and his finger found her center. She was already so wet. If this didn't end up back in his room or hers, it was going to be one of the biggest disappointments of his life. But for now, he had his charge and he was not going to fail her.

Paige looked right at him as he worked her clit in delicate circles. He could tell that she was having a hard time keeping her eyes open. She softly rolled her head to one side, then quickly righted it for appearances. "Is it wrong that I wish I could kiss you right now?"

He shook his head, wondering how much he would have to pay to kick everyone out of this bar right now, kiss her with wild abandon and take her right there and then. "That's for later. When we aren't around all of these people we know." He leaned closer and muttered into her ear, "For now, I want to watch you come."

She whimpered and squirmed in her seat. "It's not going to take long."

"Good." He continued with his ministrations as they held each other's gaze. It was the hottest thing Zach had ever done with any woman. He watched the constellation of reactions on her face as her lips went softer and her eyes blazed with intensity and then finally, her jaw went tight as she clamped her eyes shut and she reached under the table to grab his wrist. Her shoulders shuddered slightly. He couldn't wait to find out what that moment was going to be like, deep inside her. Especially if she called out his name.

"Okay?" he asked.

She nodded, composing herself. "Better than okay."

He slowly pulled his hand away and Paige straightened her dress under the table. They both sat back and each took hefty sips of their drinks. Zach was more than a little concerned about how he was going to walk out of this bar without embarrassing himself. He had the fiercest hard-on he'd had in quite some time. But the reality was he didn't really care right now. He just wanted to get her alone.

"Uh. I don't want to sound like a cliché, but your place or mine?" he asked.

She smiled. "As long as we have a bed and the rest of the night, it doesn't make a difference to me. I'm thinking we're going to have everything we need." She finished off her drink.

"I am *so* glad we finally made a plan to have drinks."

"Yeah. Me, too."

As Paige and Zach walked down the hall to their rooms, she had only one thought—she could not believe she was doing this. Then again, she could hardly believe what had just happened down in the bar. She'd let Zach put his hand inside her panties under the table, in a crowded room that was full of their colleagues. Paige didn't do a lot of spontaneous things. She certainly wasn't daring very often. But she could get used to this. Her blood was pumping. She felt alive, after so many years of feeling far less than that.

"Let's go to my room. It's closer," Paige said. "Probably ten whole feet."

Zach laughed. "I like how you think."

She fumbled for her key card as he stood right behind her and placed his hand on her hip. The light went green so she turned the door handle, and the two of them nearly stumbled into the room. Paige dropped her bag on the floor.

"We're all alone," he said with a clever grin on his face, moving in on her. The only illumination in the room was the ambient glow of the Las Vegas strip, filtering through the window.

Everything about him was a feast for the senses and she didn't know where to start—his hair begged to be touched and his chest was hiding under his dress shirt while the knowledge of what it looked like bare was filtering through her head. "We talked about kissing in the bar." She bit her lower lip in anticipation.

"Like this?" He cupped her shoulders with his hands and placed the softest kiss on her lips. It was a tease. A taste. It made her light-headed.

"That's a good start." She grasped his biceps and pulled him closer, peering up into those beguiling blue-gray eyes. "But I was thinking something more like this." She closed her eyes and pressed her lips against his. Zach immediately upped the ante, reining her in with his strong arms and holding her close while his lips parted and his tongue explored her mouth, then tangled with hers in an endless loop. The kiss was like a storm, chaotic and raw and unpredictable. It was everything she wanted.

He wasted no time pulling down the zipper at the back of her dress, his determined fingers traveling lower while want and need raged inside her. He peeled her dress down her arms and left it loose around her waist to reveal her black lace bra. She was so thankful she'd put on some of her best, sexiest underwear today. On some unconscious level, she must've been hoping that this would happen. He slipped the bra strap from her shoulder, then pulled one of the cups down from her breast before lowering his head and drawing her nipple into his mouth. He held on to her rib cage with a firm grip. He wasn't letting go. Not anytime soon.

Paige gasped when he gently tugged on the tight bud with his teeth. A sizzle of electricity traveled straight to her clit. She was already close. How was that possible? She needed him so badly she could hardly think straight.

Zach unhooked her bra and cast it aside, then pulled her dress down from her hips. She was all ready to start on his shirt or maybe go straight to his pants, but she didn't get the chance. Zach dropped to his knees before her, holding on to her hips and then digging his fingers into the fleshiest parts of her ass. He gazed up at her with a look that was indecipherable, making her feel even more overheated than she had a minute ago. His eyes shifted darker and he tugged her panties to one side to revisit the place his hand had been in the bar. He nestled his face between her legs, his tongue quickly finding her apex. Another zap of electricity hit her hard. So hard that she could hardly stand. She reached for the dresser that was right behind her, but bracing herself only gave him better access. She was at his mercy.

"Zach. Come here. Let's get you out of those clothes." As good as it felt, everything they'd done together was so focused on her pleasure... She wanted her turn.

"I couldn't agree more." He rose to stand and took her hand, then tugged her to the bed while he used his free hand to untuck his shirt.

Paige quickly took the opportunity into her own hands, turning him around and smashing her mouth against his, tongues swirling while her fingers scrambled through the buttons of his shirt. She shoved the garment from his shoulders, never letting go of the kiss. His pants were the next to go, slumping to the floor, leaving nothing before her but his long, lean, hard body. She tugged his boxer briefs past his hips, then took his erection in her hand, stroking firmly from base to tip.

Zach groaned in ecstasy and dug his fingers into her shoulders. "That feels so good."

"Oh, that's only the beginning." She gently pushed him back on the bed. "Stretch out. In the middle."

"I feel like you've done this before."

"Very funny." Of course, it was humorous to Paige on one level, but only in that she wasn't normally much of a talker in the bedroom. Something about Zach made her want to make him feel good. So good. Perhaps it was because he'd been so focused on her from the start. She climbed onto the mattress and kneeled between his legs, stroking his lower belly with one hand while she raked her fingers along one of his thighs. She studied his handsome face, looking for clues as to what he liked. The answer was: all of it. She took his length in her hand again and stroked hard, then lowered her head and slipped his erection into her mouth. He was so hard and quite a lot for her to contend with, but she took her time, letting her lips glide along his length, swirling her tongue around the swollen head with every pass. She felt the tension in his hips and legs. It was radiating from his body. She could relate. She had quite a lot of that to deal with from her side of things. The need was centered between her legs, but she felt it in her breasts and stomach. She felt it on the tops of her thighs.

From the sound of his breaths, which were getting shorter and choppier, she needed to move things along or Zach was going to reach his peak and she'd have to wait even longer while he recovered. She slowly released him from her lips, then rolled onto her side next to him. "Please tell me you have a condom." She could hardly believe that she'd been so irresponsible as to let them get this far without having had this discussion. Certainly there were other things they could do that didn't require protection, but she wanted Zach. All of him.

He sat up slowly and turned to her. "Confession time."

"Okay…" She heard the uncertainty in her own voice as she traced his abs with her fingers. What was he about to say?

"I do have one. Well, a few actually." He got up from the bed and shuffled over to his pants, which he picked up. Then he started searching the pockets. "I don't normally do this, but…" He turned to her with the foil packets in his hand.

Paige beckoned him closer with a curl of her finger. "You were hoping you'd get lucky?"

He laughed quietly. "Busted." He stooped down and kissed her softly. "Happily busted."

She took the packets from him and opened one as he crawled onto the bed next to her. She tore it open and rolled it on as he kissed her with renewed passion. Then he shifted to his knees and took charge, spreading her knees wide for him. He took his cock in his hand and stroked himself a few times, then lowered his body, slowly driving inside. She couldn't contain the groan that came deep from her throat. He felt impossibly good. Even better than she'd dared to imagine. As he started to thrust, she couldn't help but notice how careful his strokes were—deep and strong with a super sexy rotation of his hips. She raised her pelvis to take him deeper and he settled his body weight against her center, sending her closer to the edge. The pressure built quickly as he ground against her a little harder and lowered his head to lick and suck on her nipples. Paige arched into him, first wondering if they could get closer, then curious how long they could stay this way, even when both of their breathing became shallower and faster. She reached down and grabbed his firm ass and then wrapped her legs around him tightly, wanting it harder. Faster. Forever.

Their rhythm was unparalleled, everything in perfect sync—breath and pulse building to a crescendo that she felt coming for her. She was stuck in that place where she wanted more but was desperate for the peak, and then finally it had her in its grasp, shaking her to her core with wave after wave of heat and pleasure. Zach followed right after her, calling out, and she took his head in her hands and kissed away the sound, wanting it all for herself. Zach collapsed on top of her, weighing her down. Part of her wanted to be pinned to this bed by him for all eternity. Nothing in recent memory had felt so good.

"That was incredible," she muttered into his ear, stroking his back and still holding him tight with her legs wrapped around him.

"So good. So fucking good." Zach raised his head and kissed her with all of the heat he'd delivered from the first time their lips had met. "But I'm going to need more. I need more of you, Paige Moss."

A grin bloomed across her face as she smiled to herself. "Really?"

"Yes. I want to have you all damn night."

Six

Everything around Zach right now was soft and inviting—the sumptuous hotel bedding, the faint early morning light and most tempting of all was Paige's bare skin. Every atom of his body was waking now to the memory of last night and the awareness that she was right there, next to him in bed, available to touch and caress. Her quiet, even breaths told him that she was still asleep. She was on her side, with her back to him, so he scooted closer and pressed his chest against her shoulder blades. Beneath the silky sheets, he smoothed his hand over the velvety bare skin of her waist, then up over the slope of her hip and down to the yielding flesh of her thigh. He molded his body around hers, his fierce erection nestled against her impossibly soft backside.

Last night had been a revelation for Zach, and all he wanted was more. Even when he knew it was wrong. Even knowing with a fair degree of certainty that if Tom ever learned what had taken place in Paige's hotel room over the last ten hours, he would absolutely blow his stack.

Or maybe that was part of what made it so hot.

He nestled his face into the back of her hair, pressing his nose against her neck and inhaling her intoxicating scent. Paige stirred and hummed softly, but didn't utter a word. As much as he liked her, she was a mystery to him. She didn't show her cards. She kept things locked up inside that beautiful head of hers. Sex seemed to be the only thing that could get her to shed her perfectly composed exterior. In bed, she was free and unguarded. She knew what she wanted, she wasn't afraid to ask for it and last night, all she had wanted was him. It was such a turn-on.

"You awake?" he muttered, kissing her neck, then her shoulder. He smoothed his hand up along the tempting terrain he'd traveled a moment earlier, then slipped around to her breast and lightly teased her nipple with a fingertip. The bud tightened beneath his touch. How he loved feeling her body respond to him that way.

"Getting there." A warm and gentle murmur followed her answer, suggesting she appreciated his touch.

"Good. Because I need you, Paige. I need all of you." He propped himself up on his elbow, pulled her hair back from her neck and kissed her shoulder.

Paige tensed. She cleared her throat. "What time is it?" Her voice was clear. Almost cold.

"It's a little before eight. Are you okay?"

She eased herself to the edge of the bed, then stood, taking the duvet and wrapping up her luscious body in it. The disappointment was so instantaneous, it made his stomach sink. "I think it's probably time for you to go."

"Oh. Okay." He sat up in bed, tugging the remaining sheet up to his waist to cover up his hard-on. There was nothing worse than your body telegraphing your readiness for sex while the other person in the room wasn't in the mood. "Is your flight soon?"

"It's this afternoon. Hold on. I need to pee." She marched off to the bathroom and closed the door behind her.

Zach was more confused than he'd been in quite some time. What in the hell had he done or said to deserve this treatment? Had he shown too much enthusiasm? That didn't seem possible. She'd been fully into every minute of their night together.

When Paige emerged from the bathroom, she was wrapped up tightly in the white terry cloth hotel robe. "Last night was great, but like I said, you should probably go."

"Really? Don't we have a little time?" He patted the empty spot on the mattress next to him.

"Not a good idea." She shook her head.

"Did I do something wrong?"

"No. Not at all. You're amazing and last night was super fun. But everyone staying on our hall is either an agent or an athlete. Nothing good comes from someone spotting you walking out of my room. It wouldn't be good for business. For either of us."

He supposed she had a point, but he still didn't like it. "You know, Moss and Armstrong don't have to feud forever. I don't know about your company bylaws, but that certainly isn't written into ours."

Paige stepped closer and perched on the edge of the bed. Although he was happy to have her closer, it didn't feel like a warm or welcoming gesture. "Look. Last night was awesome."

"It was better than awesome," he interrupted.

"Excuse me?"

"Paige. I made you come at least five times. It might be more. I lost count." He remembered reading an article in a men's magazine about when a woman reached her sexual peak. It had said it could go well into her forties. After last night, he was certain that was true.

She raised both eyebrows and pinched the bridge of her nose. "Leave it to a guy to keep score."

He shrugged. "I'm competitive. What can I say?" He scooted closer. "Tell me last night wasn't better than awesome."

Her cheeks colored with pink and she looked up at him with her deep blue eyes. "Fine, it was incredible. Out of this world. Is that what you want to hear?"

"Only if it's true."

She sucked in a deep breath. "It's true. Okay? You are unbelievable in bed. But you and I are on a work trip, and this was not a great idea given the history of our two agencies." She cleared her throat again, then stood and wrapped her arms around her waist. "Plus, we need to be realistic. You're twelve years younger than me. This could never be anything more than sex."

"I wasn't aware I'd asked for anything more than that." He knew it probably came off as rude, but it was the truth. It wasn't like he'd asked her for a relationship. They'd had sex. And he wanted a whole lot more of it. With her.

"Right. So let's chalk this up to what it was. Just sex."

"Which means what?" He knew he probably sounded as though he was being obtuse, but he wanted her to say it. Out loud. Whatever was circulating in her head.

"It means that we can't see each other again. And we can't tell anyone about this. No one."

"I guess I don't understand why any of this means it has to be the end. I'm totally up for just sex. We both live in the same city. Hell, our offices are only two blocks away from each other."

She padded to the corner of the room and plucked his shirt from the floor, then marched it back and thrust it in his direction. "Absolutely not. Last night was the beginning, middle and end."

Zach calmly took his shirt and climbed out of bed, opting to stand in front of her completely naked, with the hard-on that was still very much present. Let her see what she was saying no to. Let her look at what she'd be missing. "Okay, Paige. Whatever you say. I'd like to use the bathroom before I go. If that's okay with you." He tossed the shirt on the chair instead of putting it on and calmly stepped into the bathroom to hide his annoyance. He splashed ice-cold water on his face and chest to help abate his body's excitement over the prospect of sex. He dried his skin, then used the bathroom and washed his hands, all while wondering if Paige Moss would ever take him seriously. Was he doomed to be dismissed by her forever? What more could she possibly want from him? A connection with a deep-pocketed sponsor and five orgasms in one night should have been more than enough to keep her interested. Apparently not.

He stepped out of the bathroom, then fetched his boxer briefs and tugged them on. Paige was standing near the door to her room, still wearing the robe and not saying a word. The silence was beyond awkward. It was painful. He put on his pants, then his shirt, telling himself that this might just be for the best. Tom's approval and his personal success were most important to him. He needed to focus. His night with Paige had been all kinds of fun. But that was in the past now. At least according to her.

He picked up his shoes, but didn't put them on. Instead, he tucked his socks inside of them. "Okay, then. I guess I'll see you around."

"You're going to walk out of my room barefoot?" she sounded panicked.

"I am. And I'm going to do it slowly, too. Just in case I run into anyone we know while I'm out in the hall."

She frowned at him, but that only made him think harder about how badly he wanted to kiss her. "You realize this could be just as bad for you as it would be for me. I mean, if anyone found out."

He shrugged. "I like living on the edge. It makes life more interesting."

"Don't you want to be taken seriously, Zach? You've just taken over your father's company, and I know for a fact that there are agents who have been there as long as you've been alive. You have to know that some of them resent you. I'm sure they'd do anything they could to railroad you. Do you really want to give them ammunition?"

Zach hadn't thought about that, but that wasn't what was really bothering him right now. It was the confirmation, from Paige, that some people didn't take him seriously. He was deathly afraid she might be part of that contingent. "It's just next door. I think I can make it that far."

"It's your career. I can't tell you what to do."

He stepped closer to her, their gazes connecting before he let his focus drift to her lips. He couldn't escape the sense that this wasn't the end, even when she was telling him it was. There was more between them. He knew it. "Let me know if you change your mind, Paige."

"I won't. Change my mind."

He turned the doorknob, then leaned over and kissed her on the cheek. "Well, I certainly appreciate a woman who knows what she wants."

Paige slumped against the door of her hotel room as soon as Zach was gone. She was so turned on right now that she could hardly see straight. Zach had been wrong about five orgasms. It was actually seven. Of course she'd kept score. Hell yes, she had. If only because he was light-years ahead of any other guy she'd ever gone to bed with.

And how had she responded? She'd sent him away.

"It's for the best. Right?" she asked herself as she took several steps ahead and dramatically flopped down on the bed face-first. Unfortunately, the sheets were perfumed with a beguiling mix of Zach's heady smell and the familiar scent of sex. Visions of last night rushed through her consciousness—his strong hands all over her, his unforgettable mouth visiting everywhere his hands had been. Being with him was intoxicating. He left her entire body buzzing with electricity. The longing for more of Zach was so strong that it created a burning sensation in the center of her chest. Despite everything she'd just said to him about how it would never happen again, she could be easily convinced to show up at his door stark naked right now.

But no. That was not a good choice for her. Not now. Not tomorrow. Or next week. Just because she'd slept with Zach, didn't mean that she suddenly trusted him professionally. And her history with his stepdad had proven time and again that there was no cozying up to anyone involved with Armstrong Sports, unless you wanted to eventually get stabbed in the back.

And then there was the personal side of her inner

conflict over Zach. He was *twelve* years younger than her. More than a decade. He had his entire life ahead of him. He probably wanted a marriage and children—one thing she'd already failed at, and the other she was certain was no longer in the cards for her. All of which meant he would eventually reach a point where he no longer had a use for her. She didn't get involved because she refused to get hurt. That was a good choice. It was smart. And all of that aside, did he even like the same music and movies she did? If they were together, what would happen when the sex faded? Did they actually have anything in common?

"Cut it out, Paige," she said into the emptiness of her room. Why was she tormenting herself with hypotheticals? She needed to get a grip. Her brief time with Zach had been amazing. Full stop. She'd had her fun. And now it was time for a return to reality, and that was not possible in this room, this hotel or this city. She needed to get to the airport as soon as possible. Maybe she could hop on an earlier flight. Was she running away? Absolutely. Running back to her normal, everyday life where she worked hard and didn't give a man a chance to stomp on her heart.

She crawled across the bed until she could grab her phone from the nightstand. She pulled up the airline app, tapped her reservation, then scrolled down to a button at the very bottom of the screen that would allow her to change her travel plans. With a little luck and a fee of several hundred dollars, she grabbed the last first-class seat on an earlier flight to

New York. It made her feel slightly better about her lot in life. This was the version of herself she most appreciated—the Paige who took charge, changed her circumstances and moved forward.

She rolled off the bed and hustled into the bathroom, then started the shower. Moments later, she stepped into the warm spray, but the instant she spread soapy bubbles over her skin, her mind flew to Zach. *Dammit.* If she'd been smart, she would have convinced him to take a shower with her before he left. That would've left her with an expanded treasure trove of white-hot memories. The downside of a one-night stand was having to accept that there would always be things left undone. It was baked into the concept. Not that she'd done this very often. It wasn't her thing. When she was younger, her response to sex had always been to pull the other person closer and hold on tight. That was how things started with Andre. But there would be no holding on to Zach. It was a losing proposition.

She turned off the water and got out of the shower, dried off, then dressed in a comfortable knit dress for her return trip back to New York. She quickly packed up her suitcase, being far less careful than she would typically be by allowing her dirty clothes and the clean ones to intermingle. She was not going to miss her new flight.

Still, she hesitated for an instant out in the hall. Was Zach still next door? Was he angry or upset with her? Or had he already moved on? His cavalier attitude when he'd left made her think the latter. In this instance, she needed to be more like Zach.

She ducked down the hall with her roller bag and was relieved when there was no one else waiting for the elevator. After a quick ride downstairs, she stopped by the front desk to drop off her key card, then hurried outside to the cabstand. She'd been in line for only a few seconds when there was a warm hand at her waist. *Zach.* She quickly flipped around. The disappointment hit her all at once—she sighed and her shoulders dropped. It was Andre. "Hey."

"Heading out already?" he asked.

"Yes. I have a ton of work to do. I really need to get back home and catch up on everything I've been ignoring while I've been in Vegas." She looked down and saw that he had his suitcase as well. "You're leaving, too."

"I promised Casey I'd get back as soon as possible. Between work and her school schedule, Sundays are usually the only days we get to spend any time together at all."

Paige couldn't deny the anger bubbling up inside of her. It wasn't jealousy. She simply didn't understand the universe's criteria for doling out life circumstances right now. Why did Andre get to find love so effortlessly while she was completely frazzled after a one-night stand? "That's nice."

"Share a cab to the airport?"

She tried in earnest to think of a reason to say no. The thought of a solo ride to the airport sounded peaceful. But she couldn't come up with a single excuse. "Sure."

As the couple at the front of the line climbed into a taxi, she and Andre stepped forward.

"I saw you and the kid in the hotel bar last night. You two looked very cozy," he said.

A ribbon of panic ran through her. She hadn't seen Andre at all. Had he noticed that Zach had his hand up her skirt? Had he seen the moment she'd given in to his touch? She'd been so sure that the table at their booth and the dim lighting had obscured it all. "Don't call him a kid, Andre. That's very demeaning. The man is thirty years old."

He bugged his eyes. "Defensive much?"

"It's the truth."

Andre leaned closer. "You had sex with him, didn't you?" he asked straight into her ear.

"Excuse me?" Paige yanked her bag as they moved another spot closer to the front of the line.

"I can always tell when you've had sex, Paige," he muttered under his breath. "Judging by the way you look right now, I'd say that you had quite a night."

Was it really *that* obvious? Hopefully it wasn't to the rest of the world, and this was simply the product of having been married to Andre. He could read her like an open book. She hated feeling so exposed. "If you're expecting me to admit to anything, you can forget it."

"It's a compliment. You look spectacular. I don't mean anything nefarious by it."

"And this is weird coming from my ex-husband."

The man in front of them in line got his cab, which meant she and Andre were next. She was so ready to get to the airport, break away from Andre, get on her flight and escape all of this.

"Paige!" a man's voice shouted.

Paige and Andre turned in unison. Zach, his suitcase and a big old grin approached. Unfortunately for Paige, his smile alone was enough to make her tingly.

"You guys headed to the airport?" Zach asked.

"Yes. You, too? You should join us," Andre answered.

What in the hell was going on? Paige had lost all control of her world.

"Perfect," Zach replied breathlessly then thrust his hand in Andre's direction. "I'm Zach Armstrong."

"Andre Held."

Paige watched the two of them shake hands and silently wished for lightning to strike her dead. Her ex-husband and the too-young-for-her guy she'd just hooked up with had now befriended each other. What was next? Was her high school boyfriend hiding in the bushes?

"You three together?" the doorman tending to the cabstand asked.

"We are," Andre answered.

Apparently, Paige thought.

"This is you," the doorman said.

A taxi pulled up and the driver got out to help with the bags.

"Do you have a spot in the front seat for me?" Andre asked.

"Sorry," the driver answered as he tossed the suitcases into the trunk. "I've got a bunch of books up there. I'm studying for my real estate license. But there's plenty of room for three in the back."

"Looks like you're the pickle in the middle, Paige," Andre said.

"What? Are you twelve?" Paige asked. She scooted across the seat while Zach rounded to the opposite side of the car and climbed in. She left a sliver of space between them, which quickly disappeared as soon as Andre got in on her right.

"Everybody comfy?" Zach asked.

Paige wrapped her arms around her handbag, which was perched on her lap. "Never been better," she lied.

The cabdriver eased around the corner in front of the hotel, but as soon as the coast was clear to turn onto Las Vegas Boulevard, he gunned it. Paige slid into Zach, then had to wiggle herself back into place.

"Sorry," she said.

"No problem," Zach answered in a low voice that sent shudders through her.

"So, Zach," Andre said. "Where do you think Ryan Wilson will land? I gotta think he'll have his pick of teams."

Zach leaned forward to make eye contact with Andre. "You know I represent him?"

"I'd have to be hiding under a rock. Plus, I'm really hoping he doesn't end up with a team in our division."

Zach laughed. "Yeah. Well, we'll see."

"What's he going to do without Davante Diggs to throw to? Those two were pure fire together."

Zach cleared his throat. "There might be some other changes afoot."

"Whoa. Seriously?"

Zach and Andre quickly launched into an in-depth discussion of professional football, while Paige looked straight ahead and tried not to think about how damn awkward it was to be sitting between them. She had no trouble keeping up with the substance of their conversation since she followed all sports closely, even those in which she had zero clients, like football. It paid to be well versed in the entire industry. Still, she couldn't ignore the way Zach and Andre got along from the word *go*. They were a flurry of chatter. They made each other laugh. At one point, Paige nearly asked if they wanted her to sit by the window so they could be closer, but that would have required her crawling over either her ex-husband or the man she was trying like hell to resist. One lap she had no business in, and the other…well, that would've been entirely too inviting.

"Which airline?" the cabdriver asked.

"Southwest," Andre answered.

"Delta," Paige and Zach both said at nearly the same time.

She turned to him. "Which flight are you on?"

"The eleven-thirty into LaGuardia."

Paige closed her eyes and begged for some semblance of tranquility. "Do you know your seat assignment?"

"3A. Why? Are we on the same flight?"

Andre quietly chuckled as the cabdriver pulled up to the curb in front of his airline and popped the trunk. "It's been real, guys." He opened the door, then pulled out his wallet and offered a twenty dollar bill. "This should cover my piece of it."

Zach held up his hand. "Don't worry. I've got it."

"You sure?" Andre asked.

"I am," Zach said.

"Bye, Paige. Take care of yourself," Andre said, then turned his attention to Zach. "Make sure she gets home safe, okay?"

"Will do," Zach replied.

Andre winked at Paige, then closed the door. The cabdriver eased back into the flow of traffic.

Paige scooted across the seat to separate herself from Zach. "We need to set some ground rules for our flight."

"So you are sitting next to me?"

She cleared her throat. "I am."

"Worried I'm going to go for a replay of last night in the bar?"

A tremor of that incident rambled through her body. The thought that it might happen more than once had never occurred to her. She was more worried she'd fall asleep with her head on his shoulder. Or have to ask him to get up so she could go to the bathroom, only to have him say there was plenty of room for her to squeeze past him. Because of course he was going to do that. It was going to be impossible to sit next to him for five hours, watching him be adorable and heartbreakingly handsome, knowing this was not meant to be.

The driver pulled up to the curb again and Zach was quick to put his card into the payment terminal.

"Let me know the total. We can split it."

"Paige. I've got it. It's fine."

"Okay. Thanks." She climbed out of the car, grabbed her suitcase from the trunk, then waited for Zach at the curb. She couldn't be rude. They were traveling companions now, whether she liked it or not. "Ready?"

"I've never looked forward to a flight more than this one."

"Zach. Come on. Please stop messing with me."

He stepped closer and reached for her elbow. "I'm not. I'm really not. No matter what happened last night or this morning, I'm determined that you and I will be friends. Beyond that, don't worry. I will respect your boundaries. You said you don't want anything to do with me and that's fine."

"I don't think I put it that way. Did I?"

"You said it was just sex. And I said that I didn't understand what the problem was with just sex. That was the beginning of the end."

Paige quietly sighed. What was it about him that stripped away her defenses? That made her want to backtrack on every damn thing she'd said to establish boundaries? "You want to be friends?"

"I do."

"Okay. Then let's be friends. Just friends. That's it."

"I can live with that." He turned toward the terminal. "For now."

Seven

Paige had been back in New York for three days, but she was having a hell of a time focusing on work. Zach was still so present in her head that it was like he was following her around all day. Sitting in her office. Joining her on the subway for her ride home. He was certainly there when she went to bed at night and turned off the lights. It was all too easy to think about no one but him. To think about what it would be like if she'd simply given in to the idea of "just sex." If she were truly capable of not getting emotionally involved, she wouldn't have hesitated to say yes to the idea. But she knew herself. She knew what time with Zach Armstrong was going to do to her.

The flight home had been more than enough of a test. She couldn't help it—she loved hanging out with him, watching him turn on the in-flight entertainment and witnessing his genuine excitement that he could watch sports highlights. She enjoyed eating a meal with him, even if it was merely airline fare. As much as she'd been determined to create distance between them, they still effortlessly fell into conversation. They laughed together. With not-so-innocent glances, they flirted. In any other world, if their difference in age wasn't quite so great and his stepdad wasn't such a colossal jerk, she might go for it with Zach.

When it came time for lunch on Wednesday, she ordered a salad, ate it at her desk and planned to call April. The truth was that she needed some time outside of her own thoughts and ruminations about Zach. And if anyone would have some good advice, it was her.

April picked up after the first ring. "Hey there. I'm glad you called. I've been meaning to reach out and see how the rest of your Vegas trip went."

"Yeah. About that…" Paige wiped her mouth and sat back in her chair.

"Oh, boy. That's the sound of a big story coming my way. Hold on one sec. Let me close my office door."

Luckily, Paige had enough foresight to have done that already. She adored Henry, but he was not only a gossip—he had a real knack for eavesdropping.

"Okay. I'm back," April said. "I want to know everything and don't leave out the good parts."

"I don't even know where to start, to be honest. Let's just say that things got complicated."

"With Zach?"

"Yes."

"Complicated good? Or complicated bad?"

Paige hated that there was no clear answer to this question. "Mostly good?"

April squealed so loudly on the other end of the line that Paige had to hold her phone a good foot away from her ear. "Tell. Me. Everything."

Paige sighed and turned in her office chair, looking out the window. Her tryst with Zach still felt like a dream. "It started in the hotel bar."

"Oh, right. The date for drinks."

"Yes."

"Well? What happened? You're stalling."

"He was being super flirtatious. And nice. He introduced me to a potential sponsor."

"I still have the feeling you're holding out on me, Paige."

Paige realized she was indeed dragging her feet. Even though she and April told each other virtually everything, it didn't feel quite right to kiss and tell. "I am."

"Okay. Then don't tell me everything. Just tell me the highlights."

"Seven times in my hotel room."

"Whoa."

"But before that, once in the bar. That's how it all got started."

"Wait a minute. You two had sex in the hotel bar?"

"No. I'm talking orgasms."

"His or yours?"

Paige laughed. "Mine." She gnawed on her thumbnail. Merely thinking about it made her want him. "He, uh, reached under my skirt when we were sitting in a booth in the back."

"Seriously?"

"I would not make that up. I couldn't make that up."

"I told you he was going to be fun to spend some time with."

"It was definitely fun. No doubt about that." Paige quietly groaned. There was so much frustration warring inside of her. She would've given anything to have more of Zach, but she didn't see any way that could possibly end well, and she was tired of self-sabotaging and making things harder on herself. "But of course I told him that it couldn't continue."

"Why? You're both single. You're both adults."

"First off, there's all of the weirdness between our two agencies."

"That was between you and his stepdad. Zach doesn't seem to care. At all. He was flirting with you so hard at the pool that afternoon."

"What about industry gossip? If we were involved, people would talk. I don't want to be the butt of anyone's jokes. It's already hard enough to garner respect in the sports world."

"So keep it quiet. Nobody's saying you have to let anyone know that it's going on."

Paige chewed on her lower lip, wondering if that could possibly work. She knew she could be discreet, but could Zach be counted on for the same?

The man had given her an orgasm in a hotel bar. A public place that was chock-full of people they knew. "I don't know. There's my personal track record with men, too. That's definitely eating at me."

"I know, honey. And I get it. But it's not the same as your situation with Andre. It's not like you and Zach are going to get married or something. Right?"

"Of course not."

"How did he take it when you told him that it couldn't continue?"

"He said that he didn't see a problem with seeing each other every now and then."

"He has a point. It doesn't have to be a problem. If that's what you want."

She knew what she wanted—something that didn't actually exist—a trouble-free way of getting to be naked with Zach Armstrong as much as she could handle. But was there a way for her to have at least a little bit of that? "I wouldn't mind seeing him again. And we did agree to be friends."

"So? There you go. Friends reach out. Friends call each other. Just come up with a reason to chat. Then see where things go. If it's awkward or strained, just skip it. But if there's any sign that it can be fun, I say go for it. Just don't let your feelings get mixed up in it and you'll be fine."

"That's the thing I worry about most. Emotions. They always become a problem for me."

"Honey. Listen to me. You are a strong woman. So, be strong. Let him in, but only far enough to make you happy."

The very thought of that filled Paige with both excitement and trepidation. Could she manage that? She wanted to try. "I suppose that's doable."

April snickered. "It sounds to me like Zach is very doable, too."

"Now that was a bad joke."

"I know. That's part of why you love me."

"I do love you. Thank you for indulging my more nonsensical moments."

"Hey. I get you. It all makes sense to me." From the other end of the line, there was the sound of voices. "I actually need to run, Paige, but keep me posted, okay?"

"Will do."

Paige and April said their goodbyes, leaving Paige to think of a reason to call Zach. She even wrote down a list, but most of her ideas seemed incredibly lame, especially considering that she'd been the one who was so adamant about not continuing with their physical relationship. And then, as if the universe heard her plea, she got a phone call.

Henry buzzed her line. "Ms. Moss. Enzo Bartolli from Maverick Motors is on the phone for you."

Paige had been waiting on this call. She'd left a message for Enzo on Monday and hadn't heard back. "Great. Thank you." Paige hit the blinking button on her phone. "Enzo. Hello. How are you?"

"Very well, Ms. Moss. How are you?"

"I'm great. And please call me Paige."

"Okay, Paige. I'm sorry it took me a few days to

return your call. I forget how busy it can be after you return from a trip."

"Yes. Of course."

"Also, I wanted some time to do some research on you and your client roster. I spent some time on your agency's website. It's very impressive."

"Thank you."

"I've spoken to our marketing team and we'd like to make an offer on a social media collaboration for one of your clients. Take the partnership for a test drive, so to speak. See if our two companies work well together."

Paige's heart was beating fast. She'd waited so long for something like this to actually pan out. It was going to feel like such a triumph to bring an opportunity like this to Alexis. "For Alexis Simmons, I assume?"

"Actually, I don't think Alexis is the right one for this campaign. I was hoping we could discuss Gabby Cooper. The tennis player? We're debuting a brand-new small SUV and we think she's the perfect personality to be associated with the launch."

Paige's excitement was now tamped down quite a bit. "Oh. I see."

"There'd be financial compensation, of course, but we'd also love to give her a car. She could pick out the colors and options."

"That sounds amazing. Can you send me the details so I can discuss it with Gabby?"

"Yes. Of course." Enzo cleared his throat. "You sound disappointed, Paige."

"I'm not at all. I would just really like you to take a long hard look at Alexis. She's a star. I believe that."

"Oh, we will. We definitely will. We just didn't think this was the right project for her. This particular car is quite small and Alexis is so tall. Buyers like to see a spacious interior. It won't look right if she's behind the wheel and her head is practically rubbing the roof."

Now Paige felt a little more heartened. "Of course. That makes perfect sense."

"Let's see how this goes. If all is well, I think we will find something for Alexis. It just might take some time."

"Perfect. Send over the details and I'll speak to Gabby today. I'll try to get you an answer as soon as possible."

"I appreciate it, Paige. I really do."

"And I appreciate the offer. Thank you." Paige ended the call with Enzo and immediately knew this was her excuse to call Zach. Just like April, he answered right away.

"This is a surprise," he said.

Paige clamped her eyes shut. How had she already forgotten how much she loved his voice? "Is it? Really?"

"I mean, my ego wanted to believe that I'd worn down your defenses during our flight, but I wasn't quite sure."

Paige laughed quietly. "I'm calling to say thank you for the introduction to Enzo. He just called with an offer."

"I knew he'd be quick to jump at the chance to work with Alexis."

"It was actually for one of my other clients. Gabby Cooper."

"Really? That's surprising. Alexis seems like such an obvious choice."

Yeah. That's what I thought. "He has something else in mind for her."

"I'm sure it'll all work out. Enzo is a great guy. I think I mentioned before that he's a straight shooter. He doesn't throw around ideas he doesn't plan to pursue."

"Look. I really want to thank you again for the introduction. It was incredibly generous of you to do it. I worry that I might not have fully expressed my gratitude when we were in Las Vegas. So, thank you."

"If you're going to say thank you, I'd rather hear it in person. Can we have dinner?"

Paige felt the heat rising in her cheeks. It frightened her that he could have this effect on her with so little effort. "I'd love to take you to dinner, but we've talked about this. What if someone saw us together? You know it would get back to Tom. That might not be great for your relationship—personal or professional."

"It's true. It's nearly impossible to be anonymous in this city."

"Right." Maybe this wasn't going to be possible.

"I think we're better off if we're alone. Come to my place. I'll cook."

"You can cook?"

"Don't sound so surprised. I can absolutely kill it in the kitchen."

In truth, she was almost aggrieved. The talents Zach possessed were too many to count. What was next? Was he also a master woodworker? Perhaps an aspiring botanist? "Is there anything you don't know how to do?"

"Plenty. Aside from a few insults and tawdry phrases I know in French, I don't speak any foreign languages. I don't have the slightest clue how to repair a car. And I...well, this next one is downright embarrassing. I don't think I can tell you."

"What is it?"

"No. No. It's too humiliating."

"Oh, come on. You can trust me."

He sighed. "Fine. I don't know how to whistle."

Paige laughed. He was so clever and quick. "This is perfect. I can teach you."

"I don't know. I'm worried it's too late for me. I'm turning thirty-one in a month."

Just like that, Paige felt as though she'd dropped back down to earth. An age difference of over a decade might not seem like much later in life, but it was significant now. "Are you sure you want to cook for me? This was supposed to be my way of thanking you. I could bring takeout."

"Paige. I want to make you dinner. Please. And I'm sure I can think of some way for you to express your gratitude."

Waves of impossible heat radiated through her body. Part of her loved it. Part of her worried she was only going to get burned. "Zach. Come on. We've talked through this. It's not a good idea." She hated pointing out the problem again—it only made her feel weak—but she also knew that honesty was the best policy with Zach.

"*You've* talked through this, Paige. Not me. I mostly listened and agreed because I didn't want to argue with you. I always want to be respectful of a woman's boundaries."

That gave her pause. He was dead-on about that. She'd dictated everything and had given him very little say. "Thank you. I appreciate that."

"But for the record, I think the reasons you've given me are silly. Nobody cares that our two agencies have a messy past. Tom has very little involvement in the day-to-day operations of Armstrong, and he's far more focused on his life with my mom than the company. A heart attack will do that to a guy."

Paige pressed her lips together tightly. Zach's rosy view of their situation was due in part to him not knowing the full breadth of her grievance with Tom, but maybe his stepdad really had changed. She knew from experience that traumatic experiences could make a person rethink their priorities. Her mom had certainly changed when she got sick. "How about this? We can talk about it when I come over. What can I bring?"

"A bottle of wine? I've already got a whole collection of bourbon. I can even pour you the one you had in Vegas."

Memories of their tryst during the expo played

in her head in a hot and constant loop. Would she be able to have dinner with him at his apartment and keep things platonic? It wouldn't take much to change her mind—a sexy glance or a flirtatious turn of phrase, which she already knew Zach was more than capable of. "It's a deal. When?"

"Tonight. Seven?"

Her vision flew to the clock on her computer screen. She was going to have to go home early to get ready. Her hair would need tending, as well as her makeup and of course a bit of perfume. And there was no telling how long it would take her to pick out something to wear. "Text me your address."

"Will do."

She took one final deep breath for courage. "Perfect. I'll be there."

"I knew you would."

Eight

Zach was finished getting ready for Paige's impending visit, but he was also such a ball of nerves that he needed to give himself a pep talk. "Just keep it together," he muttered as he checked himself out in the mirror. "It'll be fine. You've got this." He'd gone with tailored gray trousers and a crisp white shirt, no tie. It was a bit more casual than he'd wear to work, but far more polished than what he might wear on a regular evening at home. Paige not only deserved the best version of him, he wanted to impress. He wanted to erase any reason she might have to dismiss him. He only hoped that these carefully chosen clothes ended up on the floor by the end of the night.

He'd had his taste of Paige in Vegas, but after the flight home together, during which they eventually flirted like crazy, he knew that there was something more between them. The spark was unlike anything he'd ever experienced. And who in his right mind would stay away from that? Certainly not him.

He clicked off the bathroom light, wound his way through his bedroom and made one last pass through the apartment. Of course, he'd already done his part to ensure that the evening went smoothly. He'd kept dinner simple. A bottle of wine was at the ready. Every room was pristinely clean and tidy, while the lighting was soft and moody, allowing his stellar view from the floor-to-ceiling windows on the fifty-ninth floor to shine. Outside, the night sky was darkening, the only light coming from the sparkle of the city. This was seduction, Zach-style.

His doorbell rang and his heart jumped into his throat. Paige was there. He hurried to open the door and was instantly overwhelmed by the sight of her. His eyes traveled the length of her gorgeous body and blood coursed through his body so fast it made him light-headed. As much as he'd prepared, he wasn't ready for a snug-fitting dress the color of cabernet wine, following her sumptuous contours and curves. Her lush blond tresses tumbled over her shoulders in sexy waves. She was the whole package. For him, she was the beginning, middle and end.

A smile bloomed on her face and she held up the bottle of wine she'd promised to bring. "Hi there. I come bearing gifts."

"Hi there, yourself." Clearly his brain was too busy processing Paige's beauty to bother with things like a clever greeting. He took the bottle from her. "Thank you for this. Please. Come in." He stood back and she stepped past him, filling his nose with her sweet smell and further clouding his thoughts. *You've got this. Breathe.*

"You have a beautiful apartment. I mean, what I can see." She craned her neck, peeking around the corner.

"Come on. Let me give you the tour." His instinct was to reach for her hand, but he caught himself for a split second. Was it a good idea? Would he be starting off the evening with rejection? He knew the answer to neither question, but if he didn't demonstrate his intentions, he'd be mad at himself later. It was time to go for it. Tonight was about romance. This was *not* a work meeting.

Paige peered down as he wrapped his fingers around hers. Slowly, she raised her chin and delivered a questioning look. "Zach. I thought we were going to talk about this. Are you ready to dive into this subject already?"

"I am." He set the bottle of wine she'd brought on the side table in his foyer and then stepped a little closer, watching a sexy smile play at the corners of her tempting lips. Having her all alone again was all the fuel he needed to formulate his argument. "I know you're worried about what people will think. But no one else is here. No one else has to know that we're together. No one else has to know how I feel about you."

"And how is that, exactly?"

He scanned her stunning face, feeling as though he had the makings of a dictionary in his head. There were so many words fighting to leave his mouth. "You're incredible and gorgeous and so damn smart. I'd be a fool not to want to be with you." He raised her hand to his lips and kissed the back of it softly, then kept it close to his mouth. "We work well together. We mesh. We learned that in Las Vegas. Don't you want more of that?"

She inched closer as he kissed her hand again. When he glanced at her face, her eyelids were getting heavy, exactly like they had in the bar in Vegas. It made his whole body draw tight with need and want. "I feel like I should be stronger than this. But I don't know how to do that around you. You make me want to give in."

"So give in." He turned her hand in his and kissed the underside of her wrist, feeling her pulse against his lips, then continued along the tender skin of her forearm.

Paige sighed and took one final step, bringing her within inches of him. "If we do this, you have to promise not to hurt me. I've had my fill of that, okay?"

"Promise." He smiled, knowing that he was on the right path. With his other hand, he reached for her silky hair, gently combing a few strands over her ear. Then he trailed his fingers along her jaw, watching as her lips parted and she seemed to struggle with desire. Good. He was grappling with it, too. He'd wanted this since the moment they parted at the airport, and now that Paige was right in front of him, it couldn't happen fast enough. Heat stormed through him, making him impossibly hard.

He took her hand and led her down the hall to his room, but the instant they were inside, Paige took the lead, stepping in front of him and walking backward to the bed, towing him along. When she reached their destination, he wrapped her up in his arms and drew down the zipper of her dress as he kissed her. With every inch, he was closer to his prize, and that mix of anticipation and gratification was so damn delicious it made his head spin. He pulled her dress from her shoulders, then she wriggled out of it. He quickly unhooked her bra and she ruffled it from her arms, revealing her stunning breasts. They were so full and perfect, he could hardly believe that he got to touch them as he cupped them with his hands and she responded with a low hum. He could hardly believe he got to taste them as he lowered his head and wound his tongue around her nipples, which drew tight beneath his touch.

He slowly skimmed his hands along her waist and hips, then slipped his fingers into her panties and pushed them down to the floor. "Go ahead, Paige. Lie down."

"No. You. Let me take off your clothes." She kissed him softly as she unbuttoned his shirt and tugged it up and out of his pants. Every loop of her tongue and brush of her fingers against his overheated skin was only confirmation that this was right. They worked together.

As soon as she'd shucked his pants and boxer briefs, she took his cock in her hand and stroked from base to tip, only amping up his need for her. He wrapped his arms around her waist and delivered a passionate kiss while placing a knee on the bed and pulling her along with him. Paige stretched out before him, raising her arms above her head—an invitation he was so ready to accept. Gathering her wrists in his hand, he pinned them against the bed as he straddled her waist. He wanted so badly to be buried inside her right now, but that would have to wait.

He lowered his head, and he licked the velvety skin of one breast, then the other, over and over again. Her nipples were impossibly taut and tight, and every time he touched them, her skin flooded with warmth and she moaned her approval. He'd never wanted a woman the way he wanted her. It didn't take much to imagine a lifetime of exploring her luscious body, learning what she liked and delivering it every time.

He released her wrists and shifted himself until he was kneeling, bracketed by her legs. He reached for one of her ankles, lifted her leg and trailed his other hand along the creamy skin of her inner thigh, traveling down toward her center, but only teasing and tempting by stopping for a second or two before retracing the trail back to her knee. Paige bucked her hips and closed her eyes. His heart worked its way up into his throat, knowing he had her at his mercy. With every pump of blood through his body, he needed her a little more. He was that much more willing to give her everything.

But because of that, he needed everything from her. He lowered her leg, then himself, kissing her deeply. He skimmed her jaw with his lips as she combed her fingers through his hair, curling them possessively. He continued down along her throat, then brushed the undersides of her breasts, coaxing sharp breaths from her. Every kiss, soft or hard or somewhere in between, felt like it was bringing him closer to her. It was hard not to believe that he was erasing the reasons they shouldn't be together and creating new justification for why they should.

"I need you, Zach. So bad," Paige muttered.

It was sheer music to his ears. He pressed a few gentle kisses against her belly. "Let me get a condom." He got up, hating even a moment away from her, and reached into his bedside table for the packet. It was so hot to have her do it, but the truth was that he didn't want to wait any longer, so he tore open the packet and rolled it on himself. His own touch made the tension in his hips nearly impossible to take. Things were going to be so fiery and intense once he was inside her.

Paige pushed up on her elbows and smiled at him. "Get over here."

"Gladly." He stretched out next to her on the bed, his pulse beating wildly.

She rolled to her side to face him, and she pulled her leg up over his hip and kissed him with an open mouth and eager tongue. Heat did more than radiate through his groin and belly, it steamrollered him, enveloping his hips and racing down his thighs. He cupped the side of her face as he took the kiss even deeper, wondering if this was the way to unravel the mystery of Paige. The way to figure out what she wanted and if that thing could ever be him. She rolled to her back and brought him along for the ride. With little effort, he positioned himself at her entrance and drove inside. The moment felt monumental. Las Vegas had been a spur of the moment hookup; this was something more. His heart pounded in his chest as he tried to wrap his mind around her impossible warmth and the way she held on to him so tightly.

Now that their bodies were joined and moving in near-perfect sync, he drew in her sweet smell and kissed her neck. She wrapped her legs around him tighter and slanted her hips whenever he was deepest. It was that extra inch of closeness that left him meeting on the edge of release. His breaths became so shallow that they redefined the word *gasp*. Paige's were coming hard and fast now, her lips open and begging for another kiss while her eyes remained closed, lost in the utter bliss of that moment. He willed his peak away while he waited for hers, then she began to claw at his back and he took his chance to capture her mouth as she gave way. It gave them one more way to be impossibly close while they were both at their most vulnerable.

The kiss was chaotic and frantic and he couldn't imagine anything better as the pleasure barreled through him, causing his muscles to freeze and relax, freeze and relax, over and over again. His mind was a torrent of sensations and feelings, making him feel like he was being hurtled through space. Then he suddenly went into the floating feeling of a free fall, bringing him back to the present, where Paige was beneath him and all was perfect with the world.

He eased off her to catch his breath and she was quick to curl into him. As their breaths became more even, she smoothed her hand over his chest and nudged at his cheek and chin with her nose. Then they fell into another kiss, and he realized that he didn't want to be anywhere other than with her. He only hoped that she would eventually feel the same way.

Whoa. Paige was startled by how quickly things got hot with Zach. It was as if someone had poured a gallon of gasoline on them, then lit a match and walked away. Even so, it wasn't like she'd had the inclination to fight it. Zach was right about one thing for sure—no one needed to know. And for now, naked in Zach's bed, she was perfectly happy with that idea.

"Hungry?" he asked, pulling her closer.

She laughed. "Oh, right. I forgot I'd come over for dinner."

"I'm not sure if what just happened makes me a terrible host or a great one…" Zach got up from the bed and stepped into his boxer briefs.

Paige followed suit, scooting across the mattress

and finding her bra and panties on the floor. "I lean toward great."

He glanced over at her. "Do you want something else to wear? I mean, you look spectacular in that dress, but maybe I have something more comfortable for you?"

"Yes. I would love that. Thank you."

Zach headed into his closet and Paige followed. He headed straight for a shelf where there were several stacks of T-shirts and a few sweatshirts. "How about this?" He presented a large gray pullover sweatshirt with a Harvard logo on it.

"Definitely the closest I'll ever come to getting into Harvard."

"Perfect." He tossed it to her. "Now to find you some pants."

She threaded it over her head and pushed up the sleeves. It was a little big on her, but not too much. When she looked over at Zach, he'd put on a pair of gray pajama pants and was sifting through a drawer. She stepped closer to him and put her hand on his bare back. She loved being able to touch him like that, without reservation. "Any luck? I mean, I don't *need* to wear pants."

Looking her up and down, he sent ripples of heat through her. "You do look spectacular just as you are." He fished out a plain T-shirt for himself, then shut the drawer. "So that's settled. Now let's go get you fed."

After he put on a shirt, which was a bit of a disappointment for Paige, they exited his bedroom and padded down the hall to grab the bottle of wine she'd brought, and eventually they walked into his kitchen and great room. Everything was of the finest quality, with high-end chef's appliances, marble countertops and custom cabinetry. He flipped on the light above the range, but the lighting was otherwise quite soft and romantic.

"Can I open the wine?" she asked.

"Yes. That would be great." He pulled a corkscrew out of the kitchen drawer, then two glasses from an overhead cabinet. "I'll get going on dinner. It won't take long."

Paige tackled her one job while Zach got out a large, deep pasta pot and filled it with water from the pot filler at the back of his range.

"I made puttanesca sauce before you came over." He went to the fridge and brought out a glass bowl, which he emptied into a medium saucepan.

"Yum. That's one of my favorites. I love the olives and capers and chili flakes. I'm impressed." Paige poured the merlot she'd brought into the two glasses. Then offered one to Zach.

"It's really simple." He clinked his glass with hers.

"I'm still impressed." They both took a sip, maintaining eye contact the whole time. How a small drink of wine could be so hot, Paige did not know. She was loving it, though. "So, I didn't realize you went to Harvard."

"Business school. My dad insisted."

"Ah." She didn't really care to discuss Tom, so she didn't offer more.

"Where'd you go to school?"

"U Conn, of course."

Zach looked at her and his eyebrows drew together. "Why 'of course'?"

"Because that's where my mom coached. For her entire career in women's college basketball." The confusion was still clouding his face. "My mom. Elaine Moss?"

His eyes grew as large as saucers. "Your mom is Elaine Moss? How did I not know that?"

"Was. She passed away almost two years ago." Saying it out loud still hurt, even after all this time.

"Oh. Right. I'm so sorry."

"Thanks." She shrugged. "As for how you didn't know, I have no clue. I figured everyone knew that about me."

"I don't know why I didn't put two and two together, but I didn't. That is so impressive. What a career she had. An absolute legend."

Paige took another sip of her wine and leaned against the counter, watching Zach tend to the food on the stove. "She was an amazing woman. She's the reason I got into sports. I idolized her. I wanted to be her." It was the absolute truth. Paige's mom had been her north star for her entire life, and she'd frankly felt a bit aimless since her death. Even though things were going well with her career and business, it still felt like there was little reward at the end of the day.

"Did you ever think about going into coaching?"

"I didn't. I guess I felt like I needed to have been

a player if I was going to go that route. That didn't really pan out, even though I tried like hell."

"No talent for it?"

Paige glanced down at her chest, then pointed. "These got in the way. As soon as I hit puberty, which was pretty early. Having big boobs made it really hard."

"Well, I'm sorry your dream of being a player didn't pan out, but I'm thankful you turned out the way you did." He cleared his throat. "Was that weird of me to say?"

She laughed quietly. "No. It's actually pretty adorable."

He smiled. "Good. Because I'm definitely going for adorable."

"What about you? Did you play any sports?"

"Everything. Baseball, basketball, golf, lacrosse. You name it, I tried it. I wasn't particularly good at any of it, but I always thought it was fun."

"No football?"

He shook his head and opened a cabinet door to pull out a box of pasta. The water in the pot was steaming, but had not yet reached a boil. "No way. My mom wouldn't go for that."

"Smart. The head injuries can be terrible." Once again, they'd circled around to the subject she had wanted to avoid, but she did want to get to know Zach better. "When did your mom and Tom meet?"

"Oh. I was pretty little. Only two. My mom was working as a hostess at a restaurant out on Long Island and Tom walked in one day. I guess it was love at first sight."

Paige struggled with the notion of anyone falling in love with Tom Armstrong, but Zach thought the world of Tom, so surely he had some sliver of a nice personality. She'd simply never had the pleasure of encountering it. "What happened with your dad? If you don't mind me asking."

"He and my mom were never married. They met right out of high school. It wasn't serious. She got pregnant and he took off."

Paige shook her head. "I'm so sorry."

"It's hard to miss someone you never knew, if that makes any sense." Indeed, Zach didn't seem to feel sad about any of it. He shared it in such a matter-of-fact way. "What about your dad? Your mom raised you on her own, didn't she?"

Paige nodded. It was funny how similar her own story was to Zach's. "My parents did marry, but it didn't last. Only a year. Just long enough for her to have me. By all reports, he couldn't deal with my mom's career. It was all-encompassing."

"Of course. You don't win a whole bunch of national championships without being fully in it."

"Seven championships to be exact." Paige nodded in the direction of the stove. "Water's boiling."

"Oh. Thanks." Zach hustled over and dumped the entire box of pasta into the water, then gave it a stir. "So, do you want to tell me about what happened between you and Tom? Because knowing both of you, I really don't get it."

Paige rolled her neck, instantly feeling tense. "I don't know. Do you really want to hear this?"

"I do. I absolutely do. I want to understand why you hate him and I want to figure out why he thinks you're a pit viper."

Paige reared back her head in shock. "A pit viper? He called me that?"

Zach squinted and offered a sheepish smile. "I probably shouldn't have shared that little detail."

Paige shook her head and poured herself another glass of wine, then topped off Zach's glass. "Here's the story. Ten years ago, when my agency was still very much in its infancy, one of Tom's clients came to me and asked if I might be interested in representing him."

Zach stepped closer, seeming engrossed. "Who was it?"

"Roger Fielding. The tennis player."

"I know who he is. He was still on our roster until he retired a few years ago. So obviously you didn't actually steal him away."

"Exactly. It never came of anything. The only reason Roger approached me at all was because his daughter, Laurie, showed so much promise in the sport. He was hoping I would take them both on, since Tom had been hesitant to sign Laurie."

"Ah. Right."

"But Tom thought I was trying to poach his client. So he had it out for me after that. Not that he'd been particularly welcoming or kind to start."

Zach sighed, seeming more resigned than disappointed. Perhaps Tom had always shown this side to Zach. "Professional jealousy. He really did view all other agents as the enemy. I think it was the way his dad raised him, and he started the company."

Paige took another drink of her wine. "I went for years just thinking we would hate each other and that would be that. Then, apparently Tom saw his chance to get back at me. He tried to hire my husband, Andre. While we were still married. And while Andre was working for me."

True surprise crossed Zach's face. "Whoa. Seriously?"

Paige nodded, trying not to think too hard about how badly she'd felt betrayed. "Yes. It was the beginning of the end of our marriage."

"But you don't actually blame Tom for that part, do you?"

The question froze Paige in her tracks. Because the truth was that she did on some level blame Tom. But hearing it worded in that particular way, by Zach, made her second-guess this old assumption she'd made. Just then, the timer went off.

"That's the pasta. One sec." Zach grabbed some oven mitts, then drained the noodles into a strainer in the sink. "You didn't answer my question."

"I know. I'm thinking about it."

Zach turned the pasta out into a deep skillet, then poured in some of the sauce he'd made, rich with tomatoes and its lovely accompaniments. "No worries. I've got all the time in the world."

"I do blame Tom, to be honest." Paige approached the stove to better watch him work as he tossed the noodles and adjusted the seasonings. "There was no reason to recruit Andre other than revenge. But when I talked to Roger, he approached me. Not the other way around. And I told Roger that he would have to separate from your firm before I would sign him. I wasn't going to steal him away."

"You mean like I did when I signed Ryan Wilson? Because, technically, that's what I did." Zach began coiling pasta into two large bowls.

"But you're genuinely friends with Ryan, right? So it's not exactly the same." Paige could see precisely how blurry the lines could get. "I guess I shouldn't blame Tom. But it's hard not to hold a grudge. Especially when he apparently still holds one against me."

Zach went to the fridge and pulled out a wedge of Parmesan cheese. "He definitely does. Although I'd like to think I could do something to make that go away."

Paige reached for his arm. "No. Don't do that. Really. I can't imagine it ending well."

He grated the cheese over the steaming bowls of pasta. "Well, you obviously came to an understanding with Andre over the whole thing. Why not Tom?"

"Maybe because it always seemed like he thought the worst of me? It really made me hate the name Armstrong. I'll tell you that much."

Zach leaned over and kissed her on the forehead. "Well, this Armstrong likes you a lot, Paige Moss.

Nine

Henry appeared in the doorway to Paige's office with a huge arrangement of red roses and deep purple iris. "Guess who got flowers again?"

Paige jumped up from her desk and rushed over to retrieve the gorgeous blooms. This was the fifth or sixth delivery in the last two weeks, the length of time which she and Zach had been seeing each other. "Seriously?" she muttered quietly. She really didn't want to call any attention to the delivery. People in the office had definitely taken notice, and she didn't want to answer any questions about it.

"I'd say someone is smitten." Henry shot Paige a discerning look. "I know. I know. Not that you asked me."

"Thanks for bringing them in. Please don't tell

anyone who they're from." Paige set the flowers down on the coffee table in front of the sofa in her office. Zach was still a secret and she preferred it that way.

"You know me. I am discreet to a fault." Henry disappeared through the door.

Paige plucked the enclosure card from the flowers. They were indeed from Zach. *The terrace was magnificent. Love, Zach.*

Despite wanting to keep this all to herself, Paige couldn't ignore the rush of pure white heat that crept up her chest and down her back. It was making her feel so flushed that she had to breathe her way through it. Paige had gone to his place last night. They brought a bottle of wine out onto his apartment's terrace, and although they did quite a lot of talking, it eventually turned to kissing, which then led to sex—on a lounge chair, barely wrapped up in a blanket. It was the most adventurous thing Paige had *ever* done in the sex department.

Paige wasn't a person who took big chances. She'd never once accepted a dare. But something about Zach made her okay with living closer to the edge. He made her want to try new things, which quite frankly made her incredibly nervous. She was already flirting with disaster by seeing him. If anyone at her agency found out, she would lose so much credibility, especially with everyone who knew firsthand the way Tom Armstrong had treated her. There was even more on the line for Zach—he was jeopardizing his relationship not only with his employer, but with his family. And yet, he seemed too eager for more time with her. It defied logic. Which made Paige think that for Zach, this was all about the thrill. The taboo of professional rivals getting into bed. Or perhaps it was because she was an older woman and he a younger man. The bottom line was that she found herself questioning his motives. Not a lot. But a little. Just enough to bother her. Even when he sent flowers.

Henry appeared at Paige's doorway again. "Alexis is on line two for you."

"Got it. Thank you." Paige stepped away from the flowers, sat at her desk and picked up her office phone. "Alexis. Hey there. How are you?"

"Confused, to be honest. It's been three weeks since you went to Vegas and I haven't heard a thing. No endorsements. Nothing. Meanwhile, I find out that Gabby Cooper is doing a campaign for Maverick Motors? What gives, Paige?"

Paige was taken aback by Alexis's tone. She'd never heard her so angry. "Alexis. It's okay. Take a deep breath."

"Don't tell me to take a breath. I'm upset. This isn't what we talked about."

Paige knew very well that it wasn't what they'd discussed. It wasn't what Paige had anticipated, nor was it the way she would've wanted it to go. But it was the reality they both had to live with. "I have several things in the mix right now. I just haven't gotten to the point where I wanted to tell you about it. I don't want to get your hopes up. These things fall through sometimes and I don't want to promise something I can't deliver."

"From where I'm sitting, you've already promised and not delivered."

Paige's mouth went dry. Her stomach wobbled. "You're right. You're absolutely right. Do you want me to send over the list of everyone I've been talking to? Will that help—if you can see what I've been working on?"

"Yes, actually. I would like to see that."

"Give me a day or two to pull something together and I'll send it over, okay?"

"Paige. No. I want to see it now. Whatever you have. You don't have to polish things up for me. We've been working together too long for that."

Paige nodded to herself. "You're right. No problem. Let me put you on speaker and I'll e-mail it to you while we're on the phone." Paige pressed the button for speakerphone and set down the receiver, then started a new e-mail to Alexis and attached Paige's notes about sponsor meetings and calls. She quickly hit Send. "Okay. It's on its way to you. It's the unvarnished truth, okay? There might be some things in there that you won't like. I'm not going to take a lowball offer on your behalf, Alexis. Your time, name and talent are precious commodities. They should only go to the highest bidder. I feel strongly about that."

Alexis sighed. "Okay. Thank you. Thank you for doing this. I guess I just panicked when I saw the thing about Gabby."

"Just so you know, Maverick Motors is looking at you. They just don't have the perfect thing for you right now. It's still very much in the mix. And the kind of money they offered to Gabby is not what you're worth. I'm working up to that, okay?"

"Okay. That sounds like it could be good."

Paige felt as though she could breathe a little easier. "I've got your back. I will not let you down."

"Thank you. I appreciate it. I do."

"Good. Well, go ahead and read what I sent, then get back to me with whatever feedback you have. If you feel strongly about one of those opportunities, I'll go after it twice as hard."

"Will do. I'll send you an e-mail after I read yours."

"Are we good, Alexis?"

"We're good. I can't forget that you're always straight up with me. Not all agents are like that."

"It's the only way I know to be."

"And that's why I love working with you."

"It's the same reason I love working with you. I hope you enjoy the rest of your day."

"You, too."

Paige hung up the call and took a cleansing breath. Everything she'd told Alexis was the absolute truth. But could Paige be working harder on Alexis's behalf? There was always more work to be done. Always. She turned to her to-do list, but a text on her cell phone pulled her attention from that. It was from Zach.

Did you get the flowers?

She sighed and smiled. She wasn't doing a great job keeping up with things today. I did. They're beautiful. Thank you so much.

You're welcome. What are you doing for lunch?

Paige tapped out her response. Having a salad at my desk. Why?

Wanting to see you. Swing by my place?

Paige knew exactly what this was—a booty call. She knew because she and Zach had already done this twice: gotten together under the guise of lunch, only to end up naked and doing each other in the most unconventional of places, like her kitchen or his living room. Part of her wanted to say no. Pump the brakes. Was this turning into too much, too fast? Another part of her wanted nothing more than to forget about work for an hour and have Zach give her a mind-blowing orgasm or two.

He sent another text. Confession time. I'm already on my way home. I was in my office thinking about you, and got so hard. I need you.

A vision of Zach and his physical predicament popped into her head. Paige nearly bit the heel of her hand.

I won't lie. That's hot.

Get in a cab. Charter a plane. I don't care. Just get here.

On my way. She got up from her desk, grabbed her bag and rushed out into the hall. This was what Zach did to her. She could be thinking one thing and end up doing another.

A quick ride in the elevator and she was down in the lobby, then out on the street, where she was lucky enough to flag a cab right away. Fortunately, Zach's apartment was only ten minutes away. She trailed a finger up and down her thigh, looking out the window and thinking about what was waiting for her—Zach, his rock-hard body, his heartbreaking smile and his endless determination to please her. Even though she sometimes wondered what in the hell they were doing, she was a lucky woman. Damn lucky.

She paid the driver quickly when they arrived and then rushed into his building. Zach's doorman, Jorge, knew her by now and greeted her with a smile, then held the elevator for her. "Ms. Moss. It's nice to see you. Mr. Armstrong just went up to his apartment a few minutes ago."

"Good to see you, too. Zach and I have a lunch date today." She stepped onto the elevator.

"Interesting. He told me he was going to show you some fabric swatches for a new couch," he replied.

Paige simply smiled. "Right. That, too." She and Zach would've taken the time to get their stories straight if they'd planned this in advance. Perhaps this was the price of an impromptu rendezvous.

"You two have fun."

Oh, I think we will. The doors slid shut and she watched the floor numbers on the display like a hawk. As she traveled higher, her anticipation ratcheted up, her body buzzing with electricity. Her thighs felt tingly. Her chest and face flushed. Her nipples drew tight. All because she knew Zach wasn't far away. When she finally reached fifty-nine, she practically launched herself out into the hall. It took a single knock on Zach's door for him to answer. Completely naked.

He grasped her arm, tugged her into the foyer and closed the door behind her. Paige dropped her bag on the floor and in a flash, Zach had her pinned against the wall and was kissing her harder than ever before. One of her hands dug into his muscled back, while she reached down with the other, wrapped it around his impressive erection and began stroking hard. He groaned into her ear, then nipped at it. It stung, followed by a wave of pleasure.

Zach tugged her dress up, almost to her waist, then slipped his fingers into the front of her panties. He knew exactly where and how to touch her. Just a few rotations against her clit and she was already teetering on the brink. "You are so wet."

"You aren't the only one who engaged in mental foreplay. I couldn't stop thinking about you in the cab. And the elevator."

He groaned again and reached over to the foyer

table. "I'm prepared." He fumbled with the condom packet, then used his teeth to rip it open. "Here. Put this on me. I'll unzip you."

They were a tangle of limbs while she rolled on the condom and he frantically drew down the zipper of her dress. She pushed the garment to the floor, ditching her panties at the same time, while Zach unhooked her bra. He tugged it from her arms in a single motion, cast it aside and, again, pushed her against the wall. All that was left between them was the heat they were generating together.

He hooked his hand behind her knee, then raised it up to his hip and drove inside. Paige gasped as he filled her so completely. With her back braced against the wall, Zach raised her other leg until she could wrap them both around his waist. So *that* was how that particular position worked. His thrusts came hard and fast, and with so much of her body weight resting against him, the friction and pressure on her clit quickly sent her straight for the edge. Every muscle she had felt like it was tightening, coiling, ready to spring. And then, just like that, she unraveled, digging her nails into his shoulders and muffling her cries in his neck. Zach followed, tossing his head back and loudly moaning his approval.

Zach gently set her back down on the floor. Paige leaned against the wall, breathless. "Whoa. That was the hottest three minutes of my life."

"Oh, come on. It was more like five." Zach turned and grinned, his chest heaving. "I'm guessing it was better than a salad at your desk."

She laughed quietly and stole a kiss. "Way better."

"Hold on one sec. Let me run into the bathroom and take care of this." He stepped down the hall and ducked into the half bath off the great room.

Paige plucked her bra and panties from the floor and put them on. "That really was fun," she pronounced loudly. It was enough to help her shake the stress of her call with Alexis.

Zach emerged from the bathroom. "I spent my whole morning thinking about you. It was exactly what you called it. Mental foreplay. Three hours of it. I was more than ready to go."

"What would you have done if I hadn't been able to come over?" Paige hooked her bra.

Zach grabbed his clothes from an armchair in the corner. He'd apparently disrobed in the foyer? He wasn't kidding when he'd said he was ready. "I'm not sure. Take care of the problem myself? It wouldn't have been nearly as much fun." He stepped into his pants, then pulled on his dress shirt.

"I'm glad it worked out." Paige wiggled into her dress.

"Me, too, Paige. Me, too." Zach tucked his shirt into his pants, then stepped behind her to pull up her zipper. "I was hoping we could talk about something."

"Fabric swatches for your new couch?"

He snickered. "I panicked. I don't know why I felt like I needed to come up with an excuse for being home in the middle of the day and inviting you over."

"I told Jorge we were having lunch."

"Now that would have been a more plausible explanation." He cleared his throat and looked down at the floor for a moment, like he was gathering his thoughts. "But I do hope we can talk through a few things. Real things. Maybe tonight?"

Paige didn't like the unknown in her life. She needed to know what he wanted to discuss, especially since it sounded important. "About?"

Zach reined her in with his arms. "Us, of course."

She instantly smiled, even when this felt like absolute confirmation that they were getting in too deep, exactly the thing that she'd said she wouldn't do. "What about us? Please don't tell me you want to get married. It's been two weeks."

He laughed. "Would you consider it if I asked?"

"No. See my previous comment about two weeks."

"Well, it's actually been over a month since we started flirting and Vegas was like three weeks ago."

"You're funny." She loved seeing him so eager to grin. He was so sincere. And so good at bending any argument in his direction. It was part of what made him a good agent. "What did you want to discuss regarding us?"

He carefully brushed a tendril of hair from her face. "I just keep thinking that the things that are standing between us don't have to be a big deal. My family. Your history with Tom. These are things that can be overcome. I think we should clear the air. Then you and I can be together for real. Go out to dinner. Go to work events together. I hate that we have to hide."

Paige took a moment to formulate her response. She didn't want to discount what Zach was saying, but he was being incredibly naive if he thought Tom would set his grudge aside. "You're already flirting with all of that by sending me flowers all the time."

"I know I am. Honestly, I would send you flowers every day, Paige. You're the best thing that's happened to me…" He scanned her face, his eyes so honest and full of hope that it broke her heart a little. "Ever."

Paige's heart jumped up into her throat. What defense could she possibly have for that? "I love our time together, Zach. I do. And I'd be lying if I said that I didn't want it to continue."

"But? I sense a 'but.' And not the good kind." He reached down and squeezed her ass to punctuate his point.

"*But* I know a side of Tom that you don't. And I can't fathom him being okay with this."

"I think you're wrong. He's changed."

Paige didn't know how she was supposed to argue the point. She had her evidence and Zach had his. They contradicted each other, but the way she saw it, he had a lot of familial bias mixed in with his. Whereas hers was based purely on events she'd personally endured. "You aren't thinking about telling him, are you?"

"Well, yeah. You make me happy. I want to share that with the people I love the most. That means my mom and Tom."

"I really don't think you should say anything. In fact, I'm begging you *not* to tell him."

Disappointment crossed his face. "Really?"

"Really."

"Okay. If that's what you want. But I can't keep it a secret forever. At some point, I'm going to tell both of them. And we'll just have to deal with the fallout, okay?"

Paige pulled him closer for a kiss. She had a bit of a reprieve, but something told her that this wouldn't last. Either he was going to slip or she was, and the secret would get back to Tom. When it happened, it would be the end of the road. Her fun with Zach would be over, and she wasn't ready for that. Not yet. "Look. I trust you. But I would be happier if you didn't say anything. At least for a little while longer."

He hesitated. "Okay. I can do that."

She decided a change in subject was a good idea. "What do you have going for the rest of the day?"

"I'd love to work from home since it's Friday, but I really need to go back in." He cleared his throat. "Tom is coming in Monday morning for a meeting. It's his first time in the office since his heart attack, so it's a big deal. People are excited to see him. I just want to be sure I'm fully prepared so I can relax over the weekend."

From where Paige was sitting, Zach's upcoming meeting with Tom was reason enough to stay quiet about them. No reason to rock the boat when there were other, bigger things to discuss. But she had to put her faith in Zach. She wasn't going to offer her advice. "I'm hoping that your relaxing weekend will include me."

Zach snaked his arm around her waist. "Are you kidding? I'm expecting nothing less."

Ten

This was the first time Zach had ever been truly both nervous and excited to see Tom. That day when he'd gone out to Long Island to pitch his expansion of the agency had been one thing, but it was all hypotheticals at that point. Today would be Tom's first time back in the office since stepping away from the agency, and he was coming in for an update on the progress of Zach's big plan. Zach needed to impress.

He paced in reception, glancing at his watch. It was 10:03 a.m. Tom was three minutes late, which wasn't like him at all. Was everything okay? Zach sure hoped so. By 10:07 a.m., he was really starting to worry, but then the elevator dinged, the doors slid open and Tom appeared. To Zach's great surprise, he was wearing a suit. It looked like any other day at Armstrong Sports before Tom's heart attack. It made Zach feel like he was in a bit of a time warp.

"Morning. I was about to send out a search party." Zach hugged Tom.

"Traffic is horrible. I don't miss that part of the job," Tom replied.

"Exactly why I live in the city." Zach spread his arms wide. "Welcome back. Everything is pretty much the same."

"Except that I'm not here."

"Right." Zach nodded. "Let's go back to my office. We can talk over things, then I figured you'd want to make the rounds and catch up with folks."

"Sounds good to me."

Tom and Zach headed off down the hall, Zach purposely slowing his pace to allow for Tom to keep up. Tom had been steadily recovering since his heart attack, but he wasn't one hundred percent healed yet. When they approached Zach's office, Teri got up from her desk and gave Tom a big hug.

"Tom. It's so good to see you," she said.

"Same to you, Teri. I hear you've been taking very good care of Zach here."

"More like he's taking very good care of me," Teri quipped.

Tom smiled and delivered a sideways glance to Zach. "Glad to hear it."

Zach waved Tom into his office and they got settled on the large leather sectional in one corner. Zach handed over a binder with a full report of his progress to date. It hadn't taken as much time as the original proposal, but it had still been a real labor of love.

Tom sat back and opened the cover, then fished his reading glasses out of the breast pocket of his suit jacket. "Let's see what we've got here."

Zach opened his own copy to follow along. "Obviously these are all projections, since we've only signed seven new clients. But I've already put together endorsement deals for four of the seven and we're working on new revenue streams for the others."

Tom flipped through the pages, nodding as he consulted the numbers. "It's definitely proving to be exactly what you told me it would. Have you done any projections longer than two years for these new clients?"

"I haven't, but I can. What would you want to see?"

Tom shrugged. "Five years? Just to get an idea of the full scope."

"Sure thing. I can do that."

"I noticed that all of the new clients are in golf and tennis. I thought you were looking at other sports. We talked about basketball, right? How's that coming along?"

Zach held his breath, knowing that Tom was essentially asking about Alexis Simmons, a topic Zach did not care to discuss. "It's a work in progress. I'll put it that way. But I have made some strides in other big sports. I've started talks with Aida Niemenen, the Finnish race car driver. She's likely going to be the first woman in Formula One. So that's exciting.

There will be so much attention on her. She'll truly be breaking new ground."

Tom nodded slowly, then returned to the binder and looked through several more pages before closing it and resting his hands on top of it. "I'm proud of you, Zach. You stood up to me. You fought for something I resisted. And you're making it work. You're putting your stamp on the agency, which is something I'd once thought I didn't want, but I can now see that it's a good thing." He reached over and patted Zach's knee. "Great job. Truly."

Zach felt like he was floating on air. Tom had always been generous with praise, but this was a whole new level. "Thank you so much. It means the world to me."

"And I have to say, the new job agrees with you. You seem much more relaxed and confident. You seem..." Tom scanned Zach's face. "Happy in a way I've never seen you."

Those were all very nice things to hear, but Zach knew very well it was about far more than his job. His demeanor and happiness were all due to Paige. "I need to tell you something."

"Of course. Anything."

"I know you were trying very hard to not mention Alexis Simmons just now."

"I didn't want to force the issue. You're doing so well on other fronts. Not that I don't want you to pursue her. I do want that."

"Well, there's a reason I haven't done that." He sucked in a deep breath for courage. "Paige Moss and I spent some time together in Las Vegas, then we spent more together after we got back and, well, you should know that we're involved. Romantically."

Tom didn't respond immediately. In fact, it was a struggle to read his facial expression, leaving Zach feeling like he was floundering.

"She's so great," Zach continued, overwhelmed by an irrational need to fill up space. "And I know about the bad blood between you two, but it just seems like it's all in the past and maybe it's better if we all let bygones be bygones. You know? Water under the bridge and all of that?"

Tom nodded. He even smiled, which helped to relax Zach ever so slightly. "I see."

"And?"

"Of course your mom and I want you to be happy. We want you to find love and have a family and all of the things that have made our lives so rich and rewarding."

Zach's shoulders relaxed. "Thank you. I appreciate it. We're not there yet. It's new. But it's special. We absolutely love spending time together."

"If I were you, I'd take things slow. Keep your options open. Paige is quite a bit older than you. She's probably not interested in the same things you are. You know, as far as life goals and things like that."

Zach had never considered keeping his options open. He only wanted to be with Paige. "I'm happy with the way things are, Tom. I don't plan to date other women."

Tom frowned, then tried to cover with a forced smile. "Just don't do anything rash, okay?"

Zach was so tired of that sort of advice. It was remarkably similar to what Paige had said to him. "I've got it under control. Everything."

Tom nodded and looked at the binder again, then handed it over to Zach. "Well, you're certainly hitting it out of the park with this."

"Thanks."

"I'd like to go ahead and make the rounds in the office. There are so many people I want to see and talk to." Tom slowly got up from the couch.

"You got it?"

"I do. I need to do these things on my own. I'm getting stronger every day."

It took everything in Zach not to help Tom, but he'd been told by his mom to only lend a hand when Tom was struggling so badly that he might fall. "You are. You definitely are."

Tom started for the door and Zach trailed behind. "I'll see you soon, okay? I'm sure your mom would love to have you out for dinner again soon."

"Yeah. Sure. I'll give her a call and set something up." Zach opened the door and followed Tom out to Teri's work area. To Zach's surprise, Derek was standing there. An even bigger surprise was the odd look on Teri's face. It was like something was wrong.

Derek stepped forward and held out his hand for Tom. "Mr. Armstrong, I'm such a big fan. I'm Derek James, one of the newer agents here. I really wanted the chance to meet you."

Tom shook Derek's hand. "Zach tells me you're a real go-getter."

Derek grinned. "I'm working on it. For sure."

Tom clapped Derek on the shoulder. "Good man. Just keep working hard and you'll find your place."

"I will, sir."

Tom turned to Zach and gave him a hug. "Great job, again. I'm sure I'll speak to you soon."

"Thanks." Zach watched Tom as he started down the hall, then turned to Teri. "Everything okay?"

"There's a call on hold for you," she said.

"Is it important?"

"Sounds like it." Teri glanced at Derek. "Can you excuse us, Derek?"

"Oh. Yeah. Of course." Derek turned on his heel and disappeared in the direction Tom had gone.

Teri stepped closer to Zach. "I didn't want Derek to overhear. She made me promise to be discreet."

"Who? Paige?"

Teri pursed her lips together tightly and shook her head. "Alexis Simmons," she whispered.

Zach felt the blood drain from his face, even when he had no idea why Alexis might be calling him. For a moment, he considered asking Teri to tell Alexis that he couldn't even speak to her. Agents only spoke to other agents' clients when there was trouble afoot. Then again, as far as Zach knew, Alexis and Paige were doing great. Perhaps the secretiveness was for a good reason. "Put her through."

"Okay. Two secs."

Teri hustled back to her desk while Zach returned

to his office and closed the door behind him. A moment later, his office line rang.

"Alexis. How are you?" Zach answered.

"Good. How about you?"

"Also good. What can I help you with today?"

"I need to ask you a question. Or maybe it's a couple of questions. But you have to promise me that you won't say anything to Paige."

"Not sure I can promise you that. It depends what you're going to ask. Paige and I are close. I'm not sure if you're aware of that."

"I knew you guys were friends. But I figured all agents secretly hate each other."

"That's not the case with Paige and me." *Not even close.*

"Okay, well, I'm just going to go for it because I'm frustrated. I want to know if you'll represent me. Paige isn't cutting it. It's been nearly six weeks since I went number one in the draft and there have been zero endorsement deals. And it's been nearly a month since the expo in Las Vegas. Meanwhile, a bunch of players who were drafted after me are filming commercials and doing photo shoots and social media partnerships. It's more than just the money. It makes me look bad."

Zach's mind was reeling at full tilt, like his brain was on a carnival ride—one of those spinning ones that make you feel a bit sick. "I can't represent you, Alexis. I could never do that to Paige."

"Then can you talk to her? Because I'm at the end

of my rope. Do you understand why I might want to make a change?"

Zach could just imagine that conversation with Paige. It would not go over well. "I know Paige is working hard on your behalf. Things just haven't been coming together the way she'd hoped they would."

"Tell me about it."

"I also know that she's holding out for top dollar. I'm sure she doesn't want you bogged down with commitments. All of those things, like filming commercials and photo shoots, can really eat into your time. You've got basketball to think about, too."

"Yes. She's told me all of that. But I've got my bottom line to think about. If I'm lucky, my career is going to last seven or eight years. Ten if I'm really, really lucky. But I could also get hurt. Or go through a slump. Or end up on a terrible team. My stock is never going to be higher than it is right now."

"You don't know that. What if you win a championship? End up being MVP? What if you become an all-star?"

"That's a lot of what-ifs, Zach."

"Life is full of that, unfortunately." Zach knew that all too well. What if Tom had given a full-throated endorsement of his relationship with Paige? What if Paige was willing to tell the rest of the world that she didn't care what they thought?

"Let me ask you this," Alexis said. "If I had been your client all along, would I have endorsement deals right now?"

Zach knew the answer was yes, but it wasn't a fair question. He had relationships that Paige hadn't had the chance to build yet. He also had superstar male clients who he could use for leverage. It really wasn't a level playing field for Paige or Alexis. "I try not to deal in hypotheticals. But I understand your frustration. And you're right about all of it. You should be getting those big deals. I'm just begging you to stick with Paige."

"I'm not sure. Part of me thinks I need to be a smart businesswoman and strike while the iron is hot."

Again, Alexis was making all kinds of sense. But Zach had to save this. For Paige. He couldn't help but think about the night of the women's draft, when Paige had found out that Zach had sent congratulatory flowers to Alexis. He remembered how passionately she'd told Zach to step off, and the reasons why she had earned the job of Alexis's agent. "Paige has been with you from the very beginning, hasn't she? Since high school? Since before any of the hype. Since before college."

"She has. But some working relationships run their course. Plus, it's not like she hasn't had her payday. I signed a fat contract with Phoenix. She got her cut and she will continue to do so as long as I'm playing there."

Zach swallowed hard. He'd run out of reasons to stop Alexis from doing the unthinkable. "I can't represent you, Alexis. My relationship with Paige is too important to me. But I do hope you'll think about what I said. Close personal ties in this industry are few and far between. I know that Paige genuinely cares about you and your career. That's worth something."

"You know, Zach, I have to say that I really expected you to jump all over this. I'm not happy with your answer, but I get it. There aren't enough people in this world who are straight shooters. You clearly are. So thank you for that. And for your time."

"No problem. I hope you know that I'm rooting for you. From the sidelines, of course."

"Thanks. I'm hoping you'll keep this conversation between us."

The thought of keeping this from Paige deeply bothered him, but the idea of telling her about it was even more unpleasant. "Absolutely. As far as I'm concerned, we never spoke."

"Perfect. Thanks."

"Goodbye." Zach ended the call and put the phone receiver in its cradle. Slumping back in his chair, he scrubbed his face with both hands. His mind was running one million miles a minute. He could not believe what had just happened. Now what?

He took a deep breath, replaying the conversation in his head. He'd done the right thing, right? He'd taken Alexis's call, politely turned her down and defended Paige. How he wished he had a confidante right now, someone who he could talk to about both work and his personal life. If all was right with the world, that person should've been Tom. But Tom believed Zach had no business being with Paige, and he sure as hell wasn't going to agree with Zach's approach with Alexis. After all, Tom had told Zach to pursue Alexis as a client.

As if he wasn't on edge enough, Zach's cell phone rang. Flustered, he reached for it and looked at the caller ID. It was Paige. She was his real confidante right now. And he couldn't utter a word about this to her.

"Hey there," he said when he answered.

"Okay. So I know it's Monday, which is usually pretty low-key for us, but it's the Eastern Conference Finals tonight and I'm thinking pizza is in order."

He sat back in his chair and smiled. Simply hearing her voice and knowing that she wanted to make plans filled him with such joy. Especially since it involved basketball and pizza. "Sounds amazing."

"I got an incredible bottle of red wine from a client. It'll be perfect."

It sounded better than perfect to Zach. It sounded like sheer heaven. "Absolutely. I'm in. What do I need to do?"

"Nothing. I'll bring the pizza and the wine. Meet at your place at seven? Tip-off is at seven thirty."

"Okay. I'll see you then."

"It's a date."

Zach hung up the phone, now even more conflicted. He couldn't wait to see her tonight, but it was going to be sheer torture to talk to her, knowing that he was hiding the secret of his call with Alexis.

"Zach?" Teri buzzed his line.

"Yep."

"Sorry to interrupt, but Ryan Wilson is on the phone for you."

"Great. Put him through."

Zach got back to work, talking to Ryan, then answering e-mails, followed by several phone calls to other clients. Next came a staff meeting, which Tom unexpectedly stayed for, followed by a quick lunch, then even more calls and e-mails. By six o'clock, Zach was more than ready to head home.

He decided to walk the fifteen or so blocks to his apartment, if only to clear his head. It was a gorgeous evening with the hint of warmer days to come. He arrived at his apartment with a few minutes to spare, so he changed into jeans and a T-shirt, then tidied up a bit. Paige was right on time at seven.

"Pizza delivery," she said when he opened the door.

He quickly took the extra large cardboard box from her. "Whoa. It's still hot."

"Just like you." Paige leaned over to deliver a soft kiss. "I like you in jeans. It's working for me."

Zach laughed quietly. "Come on. I've got the TV on in the great room." He led the way and placed the box on the center island in the kitchen when he arrived.

Paige immediately went for the cabinet that had the wineglasses. By now, she knew his apartment like the back of her hand. She opened the bottle and poured two glasses, then handed him one. "Cheers. To basketball and pizza."

"To a woman who will make plans to watch basketball and eat pizza." He clinked his glass with hers, then took a long sip, transfixed by her. It wasn't that she was any more beautiful today. Or somehow more sexy. But there had been a shift today—a monumental one. Everything he'd been feeling during that meeting with Tom and that awful phone call with Alexis was pointing him toward one thing—he loved her. He was in love. He wanted to tell her. He wanted to shout it from the rooftops. The only trouble was he wasn't sure she would ever return the words.

For a man who'd always felt fortunate, Zach seriously doubted he could be lucky enough to have Paige for good.

Eleven

Paige was feeling extraordinarily lazy. Maybe it was because it was Friday. Or perhaps it was because Zach was being so ambitious. "Don't get up. Come back to bed," she said.

He laughed as he threaded a T-shirt on over his head. "I love how I'm the responsible one in this scenario."

"I'm still naked under here, you know." She stuck one bare leg out from under the covers to prove her point.

Zach rounded to what had become her side of his bed and leaned down to kiss her forehead. "You're killing me. But I have to get in a workout before I head to the office. My day is jam-packed and my whole schedule will be thrown off if I don't."

She sighed and smiled up at him. Dammit, he was

handsome. And responsible. "Okay. Fine. Maybe I can help you wash off that workout when you're done."

"I love the way you think."

Zach disappeared and Paige rolled to her side and grabbed her cell from the bedside table to unplug it from the charger. She was surprised to see a missed call from April, but no message. She sat up in bed, leaned back against the headboard and called her best friend.

"How are you?" April asked in greeting.

Paige ignored the odd tone April had taken, which was much the way you ask a very ill person how they're holding up. "Hello to you, too. I'm good. What's up?" Paige combed her hand through her hair. It was a bit of a tangled mess after last night with Zach.

"Good? How could you possibly be happy?"

Paige had to think about that for a moment. No one had ever called her out for being happy. "Because I am." In truth, she was better than happy. She was in a great place, something she hadn't dare to imagine after her divorce or after her mom passed away. Things were going well at work. She'd gotten closer on a new shoe deal for Alexis. She and Zach were humming right along. They had their hurdles and Paige wasn't sure how long it would last, but overall, things were, for lack of a better word, *good*.

"Oh, my god. You haven't heard, have you?"

Paige was beyond perplexed. And now getting frustrated. "Heard what? What's up with you?" Perhaps there was some juicy gossip April had become privy to?

"I was calling to tell you I'm sorry. I just assumed you would've heard about everything with Alexis by now."

Her spine stiffened. "Everything with Alexis? Is she okay? What happened?"

"There's a credible rumor that she's signing with Armstrong. According to our source, she's leaving you, Paige."

"What are you talking about? Alexis wouldn't leave me. At least not without talking to me first." Or would she? The question popped into her head and would not leave. Alexis was not a confrontational person, and she'd called Paige and given her an earful about the distinct lack of sponsorships after Las Vegas. Maybe she was unhappy enough to leave. "Plus, Zach wouldn't do that. He wouldn't." She wanted to be confident in that answer. Their relationship felt rock solid. But was it? They'd only been together a little over a month, just long enough for her to let down her guard. And if he'd shown ruthlessness in one area of his life, it was in work.

"Paige, he's in charge of the agency. You know that something like this wouldn't happen without his knowledge. It's impossible. The buck stops and starts with him."

Oh, god. April was so right. About all of it. Zach had total control of the company. Paige didn't know whether she should cry or scream. Or both. Maybe at the same time. "What do I do? I don't know what to do."

"Are you two still seeing each other? You kept things casual, right?"

Paige's stomach rolled, making her queasy. She shifted in the bed, which only reminded her that she was naked under Zach's fluffy duvet. "We see each other all the time, April. It's about as far from casual as it could possibly be." *I'd go so far as to call him my boyfriend. I think I might be falling in love with him.*

"Why did you do that? That wasn't the plan. You were supposed to have your fun and not get too close."

"Yeah, well, life doesn't always go according to plan. Case in point—today and the news you just delivered." It was the truth. She'd gone into her situation with Zach trying to be cautious. But he was so disarming. He was so much fun. And they understood each other in ways she'd never anticipated. "It just happened. Everything made sense at the time." *At the time.* The thought made her feel even more sick. She was already speaking about Zach in the past tense.

"I'm so sorry. I don't know what to tell you. I really wish I hadn't been the one to break the bad news."

She told herself to get it together. She was stronger than this and there had to be an explanation. Bad rumors went around all the time. Misinformation was everywhere. "Are you going to be reporting on this? Have you verified through a secondary source?"

"It's not my story. Brett Daniels has a source at

Armstrong who leaked the information to him. I don't know when it becomes official. All I know is that Alexis wasn't happy and decided she needed to make a change. I'm sorry. So sorry. I know how hard you've worked with her."

An old familiar feeling settled over her—betrayal. She wanted it to go away, but it seeped into her pores. It threatened to smother her. This was how she'd felt when she discovered that Andre was thinking about leaving her employ and going to work for Armstrong. When she'd discovered that her own husband cared more about his professional fortunes than her. It was when she'd learned that Tom Armstrong was not afraid to play dirty. "Do you think Tom Armstrong could be playing a role in this?"

"Isn't he just serving an advisory role now? This seems like a big move for someone who isn't in charge anymore."

"It's still his company. Everything has his finger-prints all over it."

"I wouldn't put it past him, but are you just saying that because you're in deep with Zach?"

As much as Paige adored April, she was bringing up far too many unpleasant realities this morning. "I don't know. Maybe." She remembered thinking that Zach was naive for wanting to tell Tom about their relationship, but perhaps she was the one who was naive. Perhaps she was the person who hadn't considered every possible pitfall, like the fact that he might jump at the chance to sign a premiere athlete like Alexis. He'd certainly gone in for the kill when Ryan Wilson became unhappy with his agent.

"It sounds to me like you have some detective work to do."

"Is there any way you can convince Brett to sit on the story? Just for a little bit until I get this straightened out?"

"Honestly, I doubt it. There's nothing Brett loves more than a scoop. And it's only a matter of time before other networks pick up on it. A story like this can only be contained for so long."

Paige blew out a breath of frustration and threw back the covers. "I need to track down Alexis. Can I talk to you later?"

"Of course. Whatever you want or need. Just let me know. I'm so sorry, Paige. Truly."

"Thank you. It's nice to know someone is in my corner."

"Of course. You know, you'll get past this. You will get to the other side, stronger. You did it with Andre. You did it when your mom passed away. You can do it again."

Paige appreciated the pep talk, but it only served as confirmation that Paige's entire life had fallen apart in the time it took to have a short phone call with her best friend. "Thanks. I hope you're right."

"I am. I'll let you go, but don't forget that I love you."

"Love you, too, April. Goodbye." Paige ended the call and got out of bed. She grabbed a pair of leggings and a long-sleeved top she had in the drawer

Zach had emptied out for her. She wrapped her arms around her midsection and wondered what to do next. Logic said she should confront Zach, but maybe she should do the detective work first. Thank goodness he hadn't given in to her plea for sex. He'd be busy in his home gym for at least the next half hour until he finished his workout.

To start, she sent a text to Henry. Sorry to text you so early. Can you reach out to Shonda in legal and have her pull Alexis's contract?

Is there a problem?

Not sure.

Okay. I'm on it.

Paige next pulled up Alexis's number on her phone. She had to hear this from the source. Was there a chance April had gotten some bad intel? Paige knew it was unlikely, but it wasn't impossible. More than anything, she needed to hear it from Alexis herself. The number rang and rang, and then she got Alexis's voice mail. *This is Alexis Simmons. You know what to do.*

Paige ended the call. She knew for a fact that Alexis never listened to her voice mail. She sent Alexis a text. Please call me. I hope everything is okay.

A text from Henry appeared. Shonda is getting oral surgery. Not due to be back in the office until Monday.

Is there anyone else who can help me with a contract?

I'll ask.

Thanks.

Paige ventured into Zach's kitchen and poured herself a cup of coffee, pondering her next move. She really, really did not want to accuse Zach of anything until she verified what was actually happening. Then she got an idea—Alexis's mom. She and Alexis were impossibly close. If anyone would know what was going on, it was her.

Paige felt a small glimmer of hope. "Yes. Perfect," she muttered to herself as she scrolled through her contact list and found the number for Anna Simmons. The call rang once. Then twice.

"Hello?"

"Anna, hi. This is Paige Moss. I'm sorry to call so early, but I've been trying to reach Alexis regarding an important work matter. I called her cell and got voice mail. I'm wondering if you know how I can reach her. Or if you know what she's up to right now."

"Oh, Paige, I'm so sorry. So very sorry."

"About what?"

"I was told not to talk to you."

Paige felt like she'd been punched in the stomach, hard, by someone much bigger than her. "Anna, please. I need you to talk to Alexis…"

"I'm sorry, Paige. I can't." The line went dead.

Paige stared at her phone in disbelief. "She hung up. This is real. It's happening." And the only logical explanation was that Zach was behind it. Was everything she'd thought about him the night they met proving to be right? And had everything she'd thought about him since that fateful night in Vegas been wrong? Was she the naive one? Had everything she'd done to protect herself and her business been in vain? A complete waste of time and effort? She couldn't begin to wrap her head around the present moment and the deluge of questions that accompanied it. It was like she was outside of her own body, observing what was happening to her. It felt that unreal.

The only step forward was to confront Zach. She had to do it. She took another sip of coffee for courage, left her mug on the counter, then walked down the long hall that led to the back of his apartment. The last room on the right was his home gym. When she reached it, she stood in the doorway, watching him run on the treadmill. He had his earbuds in and was in his own little world, undoubtedly listening to music too loud. Every swing of his arms was relaxed, his back perfectly straight while the muscles of his toned legs were fully engaged, showing off his lean strength. He didn't look like a man who was hiding a big secret, but she questioned everything in her life right now.

Eventually, he started to slow down the pace of the machine until it brought him to a brisk walk. He took out his earbuds and that was when he noticed

Paige. A smile instantly bloomed on his face. It felt like her heart was being cleaved in two. "You were really serious about that shower, weren't you? I'm going to need at least fifteen minutes to cool down."

She ventured into the room. "Zach. We need to talk."

His brows drew together and his forehead wrinkled. "Sounds important. Is everything okay?"

She wrapped her arms around her middle, needing to protect herself. "Is there anything you want to tell me?"

"About?" He stepped off the treadmill and approached.

Paige reflexively took a step back. She needed distance between them. It was the only way to keep her head straight. "Work. Armstrong Sports. New client signings, perhaps?"

"I honestly have no clue what you're talking about right now."

She didn't want to feel so irked, but she was. She expected Zach to be honest with her and all available evidence pointed to him being anything but. "You don't know a thing about a rumor that Alexis is signing with your agency?"

He reared back his head. "You're joking, right?"

"I just got off the phone with April. They have a source inside Armstrong Sports. They're going to report the story."

Zach wiped his forehead with his towel. "No way. They're wrong. Who do I need to talk to? Is it April's story?"

"Don't you think you should first speak to Tom? Make sure he isn't up to something?"

He shook his head in dismay. "You just always think the worst of him, don't you?"

"Hey. That's not fair. I have more than enough history with Tom to justify my opinion of him. And if you think the story is wrong, then why did Alexis's mom just tell me that she was instructed not to speak to me if I called her?"

Zach's eyes doubled in size. "Seriously? Have you spoken to Alexis?"

"No. She didn't answer when I called."

Zach stepped over to the weight bench where he'd left his phone. "I have two missed calls from a number I don't recognize."

"Reporters, maybe?"

"You really think this is real?"

"Yes, Zach. I do. At the very least, I think we need to find out."

"Okay. Yeah. Let me call Tom right now." He dragged his finger along the screen. "I'll straighten this out. Don't worry about it."

Paige was still processing, but things were starting to feel real now. She tried to imagine what was ahead for her and Zach, but she couldn't see a thing. Logic said that this was the beginning of the end. She'd known this moment would eventually come, but she'd had no idea it would be today. "Let me know what he says."

"Do you want to stay?"

"For your conversation with Tom? No." Yes, she

was supposed to be stronger than this, but she didn't have the courage to actually witness the moment when everything truly fell apart.

"Paige. Come on." Zach's tone was so plaintive. It was hard not to infer that no matter the outcome, he expected her to be a good sport about this. She couldn't imagine that. Not at all.

"I'll be getting ready for work if you find anything out."

As Zach watched Paige walk away, he could not believe what was happening. It had to be wrong. It simply didn't make sense. Which was why he wasted no time calling Tom.

"Morning," Tom said when he answered. "How are you? Is everything okay? It's not like you to call so early in the day."

Zach glanced at the time on the clock on the wall. It wasn't even eight o'clock yet. "Did I wake you? I hope not. I know you still need your rest."

"Oh, no. I'm up. Having coffee with your mom in the breakfast room right now. What can I do for you?"

Zach cleared his throat. "A reporter at one of the sports networks is about to break a story that we're signing Alexis Simmons. They claim to have an inside source. I'm trying to figure out what this is all about. Do you have any thoughts?"

"Oh, no. Really?"

An intense wave of relief washed over Zach. Tom wasn't involved. He didn't know about it, either. "Right? It doesn't make any sense. The reporter must have some bad intel. That's all I can think."

"No. Zach," Tom said. "That's not what I'm saying."

"Then what?"

Tom sighed heavily. "I didn't want this to get out now. Especially not to you. You weren't supposed to know. Not yet."

"Know what? You have to tell me what's going on. This is my ass on the line." *And my heart.* Zach had such a bad feeling about this. His pulse was speeding up and slowing down. His entire body was filled with unease.

"I didn't want you to find out until it was a done deal. I don't know who decided to talk, but I have a pretty good feeling it was Derek. He's hungry, but he's very young. I should've known better than to keep him in the loop. That was my bad. I fully own it."

Zach was in such shock that it was hard to breathe. "What are you saying? It's true? You've signed Alexis to a contract with our agency?"

"Yes, Zach. It's true. The preliminary agreement is complete and we're hammering out the details now. It should be done by the end of the day. I was hoping we could announce it next week."

"Why in the world did you do this? And without telling me?"

A long silence played out on the line and Zach wished he could see Tom's face right now to read his expression. Had he been making moves behind Zach's back?

"I did it because you wanted Alexis, but you were also involved with Paige Moss. I figured there was no way for you to get yourself out of the predicament you were in, so I did it for you. I found out from Derek that she'd called you. I guess he overheard Teri on the phone when she answered the first call. And it was a safe assumption from my end that you'd turned Alexis down because of Paige. Sure enough, Alexis confirmed exactly that."

Zach needed to sit. He was about to be sick. He perched on the edge of the weight bench, so thankful that Paige hadn't stayed to listen to this conversation. "This can't happen, Tom. We have to stop this."

"Zach, we can't stop it."

"Why not?"

"Because this is what Alexis wants. It's what she wanted when she called you. So I stepped in because this is what's best for the agency. And also happens to be better for her, too."

"It's not better for Paige. And you put me in charge of the agency. It's like you don't trust me to make decisions."

"It's not that I don't trust you. I understand. You've let your judgment be clouded by infatuation. It happens."

Had Zach allowed Paige to cloud his judgment? Zach preferred to think of it as Paige's influence steering his decisions. Sure, if he and Paige hadn't been involved, he might have jumped at the chance to work with Alexis. But Paige was important to him and he wasn't about to throw that away.

"And, I have to tell you, being back in the office that day really made me realize how much I miss it," Tom continued. "So I dipped my toes back in the water just to help everyone out. I'm happy, Alexis is definitely happy and now you can be happy, too."

"How am I supposed to be happy?"

"This advances your plans for the agency in a major way."

"But it's going to destroy my relationship with Paige."

"It doesn't have to. You have plausible deniability. Tell her you didn't know. It's the truth. I'll be the bad guy, which you know she'll believe. It's a win-win if you look at it the right way."

Zach grumbled under his breath. He could not believe Tom was being this flippant about it. Paige was already devastated when she thought losing Alexis was merely a possibility. Now it was happening, which meant only one thing—she would be destroyed and she would want nothing more to do with Zach.

"And let's be honest," Tom continued. "We all know your fling with Paige isn't going to last."

"It's not a fling, Tom. I love her."

"Do you? I'm not so sure about that. Can she make you happy? Long-term?"

"She can." If only Tom knew the future Zach had fantasized about. It was one where he and Paige were together, possibly married. He'd even wondered if there was a way they could work together. That would've been perfect. It would've been everything he'd ever wanted. Now it seemed utterly impossible.

"I'm sorry to say this, and I know this won't be easy for you to hear, but I think you're being very shortsighted. You have your entire life ahead of you. Don't sell yourself short because you think you're in love with a woman who's probably not right for you."

Zach shook his head, knee-deep in disbelief at how quickly his idyllic world had crumbled down around him. He'd always thought of himself as lucky. Now he wasn't so sure. "Tom, do you realize that you basically made sure that there's no way that my relationship with Paige can work? Even if she decided to forgive me for what has happened, she'll never forgive you."

"And what's the problem there?"

"You're my family, Tom. If I'm going to be with someone, they need to be part of my family. How freaking uncomfortable would Christmas morning be if the woman I love and the man who is the only father I've ever known don't like each other?"

"You're that serious about her?"

"Yes. I am. That's what I've been saying all along."

"I just assumed this would eventually run its course."

"Well, that's probably going to be proven to be true. But just not in the way you imagined it." Zach got up from his seat on the weight bench, but it took some effort. His entire body was weighed down with a heavy mix of anger and sadness. "Tom, I have to go and try to salvage this situation with Paige."

"I know you're upset now, but, Zach, I'm telling you that these things have a way of working out for the best. Five years from now, you'll be happy it played out this way."

"Somehow, I doubt that. But thanks for the kernel of wisdom anyway." Zach eagerly ended the call. He couldn't endure any more of Tom's misguided logic. Unfortunately, his phone rang again right away. It was Teri. "Hey. I'm glad you called. We need to talk."

"What in the world is going on, Zach? Three different sports reporters called for you in the last five minutes and they all said it was urgent. And Derek came by wanting to see about getting a bigger office?"

Zach wanted to punch a wall or at least tear his hair out. "It's a long story. For the moment, just tell the press that we have no comment at this time."

"And Derek?"

"Tell him to go back to his tiny, appropriately sized office and get back to work."

Teri snickered. "Got it. Anything else?"

"I might not even be coming in today. We'll see how things go. Can you manage?"

"Of course, Zach. Always."

"Thank you. You're the absolute best." Zach ended the call and started down the hall. "Paige? Are you still here?" he called. No response came. Had she left? He wouldn't blame her if that was the case. But when he walked into his room, she was sitting on the edge of the bed, fully dressed, staring at her phone and shaking her head. "Hey," he said.

She looked up with an unimaginable amount of pain on her face. He wanted so badly to make it go away. "They broke the story. It's over." She handed over the phone, which had a video from April's network on it.

Zach didn't watch it. He had too much to save in this room. "I'm so sorry. I didn't know. It was all Tom's doing."

"Is that cover for you? I'm sure Tom will protect you at all costs." She got up from the bed and marched into the bathroom, where she started chucking various toiletries into a zippered bag.

"It's not. I had absolutely no idea this was happening. None. I swear."

"I watched the video. Their source on the story says Alexis called you on Monday." She turned to him, her eyes ablaze with betrayal. They held no softness for him. Not anymore. "That was the day I brought pizza over so we could watch basketball. You didn't say a peep about it to me that night. We made love that night. And you continued to keep things quiet. You were keeping a secret from me the whole time."

He stepped closer, even though he could feel the anger radiating off her. "I didn't tell you about the phone call because I figured no good would come of it. I told her no. I defended you. I did everything in my power to keep things exactly as they are. And then I left it alone."

"Well, it didn't work because Tom apparently decided to step in. And now I've lost my biggest client and my boyfriend, all in one fell swoop."

That word—it made his heart leap. Despite the seriousness of their situation, it made him so happy to hear her call him that. "You've never called me your boyfriend before."

"And you won't hear it again. We're done, Zach."

Just like that, the air was sucked from his lungs and his heart started shrinking into a tiny ball. "Don't say that. We can work this out. I love you." For an instant, the room went still. It nearly felt like the world had stopped spinning, too. He hoped the words would fix this, that they would prove to her just how serious he was about her.

Paige zipped up the bag, flipped off the bathroom light and stalked out of the room. "You know, I thought I was falling in love with you. I did. But then this happened and I told myself that it's been five weeks. You can't be in love with someone after five weeks."

Zach followed her as she went to the closet. "I was in love with you after five minutes."

Paige froze in the doorway. Her shoulders dropped. "Zach, don't."

He rushed to her side and grasped her arm, hoping to hell that this wouldn't be the last time he got to touch her. "Those five weeks were just the confirmation that my first feeling for you was real." All Zach could think was that if his job was turning into a nightmare and his relationship with his family was about to get rocky, being with Paige would make all of that misery okay. But that wasn't going to be the way things played out. She didn't feel what he did. He could see it on her face, and it was like a red-hot poker right through the center of his psyche.

"What you're feeling isn't love. It's infatuation. And it'll go away as soon as you meet someone else." She drew in a deep breath and scanned his face. It was like she was looking right through him. "And even if it was love, it wouldn't matter. You and your family have destroyed me. Maybe it's all Tom. I don't know. But I do know that family is incredibly important to you, just as it is to me. I don't have any family anymore and it's a very lonely feeling. I don't want you to lose that on my account." A tear leaked from the corner of her eye.

"Please let me find a way to fix this."

She shook her head. "No. It's already done. Alexis is leaving me because I failed. And if there's one thing I learned from my mom, it's that accepting failure is the only way to move forward in life. I need to look ahead. I'm tired of feeling stuck."

He inched closer, wanting so desperately to wrap her up in his arms. "You weren't stuck when we were together. We were happy. We can have more of that."

"I wish that was true, but you know that you would have to give up far too much to be with me. In the end, family is all that matters. Work things out with Tom and be happy. That's all I want for you. Be happy." Paige stepped closer and kissed him on the cheek. "Goodbye, Zach."

She picked up the overnight bag she'd brought to

his apartment when he'd first cleaned out a drawer for her. It was so full that the zipper was straining. She was leaving and there wasn't a damn thing he could do about it. When Paige set her mind to something, it was impossible to keep her from her aim. It was part of what made him love her so much.

But in the end, apparently love wasn't enough to save either of them.

Twelve

It wasn't until Sunday at noon that Alexis finally called Paige back. "Hey," Alexis said, followed by a long and painful silence.

"Hey," Paige eventually replied, in an attempt to move the conversation ahead. She muted the TV and curled up on one end of her living room sofa. She'd been there since Friday morning, off and on. She did get up to answer the door for takeout, to get a glass of water or to go to the bathroom. She'd even slept on the couch. Her bed was just another reminder of Zach.

"I'm guessing you'd like to know what happened."

Paige cleared her throat. "I would. Yes."

"Of course. I definitely owe you an explanation." Alexis went on to tell the whole story, detailing how she had reached out to Zach and asked him to represent her. She then repeated the exact information Zach had relayed to her—he'd defended Paige, he'd turned down Alexis's overture and he'd made a promise not to speak a word of it to anyone. "He really went to bat for you. I want you to know that."

Paige felt like her heart was breaking all over again, just when she thought it couldn't possibly be more broken. "Then what?"

"I got a phone call from Tom Armstrong on Thursday. He'd heard from one of the junior agents in their office that I'd called Zach. Tom asked why I'd called and I told him. I told him everything. I told him that I wanted new representation."

Paige winced. That was the moment when everything had changed. It was also the moment when it became official that she'd failed. "And Tom offered to step in."

"He did. And I agreed. But I need you to know why I had to make a change."

Paige braced herself. This wasn't going to be easy to hear, but she had to suck it up. "Yes. Please."

"I know you've stood by me for a long time. You were there before any other agent. And I'm thankful for that. But you weren't there before my family, and this is all about them. They're the ones who really, truly, stood by me. My mom and dad made so many sacrifices for me. I would not have the success I have without them."

Paige related to that sentiment to her very core. She wouldn't have made the strides she'd made in her life without the steady hand and unwavering love of her mother. She wouldn't have learned the value of independence or hard work, and she wouldn't have found her love of sports, either. She and Zach had that much in common—Tom had guided him, and Paige's mom had done the same for her. "Why didn't you say something?"

"I tried to, Paige. That day when I called you, I was telling you I was unhappy. But it was like you didn't hear me."

"I thought I did."

"I think you thought you were listening. But you didn't want to believe me. There's a big difference."

"And why didn't you call me after you talked to Tom?"

"Because I felt like I already knew how the conversation was going to go. It was just going to be a repeat of what we'd already talked about. I'd already made up my mind. I need to make the most of this time in my life and this stage of my career. I don't know how long it will last. I need to take care of my family. Like, really take care of them. I want to pay off my parents' house and buy them each a car. I want to make sure they never have another worry for the rest of their lives. I feel like I owe them that for everything they've done for me, but also because I love them. I love them more than anything."

Tears started to roll down Paige's cheeks. It was impossible for her to begrudge Alexis any of these things. In the end, it was *her* talent, hard work and dedication. It didn't belong to Paige, no matter how much she'd been there along the way. "I understand."

"You do?"

"I do. You'd do anything for your family. I felt the same way about my mom when she was still here." And Zach felt the same way about his family. That was so much of the reason why Paige was resigned to the idea that they would not work. Even though she missed Zach in a way she'd never missed anyone before. She kept hearing his laugh. She kept thinking of things she wanted to tell him. And he wasn't there to make her life better. To make it sweeter.

"There's something romantic between you and Zach, isn't there?" Alexis asked.

Paige laughed. It was the only way to keep from breaking into a sobbing fit. "There is." *Or there was, at least.*

"I could tell when I talked to him. He thinks the world of you."

That should have buoyed Paige, but in reality, it made her stomach sink. The words he'd had the courage to say to her were still echoing in her head. *I love you.* They'd said a lot of things to each other on Friday morning, all of which conveyed a broad range of emotions, but none were louder and more impossible to ignore than *I love you.* "I think the world of him, too."

"So what's next for you two? How do agents at rival agencies make it work?"

"That's the million dollar question." Of course there was more to it than that. She and Zach had so many obstacles, and unfortunately, Paige had created one on her own when she'd skirted the fact that she loved him and had failed to own up to it.

"I hope you figure it out because I like you both. A lot."

"We'll see. For the moment, we aren't really talking."

"You know how to fix that, right? Talk to him."

"I wish it was that simple."

"Paige. For all of the advice you've given me over the years, it's time for me to return the favor. It is that simple. Call him. I promise you he will be excited to talk to you."

Paige drew in a deep breath and blew it out slowly. "I'll think about it. Okay?"

"Fair enough."

"I hope we can be friends, Alexis."

"Really? I'd love that."

Paige smiled. "Good. I'd love that, too."

Paige said her goodbye to Alexis, then decided to clear her head with a walk. She covered a lot of ground, wandering all over the place, soaking up the sights and sounds of life all around her. The sun was bright. The air was warmer than yesterday, which had been warmer than the day before that. There was so much to be thankful for. So much to look forward to. Summer would arrive soon. Another season. And yet none of it meant a thing to Paige. It all felt like a reminder that her life had become a hollow shell. She loved her work, but did it love her back? After everything that had happened with Alexis, she could say that it definitely did not.

When she got back to her apartment, she looked at her phone and rolled it around in her hand. She knew what her heart wanted, and she knew very well what her gut was telling her, as well as what Alexis had told her. She wanted Zach and she needed to try again with him. It might not work, but she'd forgiven Alexis, so why couldn't she forgive Tom? And if she could forgive Tom, she and Zach might have a future together. As long as Zach would accept her apology.

She decided to test the waters. Just a text. If no response came, she would know her fate and she'd move on. Just like she'd moved on hundreds of times before today.

I miss you. And I need to apologize. Her heart skipped a few hundred beats before she hit Send. But eventually she did.

Her phone rang only a second or two later. It was Zach.

"Hello?" she answered, in shock.

"On the long list of things I fantasized about you saying to me, 'I need to apologize' didn't make the list," Zach replied. "Then again, I've never been one of those guys who needed to be right."

Her entire body was blanketed in warmth. "God, I missed your voice."

"Considering the fact that I wasn't sure you'd ever speak to me again, I'd say that I more than missed yours. I've spent the last two days trying to commit it to memory."

"That is so sweet. It's the sweetest thing I've ever heard." Paige plopped down on the couch, but in a different spot from the one she'd been inhabiting for the last two days. "What are we going to do, Zach? How do we fix this?"

"Funny you should ask. I actually made a plan. I thought I was going to have to carry it out on my own, but I think it would be better if you were there."

"Plan? What kind of plan?"

"How much fun would it be if I actually told you?"

"Can I get a hint?"

"We're going to need to go to Long Island to talk to Tom and my mom."

Paige needed a second or two to think about that. What an uncomfortable situation that was going to be. "Are you sure that's such a good idea?"

"No idea. But do you want to try?"

"I do."

"Then I'll pick you up at your place in an hour."

Paige looked down at herself. She was a wreck. She hadn't showered in twenty-four hours and she was wearing sweats. "Today? We're doing this today?"

"It's now or never, darling. I'm tired of waiting for my life to start."

"I was hoping to tell you I'm sorry."

"It can wait until I see you. An in-person apology is always better."

Paige grinned. "Deal." She got off the phone with Zach and quickly showered, then spent a fair amount of time doing her hair and makeup. She wanted to look as good as humanly possible. The next several hours held a lot of uncertainty, but she hoped for the best. In her closet, she deliberated over an outfit. Eventually, she settled on slim black pants, ballet flats and a blue silk top. It wasn't her sexiest attire, but she wanted to be presentable to meet Zach's mom.

As she waited downstairs for Zach to arrive, Paige's heart was beating so fast that she was surprised she wasn't dizzy. The next bit was going to require quite a few leaps. Was she ready for them? She sure hoped so. When he zipped up to the curb in his Aston Martin, a car she'd heard about but had not yet ridden in, her heart sped up even more. Zach parked the car and got out. "Don't move. Let me get your door."

"Yes, sir." Paige waited patiently.

Zach approached, wearing dark jeans and a light gray shirt with the sleeves rolled up. He was quick to snake his arm around Paige's waist and kiss her. There was no moment where they both declared that they were sorry. It was right back to where they'd been moments before Paige got that fateful phone call from April. "I missed you," he muttered between their lips.

"I missed you, too. It feels like I haven't seen you in a year."

"When in reality, it's only been two days."

"Funny how time drags when you're miserable."

Zach kissed her temple, then opened the car door. "No more of that, if I have anything to say about it."

Paige climbed into the passenger seat and let Zach close the door behind her. As soon as he climbed in to the car, she had to say something. "Zach. My apology." She reached for his arm, quickly reminded of how much she loved the feel of his skin.

"Now? We're going to be late."

"They're expecting us?"

"I didn't think an ambush was a good idea."

Paige had the distinct impression that if she didn't get this out now, she might explode. And she didn't want to make her admission while he was driving. "I love you, Zach. I messed up by saying whatever it was that I said on Friday. Even worse, I tried to dismiss your feelings, which was horrible of me. I'm so sorry."

He smiled wide and leaned closer to deliver a soft and sensual kiss. "Perfect. Apology accepted." He turned on the engine and quickly pulled the car out into traffic.

"That's it? Apology accepted?"

"I knew you loved me, too, Paige."

"How is that possible? I wasn't sure myself."

"The minute you made plans with me for the Eastern Conference Finals. I know how important sports are to you, and you were thinking about me because you came up with an idea for a very thoughtful date night. If that's not love, I don't know what is. At least for us."

She laughed quietly and nodded. "I suppose you're right." Despite all of the good things that had happened over the last few hours, Paige was still quite nervous about seeing Tom Armstrong face-to-face under these circumstances. She already knew that he didn't like her or, at the very least, wasn't predisposed to thinking of her fondly. How would this really work? She felt reasonably sure *she* could get past it, but she had the lure of Zach. What reason did Tom have to sort anything out? He already had Zach. He already had everything.

Soon after Zach reached the town limits of Brookville, he was pulling off the main road and into a beautiful residential area with majestic homes surrounded by pristine landscaping and vast green lawns. Some even had tall wrought iron fences and gates. It all spoke of old money, a life that had not been part of Paige's upbringing—although she'd been to her fair share of swanky houses, which was part and parcel of working with professional athletes. When he turned into a long driveway, she could see Zach's family's home up ahead, a white stucco mansion on an impressive parcel of land. Her nerves started in again. This was where Tom Armstrong lived, the man she'd spent so much time and effort disliking and even hating. Now it felt as if her happiness was hanging in the balance and he was the man who would decide which way it would go.

"Are you going to tell me what your plan is?" she asked as Zach parked the car.

"No. I don't want you to talk me out of it." He opened his door and climbed out.

Paige followed suit. "Zach. Come on. You aren't going to do something drastic, are you?"

He clutched her hand and began leading the way to the house's main entrance, which was flanked with fluted pillars. "Do you trust me?"

"That's kind of a loaded question," she answered as they climbed the wide stone steps leading to the tall, arched front door.

"It's really not. I have always been honest with you, Paige. The one time I kept something from you, it was to protect you."

She took a long look at his handsome face and could only come up with one answer. "I trust you."

"Good. Then here goes." He reached out and knocked, then opened the door. "Mom! Tom! I'm here."

Paige stepped into the grand foyer, then Zach closed the door behind them. Soon, a woman who bore a striking resemblance to Zach approached from the center hall in front of them. She was tall and lithe with dark reddish-brown hair and the same smile. "Zachary. I see you've brought a friend."

Paige leaned into him and whispered, "You didn't tell them I was coming? I thought this wasn't an ambush."

"It's half of one," he mumbled in return, then stepped up to his mom and gave her a hug. "Mom, I want you to meet my girlfriend, Paige Moss. Paige, this is my mom. Angie."

Angie offered a hesitant smile. "Hello, Paige. It's nice to meet you."

"It's nice to meet you as well."

"Is Tom here?" Zach asked.

"He's on his way down. He suggested we go into his office," Angie answered.

"Sounds good," Zach said.

Angie led the way, with Zach and Paige bringing up the rear. When they stepped inside, Paige was immediately drawn to the dozens and dozens of photos of Tom on the walls, all of them accompanied by legendary athletes. As if Tom Armstrong wasn't intimidating enough, there were pictures of him with Michael Jordan, Phil Mickelson and Pete Sampras. Zach stayed by her side, pointing out one photo in particular. It was of a young Zach, Tom and Angie at the Super Bowl.

"How cute. How old were you?" Paige asked. She had to smile at Zach's dorky haircut and the enormous grin on his face. She remembered him saying that day had helped to cement his love of sports, and the whole thing had been orchestrated by Tom.

"Zach was seven years old," a man's voice behind her said.

Paige turned, confronted by Tom Armstrong for the first time in probably two years. It had been that long because Paige had devoted a lot of effort to avoiding him. "Tom. Hello."

"Hello, Paige. I'd say that it's a surprise to see you, but I had a feeling this was coming." To her great surprise, Tom reached for her hand.

"It's nice to see you," she said, out of habit.

"I'm sure you don't mean that," Tom said. "I'm sorry things worked out the way they did with Alexis."

Paige nodded, taking a deep breath and reminding herself that Tom was just a man. She could stand up to him. She could stay strong. "You know, I am, too.

But I spoke to her and I think we understand each other. We'll always be friends. Some bonds are too tight to break."

Tom eased behind his desk and sat in his chair. "Please. Make yourself comfortable."

Angie perched herself on one of the wingback chairs near the fireplace, leaving Zach and Paige to occupy the tufted leather sofa.

"I take it you have something you want to tell us, Zach?" Tom asked.

Zach crossed his leg and bobbed his foot nervously. "I do. I'm quitting Armstrong Sports, effective immediately. I wrote a formal letter of resignation, but that seemed a little silly given that you're my dad."

Paige turned to Zach, silently asking how that could possibly be his plan. "Are you sure you want to do that?"

"Zach. You can't be serious," Angie blurted.

"Please. Zach. This seems pointless. Paige is here in our home. I've apologized to her. If you two are serious about each other, let's just move on," Tom said, with a voice that was plaintive and serious. "I'm sorry about what happened with Alexis, but in the end, it was just business."

"You haven't apologized to her about what happened with her husband, Andre," Zach said.

Paige's pulse started thundering in her ears. "Zach. It's okay. We don't need to talk about that right now. And I think Tom is right. There's no need for you to quit your job."

"Please, Zach. Listen to what Paige and Tom are saying," Angie added.

Zach dropped his foot to the floor in a stomp. "No. Stop it." He turned to Tom, then his mom and, finally, Paige. "I need everyone to listen to me. For real. No more talking until I've said what I need to say."

Everyone in the room sat impossibly still. Paige was afraid to move, but she was also a little turned on. She'd never seen such a demonstrative side of Zach and she liked it. A lot.

"I'm leaving Armstrong Sports because of the very dynamic in this room. There are three things that mean more to me than anything in the world. They are sports, my family and Paige."

Paige swallowed hard, having to choke back the emotion of Zach's statement. How they'd gotten so close in such a short amount of time, she wasn't sure. She only knew that they had.

"And what happened over the last week has only illustrated that those things are not compatible in the current arrangement. So, I'm going to leave Armstrong so that—Tom—you can go back to simply being my dad. And, Mom, you don't have to be stressed by being stuck between your son and your husband. And most important, so that I don't have to work at a company that stole my girlfriend's biggest client." He turned to Paige. "I love you, Paige, and I know for a fact that the only way you and I work as a couple is for us to be close and for you to be close to my family. This is the only way that happens."

Paige reached for Zach's hand. "Are you sure? What will you do?"

"I talked to Ryan Wilson. I'm going to be his manager. That will keep me more than busy enough. I might take on some other clients at some point, but this is a good start. I'm actually looking forward to it."

"But who will run Armstrong Sports?" Angie asked.

Zach turned back and shrugged. "I don't know. Maybe one of the dozen people Tom passed over to give me the job? There are more than enough qualified people. Although, if you asked me, I would get Teri to run it. You really need someone with good administrative skills, and someone who isn't an agent themselves. She has the knowledge and she's more than shown her worth over the years."

Tom nodded and sat back in his chair. "Interesting idea. I do love Teri. And I trust her."

"Trust is important," Zach said. "I think we've all learned that."

Paige smiled. She could live with this. It might take her some time to come around on Tom. She wasn't ready to fixate on what to buy him for Christmas, but she was ready to be open to the idea that he might be more the person who Zach saw and less the person Paige had a history with. More than anything, Zach cared about preserving their relationship, and that was enough to convince Paige that it was worth taking a chance on.

"So? Can everyone live with that?" Zach asked.

"If it's what you want, honey," Angie said.

"If it'll make you happy," Tom added.

Zach turned to Paige. "And you?"

Paige merely squeezed his hand. "I want what you want."

"So that's a yes?" Zach punctuated his question with a wink.

"That's a yes."

"Would you two like to stay for dinner?" Angie asked, getting up from her chair.

Zach was still making serious eye contact with Paige. "Yes, Mom. We would."

"Perfect. Tom and I will go see where we're at with that." Angie cleared her throat, making it clear she wanted him to make a graceful exit with her.

As soon as Angie and Tom left the room, Paige stood and wrapped Zach in her arms. "I'm so proud of you."

He returned the embrace, holding her tight. "Just wait until later, when we finally get to be alone."

"Oh, yeah?" A girlish titter left her lips. "What did you have in mind?"

"A whole night of make-up sex, of course."

She kissed him softly, feeling more thankful than ever before. "It's the best reason to get in a fight."

Thirteen

"I can't decide what my favorite part of football is. It's either the beer or the hot dogs." Zach finished up the last sip of his pale ale as he looked down at the bright green of the field in Philadelphia. He and Paige were currently hanging out in one of the team's luxury boxes. In just a few short minutes, the second half of Ryan Wilson's debut game as a client of Zach Armstrong Management would begin. Ryan's team was already up by twenty-one points, so Zach felt great about the possible outcome.

"Not the cheerleaders? Or maybe the actual game?" Paige countered, then finished up one of the jumbo chocolate chip cookies that were part of the catering offerings. The food in the luxury boxes was always the best.

"Oh, yeah. Those things are pretty good, too." He leaned in for a kiss, taking any chance to get a taste of her. "Mmm. Chocolate."

"Your favorite," she said with a smile.

"Do you want to go down and stand on the sidelines for the second half?"

"Sure. I'd like to say hi to April, too. She's probably almost done with her halftime interviews."

"Sounds good." Zach led the way out of the box, then down the concourse to the VIP elevator. He and Paige flashed their all-access passes, and the security guard allowed them to board.

"Do you think you're going to go to all of Ryan's games this season?" Paige asked.

"Not unless you want to come with me to all of them."

"I can come to a few, but not all. Work is so busy right now. But it's sweet that you want me to come with you."

He was disappointed, but he understood. She had a lot on her plate. "Of course I want you there. We'll work it out." Zach and Paige had become even more inseparable over the last several months. They practically lived at his place. They spent every night together. They'd even gone on a vacation a month ago. It was just a quick week in Fiji, but it had been absolutely magnificent. They stayed in a private villa on stilts over the crystal blue ocean. They lounged in hammocks and drank fruity cocktails and made love at all hours of the day and night. Phones and e-mail were a distant thought. And all he'd thought at that time was that he wanted it to last forever.

Of course, real life was not a vacation, but damn if Paige didn't make it feel like that. Perhaps it was because she was just so much fun. They laughed together. They cooked and drank wine. They worked hard, and they had serious discussions about love and life, but it always came back to a very basic premise—from the word *go*, he and Paige understood each other. Even on the rare occasions when they argued, it didn't last for long. Not a lot of discussion or persuasion was required to help each of them see the other person's point of view.

Downstairs, they got off the elevator and walked through the stadium tunnels, past the locker rooms and eventually out to the field. Out in the open air, you could really hear the roar of the crowd, the music thumping, and feel the immensity of the game. Being up in the luxury box was incredibly fun, but *this* was what he came for. The excitement. The thrill. All close up.

A stiff wind blew through the stadium, sending Paige's hair across her face. She brushed it aside and Zach caught her smile, and all he could think was that Paige, close up, was also bigger than life. Being with her made him feel alive. She made him feel centered. And lucky. So damn lucky.

"Oh, look. The players are coming back out," Paige said, pointing to the tunnel where she and Zach had just walked.

Zach turned and spotted Ryan, who was jogging along with his dozens and dozens of teammates and the coaching staff. He waved at Zach, then made his way over to them.

"I see you found your way out of the luxury box," Ryan said.

Zach laughed and clapped Ryan on the shoulder. "We had to come down to the field to see you kick some serious ass. Plus, I wanted you to finally meet Paige."

Ryan was quick to zero in on her. "I feel like I should hug you. It's like I know you. This guy will *not* stop talking about you."

"I can't believe we haven't met yet," Paige said, taking the embrace Ryan promised. "But then again, you've been busy. I've been busy."

"I heard you signed the new quarterback for Dallas to your agency," Ryan said.

Paige grinned from ear to ear. She was incredibly proud of the achievement, and she had every reason. She'd worked hard to bring him on as a client. "Yes. My first professional football player. I blame Zach. He gave me the fever for the game."

That made Zach ridiculously happy. Paige was a fan of all sports, but she hadn't been particularly keen on football when they met. Once he shared with her his favorite nuances of the game, she was quick to jump in and join the fandom he'd always belonged to. It was yet another way in which they were wholly compatible.

Ryan elbowed Zach. "Zach does that. His enthusiasm is infectious. It's why I work with him."

"Smart man," Paige said. "Very smart."

"You're friends with April Chapman, aren't you?" Ryan asked.

"I am. Best friends, actually," Paige said.

Ryan nodded. It seemed like he was hiding a smile, which made Zach curious. "April's great. Really great."

"Yes. She absolutely is," Paige agreed.

Ryan glanced over at the coaching staff. "I'd better go to work or these guys will *not* be happy with me."

"Have a great second half," Paige said.

"Yes. Go kill it," Zach added.

"I'll try. See you both later." Ryan trotted off with his helmet in his hand.

"What a friendly guy," Paige said. "No wonder you love working with him so much."

"Honestly, I'm still thinking I don't want to work with anyone else. I realize the prevailing wisdom is to keep growing a business, but I'm enjoying just keeping things small. Simple."

Paige laughed and shook her head. "Those are not the words of the guy who was working it extra hard in Vegas. What happened?" She held the back of her hand to his forehead. "Are you feeling okay?"

"Yes. I feel great." As to what happened to him, Paige was the answer. It wasn't that she'd taken away his ambition. He merely felt like he was already living a dream. Why mess with that? He didn't see the point. "Here comes April."

Paige turned and rushed over to give her friend a big hug, then the two walked back to Zach with their arms around each other.

"If it isn't Ryan Wilson's personal manager," April quipped.

"Hey, April," Zach said, waving at her. "How are you?"

"Oh. I'm great."

"When did the network decide to move you to football?" Zach asked. "I guess I think of you as doing more baseball and basketball. Hockey, too, I guess."

"It was just a switch for this season. They're trying me out," April said.

"And? You're liking it?" Paige asked.

"I love it. Absolutely freaking love it. Especially tonight." April looked at Paige and the two of them seemed to have an entire conversation with nothing more than penetrating glances.

"Is there something I don't know?" Paige's eyes were wide with curiosity.

April stepped closer to both Paige and Zach. "Ryan and I are dating," she said out of the corner of her mouth.

Paige squealed, then clapped eagerly. "Are you serious?"

"Oh, yeah. He's amazing."

Paige peered over her shoulder at Ryan, back at April, then turned to Zach. "Maybe the four of us can go to dinner some time. Wouldn't that be so much fun?"

Zach took Paige's hand. "Super fun." He loved that he and Paige continued to fold each other into their lives. That they were making each other a fixture. He hoped that was a sign of good things to come.

"Yes. Let's do that. I'll talk to Ryan about it. It'll probably take some doing to coordinate everyone's schedules, but I'm sure we can make it work." April pulled her phone out of her pocket. "Hey, guys, I need to go meet with my producer. But it was really great to see you both." April stole one more hug from Paige, then began to walk away. After several paces, she turned back. "By the way, you two are ridiculously cute together."

Paige snickered. "I was not expecting that little bit of news. Did you know?" she asked Zach.

He shook his head. "Totally in the dark."

"Well, it's good to know that it's not just me. I hate it when I feel like I'm out of the loop."

A whistle sounded. "Time for kick-off," Zach said.

He and Paige found a reasonably quiet spot to watch the game—away from the hubbub of the players and coaches, and definitely far enough away from the sidelines so that they didn't stand too much risk of getting hurt if an errant ball or tight end went flying in their direction. Zach loved watching Ryan's first drive, especially since he marched his team right down the field and had an amazing throw that rocketed right into the waiting arms of his star receiver. The crowd cheered loudly at the touchdown, but the best part was Paige flattening herself against Zach and yelling her robust approval.

During the television time-out that followed, there was a kiss cam up on the big screens in the stadium. Zach and Paige watched as each couple embarrassingly bent to the pleas of the crowd and kissed. The fourth couple did something different though—the guy went down on one knee and popped an engagement ring out of his pocket. *Will you marry me, Kendra?* flashed across the screen. Kendra clasped her hands over her mouth, then nodded a 'yes' and rewarded her new fiancé with a kiss of his own.

"Aw. That's sweet," Zach said.

"Eh. I don't know. I always feel a little weird when someone proposes like that. What if she said no?"

"She can't say no. A zillion people are watching. It's on national television."

"My sentiments exactly."

Zach looked all around the stadium. "Ah. Okay. I get what you're saying. That really isn't the best way to do it, is it? It should be a little more low-key. And not public."

"I just think it should be romantic. And personal. It should be between two people who love each other. It shouldn't be a performance."

"But what if a guy decided to pop the question somewhere public like a stadium? What if a guy brought his girlfriend to the game and they were just having a nice time and then he asked. Would that be okay?"

Paige thought about it for a minute, then nodded. "If it wasn't some big spectacle, sure."

"Maybe he would take her hand." Zach reached out and wrapped up Paige's fingers.

Paige peered over at him with a questioning look. "Sure."

Zach stepped closer, until his toes were even

with hers. He looked into her eyes, feeling so overwhelmed by the moment. "And he could say something like, 'Paige, you are the most incredible woman I have ever met. I know we haven't been together for very long, but I want to spend every day of the rest of my life with you. You are my sun and moon. You're my reason for getting up in the morning and the reason I have a smile on my face at the end of the day.' Right? A guy could say that. But would it work?"

"What are you up to, Zach Armstrong?"

"And then he could say, 'Paige Moss, will you marry me?'"

Her eyes went impossibly large. "You mean as a hypothetical."

He shook his head. "I do not."

Paige looked around, seeming bewildered. "Did you plan this?"

"Nope."

"It's just totally spur of the moment?"

"Yes. A leap of faith. A well-educated guess. A calculated gamble."

She pressed her lips together and nodded slowly. "Interesting."

"What?"

She shrugged. "Nothing. I'm just considering your proposal."

"Once an agent, always an agent. Except in my case. Not an agent anymore."

"But what if you were? What if I told you that it's silly for you to be working on your own and you should come work with me? It doesn't make any sense that you're not agenting. You're so good at it. You're excellent at making your case."

"Apparently not, since I just asked my girlfriend to marry me and it has since morphed into a discussion of my career path."

She laughed and leaned into him, peering up at him with her mesmerizing blue eyes. "Yes, Zach, I will marry you. You make me happier than I ever imagined I could be. I'd be a fool to say anything but yes."

They fell into a dizzying kiss that drowned out everything, even the sound of the crowd around them. When they came up for air, Paige felt the need to say one more thing. "I still want you to come work with me. Just think of how much fun it would be."

He smiled and pulled her close, kissing the top of her head. "If it'll make you happy, I'm in." No, he hadn't planned any of that, especially not Paige's counterproposal, but in Zach's estimation, it had all gone perfectly. Exactly as it was meant to be. And now, Zach didn't simply feel like he was the luckiest guy in the world. He knew it.

* * * * *

USA TODAY bestselling author **Janice Maynard** loved books and writing even as a child. Now creating sexy, character-driven romances is her day job! She has written more than seventy-five books and novellas, which have sold, collectively, almost three million copies. Her books have been translated into twenty languages. Janice lives in the shadow of the Great Smoky Mountains with her husband, Charles. They love hiking, traveling and spending time with family.

You can connect with Janice at janicemaynard.com, on Twitter @janicemaynard, on Facebook at janicemaynardauthor and at janicesmaynard, and on Instagram @therealjanicemaynard.

Books by Janice Maynard

Harlequin Desire

Return of the Rancher
The Comeback Heir
One Wild Wedding Weekend

Texas Cattleman's Club

An Heir of His Own
Staking a Claim

The Men of Stone River

After Hours Seduction
Upstairs Downstairs Temptation
Secrets of a Playboy

Visit the Author Profile page
at Harlequin.com for more titles.

You can also find Janice Maynard on Facebook,
along with other Harlequin Desire authors,
at Facebook.com/HarlequinDesireAuthors!

Dear Reader,

My husband and I have attended dozens of weddings over the years. Those events have run the gamut between jeans and boots in an outdoor setting with beer and ribs afterward to high fashion brides with fancy flowers and dazzling receptions.

There have been low-key practices and high-drama rehearsals. But in every instance, they included two people hoping to build new lives with a forever kind of love.

You and I both know the odds are not great. But as romance readers, we choose to focus on the percentages that come out on top. Brides and grooms who manage to go the distance and keep love alive.

I hope you enjoy this story of my hero and heroine, who are both marriage averse but find themselves caught up in a powerful, inescapable attraction. It was a fun book to write. Sometimes the hardest lessons in life yield moments of growth and great rewards.

Grab a quiet corner, your favorite beverage and settle in for *One Wild Wedding Weekend*!

Fondly,

Janice Maynard

ONE WILD WEDDING WEEKEND

Janice Maynard

To all my fellow Harlequin authors:

One of the joys of my writing career
is getting to know so many of you personally.
I love your creativity, your passion for romance
and the way you craft stories that
give readers hope and entertainment.
May there be many more books to come!

One

"Promise you won't ruin my wedding weekend fighting with Tristan."

Daley Martin glanced at her baby sister and raised an eyebrow, though her stomach curled at the mention of his name. "Don't be silly. I'm a mature adult. I'll be on my best behavior."

Tabby scowled. "I've seen you and Tristan together. It's like putting two pit bulls in a room with raw steak."

"Ew, gross." Daley touched her pinkie finger, testing to see if the polish was dry. She and the prospective bride had just finished getting expensive manicures and were now sipping complimentary mimosas before moving to the next item on the itinerary.

Tabby didn't look convinced. She sighed. "Quit

touching it," she said. "I don't know why you can't get gel like everybody else."

"It's simple. Taking gel off in three weeks is impossible to do at home. I'd rather create my own destiny."

"It's nail polish, not a manifesto," Tabby said dryly. "But let's get back to the point at hand. Tristan is going to be *family*. I need you to behave."

"Not my family," Daley muttered. Just because *her* sister was marrying Tristan's younger brother didn't mean there was going to be any fraternization on Daley's part. Not at all.

"He's not your enemy," Tabby insisted.

"How would you know?" Daley snapped. "The man is determined to poach all my clients."

Tabby opened her mouth, closed it and wrinkled her nose. "I don't think you're being entirely rational about this subject. I love you dearly, Daley. Your little ad agency is cute and scrappy and outside-the-box, but some clients want safe and traditional. If a few prospects defected to Lieberman and Dunn, it's not Tristan's fault."

Though Daley's six-years-younger sister was trying to be diplomatic, her assessment stung. Surely she hadn't meant to be patronizing when she said *little* ad agency. But it was true. Daley employed two copywriters, a web guru, one receptionist and a part-time accountant. She had come a long way in three years. Business was good.

But she wasn't in Tristan's league, and she knew it. Deep down, that was what put the knot in her stomach. Tristan was the CEO of a decades-old Atlanta ad agency. Mr. Lieberman—of Lieberman and Dunn—had died a few years back. Rumor had it that Harold Dunn would be selling the firm to his protégé, Tristan, any day now.

Tristan Hamilton: Wealthy. Handsome. Ridiculously sexy. With his tousled raven-black hair and his sparkling blue eyes, the world was his to command.

Daley despised him. If she was lying to herself, it was only because she didn't understand why the mere sight of his tall überfit body made her quiver. He was a man with all the usual parts—arms, legs, a chiseled jaw. But the way the Almighty had seen fit to assemble those various appendages and features had created a living, breathing example of stunning male perfection.

Until the stupid man opened his mouth. When Daley stormed into his office six weeks ago to air her grievances, Tristan had given her the same speech Tabby had. All about how some clients didn't want Instagram and TikTok but were instead looking for a more conventional approach to building name recognition.

Daley wasn't convinced. She'd had a couple of very promising meetings with a brand-new boutique hotel and an up-and-coming jewelry designer, but both clients had ended up with Lieberman and Dunn. That had to be Tristan's interference.

Tabby interrupted Daley's indignant *stewing*. "Time to go," she said. "The hair appointments are the last thing on the list. After that, we'll have an hour to rest, and then we'll head to the hotel."

When Daley arrived at the Westmont Country Inn, she paused to admire her sister's organizational skills. The nuptial events had been choreographed down to the tiniest detail. Nothing left to chance. Tabby and John had rented out this charming small hotel in an exclusive Atlanta suburb and had made the decision to have the bridesmaids and grooms-men and immediate family stay here for the duration.

Hence, no transportation woes. No scheduling glitches. Plenty of time for fun and relaxation.

Daley didn't object to the plan in theory. It was nice to know she wouldn't have to fight traffic during a semi-stressful weekend. She wanted everything to go perfectly for Tabby's wedding. This plan removed a lot of the unknowns.

But it also meant Daley couldn't escape.

She was stuck here until Sunday morning…like it or not.

Clearly, several people had arrived at once. No bellmen in sight. Daley hefted her suitcase and cos-metic bag out of the trunk and draped the cream silk garment bag over her arm. She shouldered her purse, scanned the area for any sight of her nemesis and walked up the front steps.

Inside the lovely inn, a uniformed employee quickly took her bags and checked her in. The main portion of the building was three stories high. A single-story wing off the back housed premium rooms. Tabby had insisted on giving Daley one of the *fancy* accommodations as a thank-you for all Daley had done to help with the wedding.

It wasn't that much. Daley had wanted Tabby to have the day of her dreams. So she had accompanied her sister on endless site visits. There had been dress shops and caterer tastings. John was a thoroughly involved groom-to-be, but his high-powered finance job involved long hours and little flexibility.

Now all the hard work of the past six months was going to be worth it.

Daley accepted her room key with a smile and turned around only to walk smack-dab into a wall of a man. A very familiar man.

Her skin heated with uncomfortable prickles. "Oh, it's you," she said, stepping back quickly. "Hello, Tristan."

He cocked his head and smiled. "What? No claws?"

She ground her teeth. "I'm supposed to be nice to you this weekend."

Blue eyes danced with humor. "*Nice.* Now there's a word with so many layers."

"No layers," she said quickly, her gaze landing anywhere but on his compelling face. "No layers. Excuse me, please. I need to go to my room."

"Daley."

The way he said her name made her mouth go dry. Only two syllables, but his rumbly voice imbued her name with beauty. "What do you want, Tristan?"

Now his smile was rueful…cajoling. "The hotel

bar is right over there. Let's kick back before the insanity begins. Bury the hatchet maybe. John and Tabby will expect us to be on amicable terms."

She scowled. "Your brother must be more of an optimist than I realize if he's going for amicable. Tabby's only requirement was no bloodshed."

Tristan threw back his head and laughed. "C'mon," he said. "We're going to be family. Let me buy you a drink, Daley."

She was trapped, and she knew it. A bellman had already spirited her belongings away. The rehearsal dinner was still a couple of hours in the future. She swallowed her misgivings and manufactured a smile. "Sure," she said. "That would be nice."

It wasn't far to the bar. A dozen steps at the most. But Tristan's hand rested briefly at the small of her back. She fancied she could feel the heat of his fingers through the fabric of her casual cotton sundress.

Once they were seated in a high-backed wooden booth that gave a nod to English pubs, she put her purse on the bench seat and crossed her arms. "Let's get one thing straight," she said. "You and I are *not* going to be family. John and I? Yes. You and Tabby? Yes. But not you and me."

He sat back and studied her. "You have something against family?"

"Of course not. But you and I are…" She trailed off, trying desperately not to break a recent promise to her sister.

"Are what?"

Before she was forced to answer, the server appeared. "I'll have a glass of your house white," Daley said.

Tristan smiled at the young woman, making her blush. "Just a Diet Coke for me," he said. "And maybe an order of wings and celery." He looked at Daley sheepishly. "Didn't have time for lunch."

When the waitress walked away, Daley frowned. "A Diet Coke? Seriously?"

He shrugged. "I'm taking the last of an antibiotic. I may have a drink later this evening, but the doc suggested moderation for the moment."

"You're ill?" The brief flare of panic made no sense at all.

"I had a bout of Lyme disease. Fortunately, we caught it early. I'm fine." He loosened his tie and pulled it free of his collar. "Had to put my suitcase in the car this morning so I could come straight here after work. But let's get back to you, Daley. I think you were saying you and I are...?"

"Strangers," she said firmly. "Only tangentially related by marriage. There's no connection at all."

"Liar." He grinned when he said it, taking the sting out of the word. But as he wrapped his fingers around her hand, his gaze heated. "We've had a connection since day one. Surely you can't deny that."

She forced herself not to pull away, nor to reveal how very shaken she was by having him touch her, even in so ordinary a context. "We don't get along," she said. "We're oil and water. I wouldn't define that as a *connection*."

His thumb settled on her pulse at the back of her wrist. "Maybe you and I see things differently then."

"Maybe." When he released her, she told herself she wasn't disappointed.

The drinks arrived, and Daley downed half of hers recklessly. Chicken wings were far too messy to eat in front of a man like Tristan, so she grabbed a celery stick, dunked it in ranch dressing and hoped the small snack would offset the alcohol.

He finished two wings and wiped his fingers. Long, masculine fingers that probably knew exactly how to pleasure a woman. *Oh, gosh, this was a bad idea.*

"Daley…" For the first time, he seemed uncertain.

"What?"

He shrugged. "I haven't poached a single one of your clients, I swear. I would never do that to you. But sometimes a person or a business is looking for conventional advertising. What you do is impressive, but maybe your flair is not for everybody."

"Tabby said something similar," Daley muttered. "You two must be in cahoots."

His lips twitched. "Cahoots?"

"You're a smart man. I'm sure you know the word."

He shook his head slowly. "I'm not in cahoots with your sister, though I admire her greatly. She's made my oh-so-serious brother very happy."

Daley frowned. "You admire Tabby?"

"Well, of course I do. She's amazing. Wouldn't you agree?"

"Yes. But I assumed you thought they were too young to be getting married."

"I don't think you know me well enough to make those kinds of assumptions."

His reply had a bite to it.

"Sorry. You're right," she muttered.

"Maybe you're the one who thinks twenty-six is too young?" He cocked his head in that way he had, giving her a whimsical smile.

"I'm six years older, Tristan. And I swear I don't ever remember being as innocently happy as those two. I'm thrilled for them. Don't get me wrong."

"But?"

She shrugged. "But it's astonishing that any man or woman finds a perfect match. Much less one for the long haul."

"I never pegged you for a cynic." His gaze was sober now. Disappointed perhaps?

"I'm not a cynic," she said. She finished her wine and wondered how soon she could exit this booth without causing a scene. Tristan's intent regard made her want to squirm. His gaze saw too much.

"Why do I get the feeling that twenty-six-year-old Daley had a bad experience?" he asked.

When she managed to meet his eyes, there was no humor in them at all, only a gentle compassion that made her feel like weeping for no good reason.

Her throat was tight. "I was twenty-four and clueless about men. It was a long time ago. I learned my lesson."

"And what lesson was that?" A furrow appeared between his brows.

"I should go," she said. "Thank you for the drink."

When she stood, Tristan did as well. "I didn't mean to pry, Daley. I'm sorry if I upset you." His expression was troubled.

She managed a snarky grin. "This was nothing. You've done far worse. I'll see you at the rehearsal. And I swear I'll be *amicable*."

Tristan let Daley Martin walk out of the bar alone, though it went against his every instinct. For once, she had lowered her habitual defenses and talked to him as more than an adversary.

To be honest, he'd been a little uneasy when he heard John was marrying Tabby. Not because of any doubts about the newly engaged couple but because Tristan realized that it was going to be impossible to avoid Daley in the future. Aside from the wedding festivities, there would be baby christenings and holiday meals and eventually school programs and sporting events.

Tristan planned to be fully involved as an uncle.

How could he do that and not betray the truth? He was wildly attracted to Daley Martin. He was pretty sure she felt it, too. But was she naive enough to think the current between them was antagonism? Maybe so.

It was just as well. Getting involved with his sister-in-law's sister would bring nothing but trouble. Which meant he had to get through this weekend without doing something stupid. He hadn't checked in yet. Seeing Daley had diverted his attention.

With an inward sigh, he headed for the lobby. He might as well find his room and deal with a few emails. The rehearsal and the dinner would take all his self-control. He was the best man and Daley the maid of honor.

They would be thrown together all evening, not to mention tomorrow.

Time to shore up his resolve. Maybe watch a Braves game.

He'd like to think he was a smart guy. But when it came to Daley Martin, he was feeling a lot like a hormonal teenage boy.

Daley considered faking a stomach virus to get out of the rehearsal and dinner. Somebody else could stand in for her. It wasn't rocket science.

Imagining Tabby's disappointment stopped that idea in its tracks.

Daley was the maid of honor. The role was an almost sacred female imperative. And Tabby was her *sister*. Daley still remembered the day her parents brought the new baby home from the hospital. Daley had fallen in love on the spot.

For a decade, she had been her mother's right hand. Nothing had been too much of an imposition or a burden. Daley loved her sister, and she loved caring for the little girl who had become her shadow. Occasionally, they might squabble, but for the most part, they were as close as two siblings could be.

As much as it pained her to admit it, she had no choice but to suck it up and put on a smiling face, Tristan or no Tristan.

After all, how bad could it be? She would have to practice taking his arm and walking down the aisle. Once they were up front, the bride and groom would separate them. Then, when the ceremony was over, Daley would have to touch the best man's arm *again*.

She could do this.

Besides, there would be at least two dozen other people present.

Daley would smile and be nice if it killed her.

On the back lawn of the hotel, two long white tents stood ready for the festivities. Tabby and John had chosen to include only family and close friends this weekend. Then—when they returned from their Polynesian honeymoon—there would be a larger, fancier reception.

Daley couldn't fault their choice. Weddings were stressful under the best circumstances. Designing this one to be intentionally small would make the whole weekend intimate and meaningful.

Unfortunately, the setup also meant that the maid of honor and best man might spend more time together than necessary.

Didn't matter, Daley told herself stoutly. She could handle Tristan Hamilton. She *would* handle him.

After a quick shower, she studied the dresses she had brought with her for the rehearsal and dinner. Tabby had seen and approved both. One was a safe choice—a teal sheath, sleeveless, with same-color embroidery at the neckline and hem. The color suited her blond hair and fair coloring.

When she stared at herself in the mirror, wearing the dress, she made a face. It was nice enough. But no wow factor. For some reason, she was feeling the need to prove something to Tristan Hamilton. Like maybe the fact that she didn't need him or his prestigious ad agency.

When she slipped into the second outfit, her stomach flipped uncomfortably. The low neckline showed off her ample breasts more than Daley remembered. Tabby was slight and dark-headed and took after their dad. Daley had inherited her mother's more voluptuous figure.

This blush-pink dress accentuated every curve. The spaghetti straps bared her shoulders—which would be a plus in the late-May heat. The waist was fitted and then flared into a poufy skirt that ended a good six inches above her knees.

It was a dress that required confidence.

Daley had embarrassed herself that day she stormed into Tristan's office. She would like to erase his memory of her semi-rant. She wanted him to take her seriously as a businesswoman. If he was sincere about not poaching, then maybe the flip side could be him sending clients her way who *did* want a more twenty-first-century approach to branding.

When someone in the hallway knocked, Daley peeked out through the fish-eye and saw her sister. She yanked open the door. "What's wrong?" she asked, alarmed.

Tabby's smile was amused. "Can't a bride come see her maid of honor?"

Daley detected a hint of strain. "You okay?"

"Yes." Tabby paced. "Is it normal that I'm not freaking out?"

"Seriously?" Daley chuckled. "You're freaking out because you're *not* freaking out?"

Tabby perched on the side of the bed. "I know. I'm an idiot. It's just that everything is going perfectly. I'm happy and excited to be marrying John. I guess it all seems too good to be true."

"You deserve every bit of happiness, hon. And it's *all* good. Your wedding party is here. Your family is here. Nothing is going to happen."

"Unless you and Tristan go ballistic with each other."

"I promise that's not gonna happen. If you must know, the two of us shared a drink in the hotel bar earlier and agreed to play nice."

Tabby's eyes widened. "I would love to have seen that."

"It was nothing really. He asked. I said yes. We were civil."

"Why don't you like him, Daley? You don't honestly believe he's waging a campaign to ruin you. Do you?"

Did Daley really believe that? Maybe not anymore. And maybe her antipathy was a defense against the way he made her feel. All woozy inside. Like something could happen. Something *sexual*. "I may have overreacted in the past," she said. "He's not the villain in this story. But he rubs me the wrong way. He's arrogant and way too confident."

"Is there really such a thing as *too* confident?" Tabby asked. "Tristan can't help the fact that he's rich and gorgeous and super talented at what he does. I like him. He loves John dearly, so Tristan and I have that in common. He's been nothing but lovely and welcoming to me," Tabby said.

Daley's throat was tight. "I'm glad. Their family is lucky to have you."

"Maybe Tristan will find someone, too."

"I'm surprised he hasn't already," Daley said. "Atlanta may be a big city, but the pool of eligible men isn't infinite."

"John says Tristan is a workaholic and too picky when it comes to women."

"Workaholic I'd believe, but isn't John the pot calling the kettle black?"

Tabby beamed. "My John has seen the error of his ways. He may have been just like his big brother, but now he has other priorities."

"Such as you?" Daley grinned.

"I'm too modest to boast," Tabby said, "but yeah. He's even talking about babies already. And he knows I won't put up with an absentee dad. Our father lived his life that way, but I want more from my husband. A child needs *two* fully engaged parents."

Daley envied her sister's almost palpable certainty about her decisions. Tabby taught second grade. School was out for the summer, so she would have a couple of months to settle into married life. Daley was happy for her.

But she couldn't escape a guilt-ridden tinge of envy.

Tabby—completely unaware of her sister's conflicted emotions—was wearing a couture *little black dress* that made her look sophisticated and beautiful. She would make a stunning bride tomorrow.

She stood and smoothed her skirt. "I should go and let you finish getting ready. I'm glad you decided on the pink," she said.

"Oh, well, I was still making up my mind," Daley mumbled.

"Nope. Consider this an edict from the bride. The teal is okay, but you look luminous in pink."

"Thanks, sis. If you're sure it's not too much."

Tabby held out her hands. "It's my rehearsal dinner. I want everyone to see how gorgeous you are. Besides, a couple of John's groomsmen are single. Who knows what might happen?"

With a naughty grin, Tabby slipped out the door and headed back to her room.

Daley took another look in the mirror. If this was the dress Tabby wanted, that ended it.

Hair and makeup took another half hour. By the time she was completely ready, it was five fifteen. Everyone had been asked to show up in the tent at five thirty.

It was dumb to feel nervous. This was a fun occasion.

Maybe she *would* flirt with one of the groomsmen.
But not Tristan.
Never Tristan...

Two

Tristan ran a finger inside his collar and wondered if Tabby would mind him removing his tie. He was no stranger to suiting up at work. His friend and mentor Harold Dunn was old-school when it came to dress codes. But tonight, they were all outside, and though the temperature was only in the low eighties, the humidity was a bitch.

When Tristan saw John, he sighed inwardly. His brother was the definition of *buttoned-up*, even if Tabby *had* taught him to cut loose now and again. A quick glance around the tent verified that all the groomsmen were dressed to the nines.

Tristan was stuck with the tie.

The wedding director hadn't convened everyone

yet. John swore the woman wasn't a dragon. She was efficient but could roll with the punches.

So far, everyone was chatting and laughing and enjoying the flutes of champagne provided by the inn. Tristan's parents were seated. He saw that many of the group paused to pay their respects. His mom and dad had gotten a late start on parenthood and were in their midseventies, while Tabby and Daley's folks were closer to sixty.

Tristan spotted Daley right off. She lit up the room, or at least the tent. Her long blond hair was caught up in a wavy ponytail that danced when she moved. Artful tendrils framed her laughing face. So far, Tristan was pretty sure she had chatted with everyone *but* him.

The bride was beautiful, as she should be, but in Tristan's estimation, Tabby didn't hold a candle to her older sister. Daley was vibrant and sexy. Her gorgeous body was showcased in a kick-ass dress.

When Tristan noticed two of John's fraternity brothers chatting up the maid of honor, he ground his teeth. He wasn't going to allow Daley Martin to ignore him. No way. They were a couple tonight, whether she liked it or not.

He didn't pause to examine why her reticence bugged him so much. Nor did he expect every woman he met to like him.

But he understood sexual attraction, and he understood women. Usually...

When he appeared at Daley's elbow, she seemed startled, as if she really had been shutting him out of her mind entirely. "How's my date tonight?" he asked, smiling blandly at the other two men.

Daley frowned. "I'm not your date," she said. The words were heated.

He whispered under his breath, "Amicable..."

Her face turned pink. Her brown eyes glowed with heat. She turned her attention back to the two hapless groomsmen. "I think we're about to start," she said. Linking an arm with each guy, she steered them toward the front of the tent, where a small podium had been decorated with lilies and greenery. "Tell me how you both met John."

Tristan let them go, but he didn't like it.

Before he could formulate a plan, the wedding coordinator put two fingers to her lips and whistled loudly. Laughter erupted in the tent. The six bridesmaids and their male counterparts hurried to take their places. Tristan and Daley made seven each.

The coordinator smiled. "Tabby and John are so glad you're all here today. We're going to make this rehearsal short and sweet. I'm hungry, and I know most of you are, too. The way this works is simple. First, we're going to get everyone comfortable with your spots. We'll practice walking out. Then back in. Then out one more time, and we'll be done."

The woman knew her stuff. Tristan was glad about that. She managed to corral her adult charges like a kindergarten teacher rounding up after recess. The ladies and Daley took their marks on the left. The men on the right. Tabby and John and the female minister stood in the middle.

The coordinator turned the ceremony over to the pastor, who briefly went over the various parts of the service. When that was done, the director cued the string quartet. "Now the recessional," she said. "Bride and groom. Then the rest of you. Last in, first out."

Tabby and John departed looking smugly happy. When it was Tristan's turn, he offered his arm to Daley, grinning. His partner looked as if she would like to stick a knife between his shoulder blades. Every bit of her temper only made him want her more. That much passion—when focused in the bedroom—would be explosive.

Unfortunately, there was no opportunity for chit-chat. As soon as the recessional was over, the director had them lining up again. This time, various groomsmen practiced seating the parents...and the grandparents who were able to attend.

Then the processional music began. Tristan had been to many weddings where the women walked down the aisle alone. But per Tabby's wishes, the couples entered together. When it was Tristan and Daley's turn, he squeezed her arm. "I can't imagine doing this in front of hundreds of people. I'm glad our siblings wanted a small wedding."

This time, Daley nodded. "Me too."

They made it to the front without incident. Then, from the side, the minister and John entered and took their spots. The music changed, and Tabby started down the aisle holding her father's arm. She had her eyes fixed on John the entire way. When Tristan glanced at his brother's face, the naked emotion he saw there made his own throat tight.

What would it be like to have that bond with another person? Tristan had never come close. He didn't think he ever would. He was probably too driven and too selfish to make room in his life for a family.

Daley was immune to his self-reflection. She watched her sister, beaming.

Mr. Martin handed off his daughter and sat down beside his wife.

The minister quickly repeated the order of the service. Tristan and Daley pretended to hand over the rings at the appropriate moment.

Then, it was time for one more practice…going out…again.

At the back of the tent, relief permeated the group.

One of the groomsmen whooped loudly, making everyone laugh.

Now, the hotel caterer took over. "The food is in the adjoining tent," she said, "Help yourself. There's plenty. Tabby and John have asked that you sit wherever you like, no place cards."

Tristan kept an eye on Daley as the group moved en masse to the adjoining tent. The buffet was sumptuous and plentiful. A beef carving station. Shrimp and grits. Garden-fresh vegetables of all kinds. The fancy fruit pyramid was a work of art. Homemade rolls.

And then the desserts. *Wow.*

Tristan's stomach growled as he took his place in line. Daley was four people in front of him, flanked by two bridesmaids.

The wedding coordinator had a spouse, as did the minister. Four musicians. Twelve bridesmaids and groomsmen. Tristan and Daley. The parents. The bride and groom. Three grandparents total. And Harold with them. The caterers had set up five tables of eight. That left a handful of empty seats.

As Tristan watched, the group settled in noisy, appreciative groups. Tabby and John ended up with the groomsmen. When Daley put herself firmly amidst a gaggle of bridesmaids, Tristan snagged one of the last empty seats. "Mind if I join you ladies?" he asked.

A tall redhead shot him a teasing smile. "Knock yourself out."

Daley said nothing, but he saw her face flush.

Not all the women had met each other. That left plenty of room for getting-to-know-you conversation. Two teachers. A cousin. Three college friends.

When the others were occupied, Tristan leaned closer to whisper to Daley, "Is Tabby staying with you tonight?"

She snorted. "Are you kidding? Tabby and John are not ones to follow either superstition or convention. They have their own room. I don't think they can bear to be apart."

Tristan frowned, hearing something odd in her voice. "You don't approve?"

She shrugged. "It's not up to me."

The woman on Tristan's right said something to him, putting an end to the quiet aside with Daley.

The older crew slipped out around eight, as did everyone else not in the immediate wedding party.

When it was only Tabby and John and their fourteen best friends and family left, John tapped his glass with a fork. "Settle down you wild people. Tabby and I have gifts."

Six women received pearl earrings. Six men opened engraved silver pocketknives. Only Daley and Tristan were empty-handed.

John came to Tristan carrying a larger package. "For my big brother," he said, putting a hand on Tristan's shoulder. "Not only my best man but the best man I know."

The words caught Tristan off guard. "Right back atcha," he said gruffly. When he opened the bag and removed the tissue, Daley peered over his shoulder.

"What is it?" she asked.

"Holy hell, John," he said. "This is too much." It was a small bronze sculpture of a horse he had seen in an expensive gallery in Florence, Italy, a year ago when he and John had taken a brother trip. John and Tabby had only been dating a few weeks back then, but he had called his new girlfriend every night.

John grinned. "You're a hard man to buy for. I thought about Christmas, but by that time, I already knew Tabby was the one, so I saved it for now."

"I love it. Thank you, John."

Then it was Daley's turn. Tabby stood behind her sister and wrapped her arms around Daley's neck. "You've looked out for me my whole life. No one ever had a more wonderful big sister."

Daley's bag was much smaller. She pulled out a

black box, opened it and smiled. "I love it, Tabby. Thank you so much."

The gift was a yellow-gold cursive D accented with tiny diamonds that caught the light. Tristan stood as well. "Here, let me," he said.

Tabby plucked the necklace from the box and handed it to him. "Thank you, Best Man," she said, giggling. Tristan realized that shy Tabby had loosened up as the evening progressed.

Daley didn't move a muscle. She sat in silence as Tristan brushed aside her ponytail and fastened the clasp. It wasn't easy. His fingers were big, and the mechanism was dainty.

It didn't help that he inhaled Daley's light perfume with every breath. Already, he regretted his impulsive offer. He had to get a handle on these inconvenient *feelings*. John would neuter him if he thought Tristan was causing problems with Daley.

After Daley's gift, the formalities were over.

There were a couple bottles of wine left. But after those were gone, John and Tabby headed back to the hotel, and the others followed. Daley surrounded herself with enough people to keep Tristan firmly at a distance. It was just as well.

He was in lust with the maid of honor, but that was as far as it could go.

Daley found herself arm-in-arm with her sister as they walked down the hall. John trailed behind them, yawning.

Tabby kissed his cheek. "I'll be there in a minute. I just want to say good-night to my sister."

John grinned a surprisingly wicked smile. "I'll be waiting."

Daley and John laughed when Tabby turned red as a tomato.

Daley unlocked her door. "You didn't have to get me such a fancy room, but I love it. Did you have a good evening? Was everything the way you wanted it?"

Tabby yawned and stretched her arms over her head. "It was perfect. I can't wait until tomorrow. The weather is supposed to be amazing. I'm glad about that."

The guest list was very selective for the 5:30 p.m. ceremony and sit-down dinner. About fifty of John and Tabby's friends and extended family would be arriving.

The wedding party would have brunch in the hotel dining room, and then everyone would have a few hours of downtime before getting ready for the big event.

Daley suddenly remembered the question she had wanted to ask. "Who was that one guy who wasn't a grandparent but was sitting with them?"

Tabby's eyes widened. "I thought you knew. That was Harold Dunn."

"Of the advertising firm?" Daley was shocked. "Why was he here?"

"Harold and his wife were godparents to Tristan and John. She died a couple of years ago. He's been lost without her. That's why John wanted to include him tonight as well as tomorrow. Harold is like family to the Hamiltons. In fact, they called him Uncle Harold when they were little."

"I had no idea."

"Harold wanted both boys to go into business with him. Tristan was premed, super smart, but Harold finally persuaded him, and Tristan's been great at advertising. John was a numbers guy from the beginning. Harold understood when he went into finance."

Daley struggled with this new information, trying to fit it into her image of the Tristan she had created in her head.

Tabby touched her arm. "Tristan can be trusted, Daley. I swear. He's not your enemy. I know you've had trouble letting men get close. Please give him a chance."

"Give him a chance?" Daley gaped at her. "What does *that* mean? I promised not to fight with him this weekend. That's all."

"But you admit you have chemistry..."

"Where is this coming from? I barely know the man."

That wasn't exactly true. The day she had stormed into his office was only one of many encounters in the last six months. She'd met Tristan at a family dinner when John and Tabby were officially engaged. There had been a Christmas party and a spring trip to the mountains. Daley had brought a date on that one. She'd dumped the guy the following week.

Tristan was like a bad encounter with chiggers. He got under her skin and couldn't be ignored.

Tabby held up her hands. "Fine. I'll hush up about it. You can stick your head in the sand if you want to. For now, I'll say good-night and sweet dreams."

Daley hugged her sister. "I love you, Tab."

"I love you, too."

"Go to your man. He won't be happy if he sees you crying."

Tabby smiled through her tears. "It's an emotional weekend. I think I'm entitled."

When the door closed, Daley sank into a brocade-covered armchair and kicked off her shoes. She was tired to the bone but also wired. Tonight had been fun. It was lovely to see Tabby so happy.

If there was a part of Daley that felt a little weepy, too, it was only because life was changing. Time moved on.

She finally summoned the energy to undress and take a shower. As she removed the necklace and laid it carefully on the dresser, she told herself she was imagining the lingering warmth from Tristan's fingers on the back of her neck.

Avoiding him tonight had been impossible. His smile, whether aimed at someone else or at her, had the power to make her insides get wobbly. She hated that. It made her feel weak and stupid and immature, but she was none of those things.

She had worked hard and pushed harder until she created the life she wanted. Tabby's marital bliss was convincing, but Daley had plans to go it alone. Men only complicated things. Being a mature woman was hard enough without that.

As she dried off, she realized how thirsty she was. At home, she made it a point to drink water all day. This evening, there had been wine, but now she needed something more basic…and cold. Had there been an ice machine in this hallway? She couldn't remember.

The hotel provided lush, soft robes. But she didn't fancy wandering in a strange place where she might run into anybody.

Grimacing, she slipped into the frothy dress again. But only that. No bra. No undies. No shoes. She picked up the ice bucket, tucked the hotel key card deep in her cleavage, opened the door and peeked out. The hallway was dimly lit with safety lights every twelve feet or so. No sign of life anywhere.

Her room was near the end of the corridor. She checked that way first. Nothing. As she turned and passed her room once again, a familiar figure appeared around the corner. It was Tristan carrying an ice bucket.

One masculine eyebrow lifted in surprise. "I thought you'd be long asleep by now."

"I'm thirsty," she said. "Where did you find ice?"

"Unfortunately, all the way back in the main hotel. I don't need all of mine. You want me to pour some in yours?"

It was a very ordinary question. The way he looked at her was anything but…

When she didn't answer immediately, he cleared his throat and rubbed a hand across the back of his neck. He had ditched his jacket and tie. His shirt-sleeves were rolled to his elbows and, like her, he was barefoot.

"I don't think I told you," he said. "But your dress—and you in it—are beautiful."

"Oh. Well, thanks."

They stood there staring at each other for long seconds. Something shimmered in the air between them. Awareness. Interest. It was after eleven. Not all that late. But clearly, they were the only ones awake and wandering.

He reached for her ice bucket. "I'll give you half," he said.

She clutched the bronze container to her chest. "We don't want to spill anything in the hall. Or make noise. Maybe we should do it in my room over the sink."

His entire body froze. "Your room?" The two words were croaky.

Daley stared at him. The problem was, she *wanted* to dislike him, but he made it impossible. His easy-going charm was seductive, even when he wasn't trying to get a woman out of her panties.

That wouldn't be a problem tonight.

She tugged the key card from its hiding place, grinning when his eyes bugged out. "Come on in."

Tristan followed her, but his posture was uneasy, his expression guarded.

She pointed to the wet bar. "Your room is probably a mirror of mine." She handed him the ice bucket. "Thanks for sharing. I can offer you a fifteen-dollar jar of macadamia nuts. If you're still hungry."

He shook his head. "I'm good." Quickly, he poured half his ice into her bucket. Then he unwrapped a plastic tumbler, filled it with ice and water, and handed the cup to Daley. "There you go," he said. "I'll see you in the morning."

Daley took a long swig and nodded. "Good night."

Tristan had to pass her to get to the door and thus the hall. When he was in touching distance, he stopped. He set his now half-full ice bucket on an end table and stared at her. "Random question," he said, his tone light.

"Yeah?"

"If I were to kiss you, what are the odds I'd end up with a bloody nose or a black eye? I'm only asking because the best man should look presentable at a wedding."

Her heart began to pound. She set the cup aside. Here it was. The moment of truth. Daley could deceive herself under certain circumstances, but she was the one who'd invited Tristan into her room. He was only responding to her overture.

There was something between them. Maybe a connection as simple as healthy lust. They were two adults in their early thirties surrounded by the trappings of an unabashedly romantic weekend. Weddings, no matter how nicely disguised, were about sex…in the end…

Her mouth was still dry. "Well," she said. "I think you're safe."

Heat flared in his gaze. Heat and intent.

Daley's knees went weak.

He put a hand on her bare shoulder. "You have the most amazing skin. I've wanted to touch it all evening."

With one step she was between his arms. Close enough to absorb the warmth from his body. "Feel free," she whispered.

Tristan always surprised her. She had expected him to pounce. Clearly, she had opened the door with a broad invitation.

But he was nuanced in his approach. He ran both his hands from her shoulders down her arms to her wrists. "You smell good," he muttered.

She felt like an awkward teenager, not quite knowing what to say. "I already took a shower. I didn't want to wander in the hall wearing a robe, so I threw my dress back on."

He pulled back and stared at her. "Only the dress?"

She nodded. "Yep."

A rush of color streaked his cheekbones. He lifted her skirt with one hand and found smooth, naked skin right where her thigh rounded into her ass. "Good lord."

When he released her and stepped back, Daley was confused. "It's not that shocking, is it?"

"I'm not worried about you in the hall," he said tersely. "We both know this is a bad idea, right?"

"The worst," she said, nodding solemnly.

"I'll go if you want me to…"

But he touched her arm again as he said it, so the words weren't convincing.

Maybe it was the late hour or the knowledge that

she was losing her sister or the fact that Tristan was rumpled and heavy-eyed and not as intimidating as he had seemed in the past. But whatever the reason, she felt a great yearning to be with him.

"I don't want you to go," she whispered. Carefully, she unbuttoned one of his shirt buttons.

He covered her hand with his. "I need to shower. Four minutes tops."

"Use mine," she said.

"Protection?"

"I'm on the pill."

"I've seen the doctor a million times in the last two months. I'm in the clear."

"Then it's settled," she said, shaking inside with a combination of alarm and excitement. He hadn't even kissed her yet. She felt the leashed hunger in him, the careful control.

His gaze darkened. "Will you change your mind while I'm in the shower? Please don't."

She ran her thumb along his jaw, feeling the late-day stubble. He was a very masculine man. Big and powerful and yet funny and sometimes sweet. "I won't change my mind."

It took him six minutes, not four. But when he exited her bathroom wearing nothing but a white towel tied around his tanned hips, Daley was standing exactly where he had left her.

He lifted an eyebrow. "You okay?"

She nodded slowly. "Yes. Maybe a little freaked out." The knot in his towel looked sturdy, but she kept an eye on it, nevertheless.

Tristan crossed the room in three long strides. When he was standing in front of her, he slid a finger beneath one of her dress straps. "Freaked out about what?"

"All of it," she said, throwing up her hands and taking a literal step backward. "I never sleep with a man on the first date."

His lips quirked. "I believe you told everyone I'm *not* your date."

"Even worse," she muttered.

"Tell me to leave or let me undress you," he said soberly.

She stared at him in silence. *Did* she want him to go? She *should*. But she really didn't. She was going to indulge herself just this once. Like an inoculation, tonight would help her get past this love-hate relationship with Tristan Hamilton.

"Stay," she said quietly. "Stay and make love to me."

Three

Tristan thought he might be dreaming. But his hair was wet, and he felt the thick pile of the carpet under his bare feet.

He sucked in a breath, praying he wouldn't wake up if this was a delightful mirage. "Come here, woman. Let's get you out of that dress."

Daley's brown eyes were huge, her pupils dilated. "Okay," she whispered.

He turned her around and lowered the zipper, watching in hushed silence as the graceful curve of her spine was revealed. Her body was like a woman's body should be, soft and lush and welcoming.

He practically stuttered when he saw what was underneath. "You weren't kidding," he said. "You threw on the dress and nothing else? To get ice?"

She peeked over her shoulder at him and grinned. "I was in a hurry."

He realized she had clutched the bodice to her chest. "Let it go, Daley. I want to see all of you."

Her smile faded. "We can't go back from this."

"Then, what the hell? We might as well enjoy ourselves."

Without warning, a pile of blush-pink tulle and satin fell to the floor in a pool at Daley's feet. With his throat dry and his heart knocking against his ribs, he held her hand as she stepped away from her finery.

Now he could take her in from head to toe. The view was something akin to seeing the Sistine Chapel for the first time: Shocking. Exhilarating. Awe-inspiring.

He exhaled sharply. "I always knew you were a knockout. But my imagination wasn't up to the task." He put his hands on her waist and slid them to her curvy hips, pulling her close. "I can't believe it's taken me this long to coax you into bed."

Daley rolled her eyes at him. "*You* didn't do *anything*. I'm the one who asked for ice."

He grinned. "Ice? And yet somehow, I never knew that was code for getting naked together."

"I think there's a little more to it than that." She put her hand on his hip. "May I?"

A dark flush spread over his cheekbones. "Be my guest."

When Tristan held his arms out at his sides, Daley took a deep breath. She fumbled with the knot in the towel. "You must have been a Boy Scout," she muttered. "Maybe I need a knife."

"No knives," he said quickly. "Here. Let me help."

And then it was done.

Tristan Hamilton stood in front of her in all his glory. Tall, handsome and fully prepared to rock her world.

She was determined not to let him think of her as unsophisticated. When she wrapped her fingers around his erection and squeezed gently, a whistling breath escaped his lips. "Easy, Daley."

"Am I doing it wrong?" she asked, feigning innocence.

"Hell, no. But I haven't even kissed you yet."

She shrugged. "I figured you would get around to it eventually."

"Smart-ass." He pulled her into his arms and pressed his lips to her temple. "This is nice."

Every bit of available oxygen had inexplicably been sucked out of the room. Daley felt dizzy and disoriented. She clung to the only steady thing at hand.

Tristan. Naked, soap-scented, hard-bodied Tristan.

He felt amazing.

He pulled the band from her ponytail. She had covered her hair in the shower, too tired to wash it twice in one day. Now, she was glad. Tristan winnowed his fingers through her heavy layers, sifting and separating. The scalp massage was almost enough to make her come.

"I have a very nice bed," she said. "King size. Great mattress."

"Not yet." The two words were gravelly. As if he had to work to find them.

Without warning, he covered her mouth with his. His tongue was bold and tasted of toothpaste. When he thrust that same tongue gently against hers, she whimpered. Somehow, deep down, she had known it would be like this.

Suddenly, they were kissing like two lovers reunited after a long, continents-apart separation. Panting. Desperate. Ravenous.

The man knew how to kiss. Which shouldn't surprise her. According to Tabby and John, he'd dated a bevy of eligible women in the Peach State. But never for more than a few weeks at a time. Tristan was not a *relationship* kind of guy.

That was fine with Daley. She didn't want to *date* him. She just wanted to…well, you know. It was hard to even say it in her head.

The world tilted when Tristan scooped her into his arms and staggered to the bed. She liked to think his lack of coordination was due to rampant sexual desperation and not her addiction to caloric coffee drinks.

When he dropped her on the mattress and followed her down, she smiled up at him. "You really are a stud, aren't you? Tell me again why you don't have a date for your brother's wedding?"

He nuzzled her nose with his. "My job is to fraternize with the maid of honor. I didn't want any distractions."

"Such dedication," she mocked him gently.

"You have no idea." He slid his hand between her legs and stroked her intimately. Daley's squeak of alarm and surprise didn't sound at all sophisticated.

Tristan chuckled. "I'm glad we decided to bury the hatchet," he said. "This is way more fun than arguing."

"It may only be a temporary détente," she warned. "I'm still not sure I like you."

He found her breast, squeezed the nipple and bent his head to taste the bud with the tip of his tongue. "I'll take my chances."

Heat flashed through Daley's body. Her back arched off the bed. Suddenly, she was uncertain. Did she want this overwhelming sexual hunger? Could she hold her own with a man like Tristan? He was bold and decisive, and he certainly was not the kind of guy who would be easily *handled.*

The time had passed for making rational decisions. At this moment, she wanted Tristan so badly, she was willing to do just about anything. Including the choice to ignore common sense and her gut feeling that she was courting disaster.

He made her come once with his hand—fast and hard—before moving between her thighs and pressing the head of his sex where she still quivered. "Are we okay?" he asked.

She managed to open her eyes. "I don't know about you, but I'm great."

His choked laugh as he pressed deep made her smile. He filled her completely, but the flex of his powerful hips was more gentle than rough. As if he wanted to make sure she was comfortable.

When he was all the way in, she tried to find her breath, but it was gone. Her body trembled. This felt good. So good. For once, she was able to enjoy the act of lovemaking without worrying about consequences. She and Tristan were nothing to each other. This was sex. Really great sex.

It didn't matter if they were one and done. Daley could relax and *feel*.

Perhaps Tristan picked up on her bemusement. He rested his forehead on hers. "You still with me, Daley? I'd hate to think you were dozing off."

She wrapped her legs around his waist, making them both groan. "I'm here," she said softly. "Just enjoying the moment. You're good at this. But I guess you know that. Given your vast experience."

Tristan withdrew and thrust harder. "Insults? Really? What happened to détente?"

"No insults," she whispered. "I like being with someone who knows women."

His frown was fleeting but noticeable. "I don't know *you* all that well. Maybe we can rectify that."

Daley closed her eyes, not answering. No point in saying sex was all she wanted from him. Men like Tristan weren't what she needed for the long run. At this point in her life, she doubted marriage was in the cards for her, and she was okay being single.

But sex? That was something else entirely.

She wrapped her arms around his neck and kissed

him. "I won't break," she said, sucking his bottom lip. "Give it all to me."

He reared back and stared at her, eyes glittering, chest heaving. "Be careful what you ask for, Daley."

"Ooh, I'm scared," she said, mocking him gently.

Her provocation pushed his control to the snapping point. He said a word under his breath, a word she couldn't catch, and then he snapped. The man was focused and talented. He had her at the edge in no time at all, and when her climax hit, he gave no quarter.

Again and again, he hammered into her until they both cried out and found what they had been seeking...

When Tristan awoke, he was momentarily disoriented.

Then everything came rushing back. John and Tabby. The wedding. One bridesmaid in particular...

He rolled over, and there she was. Daley Martin. Golden hair spread across her pillow. Body like an angel and the personality of a cactus.

Hell. What had they done? John would kill him.

In the next second, Tristan formulated a decision. *Nobody* was going to find out about this. What he and Daley did behind closed doors was their business.

His movements had disturbed her. Slowly, her eyelashes lifted, her sleepy gaze cleared and awareness returned.

She winced. "Did we...?"

"Yes." He said it bluntly, wondering how she would react.

"You're sure it wasn't a dream?"

He pinched her arm. "Very sure. And if we stay in this bed, it's going to happen again."

Daley made a face at him. "Then we'd better get up. I'm hungry." She crawled out of bed, grabbed a crimson velour throw from a chair and wrapped it around herself. The hotel was too small to offer room service, but the minibar was stocked. "How about Cokes and corn chips?" she asked.

"Works for me."

The large suite included a sitting area in front of a fireplace. As he watched, Daley pushed the AC down four degrees and turned on the gas logs before grabbing their snacks. "This is cozy," she said, smiling at him and making his sex twitch.

He was like a salivating dog in her presence.

She sat on the love seat and patted the spot beside her. "Come relax with me."

The bath towel from earlier was damp. So, he settled for tugging the top sheet loose and wrapping it, toga-style, around him. He dropped down beside her and kissed her shoulder. "I don't think relaxation is in the cards. I'm already thinking about how to take you next."

Her mouth fell open and her eyes widened. "Oh."

He cocked his head. "Did you really think we were through?"

"I thought you would go back to your room." Her cheeks were pink.

"Only if you kick me out."

"I don't want to kick you out."

Her quiet words sent jubilation coursing through his veins. He leaned back and yawned, feeling remarkably mellow under the circumstances. "Tell me about you and Tabby," he said. "What were you like as kids?"

Daley curled her legs beneath her. Her mussed hair made her look younger and more vulnerable than the Daley he knew before tonight. She picked at a thread on her blanket. "I'm six years older than Tabby. You probably know that. She was my baby doll—a living, breathing playmate. I adored her and still do."

"So you'll want a big family one day?"

Daley's expression was odd. "No. Tabby will be a great mom, but I think I'm more the career type."

"Women do both," he said, caught off guard by an odd note in her voice.

"Not easily. I knew when I started my ad agency that I was making a commitment. The hours are long, and I have a lot of responsibility. I enjoy the challenge."

"And what about men?"

Her gaze when she stared at him was bland. "What about them?"

"Do you see yourself getting married?" He had no clue why he was asking.

"Do you?" she asked sharply.

"No." He felt foolish now. And deflated. "Sorry," he muttered. "That was too personal a question."

"Well, since you opened the door—why are *you* anti-marriage?"

"Not so much *anti* as realistic. Marriage requires compromise and maturity."

"You don't strike me as immature." Her words were teasing. "So it must be the compromise thing. I suppose you're stubborn and set in your ways? Is that it?"

"You could say that." He winced. "Besides, I was engaged once. In college. When we broke up, she told me I had the emotional depth of a head of lettuce. Things like that stick with a guy."

"Ah." Daley grimaced. "I'm sorry, Tristan. That must have been awful. For what it's worth, I've seen you with John and Tabby. You care deeply about your brother, and you've made Tabby feel a part of your family. Perhaps Tristan Hamilton has come a long way, longer than you know."

"Maybe." He rubbed the back of his neck, uncomfortable with the personal flavor of the conversation. He was better in bed than dissecting his psyche. "So that's me. What's your excuse? I think I can ask that since I've bared my soul."

Daley leaned forward and set her drink can on the coffee table. She had eaten a few chips, but that was it. "If you want the truth, I'm petrified of being so vulnerable. Marriage—a good one anyway—requires letting another person get close to you. Permanently." She shrugged. "I don't think I'd be good at it."

"So what you're saying is that you and I are slated to be the doting auntie and uncle."

"That's about it."

He twisted a lock of her hair around his finger. "Shouldn't we get some shut-eye? I know the bride will be the center of attention, but those dark shadows underneath your beautiful lashes will tell people you had a sleepless night."

Daley turned her face into his palm, nuzzling him like a kitten seeking affection. "You don't really care about sleep, do you?"

Her husky voice turned him inside out. He tugged at her blanket, baring one breast. As he palmed the soft flesh, shuddering raw need choked him. "No. Not even a little bit."

He moved on top of her, easing her under him. The piece of furniture was a love seat, not a sofa, but the bed was too far. Making this happen was awkward and funny and damn serious all at the same time.

When he entered her, Daley closed her eyes and arched her neck. Her legs wrapped around his waist.

"Look at me," he demanded. He didn't entirely understand his driving need to connect with her, but he wanted to see the expression in her eyes.

She complied slowly. A tiny smile curved her lips. "I'm looking, big guy."

"Will you regret this?" he asked. The words tumbled out, surprising even him. He kissed her eyebrows, her nose, her soft cheeks.

When he withdrew and thrust again, Daley sank her teeth into her bottom lip. "Maybe." She sighed. "Probably."

"Don't," he begged. "Whatever happens, don't regret tonight. Please."

"Why does it matter? It's just sex."

Was she taunting him on purpose?

He tamped down his pique. "Pretty great sex."

"True."

He paused, resting on his elbows, studying her flushed face and bare breasts. "You fascinate me, Daley. Even when you were yelling at me in my office, I wanted to know you better."

She scrunched up her nose. "Please don't remind me of that day. It's so embarrassing. I acted like a crazy woman."

"You were passionate," he said. "I think maybe you try to hide that passion, but something pushed you over the edge that afternoon, and I saw the real Daley Martin for a few minutes. She was astonishingly full of life."

"Well, it won't happen again. You stay in your corner, and I'll stay in mine."

He kissed her lips this time, sinking deep, tasting the salt of the chips. "Where's the fun in that?"

"Do you always talk this much during sex?" She ruffled his hair with both hands, making him shiver.

"Only with you."

They stared at each other for long moments. He was deep inside her, aching to come. Daley was flushed, glowing. Also clearly on the edge.

She touched his cheek. "I won't regret it," she said. "Some things get tucked away as shining memories. They keep us going on dark days."

He liked the way she looked at him. But her words were another story. Why did this have to be nothing more than a memory?

Hell, he knew the answer to that. There was no universe in which Daley and Tristan as a couple made sense. The important people in this equation were Tabby and John. On that point, Tristan knew he and Daley were in perfect agreement.

"Well," he said, rotating his hips until she gasped, "if this is going to be no more than a memory, I'd better make it good."

He slid out, groaned and slammed into her. Daley arched into his thrusts, chanting his name. When it was almost too late for him, he maneuvered them onto their sides so he could trigger her pleasure. He stroked the little nub of nerves and held her tightly as she cried out. Then he was on top of her again, thrusting his body into hers, relishing the exact moment when fire streaked from every cell in his body and imploded in his release.

When he could feel his legs, he scooped her up, killed the lights and carried her back to the bed.

Daley was asleep instantly. He was a few minutes behind her. In the dark, he frowned. What had happened in the last few hours? Sexual indulgence? Or something more...

When he roused next, he thought he could see a faint gray light around the edge of the drapes. Daley was sprawled across his chest, tapping his forehead with her finger.

"Wake up," she said. "You have to go to your room."

He muttered a word that encompassed his feelings. "Don't wanna…" he mumbled.

That little finger didn't give up. "You have to," she insisted. "People will be stirring soon."

Rolling to his back and groaning was his only response. He breathed in and out, trying to summon the energy to stand and get dressed.

Slim fingers curled around his apparently permanent erection. "Or maybe just one more quickie," Daley said.

"Hell yeah." A jolt of heat energized him. "Come here, sweet thing."

They ended up with Daley on top, which turned out to be incredibly rewarding for both of them. Unfortunately, even the excess of the night didn't give him much staying power. He was obsessed with her.

Only when he felt the little jerk in her body and heard her sensual moan did he let himself come.

There was no opportunity for wallowing in carnal bliss.

The light was growing stronger.

Cursing beneath his breath, he loped to the bathroom, found his clothes and jerked them on, grimacing at the wrinkled, less-than-fresh items.

Daley stood by the door, wrapped in the red blanket. She shoved her hair from her face. "Sorry to throw you out," she said. "But weddings wait for no man."

He pressed a quick kiss to her forehead, grabbed his ice bucket—now mostly filled with water—and put a hand on the doorknob. "We'll talk later," he promised.

Daley frowned. "No need. It's going to be a busy day. Now go."

Fortunately, his room was the closest one to Daley's. No reason any other guest should be in this corridor. And it was too early for housekeeping.

Even so, he moved quickly, anxious to escape detection. Everything was going great until he rounded the corner and came face-to-face with his baby brother.

Shit…

John's hair was damp. He carried a duffle bag and had a towel slung around his neck. Clearly, Tristan's type-A sibling had decided to cope with wedding day stress in the workout room.

John's eyes rounded. "What are you…"

"You're up early," Tristan said, keeping his voice low.

John stopped. Clearly, his brain did the calculations. The only two rooms in the direction from which Tristan had come were the bridal couple's and Daley's.

His brother glared. "Oh, you didn't. Please tell me you didn't."

Tristan could BS with the best of them, but his sibling knew him too well. "Don't tell Tabby."

Fury reddened the groom's face. "You're asking me to lie to my wife? On our wedding day? Son of a bitch."

"It's not what you think," Tristan said. "To be honest, Daley invited me in, not the other way around."

John's anger went ballistic. "And you think that matters? Tabby adores her sister. And she knows you're a player."

"Hey," Tristan said. "That's not fair."

His brother wiped a hand over his face. "Sorry. But you know this is a bad idea."

"It was a onetime thing. Nothing to get upset about."

"You couldn't go one weekend without sex? Damn, Tristan. I don't want this to blow up in my face."

"It's more than sex," Tristan said. And then wondered what he meant by that.

"Do explain." John's stare was icy.

Tristan shrugged. "We like each other."

"And you flirted with her."

"Yeah…" Tristan was beginning to understand that John was seriously upset.

The groom-to-be visibly gathered his emotions and exhaled. "Well, it's done. But please try to stay away from her today."

"Are you serious?"

"*Yes*, Tristan. My bride wants her sister to be happy. And it's my job to make Tabby happy. All of that will be a hell of a lot easier if you keep your distance."

"Fine," Tristan said, his jaw tight.

"Tabby worries about Daley. I don't want Tabby worried on our honeymoon. That's not too much to ask, is it?"

"No." Suddenly this wedding day sounded a lot less fun.

"Get some sleep," John said. "You look like hell, and brunch is in a couple of hours."

With that, John walked off down the hall, leaving Tristan to wonder how he had fumbled this weekend so badly.

Four

Daley had never experienced an alcohol-induced hangover in her life. But sleep deprivation? That was another story. When Tristan left earlier, she had set her alarm and immediately been unconscious. Now, it was nine forty-five. Brunch started at ten thirty. And she was a mess.

With her head pounding and her stomach churning, she downed a couple of painkillers and headed for the shower. Blow-drying her hair took precious minutes, but she wanted to look her best. For Tabby. For Daley's role as maid of honor. And, if she were honest, for Tristan.

It was going to be a long day, so she had opted for comfort with this morning's outfit. The crisp white cotton sundress embroidered with tiny yellow sunflowers made her look far perkier than she felt. Yellow flats completed the outfit. She left her hair loose and clipped it behind each ear with two gold clasps. Her new necklace was the final touch.

She made it to the hotel dining room with ten minutes to spare.

The wedding party was trickling in. John spotted her first. He made a beeline in her direction with an odd look on his face.

Daley hugged him. "Happy wedding day."

"Thanks." He looked behind him, saw Tabby occupied with the hotel caterer and lowered his voice. "Please don't tell your sister about last night."

"Last night?" Daley's face went hot.

"You and my brother," he said impatiently.

"He told you?" Daley was horrified.

"No, of course not. We ran into each other this morning in the hallway. I put two and two together."

"Since when is my private life relevant to your wedding day?" Daley asked, feeling indignant and embarrassed and everything in between.

John gave her a look. "You're not that clueless. Tabby wants you to be as happy as she is. Flirting with any one of the groomsmen would be fine, but not hooking up with Tristan."

"And why is that? I thought you loved your brother."

"I do. But Tabby knows Tristan's track record with relationships. If she finds out you started something this weekend, I'll never hear the end of it. She loves Tristan, too, but she's under no illusions about his desirability as a mate."

"You know she and I share everything."

"Then tell her when we get back."

Fortunately for Daley, someone else demanded John's attention, and the uncomfortable interlude came to an end.

John had nothing to worry about. This was Tabby's day. She was the bride. Daley would do everything in her power to make sure nothing went wrong.

The brunch buffet was outstanding. An omelet bar. French toast and blueberry pancakes. Bacon, sausage and ham. More fresh fruit. And a chocolate fountain with pound cake squares and huge strawberries to dip.

Daley chose to sit with the bridesmaids again. This time, Tristan didn't join her. Had he also received a lecture from John? Possibly. Her lover from last night had barely glanced in her direction since he walked into the room.

Toward the end of the meal, Tabby stood and tapped a spoon to her glass. "I hope you all enjoyed your meal. Please remember we're meeting the photographer beside the pool at three sharp. All the pictures will be taken this afternoon. John and I want to enjoy dinner and dancing without waiting after the ceremony. You have a couple hours to relax. The pool is open. There are walking trails. Cornhole. Horseshoes. Outdoor hot tub. Or you can hide out in your room and watch TV. Take your pick."

It was straight-up noon as the group began to disperse. Daley made a beeline for her sister. "Do you need anything, sweetie?"

Tabby smiled. "Nope. Everything is going smoothly. John will meet the florist. Other than that, we're all set."

"Are you going to take a nap?"

"I thought about it. But we have a super long flight tomorrow, so I can sleep on the plane."

"You doing okay with that five-thousand-mile thing?" Tabby had never even traveled outside the US. Now she was flying halfway around the world to Tahiti.

Tabby scrunched her nose. "I'm not thrilled about it, but I'll have John. He won't let me get all panicky. I'll be fine."

"Okay. Love you, sis." Daley grabbed one quick hug and watched ruefully as her sister was spirited away by two of her college friends.

Daley sighed. She might as well head back to her room and sleep.

Before she could make a move in that direction, someone appeared at her elbow. She didn't have to glance sideways to know it was Tristan.

He folded his arms across his chest, not looking at her. "Did you get a lecture from John?"

"Yep."

"I'm only cutting him slack because it's his wedding day."

"I know!" Daley exclaimed, indignant. "I like to think he'll be embarrassed later that he came down so hard on us."

"You want to go for a walk?"

She opened her mouth and closed it. "I thought we couldn't be seen together."

"I don't really care, do you? Besides, I could use the fresh air. My brother can't legislate the great outdoors."

Daley chuckled. "You have a point. Sure. Let's walk. At least I wore flat shoes."

They strolled outside into the sunshine. Tristan pointed out the path that wound through a double row of Bradford pear trees. "They may be a stinky invasive species, but you have to admit they look bridal."

"Very true."

After twenty minutes, they found a teak bench in the shade and sat down. It was a long way back to the house. Surely no one would bother them here.

When Tristan spread his arms along the back of the seat, his fingers brushed her bare shoulder. *Accidentally?*

He sighed. "I watched your face when Tabby was talking to the group. It looked like you had tears in your eyes."

Daley bristled. "What are *you*? The emotion police?"

"Daley…"

"Okay, fine. This is a hard weekend for me. I'm losing my best friend. I'm thrilled for her, and I adore John. But it's painful being the one left behind."

He tucked a strand of hair behind her ear. "You'll still be her sister. That won't change. I've been told that love grows and widens."

Daley snorted. "Did you get that from a fortune cookie?"

"I'm serious. He's not replacing you. Tabby will always have room for you *and* John in her life."

"Maybe. Don't pay any attention to me. I'm just feeling maudlin. It's probably the lack of sleep."

"Should I apologize?"

She heard the smile in his voice, even though she was staring straight ahead, taking in the lush green pasture. "Not at all. It was an enjoyable night."

Tristan put his hands on her bare shoulders and turned her sideways to face him. "*Enjoyable?* That's a sad-ass adjective." His blue eyes sparkled.

She smoothed her thumb over his bottom lip. "Sorry. Did I insult your prowess?"

Tristan ignored her teasing. "I promised John I would stay away from you this weekend." His expression was wry. His hands continued to glide from her shoulders to her wrists and back again.

"How's that working out for you?"

He wrapped his arms around her and pulled her head to his shoulder. "I'm compromising by not screwing you all afternoon."

Laughing, she nestled closer. "You're assuming you would have been invited?"

He traced a finger down her spine, making her shiver. "Well?"

"Yes," she muttered. "I'd have invited you. Still could if we can figure out a way to avoid your brother."

"Maybe we'll wait until later. Surely he won't be patrolling the halls on his wedding night."

"We can only hope."

Daley was oddly content. The tree-dappled sunshine was warm but not too hot. A light breeze lifted strands of her hair.

Dress code for brunch had been casual. Tristan wore dark indigo jeans with leather deck shoes and a pale yellow dress shirt with the sleeves rolled to his elbows. He smelled like expensive aftershave and warm male skin.

"You're nicer than I thought," she said. "All things considered."

His chest rumbled with laughter beneath her cheek. "Thanks. I think."

"I'm serious."

"So you believe I haven't been poaching your clients?"

"Yes. I believe you. Honestly, why would you need to? Lieberman and Dunn is a household name in Atlanta." She moved away from him, acknowledging—at least to herself—the need to avoid temptation. "Tabby said you wanted to be a doctor."

"I did." He grimaced. "My mother nearly died of breast cancer when I was a teenager. She recovered, but that year and a half struck me hard. I decided I wanted to be part of saving the world. Typical adolescent hubris. I still remember the grief and panic when we thought we were losing her."

"But you let Harold talk you out of it. Have you ever regretted that decision?"

Tristan moved restlessly, rolling to his feet and

pacing. "Not really. Harold needed someone, and I didn't want to sacrifice John's dreams."

"So it's better to sacrifice your own?" She frowned.

"Don't be so dramatic. I did myself a favor. Med school would have been brutal."

"It's odd," she said. "But I think you love your brother the way I love my sister. Most teenage girls will do anything to avoid annoying younger siblings. Tabby and I shared a room until I went off to college."

"She looks up to you," he said. "I hear it in her voice when she tells everyone how wonderful you are."

"It's the same with John. He convinced Tabby—and she convinced me—that you weren't a heartless monster."

"So we're in agreement that we both lucked out in the sibling department."

"Indeed." Daley sighed. "I would love to have an affair with you, you know. Until the novelty wears off. But us being together and then breaking up would implode the families and the people we love most."

"That is the most depressingly logical thing I've ever heard." Tristan kicked a rock and watched it bounce across the path.

"But…" she said.

He whirled around. "But what?"

"If you're okay with lying to your brother just this once, we could have tonight. After all, we're stuck here in this hotel until checkout time tomorrow. Tabby and John are catching an Uber at five thirty in the morning to make it to the airport for their flight. They'll assume we're both dead asleep and won't bother us."

His cheeks flushed. "You don't think Tabby will pop in to say goodbye?"

"No. We'll do that tonight, I'm sure."

Tristan reached for her hands and pulled her to her feet. "You've just made this wedding a hell of a lot more interesting."

He really was the most appealing man she had ever met. In a rakish, naughty, devil-may-care kind of way. Was that the attraction? Was she tired of being a good girl? Was she tired of being alone?

Tristan scanned a three-sixty view around them.

"What are you doing?" she asked.

A muscle in his jaw flexed. "Making sure there's no one around."

And then he kissed her.

It was nothing like last night's lazy buildup. This kiss was desperate and hunger-driven. Their calm, rational conversation had apparently hidden a banked flame.

Daley wrapped her arms around his neck. When his hands slipped under her skirt and found her ass, she didn't stop him. He rubbed her butt over her bikini panties until she thought her heart would beat out of her chest.

She stared at him wild-eyed. "Do you think we can…"

"Here?" he asked. All the planes and angles of his face were taut and fierce.

"Maybe it's too dangerous."

"I can be quick," he swore.

She choked out a laugh. "Ordinarily, I wouldn't see that as a positive, but sure." Were they really going to do this? It was madness.

Tristan sat down on the bench and unzipped his pants.

Daley hesitated. "I've never done anything like this in my life."

He winced. "We don't have to…"

"No," she said, telling herself she wouldn't let her natural caution ruin a good thing. "No, I want this. I want you."

Tristan didn't even take off her undies. When she straddled his lap, he fingered her, drew her down on top of him and joined their bodies.

Daley couldn't stop shaking. She liked this woman, whoever she was.

Tristan took her chin in his hand. "Look at me, Daley. Can you come like this?"

She nodded. "Oh, yes. Go for it."

What happened next defied explanation. Tristan kept one arm around her waist while he drove them both insane. It was fast and furious and incredibly hot.

Daley felt dizzy when pleasure ripped through her.

Tristan buried his face in the curve of her neck to muffle his shout.

Afterward, they clung to each other like survivors of a shipwreck.

At last, he straightened and stared at her. "Good lord, woman."

She couldn't tell if his words were praise or complaint. Embarrassment ripped through her. He must think she was a nymphomaniac.

Awkwardly, she stood and straightened her clothes. She glanced at her watch. "I have to go back," she said. "It's late."

"Are you mad at me?" He cocked his head and stared at her.

"Of course not." She was sated and relaxed, but at the same time aghast and guilty. This was Tabby's wedding weekend. What was she doing?

They walked back to the hotel in silence.

Partway, Daley stopped in the path. "Do I look okay?" she asked. "I don't want anybody to guess what we've been doing."

He touched her cheek with a gentle finger. "You look great. If you want, I can stay here and let you go back alone."

She nodded. "I think that would be best. I'll see you at three."

Tristan had just experienced some of the best sex of his adult life. Why then did he feel so let down? He'd like to think it was from breaking a promise to his brother, but that didn't even make the list.

Daley liked having sex with him, but she'd been very clear about her expectations. This little wedding weekend interlude had a definite expiration date. Despite the natural chemistry between them, she didn't expect to see him again once they parted company tomorrow. With some women, that would be a relief.

Unfortunately, Daley was in a class by herself.

He gave her half an hour to get situated in her room before strolling back to the hotel. Showering and shaving took no time at all. After that, he downed a beer and brooded. It was impossible not to think about Daley, but he tried.

Despite the fact this was a small wedding, it was still very traditional. The men's formal wear was expensive and classic. Tristan owned a tux that had been hand-tailored to fit his large frame. But he had rented one for this occasion to match the other groomsmen.

He slept for half an hour and then watched TV. At half past two he got dressed and checked the mirror. He wanted to make his brother proud.

Tonight was important. Tristan wasn't discounting that. Seeing John and Tabby get married was going to be a powerful moment.

But even so, Tristan was caught up in his own dilemma. What to do about Daley...

Or maybe there was no dilemma at all. If they could pretend for the rest of today—pretend they were nothing more than friendly acquaintances—Tristan would only see her a handful of times a year.

It's possible he could find valid excuses to miss a few family gatherings here and there. It wasn't an ideal plan. He had always been an integral part of his brother's life and vice versa. But his choices were few.

He couldn't date Daley and break up with her. That was out of the question. And since he wasn't in the market for a long-term relationship, he couldn't date her period.

The reluctant introspection left him feeling frustrated and grumpy.

It was almost a relief to realize it was time for the wedding photos. He donned his sunglasses, pocketed his room key and headed for the pool area.

He knew Tabby and John had met earlier for pictures of the groom's first-time-to-see-the-bride shots. Neither Tabby nor John was superstitious, but they had wanted to catch that moment before the rest of the pictures.

When Tristan arrived, the photographer had just finished taking pictures of the grandparents with the bride and groom. Next up were the parents. Then separate group pics of the Hamilton family and the Martins. Everything went smoothly.

After that, Tabby dismissed everyone but the immediate wedding party.

Tristan had to work not to stare at Daley. She was stunning. The bridesmaids wore slim strapless navy dresses and carried bouquets of yellow and white daisies.

The photographer was a skinny guy with a shock of red hair and an expensive-looking camera. He and Tabby worked together well. Both had a vision for what Tabby wanted. The bride beamed. "We're going to have fun with this," she said. "I'm thanking you in advance for your patience."

The groomsmen sprawled in folding chairs while the bridesmaids were photographed in a dozen different configurations. Because the weather had held, the ceremony would be outdoors. A white satin runner marked the aisle for the bride's entrance later.

When the women were done, Tristan and his fellow groomsmen followed orders as they were posed and prodded, all the while trying not to sweat. The group was in a good mood. It was a great day.

Tristan assumed they were done then. But he was wrong.

Tabby had asked the photographer to document the actual wedding while it was in progress— unobtrusively from the back—but she wanted shots of the wedding party posed now…just in case guests blocked the view later.

The twelve men and women, plus Daley and Tristan, took their positions with the groom. Tabby walked down the aisle, and then she and John held hands, grinning at each other. The only shot required later would be one with the minister and also Tabby's dad giving her away.

The photographer waved his hand. "Everything looks great. Now I want to try something just for fun."

The area set aside for the ceremony was shaded by enormous mature oaks whose branches met overhead. A couple of groomsmen, when asked, snagged two chairs and positioned them in front of a bank of forsythia.

The photographer seated the bride and groom and fussed with their pose. Then he had each duo of attendants stand in a semicircle around the two chairs.

"Now face each other," the photographer said. "Tabby and John—you two kiss. At the same moment, I want each couple to fake a kiss."

Tristan and Daley were so close to each other he could see the flicker of shock in her eyes at the photographer's instruction. They stood in the exact center of the picture, immediately behind the bride and groom. John never looked up at them, but Tabby gave her sister a quick amused smile.

The photographer counted down. "Five…four… three…two…one. Now."

Tristan found Daley's lips with his. The jolt of heat was no surprise. But his partner jerked away. "Fake kiss," she whispered.

He couldn't help himself. He kissed her again.

All around them, giggles and laughter erupted. Perhaps a few of the other couples had gone beyond the *fake* kiss as well.

The photographer glanced at his camera screen. "That one looks good. But one more to make sure."

Tristan put a hand on Daley's waist. No one could see. Not even John and Tabby.

The countdown came a second time: "Five… four…three…two…one. Now!"

For a split second, time seemed to halt. Tristan was hyperaware of Daley's light perfume, the sound of his own breathing. He kissed her carefully, thoroughly. Her lips were soft and warm. She made a little noise that hardened his sex.

But the moment was all too short.

He stepped back, staring briefly at the woman who seemed as stunned as he was.

All around them, the wedding party erupted in chatter.

The photographer gave a thumbs-up. "I think that's a wrap."

Tabby stood. "Feel free to go to your rooms, everybody, and take a breather. Meet back in the small staging tent at four forty-five."

She turned to Daley. "Can I come to your room and freshen up? John and I are going to take a little break until I walk down the aisle."

Daley nodded, her cheeks flushed. "Of course."

Tristan hoped Tabby would assume her sister's pink cheeks were the result of the outdoor temperature and not because she had been kissed for real.

As the bride and groom walked away to speak to the photographer, Tristan whispered in Daley's ear, "You look amazing."

She ducked her head and smiled. "Thanks. You're pretty darn hot in that tuxedo, too."

He chuckled. "For what it's worth, I could take that literally."

Although the world bustled around them, they still stood in an oasis of quiet.

"I should go," Daley said. "Tabby will be waiting for me."

"Of course."

"Tristan, I—"

Tabby called out from across the lawn, "You coming?"

"On my way."

Daley grimaced. "Sorry."

He touched her arm. "What were you going to say?"

Her gaze slid away from his. "Not important. I'll see you later."

Five

Daley unfastened the back of her sister's wedding dress, helped her out of it and draped it over the bed. "How are you holding up?"

Tabby sighed, slipped her arms into one of the hotel robes and collapsed into a comfy armchair. "I'm great. But a little nervous, too."

"About what?"

"All the people watching me when I walk down the aisle."

"That's why you and John kept the guest list small, right?"

"Yes. But I'm starting to realize whether it's sixty or six hundred, I'm still going to be a wreck."

"But only until John takes your hand."

Tabby closed her eyes and smiled blissfully. "True."

Daley kicked off her own shoes and wiggled her toes. "It's going to be perfect."

Her baby sister sat up and yawned. "I asked the photographer to show me the funny-slash-sweet picture we all did there at the end."

Daley froze inwardly, struggling to keep her expression neutral. "Was it cute? Did you like it?"

Tabby curled her legs beneath her and rested her elbow on the arm of the chair, propping her head on her hand. Her gaze was oddly intent. "I love it. But it was surprising, too."

"Oh?" Daley turned her back and pretended to search the minibar.

"Look at me, Daley."

Daley turned around slowly. "What?" she asked, trying her best to look innocent.

"One of the kisses in that picture wasn't fake at all. You and Tristan really did it."

Daley swallowed, thankful her baby sister didn't know how true that statement was. For the space of two panicked heartbeats, Daley thought about fibbing. But she sucked at lying, and in this case, it was probably better to own up and spin the facts.

"Oh, you mean the kiss. Well, yes. You know what a tease he can be. Tristan thought it was funny."

Tabby glared. "Did *you* think it was funny?"

"It was fine. I knew he was clowning for the camera."

Now Tabby's gaze narrowed. "Didn't he worry that you might punch him?"

"Apparently not," Daley said dryly. Not for a million dollars would she explain her own eager participation in that kiss.

Tabby nodded slowly. "Okay, then. I just don't want him disrespecting you."

"Tristan and I have an understanding," Daley said firmly. "It's all good. Honest." She would have to tell her sister the truth eventually. Or at least a sanitized version of the truth. But John was right. Today was not the moment for Tabby to find out that her big sister and John's brother had done the nasty.

Tabby yawned. "I need to get my second wind."

"You want a glass of champagne? I can go find one somewhere."

"Nope. Just let me close my eyes a minute. Your job is to watch the clock and make sure I'm not late for my own wedding."

At the appointed hour, Daley tucked her arm in Tristan's and strolled along the satin runner. At the front, he squeezed her hand and took his place opposite her. The music changed, the crowd stood and Tabby came walking down the aisle.

Daley's heart caught in her throat. She had known the impact this day would have from the very beginning, but the knot of emotion in her throat caught her by surprise.

Her sister didn't need her anymore. Not only that, but Daley would no longer be responsible for making sure Tabby was happy. That was John's task now.

Tabby was as radiant a bride as Daley had ever seen. Despite her professed nerves, she walked at exactly the right pace—chin up, big smile and a clear-eyed gaze fixed on her beloved.

After that, the ceremony was a blur for Daley. She took Tabby's bridal bouquet at the appropriate moment—and later handed it back—but the words the minister uttered were little more than white noise.

She was very conscious that Tristan spent more time looking her way than at the bride and groom. At one point, his gaze showed definite concern. She gave him a smile and hoped it was convincing.

Why had she opened up to him about her feelings? Despite their recent physical intimacy, Tristan was little more than an acquaintance. She was embarrassed that she had been so vulnerable.

Suddenly, Tabby and John were kissing, the crowd was cheering, and the bride and groom were headed down the aisle.

Tristan met Daley in the middle and tucked her arm in his. "You okay?" he asked under his breath.

She nodded, smiling for their audience. "Yes."

In the chaos at the back, it was easy to elude Tristan. Daley hugged John and gave Tabby a hug and a kiss. "Congrats, you two." She barely had a moment with them before the other bridesmaids and groomsmen crowded around, extending their best wishes, too.

Soon, the wedding guests were on their feet, and everyone moved en masse to the reception tent. Daley worked the room, greeting friends and family, and directing traffic to the sumptuous buffet.

Tonight, Tabby and John did have a head table.

Tristan was seated at his brother's elbow with Daley beside her sister. The two sets of parents were on either end.

Daley was in no rush to be seated. She much preferred to mingle. But when the bride and groom finally sat down, she had no choice.

The caterer had prepared plates for the bride and groom. Daley served herself and joined them. She had managed to elude Tristan every time he headed in her direction. Now he sat mere feet away.

Once most people had finished eating, the wedding director gave Daley a nod. "Time for your toast," she said, handing over a microphone.

Daley stood with only a few butterflies in her stomach. She didn't mind speaking in public, but she wanted to say what was in her heart.

"Tabby and John," she said. When she paused to clear her throat, Tabby got tears in her eyes. Daley smiled. "I have watched the two of you fall in love, and it has been such a joy. You each make the other better, stronger. If I had picked the perfect mate for my little sister, it couldn't have been a more excellent match." She lifted her glass. "To Tabby and John…"

Glasses went up all over the tent. "To Tabby and John."

Tabby was pink-cheeked and clearly delighted.

Then it was Tristan's turn. When he stood, Daley felt a funny twist in her stomach. He was relaxed, handsome, charming. He commanded attention by his mere presence.

He smiled at the wedding couple. "I'm honored to

be your best man today. Like Daley, I saw this connection between you blossom into love. I wouldn't
call myself a sentimental man—indeed, some might
describe me as cynical—but on a day like today,
it's easy to celebrate love and forever." He lifted his
champagne flute. "May you both live happily ever
after."

Daley was astonished. It was impossible to fake
the kind of genuine feeling Tristan had infused in
his toast. Her image of him continued to shift and
morph. Was he a shallow man who jumped from
one physical relationship to the next? Or was there
more to him?

According to Tabby, John loved his older brother
deeply…and admired him as well. John was apparently a good judge of character since he picked Tabby
for his wife. So it would follow that his assessment
of Tristan might be valid, even if family loyalty did
tip the scales.

While she finished her meal and pondered the
enigma that was Tristan, the DJ cranked up the music,
and the dancing began. Bride and groom's first dance.
Daddy and daughter. Then John and his mom.

Daley was taken completely off guard when the
DJ called for best man and maid of honor. Was that
even a thing? Apparently so…

No one else could take the dance floor until she
and Tristan did their bit.

She stood and rounded the table, meeting him on
the polished but temporary surface. Stepping into
his embrace with everyone watching felt awkward

and uncomfortable. But when his hand settled on her back and steered her to the music, she exhaled.

Tristan smiled. "Relax. With that deer-in-the-headlights expression on your beautiful face, people are either going to assume you hate me or that you're covering up the fact that we're sleeping together."

"That's not true." She knew he was joking, but still she hated the attention.

Fortunately, after an acceptable amount of time had passed, the DJ invited all the wedding guests to take the dance floor. Now Daley and Tristan were insulated by the size and noise of the crowd.

His fingertips grazed the bare skin of her back. "You look smashing in this dress."

Daley shook her head slowly: "It's a nice dress. All the bridesmaids look good."

Tristan's arm tightened around her waist. "But not all of them are you. I can't wait to get you alone tonight. It's driving me nuts to think of you naked in bed with me."

She stiffened. "Maybe we shouldn't."

After a heartbeat or two, he sighed. "Why?"

"I feel guilty deceiving Tabby and John."

"I get that," he said. "I promised John I'd stay away from you this weekend and look how that ended up."

"We had outdoor sex."

"Exactly."

"So, what does that make *us*?" she asked. "People with a distinct lack of integrity?"

"It makes us horny," he said, a grin teasing his lips

upward. "Besides, it would be a huge waste to ignore such intense sexual chemistry."

"Says who?"

"Says me."

A nearby couple bumped into them and apologized. When Tristan pulled her even closer, Daley realized he was aroused. Her legs trembled. "You should probably dance with someone else now."

"That doesn't sound appealing at all."

Daley was happy in his embrace, but she didn't want her sister on her case. "At least dance with Tabby. And maybe your mother."

He grimaced. "That will kill the mood."

She laughed at him. "I think that's the idea."

"And did we land on a plan for tonight?"

Daley knew she should hold firm. Say no. Be a responsible adult. But she didn't have the willpower to walk away. She wanted one last time. One final, all-consuming interlude with the man she couldn't resist.

"Fine," she said, pretending she wasn't as interested as he was. "My room. Eleven o'clock. But for Pete's sake, be careful."

Tristan's smile was brilliant. "Yes, ma'am."

As she watched him walk away, the evening felt flatter. Less fun.

That was when she knew she was in trouble...

Everyone was aware Tabby and John were catching an early morning flight. To that end, the DJ wound things up at nine thirty. Two lines formed for pelting the newlyweds with birdseed and streamers.

And then it was over.

At least Daley had snagged five minutes alone with Tabby. The two of them cried and said mushy words and hugged each other fiercely.

Now Daley made the rounds, thanking people for coming, making sure the older guests found their way safely to the car park.

In her room, finally, she stripped to her underwear and downed two bottles of water. Though the weather had cooperated—no rain and low humidity—the day had been warm. It felt great to wallow in airconditioning.

She had too much product in her hair to do much with it, so she showered quickly and used the blow dryer. When she was done, she felt comfy and sleepy and excited all at once. What to wear was a problem.

The taupe terry hotel robe trimmed in satin was nice enough. But what about underneath?

In the end, she decided to go au naturel.

When a soft knock sounded at her door, she glanced at the clock on the bedside table. Ten fifty-five.

She checked the peephole, took a shaky breath and let him in.

"You're early," she said.

Tristan dragged her close and kissed her, pushing her gently against the closed door. "Couldn't wait."

His intensity was flattering. "Please tell me no one saw you."

His teeth flashed white as he smiled. "Nope. I was stealthy."

"And it helps that Tabby and John are otherwise occupied."

"Indeed."

Daley felt awkward suddenly. "Would you—"

Tristan's smile switched from naughty to kind. "What if we sit and talk for a few minutes? Decompress. It was a long day. Great but long."

"I'd like that," Daley said. She wasn't accustomed to having a man want her desperately. Her dating life leaned more toward companionship and the very occasional two-lonely-people hookup.

This time, she didn't turn on the fireplace.

Tristan took a seat on the sofa and patted the cushion beside him. "I won't bite," he said.

She gave him a look. "I'm not scared of you."

"Good." He yawned. "Who knew getting married was such hard work?"

"It's a billion-dollar industry, right? I remember Tabby pouring over bridal magazines when she was thirteen or fourteen. We would analyze the dresses. Study the flower choices. It's a harmless rite of passage for some girls."

"For you?" he asked, apparently serious.

Daley shrugged. "Not so much. I was an art and design major. Colors and themes interested me, but planning a whole wedding? No…"

"And if you do decide to get married someday?" His eyes danced with mischief, but his question seemed genuine.

"Well…" She tugged at the lapels of her robe, making sure her breasts and knees were covered. "I don't think I'd want all the fuss. Maybe I would elope. Not to Vegas. That's not my style. But perhaps somewhere like Cadillac Mountain in Maine…at sunrise. It's supposed to be the first spot the sun hits the continental US every morning." She wrinkled her nose. "Though to be honest, I don't know how I could avoid all the tourists."

His smile was droll. "A February wedding perhaps?"

"I'm guessing you've never been there. Even in summer, the wind can cut to the bone. I can't imagine a winter wedding." She half turned in her seat and curled her legs beneath her. "How about you? A villa in the south of France? An intimate ceremony on a yacht in the Caribbean?"

Despite the topic, Tristan looked completely relaxed. A plain gray T-shirt strained to cover his broad chest. He wore thin athletic pants and sneakers with no socks. His hair was damp. He smelled of the hotel's expensive shower gel.

He ran his hand through his hair, kicked off his shoes and stretched out his legs. "That's a good question. Honestly, if a woman and I ever decided to give things a shot, I'd be happy with a courthouse ceremony. Married is married. I'd be more interested in the honeymoon."

"I should have known."

"Liking sex is not a crime."

"I wasn't criticizing," she said quickly.

He ran his thumb along her jawbone, bringing

up the heat level, scrambling her wits. "It *sounded* critical."

"Well, then, I'm sorry. You're right. I wouldn't expect most men to care at all about wedding planning."

"But John did…"

"Because he loves Tabby. Love changes people, I think," she said.

"All the more reason not to fall in love. Change is hard and messy and painful. It's a lot easier to sail through life being yourself."

Daley heard the message loud and clear. Tristan was who he was. Woe to the woman who thought she could change him.

His philosophy didn't matter to her. She didn't desire or need to mold Tristan Hamilton into husband material. All she wanted was to have sex with him one more time.

After that, she likely wouldn't see him again until Christmas, and possibly not even then if she had enough advance warning to come up with a good excuse.

She laid her hand on his taut thigh. "It's late. Maybe we should adjourn to the bed."

A muscle in his jaw flexed. "That's what I like about you, Daley Martin. You always have the best ideas."

They stood and faced each other. Daley still felt uncertain around him. This weekend had opened her eyes to many facets of his personality, but it was far too short a time to say she *knew* him.

And honestly, she was painfully aware that *she* had started this ill-advised insanity. She had invited him inside her room last night on the flimsiest of pretexts. Fooling with ice buckets. He must have thought she was the easiest woman on the planet.

That impulsive decision wasn't like her at all, but she had no regrets. Tristan was a genius in bed. Besides, against all odds, she *liked* him. Even if he was a confirmed bachelor who thought honeymoons were more important than weddings.

He took her hand and led her to the bed. "Let's get you out of that hot robe," he said, smiling in a way that made her heart clench with *something*. Yearning, perhaps? That would be dumb. She was far too smart to *yearn* over a man like him.

While Daley held her breath, perfectly still, he fiddled with the knot in the belt, untied it and slid the robe off her shoulders. His chest rose and fell. "You're about the prettiest thing I've ever seen."

"I'm a woman, not a thing."

His lips quirked. "My bad. I should have practiced that line in my head before I said it out loud. Brown-eyed blondes make me clumsy."

"Have there been many?" she asked. "Brown-eyed blondes."

"Actually, no. You're my first."

He was staring at her body so intently, she thought she might spontaneously combust. Was it normal to feel *on fire* for another human being? For a man? She'd never experienced this level of raw, carnal heat before. And certainly not with a partner who was so unabashedly interested in sex and only sex.

To be fair, so was she.

They had skipped over all the socially acceptable dinner dates and getting-to-know-you activities. Both had one thing in common. They were living in the moment. Indulging a powerful attraction.

Daley had never picked up a stranger in a bar for a one-night stand. But this thing with Tristan came close. Despite their siblings' wedding, this fling had *temporary* written all over it. Oddly enough, though, she knew she could trust Tristan physically.

It was her heart she had to protect.

"Take off your shirt," she whispered. "Please."

His smile disappeared. A flush of color darkened his face. As he ripped the soft cotton over his head, he kicked off his shoes. The front of his pants betrayed his arousal. "Why does it feel like a lifetime since I had you?" he muttered, the words low and gravelly.

"Maybe because this afternoon was too quick to count."

"Ouch." He winced. "You're tough on my ego."

"Oh, don't be dumb," she said impatiently. "We had no choice. They're called quickies for a reason."

He closed the distance between them and cupped her face in his hands. His blue eyes darkened to deep sapphire. His lashes were long and gorgeous. "Fair warning. There won't be anything quick about tonight."

Her jaw dropped. She snapped it shut, trying not to

let him know he had destroyed her with one quiet sentence. "Is that a threat or a promise?" she asked, turning her face into his palm and nibbling his thumb.

He put a hand on her bare ass and dragged her closer, grinding his erection against her pelvis. "Kiss me, Daley."

When she was barefoot, the difference in their heights frustrated her. She went up on her tiptoes and touched her lips to his. "Gladly."

It was a great kiss. World class. As notable as the Great Pyramid or the Eiffel Tower. People should write sonnets about this kiss.

Tristan ravaged her mouth with his. Taking. Giving. Coaxing. Demanding.

Already, her legs were shaky.

He scooped her in his arms and dumped her on the bed. Then he came down beside her, still partially clothed, and took the kiss deeper still. All the while, he skated his palm over her thighs, her belly, her breasts.

When he plucked at her nipple, fire shot straight to her sex. She grabbed his hair, making him wince. "I want more than kisses," she said.

"We'll get there," he promised.

Suddenly he stopped, reared up on one elbow and narrowed his gaze. "Put your hands behind your head," he said. "If you don't touch me, we can make this last longer."

"But I want to touch you," she wailed. She was dying to touch him, restless and on the brink of something earth-shattering. Even so, she did as he asked.

Such a simple thing. Clasping her hands behind her neck. But she felt vulnerable now. Open.

Tristan moved between her legs and knelt, parting her sex with his thumbs. "I like looking at you," he muttered.

She shifted restlessly. "Well, don't. You're making me self-conscious."

He lifted his head and grinned at her. "That's not what I'm after, sweetheart. I'm more interested in you being wild and free."

Could she do that? Be wild and free? Coaxing Tristan into her room last night was the craziest thing she had ever done with a man. Besides, *wild and free* was scary.

"You need to be naked, too," she said. "It's only fair."

He shrugged. "Your call." He scooted to the side of the bed and shucked his pants. When he came back to her, his erection was full and proud.

Daley had instinctively pressed her legs together while he was gone. Tristan ended up on his hip beside her, leaning over and tracing her collarbone with his finger.

She moved restlessly. "I'm glad we scratched this itch," she said. "Your *talents* have been eye-opening."

His hand stilled on the curve of her breast. "It's not over yet. And that's not a very romantic description. *Scratched this itch*? No, I don't like that."

She moved her hands from behind her head and

reared up on her elbows. "Then what would you call it? It's definitely not romance."

Tristan's expression was thoughtful. "How about mutually satisfying pleasure?"

Six

Tristan struggled to stay a step ahead of the sexy, curvaceous, alluring woman in the bed with him. She was part femme fatale, part aloof stranger.

He wasn't a stupid man. There were boundaries in place. Erected by her. To keep him at bay.

The more she tried to devise a valley or a moat between them, emotional or otherwise, the more he wanted to breach her defenses. It was a visceral re-action on his part. Perhaps an elemental need to conquer. To revert to his caveman roots.

She pursed her lips and wrinkled her brow. "I do like pleasure," she said softly.

He moved on top of her, groaning at the sensation of skin to skin. Her soft body. His heavier, harder one. Burying his face in the curve of her neck, he inhaled her delicate scent. "I promised you slow," he said, feeling foolish. Why had he thought he could hold out?

Daley stroked his hair, making him shudder. "We can do slow the *second* time."

He reared up and studied her face. A weird shiver worked its way down his spine. He and Daley had agreed this wasn't leading anywhere. It wasn't serious. Upsetting Tabby and John when the relationship went south would be a disaster.

Tristan had no illusions about his strengths as a serious *boyfriend*. He worked all the time. He invariably found some reason to break up with a woman. Either she was too clingy or not interested enough. Or she was obsessed with home shopping shows, or she voted wrong in the last election.

Even so, there was a tiny part of him that wondered if Daley was different. If *he* was different when he was with Daley. If they might make it work beyond this one weekend.

He shook his head slightly to clear the cobwebs and dislodge those disturbing, dangerous thoughts.

Daley smiled sweetly. "I didn't mean for you to go into a trance. I want you, Tristan. Rather desperately, in fact."

"Ditto," he muttered. He slipped two fingers inside her and found her ready for him. "I can't wait. Not right now." He entered her slowly, clenching his jaw, feeling the need to come almost instantly. *Damnation*. Reciting the states and capitals didn't work.

Nothing could distract him from the pure, gut-deep *pleasure* of being inside her. What a pale, uninteresting word. *Pleasure* was too banal a description. Maybe *incendiary*. Or *mind-altering*.

Daley arched her back and gasped. "Oh, yeah," she muttered. "Just like that."

Daley bit his bottom lip, and he was lost. He slammed into her again and again, heard and felt her come, then slid over the edge into infinite, sweet darkness.

When he came to his senses, he didn't know if twenty minutes had passed or two hours. The room was dark. A warm female body lay curled half on top of him. Daley. Fast asleep. Her gentle snores made him smile.

He leaned to one side and glanced at his phone—3:00 a.m.

Daley roused. "What's wrong?"

"Nothing. Nothing at all. Go back to sleep."

The next time he checked, it was almost five. "I should go to my room," he said.

He waited for Daley to argue with him.

Instead, she turned on the bedside lamp and patted his chest. "Yes." She tested the stubble on his chin with one finger. "It's been a great weekend. Thank you for being such an entertaining best man."

Wow. That sounded like a brush-off, but under the circumstances, it was probably a valid compliment. Why did it leave him feeling disgruntled?

As he stood to reach for his clothes, a knock sounded at the door.

Panic swept across Daley's face. "It can't be anyone but Tabby. Get under the covers and lie perfectly still. Hurry." She grabbed her robe, stuffed her arms in the sleeves and belted it. "Do I look like I've been having sex?"

He winced and shrugged. "Yes." Because he knew the stakes, he hid under the comforter, feeling like a fool. The tiny bedside lamp was low wattage. It made sense it was on, right? Daley wouldn't have answered her sister's summons in a dark room.

When she opened the door, Tabby's voice was distinct. "I'm very sorry to wake you, sweetie, but I wanted to say goodbye one more time. I've never been this far away from you for so long."

John's words held humor. "She's feeling a little unsteady, I think. Too much wedding and not enough sleep."

Daley hadn't pulled back the door completely. And she was using her body to shield the view of her bed. When Tristan peeked, he couldn't see a damned thing.

As the two women hugged, the door swung a bit wider. Now, Tristan could see his brother's face. And he also witnessed the moment John grew suspicious.

Tristan froze.

If John knew, he didn't let on. "Let's go, my love. We don't want to miss our ride."

Daley hugged him, too. "Take care of her. And have a wonderful trip."

Seconds later, the crisis was over.

Daley sagged against the closed door. "Oh, my gosh. I nearly had a heart attack."

Tristan shoved the covers to his waist. "So, do I still have to go to my room?"

A slow smile lit up her face. "Absolutely not." She dropped the robe, crossed the rug and laughed softly when he pulled her down into his arms.

Sunday morning, Daley decided she needed to find a man who believed in getting eight hours of sleep. She was groggy, and the dark circles under her eyes weren't at all attractive. It didn't help her state of mind to realize Tristan was gone.

Well, of course he was. Tabby and John might have headed out early, but there was still reason to be cautious. Tristan could have bumped into anybody in the hall. People loved to gossip.

One last hurdle remained before she could get Tristan out of her mind. Tabby and John had arranged for anyone still in residence to have brunch before heading home. Other than the bride and groom, only a couple of the wedding party had checked out.

Daley showered and packed her bags. Looking around the luxurious room gave her a wistful pang. She'd had no idea at all when she checked into the hotel on Friday that she would end up in bed with her nemesis. Turns out, he wasn't half bad.

She made it to the dining room as most of the group had already arrived.

Harold Dunn spotted her and waved her over to a table for four. Tristan was already seated, looking a little the worse for wear. His expression was guarded.

Daley had been introduced to Harold at the wedding, but they hadn't really chatted.

He stood, held her chair and smiled. "Perfect timing."

There was no buffet today. A young waitress took Daley's order. The two men had just been served huge plates of pancakes, eggs and bacon.

Daley waved her hand, not quite able to look at Tristan. "Don't wait on me. You two eat before your food gets cold."

They did as she asked, but her meal arrived shortly. It was a lot. Her stomach felt queasy. If she'd had her way, she would have gone straight to her car and left. But with Tabby gone, Daley was the de facto hostess.

Light conversation carried them through the meal. When they were done, Harold sat back in his seat and stared at her with a genial smile. "I was hoping we'd have this chance, Ms. Martin. John has told me so much about you."

Daley frowned. "Call me Daley, please. He has?"

"Oh, yes. I'm impressed that someone your age has already managed to establish a viable ad agency. Starting a small business isn't easy."

"Thank you," she said. This was awkward. She didn't want to hear another explanation about why some clients wanted traditional and not trendy.

Harold reached into the inside pocket of his sport coat and pulled out a folded sheet of paper. He tapped the edge of the table with it, his expression determined. "I've been thinking about you for weeks," he said. "And I've researched your bottom line. Which leads me to a very logical conclusion."

Daley frowned, confused. "Oh?"

The older man beamed. "I'd like to buy your company and bring you under the umbrella of Lieberman and Dunn."

A split second of silence hovered around the table.

"I don't understand." When she glanced at Tristan, he looked as shocked as she was, and not happy about the situation, though his expression smoothed immediately.

Harold continued, "It would be a win-win for both of us, my dear. I'm an old fart, but even I know my company needs to lean into the twenty-first century. And I could provide you with a much wider crop of potential clients."

Daley stuttered, trying not to offend. "I don't think—"

He held up his hand. "I know we'll have to meet and hash out details. It goes without saying that I'll bring your staff along, also. One plus for them will be a more comprehensive package of employee benefits—insurance, pensions, etcetera. You've built a marvelous thing, Daley. Together, we can take it to the next level."

She chewed her lip. "Shouldn't you discuss this plan with other interested parties?" She was painfully aware of Tristan's stoic quietness.

Harold looked at his CEO. "Well, Tristan. What do you think?"

There was a heartbeat of silence. Tristan's expression was inscrutable. "It's your company, Harold," he said flatly. "You're still at the helm. Whatever you want."

"Well, there you go." Harold's smile was jovial. "It makes perfect sense, Daley. John is my godson. Now Tabby is one of us. You're Tabby's sister. Bringing you into the family business completes the circle." He tapped the folded paper again. "This isn't a legal document, but I'll stand behind these numbers. Come to my office one afternoon this week, and we'll hammer out an official offer."

Daley tried to swallow the nervous lump in her throat. Her voice still came out croaky. "I don't really know what to say."

He handed her the paper. "You don't have to look at this now. It's been a long emotional weekend, I'm sure. Go home. Think about what I've said. Take your time. I've put a phone contact for my administrative assistant at the bottom. Call her and set up a time that works for you. I'm excited about this partnership. I hope you will be, too."

Two of the wedding party stopped by the table to say goodbye to Daley. While she was speaking with them, Tristan stood, excused himself and disappeared. Perhaps he hadn't packed yet. It was almost checkout time.

When it was just Harold and Daley, she grimaced. "I'm very flattered, Mr. Dunn. But surely you could see that Tristan doesn't think this is a good idea."

Harold waved a dismissive hand. "My godson is a brilliant man. But he likes to keep a tight rein on his domain. That can be a good thing or a bad thing. He'll get used to the idea. Don't you worry."

"But I don't even know if this is what I want to do, no offense."

"None taken. You're a smart woman. When you see my offer, I feel sure you'll be interested. It's generous and good for both of us."

There wasn't much else to say. Daley said goodbye to Harold and did the same with the bridesmaids and groomsmen still lingering over their coffees. Then she went to her room, picked up her bags and walked to the reception desk to drop off her key.

Tristan was nowhere in sight. Surely, he wouldn't leave without saying *something* to her. Maybe he was more upset by his mentor's surprising business move than he let on. Though to be honest, his visible recoil at the beginning had been telling.

When she walked outside to the parking lot and put her things in the car, she looked around surreptitiously. She knew Tristan drove a flashy red high-end sports car, because John had bragged about getting to drive it one day.

No vehicle matched that description. It seemed that Tristan had simply loaded up and left the property.

Daley told herself she wasn't hurt. They had both been very clear about the parameters of this weekend's dalliance. Private and temporary.

Even so, his behavior seemed odd at best.

She drove home, glad to see her apartment and get back to normal. Tomorrow was a run-of-the-mill workday. Of course, it was going to be hard to concentrate in light of all that had happened this weekend.

Ordinarily, she would call Tabby and talk things out. But her sister was still on a flight or a layover somewhere, not to mention several time zones away. Besides, she wouldn't have mentioned Tristan. Would she?

Did Tabby ever have to know what happened?

John might tell her. At least the part he knew.

They wouldn't be home for two weeks. Daley had time to make up her mind. But not about Harold's offer. That decision was far more pressing.

Daley turned down the AC, checked the fridge to see if she needed to make a grocery run, and then *finally* steeled herself to reach in her purse and extract the folded sheet of paper Harold had handed her.

When she opened it and read the number at the bottom, her jaw dropped. That couldn't be right. Was her little company honestly worth so much? Harold was a shrewd businessman. He might be sentimental about family connections, but he wouldn't squander valuable resources on a whim.

A warm glow settled beneath her ribs. Seeing the numbers in black and white was good for her professional ego. She *had* done something impressive. And now, all her hard work was about to bear fruit.

Maybe…

She studied the paper more carefully. Aside from the cash purchase price, Harold had listed possible salary ranges for her employees and for Daley. Was that a sticking point for her? She wouldn't be the boss anymore. At least not entirely. Her employees would still answer to her, but Daley would be part of Lieberman and Dunn.

Is that something she wanted?

In the end, the startling numbers in the buyout offer were not the biggest thing to consider. Daley would be working in the same building with Tristan every single day.

How would that play out?

They had both agreed that a real relationship between them was ill-advised. Tristan didn't want to commit to anything permanent, and Daley was focused on her career. Though to be fair, with this new information, maybe she would have time for a personal life after all. But when Tristan lost interest and ended things, John and Tabby would inevitably be affected.

For the rest of the day, Daley struggled with her thoughts. Her personal life and work life had collided in a big way. Though she would try to play hard to get with Harold, she would be a fool to turn him down.

She went for a run, cleaned the apartment, prepped her lunches for the week and watched a movie she hadn't seen on Netflix. By nine thirty, she was drooping.

The man who had kept her awake for most of last night was impossible to erase from her brain. She was fond of him. More than fond, really. And the *wanting* was going to be a problem. She moved restlessly beneath the sheet, touching her own breast. Remembering his strong fingers caressing her there. What was she going to do about Tristan?

Monday morning, she made it into the office half an hour before anyone else. It was far too soon to say anything about possible upcoming developments. Harold might change his mind. The deal could fall through. Perhaps Daley, herself, would reconsider.

When it came down to the essential question of what to do, she knew she couldn't give Harold an answer without talking to Tristan first. He had put his cell number in her phone after the wedding. In case they had to coordinate their clandestine plans last night.

She closed her office door and told herself her hands weren't shaking. This wasn't some middle school romance. A business call was entirely in order.

But she would text instead.

Tristan, could we meet for half an hour to discuss Harold's offer? At Portofino's perhaps? Noon? Or one. Or even tomorrow. I can't give him an answer until you and I clear the air.

Portofino's menu offered homemade pizza and salads. The restaurant had the added bonus of being right across the street from the office building that housed Lieberman and Dunn. If she remembered correctly, the prestigious agency occupied two full floors.

Tristan's response was surprisingly quick.

I can do 1 pm. See you then.

She frowned. Not exactly a sonnet. But what did she expect? Her affair with Tristan Hamilton ended the moment he sneaked out of her room yesterday morning.

When she dove into the day's schedule, it was easier to ignore the dull ache in her chest. It had been a great weekend, but Tabby was married now. Tristan was nothing more than Tabby's brother-in-law. And Daley had a business to run.

Her staff was surprised to hear she would be out for lunch. Tabby frequently ate a sandwich at her desk. Maybe it wasn't good for her mental health, but it kept her from getting behind.

"I'll be back by two fifteen," she said. "Don't forget we have a meeting at four with the director of that dance studio."

She ran out the door, hoping they would think this lunch was personal and not business. It's possible one or two of them might be suspicious when they heard about a collaboration with Harold's firm. Her people were young and quirky, and most of them worked from home one day a week. They might not like the idea of more structure.

Daley would have to worry about that later.

Right now, she had to deal with Tristan.

She beat him to the restaurant and snagged a table, pausing to send him a brief text so he could find her. She'd been seated maybe three minutes when he strolled through the lunch crowd in her direction.

Women watched him. It was impossible not to. He carried himself with the careless confidence of a man who was handsome and successful.

Daley closed her eyes briefly and tried to think of *anything* but a naked Tristan.

"Hi," she said briskly, looking up at him. "Thank you for coming. I know it was short notice."

He took the chair opposite hers, picked up a menu and studied it. "I'm starving."

The server had been watching. She hurried over and, of course, looked at Tristan first. "May I get you something to drink?"

Tristan offered her a hundred-watt smile. "We're in a bit of a time crunch. I'll have the six-inch pepperoni with olives and a small salad. Plus a Diet Coke." He turned. "Daley?"

"A mini calzone with a side salad. Lemonade, please."

The young woman walked away. Suddenly, Daley was alone with Tristan.

It helped that they were surrounded by at least thirty other people. But not much.

He looked stressed. That was her first thought. Followed quickly by the realization that she needed to cut to the chase. He might only have half an hour.

"You weren't happy about Harold's offer," she said bluntly.

He leaned back in his chair. "Wow. You aren't

even going to sweet-talk me first? I thought we had something, Ms. Martin."

His lopsided grin was rueful.

Daley stared back at him, narrowing her eyes. "You left the hotel so fast there were skid marks on the driveway."

He rolled his shoulders. "I was upset."

"Why?" She frowned. "Are you really so against L&D buying my business?"

"On the contrary. I think it's a splendid idea."

The server set drinks on the table and batted her eyelashes at Tristan. "Let me know if you need refills," she said.

When it was just the two of them again, Daley studied his face. "I don't understand. I saw your expression, Tristan. You were pissed when Harold tossed out his plan."

"No," he said. He picked up a slender breadstick and used it to drum on the table. "I was worried and a little shocked. But not pissed."

"Worried about what?"

He shook his head slowly, those blue eyes gleaming. "Surely, you're not that blind. How in the hell are we supposed to work together and not sleep together?"

Daley stared at him, feeling her face heat. "You know dozens of women. Our thing was a weekend special. Over and done."

"You underestimate your appeal. I dreamed about you last night. Woke up with an erection the size of the Washington Monument."

Daley put a hand over her mouth to smother her laugh. "Does that kind of line get you women?" She raised an eyebrow.

"It's the truth." He scowled at the breadstick. "When Harold said he wanted to move your company into our office space, all I could think about was how miserable that would be. Running into you in the hall every day and not taking you home."

"But we both agreed that continuing anything personal would be a mistake."

"We did."

"So where does that leave us?"

He shrugged. "Was it a good offer?"

She nodded her head slowly. "It was fantastic. I'd be insane to refuse."

"I figured as much. Harold is a whip-smart businessman. He would have studied every angle before he spoke to you."

"I haven't run this by any of my staff. They may not like it."

Tristan shrugged. "It's not up to them, is it? You're the boss, Daley. That can be a lonely thing sometimes. The decision will have to be yours."

"And if I've already made up my mind?" She gave him a challenging stare, waiting for him to argue or bluster or try to manipulate her.

His jaw tightened. "If you've already made up your mind, then I assume your answer is yes. Which means I'll have to find a way to stay away from you."

Seven

Tristan knew he was screwed. He'd known it the moment Harold rolled out a fantastic business offer to Daley Martin. Everything was going to change.

Daley's skill set would be good for the company. No argument there. Tristan didn't begrudge her this opportunity. But he had no illusions about how hard this would be for him personally.

He couldn't have a serious relationship with Daley. He'd known that from the beginning. Which was why they had both agreed to limit their affair to one wild wedding weekend.

The trouble was, he hadn't expected to find himself in the deep end so quickly. She made him feel slightly desperate and embarrassingly off his game.

In his experience, sex was light and fun. He treated his partners well and always parted on good terms.

With Daley, he felt *uncertain*, for lack of a better word.

Even right now, she was staring at him as if she could see the turmoil of his thoughts. She chewed her lip. "Harold's offer mentioned a twelve-month trial period. Either L&D or I can dissolve the contract with no penalty during the first year. Surely that's enough time to see if you and I can be just friends."

Tristan already knew the answer to that. They couldn't. *He* couldn't.

He reached across the table and took her hand in his. "I've made love to you, Daley. Multiple times. Each one better than the last. I don't know about you, but for me, those experiences left a mark."

She didn't try to free herself. In fact, she turned over her hand and linked her fingers with his, making his gut twist with unexpected warmth.

"I hear what you're saying, Tristan. But I'm sure if we set boundaries, this attraction we're feeling will fizzle. You know John and Tabby will expect us to be smart about working together. We love them both. We don't want to drag them into the middle of a tempestuous affair that at some point will crumble."

"Are you so sure it will crumble?" He rubbed the back of her hand with his thumb.

"Well, of course it will." The words were impatient. "Be honest. What's the longest you've ever dated a woman?"

He gave it serious thought. "As a full-grown adult? A month," he muttered.

"Well, there you go. I'm a novelty to you right now. But you know the old saying? *Familiarity breeds contempt?* When I'm in the building all the time, you'll find other women far more interesting. I'll be the co-worker down the hall. Nothing more."

"You're awfully sure about that. I'm not."

"You said it yourself. You're a workaholic. I'm focused on growing my brand and my business. Neither of us is interested in marriage."

"So, why can't we have a no-strings-attached affair?"

Daley sighed. "It's tempting. But people would find out. Inevitably. And aside from Tabby and John, we'd be setting a bad example in the workplace."

"I'm not going to be your boss."

"I know that. But…"

He scowled. "But what?"

Daley sat back and removed her hand from his grasp. "This opportunity is important to me. I like you a lot. And I enjoyed everything we did this weekend. But sometimes a woman needs to focus on her future."

Did she really think he would do anything to hinder her professionally?

He exhaled, trying not to notice the way her silky, cream-colored tank revealed the shape of her body. Today, there was no sexy wedding attire. She looked like an ad for the professional woman. Trim black pants. Black heels. And the black blazer she had hung on the back of her chair.

"So that's it," he said flatly. "Friends but no benefits."

Her smile was wry. "Yes, please."

"You drive a hard bargain."

"You'll find someone else, Tristan. And so will I."

The weeks after her lunch with Tristan were some of the busiest and most stressful of Daley's adult life. She met with Harold, hammered out the details of a deal and signed a million pieces of paper.

Then came the packing. So much packing. It shouldn't have been a big deal. Harold had the newest, fanciest phone systems and internet capabilities. All Daley had to do was box up files, tape dispensers and paper clips, and make sure to mark which bookcases and chairs and tables were going.

She had to pay out the last two months of her current lease, but the cost was well worth the upcoming rewards.

Unfortunately, the timeframe meant moving on July 1, which happened to be Atlanta's first triple-digit day of the summer. Not that Daley actually needed to carry anything, but she had to be available in and out of the building.

It was a Saturday. Harold had given her keys. No one from Lieberman and Dunn was at work. That was a good thing, because Daley was red-faced and drenched in sweat. Tabby had wanted to come along for moral support, but she and John had to make a quick jaunt to Asheville for a friend's wedding.

So Daley handled the transition on her own.

By the end of the afternoon, her new office space looked great. The brass placard on the door in the hallway had her name. She paused to polish a smudge with her sleeve. *Daley Martin, VP, Digital Specialist.* That had been Harold's doing. The title didn't exactly reflect her skill set, but it was a start.

When the movers left, she plopped into her chair and gave it a spin.

She was excited and scared. The hollow feeling in her chest would go away once she started working next week. None of her current clients had batted an eye about the change in venue, nor the fact that Daley was now affiliated with Lieberman and Dunn.

They all assumed it was a step up…which it was.

It was time to go home and take a shower, but she wanted to stay for a little while and see if she could pretend this was where she belonged. All transitions were hard, even good ones. Soon, this building would seem like her new nest. She hoped.

She had done more than work in the last month. Tabby and John had finally returned from their honeymoon. Daley had spent part of a Saturday with them, hearing all about the trip. Tabby had gifted her with a stunning red-and-gold silk pareu, along with a cultured pearl necklace in shades of gray and black.

Daley's baby sister glowed. She was tanned and relaxed, and she radiated happiness.

It was hard not to feel a twinge of envy.

The one thing Daley had *not* done was see Tristan. Though she visited Harold's office on at least four separate occasions, Tristan had made himself scarce.

Daley knew she should be glad about that. He was keeping his end of the bargain. But the truth was, she missed him. Still, it was clearly for the best.

A week before Daley had moved her office to Lieberman and Dunn, John had showed up at her old office. He quizzed her at length about her relationship with his brother. Daley told him politely to mind his own business.

But John had been like a dog with a bone.

"Either you tell Tabby what happened at the wedding, or I will," he said. "I don't want her finding out later and thinking I deliberately kept her in the dark."

Daley glared at him. "Then you tell her."

John shook his head. "No. It will be better coming from you. I'd rather not get involved."

As much as it irritated Daley to have her personal life dissected, she knew in her heart John was right. So she found a quiet moment one day over lunch to tell Tabby a much edited version of the truth.

Daley had spun the encounter as an impulsive hookup born of wedding excitement and one too many glasses of champagne.

That last part was a lie. Daley and Tristan had been dead sober. But Daley had to offer some excuse for her aberrant behavior.

She might have also left the impression that intimacy with Tristan had happened only once. No need to go into details that might shock her little sister.

Tabby hadn't seemed too surprised or upset. But she had issued a warning. "He doesn't do long-term. You know that, right?"

Daley had laughed it off. "Of course," she said. "You don't have to worry about me. It was a weekend fling. Over and done with. But let me tell you about the guy I met at the coffee shop last week..."

Now, Daley sat in her new office feeling slightly guilty about how she had misled her sister. But she didn't regret it. Daley and Tristan were no longer an item. No need to make a big fuss about what had happened between them. It meant nothing. It was only sex.

In her car driving home, she pondered all the reasons that calling it *only sex* made her uneasy. She had never been a woman who chose reckless physical encounters. She was more comfortable getting to know a man before she was intimate with him.

And even then, there had been only a handful of guys who made it into her bed.

Tristan was different. She knew that.

She didn't like it. But she wasn't going to lie to herself.

They had Monday and Tuesday off for the Fourth of July, so it was Wednesday before she and her staff met up in the new digs. Audra, one of her copywriters was visibly awed. "This place is off the charts," she said, keeping her voice low. "They even have two-ply toilet paper in the restrooms."

Daley grinned. "Our old office wasn't that bad. Try not to look like a country bumpkin in the big city. We might have been slumming it, but we were successful enough to catch the attention of Harold Dunn. That's something to brag about."

The phone rang, and soon the day was in motion. Daley was pleased to see her team pick up where they left off without missing a beat. There would be new clients soon. Or so she hoped. It was important not to fall behind.

At five o'clock, everyone went home.

Daley lingered to straighten her new desk.

When there was a knock at her open door, she looked up and saw Harold framed there. He smiled at her. "How was day one?"

"Very good, I think."

"I thought I'd give you time to catch your breath. Tomorrow at ten, though, we'll have an all-staff meeting, and I'll introduce you to the rest of our folks. They're eager to meet you. We'll have a few light refreshments, and you can give them a brief pitch about what you do with your social media focus."

"I hope that won't ruffle any feathers. I don't want anyone to think I believe my way is best."

"Relax," he said. "It will be fine."

"I thought Tristan might drop by today," she said. "To wish me luck. Is he upset that you've done this? Or maybe out of town?"

"Neither. The Lyme disease thing flared up late last week. The doctor has told him to rest. He's hoping to be back on Thursday."

"Oh. I'm so sorry." Her brain spun. "Do you think he'd mind if I dropped some dinner by for him?"

"I'm sure he'd be thrilled."

"I don't have his address."

"I'll text it to you," Harold said. "Give him my best."

And that was how Daley found herself on Tristan's doorstep an hour later holding a bag of food and getting drenched in a sudden thunderstorm. The small fold-up umbrella she kept in her car was nowhere to be found, not that it would have helped. The wind blew sideways, and lightning danced all around her. This attempt at "loving her neighbor" fell under the heading "no good deed goes unpunished."

For ten seconds she thought about getting in her car and driving away. The food was probably cold anyway. Her vanity urged her not to let Tristan see her like this. She was soaked through to the skin, and her mascara had probably run.

Before she could decide what to do, the front door swung open. Her heart stopped.

Tristan stood there frowning. "Daley? What are you doing? I saw you through the window."

Another bolt of lightning hit—followed a split second later by a huge boom. She had to raise her voice. "Harold said you weren't feeling well. I brought you dinner." She thrust the soggy bag at him. "I'll see you at the office later in the week."

She was desperate to get away. This was a very bad idea. Just seeing him brought back every delicious, naughty detail of their tryst during Tabby's wedding weekend.

He looked pale and tired. His navy shorts and

Braves T-shirt were wrinkled and faded. It was a shock to see him looking less than perfect, though a rumpled Tristan still turned her bones weak.

When she turned to leave, he grabbed her arm. "Don't be stupid. I'm not letting you go out in this."

Daley shoved a hank of wet hair out of her face. "In case you haven't noticed, I'm already soaked. I'll be home in no time."

"If you don't get struck by lightning." His impatient retort underscored his attempt to drag her inside.

The next lightning strike convinced her.

As she stood shivering in his foyer, he set the bag on a small table. "I'll find something dry for you to put on."

"That's not neces—"

She was too late. He was already gone.

Tristan returned less than five minutes later. "These sweatpants will be huge on you, but they have a drawstring waist. The T-shirt should be okay." He pointed. "That door is a guest bathroom."

Daley didn't bother to argue. Despite the fact that it was July, she was freezing and miserable. Her new-ish sandals were probably ruined.

When she ducked into the small half bath and glanced in the mirror, she groaned. Dreadful. Absolutely dreadful.

She stripped off her simple navy cotton dress, kicked off her shoes, and decided her damp bra had to go as well. Maybe he wouldn't notice.

Tristan's pants looked ludicrous on her, but they

were soft and warm. So was the T-shirt. She rolled up the pants legs as best she could. When she stepped out of the powder room, he was staring into the paper sack, frowning.

"There's only one burger in here," he said. "Where's yours?"

"I hadn't planned on staying. I didn't even mean to come inside." Being so close to him jangled her nerves. Made her doubt her choices.

He shrugged. "We'll share this one. Follow me."

Protesting would be useless. Tristan was a man accustomed to being in charge. In his beautiful modern kitchen, he grabbed two plates out of the cabinet. "Have a seat," he said.

The table in the breakfast nook was covered with mail. She moved some of it to one side and perched on a chair. "You don't look good," she said.

For the first time, a small smile curved his lips. "Neither do you."

"You know what I mean. Harold said you've been ill again. Lyme disease?"

Irritation painted his face. "The doc says my symptoms may flare up occasionally for six months or more. I'm supposed to get eight hours of sleep every night, avoid stress and eat a balanced diet."

"How's that going?" She dared to tease him.

His sharp glance made her shiver. "How do you think?"

He cut the burger in half and grabbed two water bottles from the fridge. "I haven't been to the store," he said. "Sorry."

"You're a grown man. Eat the whole burger. I have stuff at home."

"My appetite is nonexistent right now. You might as well share."

As meals went, this one was high on the awkward chart. She wanted to reclaim the affectionate banter they had shared during the wedding weekend. And to enjoy the simmering hunger. But Tristan's wishes were a mystery.

Both the burger and the hand-cut fries were cold. Still, they tasted good. She had been so busy with her first day at the new offices, she hadn't even paused for a pack of crackers at lunchtime.

They ate in silence for several minutes. His mood seemed volatile.

"What are your symptoms?" she asked quietly.

He shrugged. "Fatigue. Muscle aches. Some joint pain. They've got me on one more round of antibiotics as a precaution."

"I'm sorry."

"It's not that big a deal. I'm just impatient to be done with this."

"I think I understand that."

He finished everything on his plate, drained the bottle of water and sat back. For the first time, his mood and his expression shifted to intimacy. "Thanks for taking pity on me. I mean that very seriously. I haven't felt like fixing anything, and food delivery around here is iffy. The burger was great."

"You're welcome."

"How was your first day?"

"Decent. Stressful. Exciting."

"I've missed you, Daley."

She froze, sensing danger. Or was that why she had come? "Um… I've missed you, too. But honestly, I've been so busy I haven't had much time for…"

He lifted an eyebrow. "Memories?"

If there was a trace of sarcasm in that word, she didn't take it personally. "Something like that."

He stood up and stretched, revealing a strip of taut, muscled abdomen at his waist. "Leave the dishes. Let's go into the den."

Daley stood, too, tugging at her pants that wanted to end up on the floor. "I should go," she said. "It's been a long day."

"Take pity on me," he said. "I'm bored and grumpy."

"And that's my problem how?"

He was adorable when he was vulnerable. But he was also gorgeous and fun and sexy, and something about him did bad things to Daley's best intentions.

"C'mon, woman. Watch a movie with me."

"I can't stay that long," she said, trailing in his wake.

He turned on a single lamp and sprawled on the sofa. "Come sit, Daley."

She stood in front of him. "You and I both know that's a terrible idea. I was trying to be nice."

"Were you?" He cocked his head and looked at her until she flushed.

"Yes," she muttered.

"Or maybe you wanted to see me as much as I've wanted to see you. Five or six weeks is a long time."

"We agreed not to do this," she said, her heart beating faster.

"Do what?"

"You know exactly what."

There was a lot at stake here. During Tabby's wedding weekend, Daley had technically started all the fooling around with Tristan when she asked him to come inside her room and pour ice from his bucket into hers.

Now, Tristan had kept his word. He had avoided her for days on end. Was she going to be the one to break their run of common sense?

"I'm leaving," she said, urging her bare feet to move.

He put his thumb on her knee, rubbing in gentle circles. Who knew that spot was one of her erogenous zones?

"Don't go," he said, the words husky. "I'm not contagious." His blue eyes gleamed as he looked up at her.

"I need to be in bed early. Tomorrow is a workday."

What a dumb thing to say. But at least it made him smile.

"It's only seven, Daley. Live a little. Besides…"

She frowned. "Besides what?"

An odd look crossed his face. Discomfiture?

He rolled to his feet. Because of how close she stood to the sofa, they were now practically nose to nose. Tristan tucked her damp hair behind her ears. "I've missed you," he said, his breath warm on her cheek. "And not just the sex. I've missed talking to you and laughing with you. What do you think that means?"

"It means nothing," she snapped. He was scaring her. Because he was saying words she wanted to hear, and that was dangerous.

"Don't I deserve a reward for good behavior?" His lopsided smile was filled with sensual intent.

"Maybe." She sighed. "What do you think is fair? I brought you dinner."

He kissed her forehead. "I was imagining something more personal." He cupped her breasts in his hands. His touch was gentle through the soft cotton of the T-shirt, but it was like pouring gasoline on a fire. Her nipples tightened, and heat coiled between her legs.

She was embarrassed at the noise that escaped her throat.

When he heard it, Tristan's eyes glittered, and his cheeks flushed. "You like this?" he asked, squeezing carefully.

"You know the answer to that," she said, resting her cheek against his hard chest.

"I want to make love to you, Daley. Please."

The silence in the room filled a vast canyon of doubt. Nothing had changed. All the reasons for Daley to keep Tristan Hamilton at arm's length still existed.

She wasn't a careless or destructive person. Her priorities were clear: Family. Career. Self-care. And self-improvement.

Having a wild, illogical affair didn't make the list.

But, oh, how she wanted him. She cupped his wide shoulders in her hands, feeling his strength, his undeniable masculinity.

She had never met a man more interesting, more entertaining, more able to make her yearn and burn for him.

"Just this once," she said, rationalizing wildly to get what she wanted. "We're not changing our status."

His entire body tensed. "Of course not," he said quietly. "Whatever you think is best, Daley."

She rolled her eyes at him. "Go ahead. Tell me I'm a spineless, weak-willed, ridiculous woman."

He slid his hands into her hair and dragged her mouth to his. "I would never say such a thing. I think you're perfect."

Eight

Tristan scooped Daley into his arms and carried her down the hall to his bedroom. Earlier tonight he had felt like hell. Apparently, lust was a powerful narcotic. Now, he was invincible, all his aches and pains forgotten.

Daley smiled up at him. "I had no idea you were so strong. All my girly parts are impressed."

"Brat." He kicked open the door, strode to the bed and dumped her on the mattress. "I'm just getting started," he promised.

When he sprawled beside her and yanked at the knot in her pants—technically *his pants*—he cursed as his fingers fumbled.

Daley tried to help. "Sorry. I double-knotted it."

Finally, the knot gave way. He dragged the soft

fabric to her ankles and tugged it free. "Lift your arms." Soon, he had the T-shirt on the floor as well. He stared at her, his gaze roving greedily from her damp hair and appealing face to her feminine toes. "You're incredibly alluring, Daley."

Her cheeks had turned a delicate pink. "I'll bet you say that to all the girls who wear your clothes."

"You might be the first," he said.

"I find that hard to believe." The words were quiet. A shadow of *something* flickered in those deep brown eyes.

He leaned over her, supporting himself on both hands. "Then believe this," he said. His breath sawed in and out of his chest painfully. Desperation edged his words. "I have never wanted a woman as much as I want you. I fantasize about you every night. I've jerked off more in the last six weeks than the last six years. You're a drug in my system. And I can't go cold turkey. Lord knows, I've tried."

"Get undressed," she said, her gaze filled with the same spiraling need. "We're wasting time."

She didn't have to ask him twice. "I'm not as grubby as I look," he said, panting. "I showered this afternoon."

"Not important." She pulled his head down for a kiss.

Tristan moved his tongue against hers, trying to go slow, trying to be tender. But Daley was having none of it.

She curled her legs around his waist. "Hurry," she begged. "Hurry."

He entered her with one strong thrust. Little yellow spots danced in front of his eyes. The way her tight passage squeezed him was sheer magic. Beneath him, she was soft and impetuous—feminine and demanding.

Strong slender arms wrapped around his neck, threatening to strangle him. Not that he minded. What a way to go.

He moved in and out of her, setting up a rhythm that pleased them both.

Daley had closed her eyes at first, but now, she looked at him intently. As if she were searching for answers in his gaze.

Her eyes mesmerized him. The chocolate irises were almost eclipsed by her pupils. She sank her teeth into her bottom lip as if she were trying not to make noise.

He nuzzled her nose with his. "You can scream my name, darlin', as loud as you want. No one will hear you."

Somehow, she managed to lift her chin and give him a superior look. "You're not *that* amazing, Mr. Hamilton. I think I can control myself."

"We'll see about that."

He teased her with shallow thrusts, nibbled her neck and then lost control. He shouted her name there at the end, but Daley only moaned. Even so, the sound caused his skin to erupt in gooseflesh.

"I like making you come," he said, breathing hard. "And I like *watching* you come. You're even more beautiful than usual in that moment."

She stretched her arms over her head. "You're better than two glasses of wine. Plus, I can drive afterward."

He frowned. "Thanks? I think?"

Rubbing her thumb over his bottom lip, she grinned. "I'm sorry you've not been feeling well. If you're this good when you're ill, it's no wonder you have women panting after you all the time."

Tristan rolled onto his back beside her and rested an arm across his forehead. He wasn't functioning at a hundred percent, but having Daley here was good medicine. Who knew if this would ever happen again? Tonight was a surprise. He'd better take his chance.

"Daley," he said quietly.

"Hmm?" She might have dozed off.

"May I ask you a personal question?"

He felt her body stiffen. "I suppose."

"I asked Tabby when she and John were here recently, but she said it was your story to tell. You alluded to something bad that happened when you were young. In your early twenties. Will you tell me what it was?"

She rolled to face him and propped her head on her hand. "Why?"

That was a good question. He wasn't sure. But he felt an urgency about it.

"I want to know you," he said slowly. "We've gotten things turned around in this friendship. Maybe I'd like to back up and remedy that."

Her gaze was steady. "And you'll be willing to be as open with me?"

His stomach clenched. "I'll try."

"Okay." She nodded. "But do you mind if we go back to the den?"

Without waiting for an answer, she gathered her clothes and ducked into his bathroom. When she reappeared a few minutes later, he was waiting for her down the hall.

He let her have her own seat this time. No point in tempting fate. Even wearing his ridiculously oversize clothes, she looked adorably appealing.

"Would you like something to drink?" he asked.

"I'm fine," she said.

"Daley?"

"It's embarrassing," she said. "Or maybe I've always been embarrassed because I was so caught off guard."

"Tell me," he said softly.

"I had my own apartment when I was twenty-four. And a good job at an ad agency. I was already thinking about starting something on my own, but you know…baby steps."

"So Tabby would still have been in college?"

"Yes. It was her freshman year. We didn't get to see each other as often as before, and I missed her. My parents had invited me over for dinner. I think empty nest was catching up with them, and they liked to hear about my life and see how I was doing."

"Was your mother a good cook?"

"Not as good as my grandmother, but yes. I got to

the house early that day. They had run to the store to pick up something she had forgotten. Daddy drove her. I had a key, of course, so I let myself in. I think I was going to watch TV or scroll through Instagram. It was the house Tabby and I had grown up in, so it was nice to be home."

Tristan didn't know where this was going, but he could hear the tension in her voice, as if even now, the telling wasn't easy.

"Were they gone long?"

"No. Maybe forty-five minutes. I had just parked my car in the driveway and gone inside when the doorbell rang. I peeked out. It was our neighbor, Mr. Spalding. He and his wife have lived next door since Tabby and I were little. I thought maybe he needed to borrow something. I opened the door. He said my father had promised to loan him a book—a novel Daddy had just finished reading. It was in the office, probably. All he wanted to do was get it and he'd be on his way. I honestly never thought a thing about it. It was an ordinary day, and he was an ordinary man I'd known my whole life."

Tristan's stomach cramped with dread. "What then?"

"I saw the book immediately. My father was very organized with his library. I had to reach up to the top shelf. When I did, Mr. Spalding came up behind me and slid both hands under my shirt. He pushed my bra aside and hurt my breasts, pinched them hard. I was so shocked it took me a moment to react."

"God, Daley."

She curled into a ball in her chair. Tristan wondered if she realized how defensive her posture was...

There was silence for a moment. Then she grimaced. "I understood later when I had time to think it through. He saw my parents drive away. And he saw me arrive. He must have made a split-second decision. A crime of opportunity."

"Did he..."

"Rape me? No. I took a self-defense course in college. When I caught my breath and managed to react, I whirled around, kneed him in the balls and shoved the heel of my hand up into his nose. I may have broken it. I don't know. But it bled a lot."

"I'm glad. The bastard deserved much worse."

"I told him if he didn't get his sleazy ass out of the house in thirty seconds, I was calling the police." She smiled for the first time. "He ran like a scared little boy being chased by rabid dogs."

Tristan exhaled sharply. "I'm so sorry that happened to you."

She played with a strand of her hair, not looking at him. "Nothing happened. Not really. I was lucky. I realize that."

"You're wrong," Tristan said flatly. "Something did happen. You were sexually assaulted. Did you tell your parents?"

"No." She shot him a look. "I know you think that's stupid. But Mr. Spalding and my father were friends. And to be honest, Tabby and I didn't have the greatest relationship with our dad. He was distant. Hard to know. All the hugs came from our mom."

Tristan tried to come to terms with the story Daley had told him. Clearly, it had marked her. Surely any woman would have been affected.

Did she have trouble with intimacy after that? He couldn't bring himself to ask that very personal question. Something she had said to him at the wedding made him think her sexual experience wasn't extensive.

It made sense. She might have had a hard time putting herself in physically vulnerable situations. "Thank you for telling me," he said quietly.

"It's no big deal." Daley stood and hitched her pants. "I'll go now," she said. "Thanks for dinner." She gave him an impudent smile for the little joke she made.

He didn't try to stop her. They had reached uncertain ground. "You have a kind heart, Daley Martin. I appreciate the food and the company." He followed her as she walked back to the foyer and collected her wet clothes.

She slid her feet into soggy sandals and clutched the rest of her belongings to her chest. "And don't forget the sex," she said. "Are you going to thank me for that?"

"No," he said bluntly. "That was for us. Equally. It was mutual at the wedding, and it was today. We may not be the perfect couple—or a couple at all—but we sure as hell have chemistry."

She nodded slowly. "You're not wrong. But to be honest, I almost flunked chemistry in college, so I wouldn't put too much stock in that."

He chuckled. "I stand fair-warned."

Daley ducked in close to give him a quick kiss. Her lips were warm and sweet. He could have put an arm around her. Held her tight. But he sensed she wasn't comfortable with the situation, so he let her go. She smiled as she stepped outside. "See you at work when you're better. Good night, Tristan."

At home, Daley stripped off Tristan's clothes and took a hot shower. After the storm, the heat had returned, but it didn't matter. She was cold to the bone.

She needed to go straight to bed so she could get a solid eight hours of sleep. This week at Lieberman and Dunn was turning out to be stressful in multiple ways. Tomorrow morning would come early. Unfortunately, she was keyed up, and the knot of worry in the pit of her stomach wasn't conducive to peaceful sleep.

Tonight, she had stepped over an invisible line. It was fine to pretend she took food to Tristan out of altruistic motives. But the truth was hard to avoid. At least on some subconscious level, she must have assumed they might end up in bed.

If Tristan was not boyfriend material, why did she go to his house?

He'd been a perfect gentleman at work. Their paths hadn't crossed.

Daley was the one who broke their unspoken agreement.

Maybe Tristan was okay with that. What man wouldn't be?

But now, she faced the fruits of her impulsive choices. Seeing Tristan ill and pale tonight had shaken her. If he was vulnerable and not just a convenient sex partner, she had to see him as more than her sister's new brother-in-law.

And seeing him—really *seeing* him—raised a scary specter. Daley Martin might find herself falling in love. She already liked him. He was an entertaining companion. She adored the way he made love to her. He was smart and funny and though he had a healthy ego, he wasn't a jerk like some guys.

Tristan Hamilton was a catch.

Except he wasn't.

He didn't want to be caught. He'd made that very clear.

Her head ached from wrestling with impossible questions. After her shower, she rummaged in the kitchen cabinets until she found a packet of cocoa mix that wasn't out of date. Who said you couldn't have hot chocolate in July?

She nuked the water in the microwave, stirred in the powder and added a few miniature marshmallows. All in all, it wasn't half bad.

In the living room, she curled up on the sofa intending to read a chapter or two of the funny romance she was enjoying. She had started it weeks ago but had set it aside because of her busy schedule. When she opened the book, a card fell out. Flat. No fold. Beautifully printed in navy and gold ink on a coffee-colored heavy stock.

Tabby and John's reception invitation.

In all the chaos of moving her business, she had almost forgotten. A week from this Saturday. At a fancy downtown hotel. There would be dancing and frivolity. Daley would be expected to bring a date.

She panicked. It couldn't be Tristan. It couldn't. At the wedding John had been upset that his brother and sister-in-law might be hooking up. If Daley and Tristan showed up together, their siblings would have questions. So many questions.

Tabby wasn't the kind of woman who endorsed recreational sex. Not that she would judge Daley. But she would worry.

Besides, Daley had worked hard to pretend the wedding weekend fling with Tristan had been a one-time lapse in judgment. If Daley showed up with Tristan, Tabby would know Daley had lied.

This called for preemptive action. It was still relatively early.

She grabbed her phone and sent a text to her friend who lived in the apartment two doors down. You awake?

Yeah. What's up?

I'm already in my jammies. Do you mind coming over for a minute?

When she answered the door, her neighbor raised an eyebrow. "Is there a bug you need me to kill?"

She laughed. "No. And besides, that's sexist."

"But true."

Six-foot-three Jared Perlman had skin like polished mahogany and worked as a pediatric surgeon at Emory. He was also gay, but that was a bit of personal information he didn't share widely. He was a very private man.

He and Daley had become acquainted when he moved in down the hall three years ago. She sometimes cooked for him after he'd worked a long, brutal shift. He was the big brother she never had.

He sat in her best chair, sighed and stretched. "What's the emergency?"

"How do you know it's an emergency?"

"It's almost ten. You're usually in bed by now."

She perched on the edge of the sofa and chewed her fingernail. "I need a decoy date," she said bluntly.

"Seriously?" He straightened, his gaze interested. "Why?"

"It's a long story."

"You invited me over here. I think I deserve to hear it. Especially if I'm going to be your straight man for an evening."

"That's a terrible joke," she said, scowling at him.

"But accurate?"

"I've met somebody," she said, trying to keep all emotion out of her voice. "But he's not an appropriate date for my sister's big wedding reception."

Jared stared. "Is he a male escort? A stripper? A drug kingpin?"

"Where would I meet a drug kingpin?"

Jared grinned. "But you thought the first two were feasible?"

"This is serious," Daley wailed. "Tristan is Tabby's new brother-in-law. She and John have both warned me he's *unsuitable*. I'm guessing Tristan will suggest he and I go together to the reception. I won't be able to say no to him. That's why I need you."

"As a decoy date."

"Do you mind?" she asked anxiously. "I know this is a big ask."

"So you're sleeping with this guy, but you can't be seen in public with him?"

"Something like that..." She rubbed her temple. "I think I've decided not to see him anymore. It's a dead-end relationship."

"You *think* you've decided?"

"I'm pretty sure I have. It's the smart thing to do. But I have to get through this reception thing first."

"Without succumbing to his manly charms."

She nodded glumly. "He's very persuasive, and I'm very susceptible."

"Okay, kiddo. I'll do it."

"You own a tux, right? For all those hospital fund-raisers?"

"Yes, ma'am."

She handed him the invitation. "You keep this. I already know all the details." She paused. "You'll be impressed. He's a lot like you."

Jared's smile quirked. "In what way?"

"Charming. Super handsome. Brilliant. In fact, he was premed until his uncle coaxed him into the family business. Actually, Harold is Jason's and Tristan's godfather. They're not related at all."

"So what does this guy do if he's not a doctor?"

"He's the CEO of Lieberman and Dunn."

Jared frowned. "The company that bought you out?"

"Yes."

"This sounds fishy as hell. Sure, I'll go with you, Daley. The guy must be a sleazebag. I'll protect you."

"It's not like that," she protested. "He's a decent, wonderful person. But he doesn't do relationships, and I don't want to fall for him."

Jared studied her face. "Is it already too late?"

"No, of course not," she lied. "We've had some fun, but he hasn't tried to mislead me. If anything, I'm the one who escalated things. Now I simply have to back off."

"I hope you know what you're doing."

"I don't think I do," she said wistfully. "I may regret pushing him away. But even Tabby and John have warned me not to get involved."

"Any man can change if he finds the love of his life."

"Says who?"

Jared shrugged. "I don't know. Seems like something you wanted to hear."

"It doesn't matter," she said, keeping her tone light. "He's fun in bed, but I'm at a point in my life where concentrating on my career is the thing to do. Mr. Dunn believes in me. I want to prove to everyone that he made the right choice."

"A job won't keep you warm at night."

"Says the workaholic."

Jared grinned as he got to his feet. "My work gives me something I've never found in a romantic relationship. It matters. I literally save kids' lives sometimes. If that's the only thing I ever accomplish in my life, it will be enough."

Daley followed him to the door. "I can't argue with that. All I do is find new ways to sell cookies or life insurance or dance lessons."

He stood in the hall and smiled at her. "I'll study this guy when we're at the reception. Sizing up strangers is one of my superpowers."

"What if I run into him at the office in the meantime?"

"Sounds like you'd better come up with a plan. 'Cause if you don't avoid him, I guess I'll be getting dumped."

"You won't. I swear. My plan is not to see him at all between now and the reception. That way, he can't suggest we go together."

"How big *is* this office?" Jared asked, his expression dubious.

"Oh, hush," she said. "You're making me nervous. Tristan and I work in different suites. This plan will work. I'm sure of it."

Jared waved as he headed for his apartment. "Good luck."

When she went back inside and locked her door, she saw her phone on an end table where she had left it. As she picked it up, it dinged.

Thanks again for the food.

Those five words seemed threatening. How should she respond? Did he think she was infatuated with him? Did he think they were going to pick up where they left off?

She didn't answer at first. Let him think she was busy. After turning out all the lights, she brushed her teeth and got ready for bed. It was too late to read now. Besides, with every guilty glance at that unanswered text, she found herself less and less sleepy.

This was dumb. She had to take a stand.

Before she could change her mind, she answered Tristan's text with a thumbs-up emoji. Then she set her phone to Do Not Disturb and closed her eyes.

Nine

Tristan returned to work Thursday morning feeling almost a hundred percent. His instinct was to drop by Daley's new office space, but he knew he couldn't. For several reasons. In addition to not getting further involved with her, he faced a backlog of emails and tasks that awaited his attention.

Sometimes being the boss was not fun at all.

He found several excuses to wander down the hall where Daley and her team were now located. But he didn't catch so much as a glimpse of her. He met a couple of her staff in the break room. They all seemed bright and enthusiastic and motivated.

But no Daley.

It's possible she was avoiding him. That would be the smart thing.

He shouldn't even be thinking about her.

At lunchtime, he met with a client. But it was the same restaurant where he had shared a meal with Daley. So his brain kept imagining her sitting across from him. That memory made him fidgety and compromised his focus.

When the meeting ended, he was ruefully aware he had lost a potential new account. The CEO of Lieberman and Dunn should have been embarrassed and mortified.

Perhaps he was both. But those emotions were buried beneath a layer of introspection that was as unexpected as it was uncomfortable.

When he returned to the office, he asked his executive assistant not to be disturbed. Then he locked his door and scrolled through his phone looking for a woman to call.

He needed a date tonight. Badly. Not for sex, although that wasn't an unreasonable expectation. But mostly because he needed to purge Daley Martin from his thoughts.

He narrowed his list to five. Then, because he didn't really want to *talk* to any of them, he composed a text.

Hey (insert name here). Are you interested in seeing the new Benedict Cumberbatch movie? I hear it's getting great reviews. I could pick you up tonight at seven...

The first problem was deciding which of the five to

bump to the top of the list. They were all nice women, from what he remembered. That was the *second* problem. He couldn't really remember any of them. At least not their faces. He knew one was a lawyer, another a tax accountant. The third might be a kindergarten teacher, though that didn't sound right. *Ah, hell.* What was he going to do?

He picked one of the names at random, added the phone number and felt the back of his neck prickle with unease.

This wouldn't be cheating on Daley. They *weren't* a couple.

But all he could see was the vulnerable, hurt look in her eyes when she told him about the man who had groped an unsuspecting twenty-four-year-old.

Tristan didn't want to be another guy who hurt her and gave her bad memories.

Quickly, he erased the text before he accidentally hit Send. While he was still stewing about his problems, a text from Harold popped up.

You got a minute for the old man? How about coming by my office for a drink?

Tristan frowned at his phone. That was odd. He and Harold often shared a drink after hours, but never at two in the afternoon. Something must be up.

When he made it to his godfather's office suite, the door was open.

"Come on in," Harold said. "Close the door behind you."

This was weird. Tristan took his usual seat at the corner of the desk. Harold poured himself a finger of whiskey. "You, son?"

Tristan refused with a smile. "A little early for me, Uncle Harold." The title was honorary. "What's up?"

Harold swirled the amber liquid in his cut-glass tumbler, his expression pensive. "I know you and I have talked about a succession plan…"

"Yes, sir."

"Well, the timeline may have to be accelerated."

Tristan sat up straighter, alarm coursing through his veins. "What do you mean?"

Harold shrugged, his expression pensive. "It seems I have a pesky little tumor in my lung. The doctor says my prognosis is good. But I'm facing surgery and chemo. I had hoped to work until the end of next year. But it looks like now may be the time to bow out."

Tristan leaned forward urgently. "I'll run things while you're getting treatment. No problem. But don't walk away prematurely, Harold. It's not necessary."

His godfather looked tired, his skin sallow. "I've made my peace with the diagnosis. Either I'll beat it, or I won't. But I want to leave Lieberman and Dunn in good hands. Everything I have will be yours and John's one day anyway. We'll get an evaluation of the business. I'll sell it to you for a nominal fee. And I'll give John a cash equivalent—whatever our finance people decide makes the best sense."

"But, Harold, I—"

Harold held up his hand, interrupting him. "Sorry, son. I've made up my mind. You'll be fine without me. But let's keep this between us for a few weeks."

"What about John?"

"You can talk to him. He knows how to keep a secret."

Tristan swallowed his misgivings. "You'll have my support every step of the way. You know that, I hope."

Harold nodded. "I do. And I appreciate it." He paused, taking another sip of his drink. "The only constant is change," he said. "I've come to a turn in the road. I hope it's not the end, but either way, I need to focus on my health. You've been running things admirably for years. The difference is, you'll own it all now. You deserve this chance to steer L&D in a modern direction."

"And if you get well?"

For the first time, Harold gave him a genuine smile. "If I get well, I'm going to learn how to play golf. Visit the Caribbean. Maybe find me a lady friend. I'll be okay, Tristan. And so will you."

When Tristan reached out to John suggesting dinner, his brother countered with an invitation to take the boat out on the lake. Tristan jumped at the chance. He left the office at four thirty, changed clothes at home and headed out the door.

When he arrived at John's house, he expected to find Tabby going along. But she was nowhere in sight.

"Where's your bride?" he asked.

John stowed a cooler in the trunk. "She's got a baby shower thing for one of her teacher friends. They're all going for mani-pedis, dinner and a movie. Hop in."

One thing Tristan always loved about road trips with his brother was having time to think. John opened the sunroof, cranked up the music and set off down the interstate. Neither of them had to say a word for fifty miles if they didn't want to...

Though Tristan still reeled from the news about Harold, he relished the heat and the sunshine. Summer baked his brain, reminding him of easier, more carefree days as a kid. Life as an adult was challenging. Sometimes good, sometimes bad. But never as simple as the days he and John had spent climbing trees, riding dirt bikes and staying out till dark.

In Tristan's mind, Harold was supposed to live forever. He didn't want to think about the grim possibilities. Losing the man who had been so good to him was unthinkable.

In a way, the situation with Daley felt eerily similar. She was in perfect health, but she mattered deeply to him, and he felt her slipping away.

His world was changing around him. He felt helpless. That remarkably unacceptable reaction was a jagged burr in his chest.

John kept his boat at a marina on a finger of Lake Lanier. They made it there by seven thirty. It was a perfect time of day. The simple routines of untying and easing away from the dock were familiar. Tristan felt some of his stress slipping away.

After jetting across the water at high speed, John dropped anchor in a familiar small cove. He had brought worms and fishing tackle, but the exercise was more about habit and tradition than bringing home food.

The two of them baited their hooks, propped their poles in anchored holders and sat back to enjoy the view. The gentle slap of water against the hull of the swaying boat was hypnotic. Even at this hour, the heat was fierce.

John yawned. "Man, this is the life. If I tried, I might be able to retire at forty or forty-five."

Tristan raised an eyebrow. "Is that what you want? I thought you were the driven one of the two of us."

His brother snickered. "Where do you think I learned it?" He swatted a fly from his face. "No, seriously. I've spent five years learning how to make money for myself and other people. I love the challenge, but having Tabby in my life has changed me. I don't want to live at the office for fifty or sixty hours a week."

"You mentioned a baby shower. Does Tabby have baby fever?"

"We both do," John said, smiling. "And it may be sooner than later. The only thing holding us back is the intensity of my workload. She doesn't want to be a single parent, and I can't blame her. Besides, if I have a kid, I want to be an all-in dad."

Tristan marveled inwardly how life's twists and turns sometimes spilled out into a pattern no one ever saw coming. "Well," he said. "I have news—

news that may affect your future plans." He proceeded to tell John the medical update Harold had shared earlier in the day.

His brother frowned. "I hate to hear that. Do you think he's covering up how bad things really are?"

"I have no idea." Tristan shrugged. "Somehow, I thought he'd go on for another decade at least. It's shaken me up, to be honest."

"He's eighty-five. Did you really imagine him working for ten more years?"

"Maybe I didn't want to think about it," Tristan said. His throat was tight, and his stomach churned. "He wants to sell me the business for a nominal price. Give you a comparable cash gift. Right now."

John was visibly shocked. "Wow. I don't know what to say. He's always been generous with us. But you don't look happy about this development. What's the problem? Other than worrying about his health?"

Tristan stood and stretched, surveying other boats at a distance. "I thought I had time to think about things."

"What kinds of things?"

"About whether I want to buy Lieberman and Dunn, for one. As CEO, I could walk away whenever I wanted to. But if I'm the owner…" He trailed off, fearing he sounded like a spoiled prick.

John reached in the cooler, grabbed a beer and handed it over. "Deep breaths, buddy. No one can make you do anything. You took this job as an act of love. That doesn't mean it has to tie you up forever. It's not too late for med school."

Tristan snorted. "Yeah. It kinda is. Who would even let me in? I'd be forty before I was done. No, it's not that. I made my peace years ago with not becoming a doctor. I'm good at what I do. It may not be rocket science or saving the world, but it's the life I've chosen."

"Then what's the problem?" John frowned, staring at his brother as if trying to solve a puzzle. Slowly, his gaze sharpened. "This is about Daley, isn't it?"

Tristan hunched his shoulders, kicking a life jacket that had spilled out of the locker. "Maybe."

John stood and eased the throttle into gear, backing them away from shore. The steady drift could be treacherous. Best to stay in deep water.

Then he grabbed a bag of chips and opened it. "I'm guessing there's more to this relationship than you've let on to me and Tabby. Right?"

Tristan didn't like discussing Daley behind her back. It seemed disloyal. But John was his brother, and he trusted him. "You could say that. But it's not a relationship. We've both agreed we aren't interested in anything permanent."

"Apparently, the sex is incredible. Otherwise, you'd never be in such a tizzy."

"I'm not in a *tizzy*," Tristan grumbled. His brother knew how to push his buttons. "The problem is, Harold complicated things when he brought Daley's ad agency under the L&D umbrella. Right now, I can keep my distance. But if I'm the owner of the company, the dynamics get uncomfortable."

"Do you have feelings for her?" John asked quietly.

Tristan suddenly realized the limitations of a boat. Nowhere to pace. "No. Yes. I don't know." He ran his hands through his sweat-dampened hair. "She doesn't trust men very much. So I don't know how often she's dated—even though she's six years older than your new wife."

"Tabby says Daley has a habit of picking jerks."

"Ouch," Tristan muttered, his pride stung.

"She wasn't talking about you." He paused, his brow furrowed. "At least I don't think so. I never told her about the wedding tryst."

"Listen to you…using fancy words like *tryst*."

John wasn't bothered by his brother's sarcasm. "Maybe Daley told her the truth. I leaned on her to do that very thing."

"Then I imagine she did. Those two women are close."

"Closer than close. Sometimes I think they have some weird twin-like connection. It's uncanny."

The sun hung low on the horizon. Soon, they would have to head for the dock. The fish weren't biting.

Tristan knew this was his chance. He cleared his throat. "If I start something with her and it goes south, work isn't the only problem. You and Tabby could get caught in the middle. And honestly, I don't know how good I'd be as a boyfriend."

John's gaze seemed to see through Tristan. Painfully. "Why would you say that? I think you're a decent chap." He grinned, clearly trying to lighten the mood.

"I'm used to going my own way," Tristan said. "I'm stubborn. I'm probably selfish. And hell, John, I don't know how to do any of that romantic stuff women like."

"That doesn't explain why you've never slept alone unless you want to. You're a hunk, Tristan. Even I can see that. You give off this aura of danger and bad-boy vibes. I don't know if you do it on purpose, but it seems to work."

Tristan sank down on the cushioned bench and dropped his head in his hands. "I'm so screwed. And FYI, you're not helping."

"What do you want me to say? I don't know what Daley sees in you. I don't even know if she has any interest in you aside from your body. But damn, man, take a shot if you want to. As soon as Harold gives you the all-clear, tell Daley the truth. Surely the two of you can come up with ground rules for the office."

Tristan nodded slowly. "I guess." He thought back to earlier this week when Daley showed up at his house. Had her gesture been motivated by simple kindness, or was she as drawn to him as he was to her?

Maybe neither of them had wanted or expected this. Maybe it was nothing but sex. But Tristan had to find out.

He frowned suddenly. "Wait a minute. I thought you wanted me to stay away from her. You were afraid of upsetting your wife."

John shrugged. "So sue me. I changed my mind. Any woman who can tie you up in knots is a woman who might be a keeper. Tabby and I have talked about your *situation*. She basically told me to mind my own business because Daley is a mature, sensible woman who can make her own decisions."

"I see."

"Don't be mad, big brother. My lovely wife and I have only your best interests at heart. I want you to be happy. As happy as I am."

Tristan scowled. "Why is it that newlyweds always try to drag everyone else into marital bliss?"

"Don't knock it until you try it."

John's smirk was almost enough to make Tristan regret the boat trip.

But not quite.

He sat in the bow of the boat and eyed the glass-like surface of the lake. The dying rays of the sun painted the water with soft color. "It's almost dark," he said. "Shouldn't we get back? Won't Tabby be expecting you?"

John raised the anchor. "Yep." He started the engine. "And to be very clear, I don't want to be late."

Tristan went home to his quiet empty house with an uncomfortable image of his brother's smug anticipation. Tabby had been waiting on them when they got back. She'd bubbled over with all the fun she had with her friends.

When she hugged Tristan's neck, he realized anew how nice it was to have a sister.

But now he was on his own again and wondering if a thirty-two-year-old man wanted more out of life than a series of superficial relationships. To be honest, the women in his past could scarcely be called *relationships*. More like recreational partners.

What did that say about him?

At work the next morning, he came up with a plan. Number one: ask Harold's permission to share his news with Daley. Number two: get her thoughts on the matter. Number three: invite her to be his date for Tabby and John's wedding reception in a week.

It made sense. In fact, Daley might have already assumed they were going together. In an odd kind of way, they were unrelated relatives now.

He waited until the office cleared out. It was Friday afternoon. Few people lingered past the stroke of five. Tristan had studied Daley's pattern enough already to know that she liked half an hour to herself at the end of the day to tidy her desk and make notes for the following morning.

A five fifteen, when he strolled downstairs, he found her doing exactly that. The door to the suite of offices was open. He knocked anyway. Daley's office was in the far corner, but she was in the reception area where she entertained prospective clients.

She looked up when she heard him. The smile on her face was equal parts polite courtesy and caution. "Hi, Tristan. How are you feeling?"

"Almost back to normal. May I come in?"

She nodded. "Of course."

The lobby was outfitted with two love seats and a collection of armchairs flanking a large coffee table. He chose one of the chairs and sat down with a sigh.

"How was your week? Are you and your people settling in?"

"We are," she said, taking a seat across the table from him. "Everyone here has been very welcoming."

"Good," he said.

An uncomfortable silence crept in between them.

Daley folded her hands in her lap, her gaze sliding past him. "Is there something wrong, or is this a social visit?"

She was palpably nervous. Did she think he was going to suggest hooking up this evening? The thought short-circuited his brain and hardened everything in his body. But first things first.

"I have some news," he said quietly. "Harold has given me permission to share it with you, but the situation is confidential for now. He's asked that neither you nor I talk about it to anyone else in the building. Not until he's ready."

"My lips are sealed."

Her words were lighthearted, but he saw anxiety in her eyes. "I don't mean to be dramatic," he said.

"Tristan," she said, her tone exasperated. "We're alone here. What's going on? Tell me before I expire of curiosity."

It was hard to say out loud. "Harold has cancer. I don't know how bad. He was cagey with the details."

Daley leaned forward in concern. "I am so sorry. I know how much he means to you and John. You can trust me, Tristan. I won't say a word. I understand his wanting to be private about personal health issues."

"It's more than that. He says he's done."

"Done with what?"

"The company. I tried to tell him I'd keep things running while he's out for a few months, but he says it's time for me to take over."

"How do you feel about that?" she asked quietly.

"You want the truth?"

"Yes, please."

"I'm not ready. I always thought about buying L&D as something down the road. I've been the CEO, but this will be different. I'll be tied down."

"And you never really wanted the job to begin with."

Her wry understanding soothed some of his angst. "He wants to sell it to me for a pittance and give John an equivalent cash gift. Basically, doling out an inheritance—though he swears to me it's a *small* tumor. Damn it, Daley. I'm not ready for any of this. Losing him. Taking over L&D. But this will involve you, which is why he gave me a dispensation to loop you in on the details."

"How will it involve me?" she asked quietly. "Are you planning to cancel my contract as soon as he's gone?"

"Of course not."

"Then what's the problem?"

"Right now, you and I don't have any direct working relationship. Won't it be uncomfortable for you if I own the company?"

"I don't think it has to be. You have the same options Harold laid out originally. During the first year, you can kick me to the curb if you think the collaboration isn't working."

"And if we're sleeping together?"

Her cheeks turned pink. "Don't be ridiculous."

His temper heated. "How is that ridiculous? Anytime we're in ten feet of each other, we end up in bed."

"That will burn itself out," she said calmly.

"You're so sure of that?" He wanted to prove her wrong. But this was their place of business, and he wasn't going to do anything to cause her emotional discomfort or pain.

"I don't know what you want me to say," she said. "I am a professional. I assume you are, too. We'll observe boundaries. If necessary."

He gave her a tight smile. "It *will* be necessary."

She lifted her chin. "Maybe." She glanced at her watch. "I should probably get home. I could stay here for three more hours finding things to do, but I'm trying to establish healthy work-life boundaries."

He grinned. "I know something about that struggle." He cleared his throat. "One more thing, and I'll let you go."

"Oh? What's that?"

"John and Tabby's party is next weekend."

"I haven't forgotten. Black tie. Very fancy."

"I wondered if you and I might go together."

As soon as he said the words, Daley went still. Like a rabbit trying not to be noticed.

"Um…" she said. "I appreciate the offer, but I have to pass."

His anger welled again. Was she deliberately trying to torment him? "Why?"

Daley stood, picked up her purse and backed toward the hall. "I already have a date."

Ten

Daley practically ran to her car. She had left Tristan in the building looking stunned and irritated. His jaw had literally dropped.

It was exactly the scenario she had hoped to avoid.

His invitation wasn't out of line. She had known this might happen.

What she hadn't expected was how guilty she felt about turning him down.

And how disappointed.

Thank goodness she had lined Jared up as her escort.

The next seven days crawled by. Her weekend was uneventful. Farmer's market. A bit of cooking for the upcoming week. Lounging by the pool at her apartment complex. Reading a good book.

Then Monday, it was back to work. She half expected Tristan to show up in her suite again…to try changing her mind. But he was nowhere to be seen.

For her part, she stayed in her back corner office with the door mostly closed. Work was her salvation. Otherwise, she'd be thinking about Tristan every minute of every day. It was aggravating to realize how much real estate he occupied in her brain.

She wasn't obsessed with him. Right? You could call it a healthy crush. A fluttery preoccupation with memories of their time together.

He had hinted at an ongoing *something* between them. It was sweet that he wanted to avoid awkwardness and that he cared enough to protect her from the situation.

But really, wasn't it all a moot point?

Daley was captivated with a man who could break her heart. And she had zero confidence in her ability to keep things platonic.

On Saturday, she took her time getting ready for the party, giving herself plenty of time to turn a Cinderella advertising exec into a princess. Or at the very least, a lady-in-waiting. Tabby and John had rented two huge adjoining ballrooms at one of downtown Atlanta's poshest and most exclusive hotels.

As small and intimate as their wedding had been, this occasion was all out. They had invited 350 friends, family members and work colleagues. According to Tabby, the RSVPs had flown in fast and furious. Something like ninety percent said yes.

The evening would begin with a lavish sit-down

dinner. Then everyone would adjourn to the next room for dancing.

The theme for tonight was *black-and-white ball*. The men, of course, would have no problem. Formal wear was easy. But as a fair-skinned blonde, Daley didn't look good in stark white. Plus, she was tired of black. She had found a beautiful dress in cream that would do. It was halter-necked, fitted at the waist and fanned out in a beautiful floor-length skirt.

The neckline and waist were adorned with sparkly beading. Although the design was mostly plain, the heavy damask silk-and-satin fabric took the dress to whole other level. It was a party dress. A grown-up dress.

It would also make her stand out. She wasn't sure how she felt about that. Her bare back and shoulders were lightly tanned. Her hair cooperated as she twisted it up in a complicated chignon. When she stepped into the dress and zipped it up, she stared into the full-length mirror in her closet.

Tonight was about Tabby and John, of course. But Daley was the maid of honor, and she looked forward to this chance to socialize in a way she seldom did.

Jared rang her doorbell at six thirty on the dot.

He smiled when he saw her. "Wow, Daley. Smokin' hot."

"Thanks. You're looking handsome yourself."

He bowed. "Anything for a lady running from love."

"It's not love," she insisted. "Only sex."

He gave her a knowing look. "Whatever helps you sleep at night."

Twenty minutes later, Jared parked his Mercedes in the hotel garage and held her arm as they took the elevator to the fifth floor, where the ballrooms were located.

She gripped his sleeve. "I'm nervous," she said, lingering in the hall and trying to breathe. "I don't like lying."

"How are you lying, Daley? I *am* your date. We may not be involved in a romantic relationship, but we're friends. I'm sure we're not the only people present tonight who have a platonic arrangement."

"Maybe."

"Quit worrying."

She had arrived half an hour early to greet her sister and help make sure any last details were ready. "We should go in," Daley said. "Before I lose my nerve and run home."

It was a joke. Of course, she wouldn't miss this special evening.

If only she could avoid Tristan.

As she and Jared entered the ballroom, Tristan was the first person she spotted. His commanding physicality made him hard to miss. He was standing with John and Tabby, studying the large silver fountain filled with champagne.

Daley forced her feet to move. Jared was a comforting presence at her elbow.

Tabby saw them and beamed. "You made it," she

said, hurrying over to greet them. "I was starting to get worried." John and Tristan stood behind her.

"Sorry, sis," Daley said. "We got caught in traffic. You remember Jared, right?"

Tabby took both his hands. "Of course. Thanks for coming. It's been a while, but John and I have never forgotten that chocolate cream pie you brought to Daley's potluck."

Jared's easy smile was warm. "I can't take credit. My mother cooked that. She spoils me."

John drew Tristan into the little circle. "Tristan, this is Daley's neighbor, Jared Perlman. He's a pediatric surgeon at Emory. Jared, this is my brother, Tristan. He's the CEO of the Lieberman and Dunn ad agency."

The two men shook hands.

Daley told herself she was imagining a weird tension between the five adults. Had Tristan not brought a companion? That seemed unlikely.

Tristan didn't appear in the least intimidated by Daley's faux date. Nor was he overly friendly. "Nice to meet you, Jared." Then he kissed Daley's cheek casually and smiled a warm, intimate smile that made her stomach turn somersaults. "You look stunning, Daley."

His masculine scent made her insides quiver. "Thank you," she muttered, her throat dry.

Jared had a hand at her back. Maybe he thought she might bolt.

Daley tried to gather her wits. "What can we do to help, Tabby? Everything looks beautiful."

The round tables seated eight each. Tabby's centerpieces were artistically composed of white gardenias with dark green glossy foliage. The place settings were real china and crystal. No plastic plates and easily broken forks.

"I think everything is ready," Tabby said. "The hotel has been wonderful. John and I are going to stand in the hall and greet people as they arrive. But you three relax and make yourselves comfortable. Have a drink. I'm so glad you're here."

When the bride and groom walked away arm in arm, Daley stood alone, flanked by two alpha males. Both men were incredibly attractive. Both men were incredibly charming. Both men were intelligent and cultured and confident.

Suddenly, she panicked. Her face felt flushed, and her forehead was damp. "If you'll excuse me, I need to visit the ladies' room."

Tristan watched Daley cross the ballroom to a restroom on the opposite wall. In that ultrafeminine dress, she was temptation personified. The bare skin on display was tantalizingly smooth and warm. Tristan wanted nothing more than to take her into a quiet back hallway and kiss her until she admitted the guy she brought tonight was a blatant attempt to keep him at arms' length. It wasn't going to work.

He dragged his gaze back to her companion. "How long have you known Daley?" he asked, telling himself he wasn't a caveman. The need to fight for his woman was ludicrous but inescapable.

Jared Perlman's smile was calm and friendly. "Almost three years. She brought me cookies the day I moved in a few doors down the hall."

"I see." Tristan's gut churned. His intellect told him Daley wouldn't jump from one lover's bed to another. But this tall Black man with the build of an athlete and the engaging personality was undeniably perfect.

"She's a remarkable woman. Genuine. Kind. Talented," Jared said.

"I'm aware of Daley's finer qualities," Tristan said, trying not to grind his teeth.

Jared nodded. "Nice to meet you, Tristan. I'm going to grab a couple of champagne flutes before the crowd gets here."

Suddenly, Tristan stood alone. In moments, this room would be packed with people who knew and loved John and Tabby. People here to celebrate their marriage and congratulate them on achieving that most elusive of life's goals—finding a soulmate.

Tristan felt out of place and grumpy. The woman he wanted had brought another man to dance with, have dinner with, possibly go home with. But even as those negative thoughts stole his pleasure in the evening, he wondered.

Was Daley genuinely interested in Jared Perlman, or was she fighting the current that dragged her ever closer to Tristan and he to her?

He understood running scared. He'd known the first time he met her many months ago that she was a woman who could change his life. So he had kept his distance.

His life was great. No need for a change.

That didn't explain what happened during the wedding weekend and in the weeks since.

What if Daley was the one? Did he even believe in *the one*?

All the same problems remained. John and Tabby possibly getting dragged into the dangerous rapids of a volatile relationship between Tristan and Daley. Daley's new position at Lieberman and Dunn. The fact that Harold was bowing out and would no longer be a layer of separation between them.

Maybe Tristan should take this as a sign from the universe. Daley had a great guy in her life. A guy probably more suited to hearth and home than Tristan.

Perhaps he should let her go.

Daley finished her last bite of wedding cake and smiled. Tabby and John sure knew how to throw a party. The dinner was a smashing success. Laughter and conversation filled the large room.

Moments later, she and Jared joined the throng making its way into the adjoining ballroom for dancing. An eight-member band led by a female vocalist warmed up with a medley of familiar tunes.

Jared steered her to a quiet pocket near a crystal punch bowl. "How are you holding up, Ms. Martin? Your Tristan has been giving me dirty looks all evening."

"No, he hasn't," she muttered. "I think you're exaggerating."

Jared curled an arm around her shoulders. "Pretty sure I'm not. You wanna dance? I learned most of my moves from TikTok, but my niece says I'm not half bad."

Daley managed a smile. "Sure," she said. "That sounds like fun."

The dance floor was crowded already. Jared carved out a place for the two of them and slipped easily into the music. Daley did her best, but the upbeat tempo only made her feel sad. She wanted to go home, get into her pajamas and pretend she didn't know the tall, gorgeous, irritating Tristan Hamilton.

Why hadn't he brought a date tonight? According to John, Tristan knew any number of women willing to do his bidding. Surely one of them should be here pandering to his considerable ego.

Her petulant inner monologue embarrassed even her. Tristan wasn't so bad. Not at all. Why had she gone to such convoluted lengths to make him think she didn't want to spend time with him?

The truth was humiliating.

She was scared. Scared to be vulnerable. Scared of getting hurt.

When the dance ended, Jared took her hand and led her off the floor. "May I make a suggestion, Daley?"

"Of course."

He grimaced. "Why don't I leave so you can patch things up with your brooding boyfriend?"

"He's not my boyfriend. And why would you leave?"

"Because I think you made a mistake. You and Tristan should probably be here together. Any man who makes you so hot and bothered is worth your time. I like him, Daley. Why don't you give him a chance?"

She was torn between yearning and dread. "I don't know that he wants to spend the evening with me."

Jared kissed her cheek and squeezed both her hands. "Surely, you're not that blind. The man has tracked our movements the entire evening. And he doesn't look happy. Despite this festive occasion."

Daley took a deep breath. "I would feel bad ditching you." Already, her subconscious had embraced his suggestion.

"I've had a great dinner. I danced with a beautiful woman. I'm more than happy to head home. I went in to work at 5:00 a.m. this morning. Believe me, I wouldn't mind going to bed at a decent hour."

She searched his face. "You're a very nice man, Jared Perlman."

He smiled at her. "You can reward me with a home-cooked meal one night soon."

"Done. I'll walk you to the door."

"No need." He shoved his hands in his pockets. "Don't be afraid, Daley. Once upon a time, I let fear and uncertainty cost me a relationship when I was in grad school. I've always regretted it. I don't want that for you."

She nibbled the edge of her fingernail. "I know you're right. It's terrifying, though—you know?"

"Tabby and John made it happen," he said.

"But they're perfect for each other." She grimaced. "That doesn't mean the rest of us will be so lucky."

"Is it luck or something else?" he asked. "Things like working hard at a relationship. Choosing vulnerability over protecting the status quo. Maybe Tabby and John are not so different from the rest of us."

"I hadn't thought of it that way. I've always assumed it was easy for my sister to fall in love with such a great guy."

"Is that what Tabby told you?"

"No. We never really discussed it."

"Probably because she's loyal to her husband and chooses to keep the bumps in their relationship private. You could ask her, though. Not tonight, obviously. But if you really want a chance with Tristan, Tabby might have some insight."

"Maybe. But she's already warned me that he doesn't do *permanent*."

"So change his mind. I've seen you in action. Goal-oriented. Focused. He won't know what hit him."

"Very funny. I don't want a man who has to be cajoled or trapped into a relationship. He should fall at my feet and express his devotion."

Jared chuckled. "I hope you're not serious."

"No. I'm not." She glanced across the ballroom, trying to spot the man in question. "Thanks for bringing me tonight."

"My pleasure. I'll be in touch."

When Jared exited, Daley grabbed a glass of champagne from a passing waiter and watched the dancers. She wanted to go home, too. But that meant saying goodbye to Tabby. Her sister would assume something was wrong.

It was easier to stay and smile. In another hour, her exit wouldn't seem remarkable.

A deep voice came from behind her shoulder. "I didn't expect to see you being a wallflower."

She whirled around. "Tristan…" Her heart pounded. How had he sneaked up on her? "You scared me to death." In formal clothes, he looked like the man at the wedding. The man who had made her throw caution to the wind.

He shrugged. "You were lost in thought. Is something wrong?"

"Wrong? No. I enjoy people-watching."

"Where's your date?"

Daley panicked. "He's on call. Had to head back to the hospital." The lie stuck in her throat, but she wasn't ready for this. For Tristan. She hadn't decided how or if she was going to pursue an inconvenient attraction.

"I see." His expression was completely unreadable. A blank slate. Concealing his emotions. "Would you like to dance?"

The band had settled into a dreamier, more romantic mood. Slow dances. Poignant lyrics. Perfect for a late-night rendezvous.

"Yes," she said. "I would."

He took her hand in his and drew her out onto the dance floor. The crowd was less dense than at the beginning of the evening, but there were still enough people to preclude private conversations.

That was a good thing.

Tristan pulled her into his arms and held her with that masculine confidence she so wistfully admired. He was sure of himself. Relaxed. At ease.

Daley, on the other hand, was a mess. When his big warm hand settled at her back, she let him bring her close. To an outsider, they were perfectly matched.

"You aren't being very kind," he said. His breath was warm against her ear.

She stiffened. "I don't know what you mean."

He brushed her hair from her cheek. "It's bad form to outshine the bride. You're literally the most dazzling woman in the room tonight."

"Don't be absurd." His over-the-top compliment rattled her.

"I'm only speaking the truth. Why does that bother you?"

"I've already slept with you, Tristan. You don't have to do this."

"You're the prickliest damn woman I've ever met," he muttered. "I'm not your enemy, Daley."

She exhaled, sagged against him and felt his arms tighten to hold her up. "I'm sorry," she said. "Thank you for the compliment."

"Not a compliment. Merely a statement of fact."

"Maybe we should just dance," she said quietly. "That way we won't get in trouble."

He laughed softly and took her at her word.

The room faded away as they moved across the

floor. She loved the feeling of lightness, of synchron-icity. As if this moment were always destined to hap-pen.

Tristan made her happy. Maybe that was why he scared her. To know such quiet peace when she was with him and yet at the same time to realize the ephemeral nature of their relationship was a pain-fully impossible conundrum.

Tonight, he had come to this party alone. Why? She was afraid to ask him.

She rested her cheek against his shoulder and let the music envelop her. Tristan's familiar scent im-printed on her brain. Not only that, but the feel of his big taut body. The knowledge that he was aroused from holding her and dancing with her.

What did it all mean?

Love seemed such an intimidating word. Maybe it was simpler than she expected. Maybe she needed Tristan, and he somehow needed her. Could that ex-plain their explosive sexual connection?

All her adult life, she had felt a little bit broken. As if she weren't a woman who believed in fairy tales and thus would never find her Prince Charming.

Who wanted a prince, anyway?

Daley much preferred the fallen angel. The naughty sinner. Tristan Hamilton, rogue and lover.

She lost track of the music as it changed and changed again. Had they danced through two or four songs? Or half a dozen? She was dizzy. Weak. And yet filled with exhilaration. Could Tristan feel how fast her heart raced? Did he know he was seducing her without even trying?

When the band took a break, Daley was forced to return to earth. The air wasn't scented with wildflowers. It was overly perfumed. With notes of sweat and liquor.

Even the white tulle and fairy lights someone had hung overhead—once so enchanting—now looked commonplace.

"I'm thirsty," she said. "Let's get something to drink."

"Of course." Tristan put his arm around her waist as they crossed the room.

"How long were you planning to stay?" she asked, not looking at him.

He waited until they were off the dance floor before he pulled her to a halt beside the refreshment table. "I think that depends on you."

Her eyes widened. His seemed to telegraph a message. "Oh?" she said.

His lips twitched in a small smile that still had enough power to weaken her knees. "Well, since your *friend* is out of the picture, I thought we could go back to my place."

"To watch a movie?" Her gaze settled on his tanned throat where his white shirt collar peeked out over his tux jacket.

"No, Daley Martin. To let me fully appreciate that gorgeous dress before I remove it and take you to bed. Is that something that interests you?"

The magic was back. It washed over her and stole her breath.

"Yes," she said. She searched his face. "I would like that very much."

"Will I be stepping on any toes?"

She stared at him blankly. "Excuse me?"

"Your Jared person?"

Her face flamed. Embarrassment was not a pleasant experience. "He's only a friend," she said. "I invited him because I was scared of you. And me. And you and me together."

Tristan's frown was dark. "I'm trying to be angry with you, but I can't. Not when we're about to be in harmony for once."

"There's one more thing."

His eyes widened in alarm. "Do I want to hear this?"

She shrugged. "Jared didn't get called in to work. He volunteered to leave because he knows I'm interested in you, and you didn't bring a date tonight."

"Interested?" His gaze was hot.

"I'm fond of you," she clarified. She cupped his face in her hands. "I'm sorry I lied. I won't do it again."

He kissed her. Almost platonically. They were surrounded by witnesses. "I forgive you," he said, staring down at her and memorizing her features one by one. "Let's go home."

Eleven

Tristan's mood did a complete one-eighty. Daley wasn't in a relationship with the hunky doctor. She'd used him as a decoy. *Hot damn.*

Tristan handed her a glass of champagne and watched her drink it. "None for me. I'm driving," he said. The chilled water in crystal pitchers was exactly what he needed.

Daley drained her flute and set it aside. "If we're leaving, we should say goodbye to Tabby and John."

"Of course." He scanned the room. "They're dancing now. We'll catch them when they leave the floor."

"That works."

He pulled her close and stole another kiss. "This song has at least three more verses. Why don't we enjoy ourselves while we wait?"

A pink hue stained her cheeks. Big brown eyes studied him. "Sure," she said.

Any excuse to be closer to her. His patience was hanging by the merest of threads.

On the dance floor, he was obligated to hold her. Permitted to touch her. Encouraged to twirl her in a dizzying circle until her laughter sent a quiet burst of joy sliding through his veins.

He was almost disappointed when the song ended. Almost but not quite.

Daley wiggled out of his arms. "I'm going to grab them before they get involved in another conversation." Tristan followed her.

When Tabby saw them, she smiled. "You guys having fun?" Then clearly, she processed the fact that Daley had come with another man. Both eyebrows went up. Even John looked confused. Tabby eyed her sister. "Where's Jared?"

Tristan could see Daley was flummoxed. She wouldn't want to lie to her sister. But the truth was confidential. For now. "Jared was on call," he said. "Poor guy had to report to the hospital."

Tabby made a face. "That's too bad. I really like Jared."

Tristan stiffened. Whose side was Tabby on?

John must have noted Tristan's involuntary grimace. "Are you two headed out? Tabby and I will be staying until the bitter end."

"Because we want to," Tabby said, her tone exasperated. "I think my poor husband is partied out."

John held out his hands. "I'm having a great time.

But you can't blame me for wanting to take my bride home to bed."

Daley and Tristan laughed when Tabby blushed.

Tristan gave his brother's shoulder a playful punch. "How long are you going to play that newlywed card?"

"As long as I can." John kissed his wife's cheek. "As long as I can."

In the car, Tristan had a few second thoughts. "Do we need to swing by your place?" he said. "In case you want to spend the night?"

"Am I invited?" she asked, shooting him a sideways glance as he pulled out of the parking garage.

"Always," he said lightly.

"Then, yes. It won't take me long to grab a toothbrush."

Her incredibly matter-of-fact statement had him hard and aching. He'd had no clue if she would ever come to his bed again. And now this. Plus, she had said she was fond of him. What did that mean?

He cooled his heels in her living room while she gathered whatever she needed for a sleepover.

Suddenly, he bellowed down the hall. "Please don't change clothes."

When she appeared moments later with a small overnight case in her hand, she grinned. "I wasn't going to. If a man has a fantasy, who am I to mess that up?"

"Thank you," he said. "I like it when a woman knows who's boss."

She kissed his cheek, lingering to nibble his jaw

and lightly run her tongue across his lips. "I thought we agreed you're *not* my boss. Don't get cocky."

"Yes, ma'am." His body was in shock. Having Daley be so comfortable with expressing affection, so sweetly sensual, scrambled his brain.

The little witch knew exactly what she did to him. "I'm ready," she said.

He tucked her into his car with care, scooting her skirt out of the way and closing the door. The distance from her place to his was not bad. Twenty minutes at most. But the drive taxed his control.

At his house, things took an unexpected turn. As Tristan struggled to play host, Daley took matters out of his hands. "We don't need anything to eat or drink. I'm ready for that unveiling you promised me."

He shoved his hands in his pockets to keep them out of trouble as his libido battled with his sense of what was right. "It would be bad manners for me to jump you the moment we come inside."

She put both hands on his chest. "Screw manners. We both know what we want. I want *you*, Tristan."

He closed his eyes briefly. *Dear lord.* "Yes." He covered her hands with his. The croak of agreement was the only word he could squeeze past the lump in his throat. Unexpectedly, he saw that tonight was far more than one episode in a casual affair. This woman meant something to him. The searing revelation was as profound as it was terrifying.

He scooped her up in his arms. A glance in the foyer mirror showed him the graceful way her skirt spilled over his arm. Daley's gaze was locked on his face. A tiny smile curved her lips. She was like sunshine in his home.

How had he not recognized how very much he needed sunshine?

In the bedroom, he set her on her feet. The dress was not complicated. A small fastener at the nape of her neck was easily conquered. When he drew the bodice of the dress to her waist, he sucked in a sharp breath. Surely, he had known she wasn't wearing a bra. The design of the gown precluded one. But seeing her ivory skin and pink-tipped breasts was like getting whacked in the head with a baseball.

He felt dizzy and disoriented.

Daley reached for his hands and placed them on her body. He cupped lush curves and gently touched nipples that puckered beneath his fingers. "You make me ache," he muttered. "Every time it's like I'm seeing you fresh and new." He bent his head and kissed the valley of her cleavage. "I'm glad you came home with me."

Her hands cupped his head, ruffled his hair. "Me too."

The room was silent, too silent. He could hear himself breathe. The cadence was revealing. She had to know how desperately hungry he was. Music would have eased the moment, but it was too late now.

When he reached behind her to find the hook at her waist, she rested her cheek on his chest and sighed. "This is nice."

It wasn't the adjective he would have chosen, but the dreamy pleasure in her words was enough. Carefully, he lowered the zipper until she could step out of the voluminous skirt. He steadied her and set the dress aside on a chair. When he turned back, Daley had wrapped her arms around her breasts. She wore nothing but a pair of sexy undies—black lace—cut high at the leg and low at the waist.

Her posture and her gaze were wary.

"What's wrong?" he asked, frowning.

"Nothing. But I'm at a disadvantage. May I take over now?"

He held out his arms. "Be my guest."

Her expression was endearingly intent as she fumbled with the knot in his bow tie. When she finally had it free, she started in on the buttons of his shirt. He realized he was holding his breath. He tried to exhale without making it obvious.

Soon, she had him bare from the waist up. The air-conditioning in his house was plenty cool, but his skin was hot. Especially where she touched him.

When she managed to get his pants unzipped, his patience snapped. He backed away from her, ripped them down to his ankles and then had to hop around when everything got tangled up.

Daley had the audacity to giggle.

While he fumbled to free himself, she ditched her undies, crawled onto the bed and stretched out on her back, tucking her hands behind her head. The smug little smile on her face drove him crazy—urged him to work faster.

At last, he was free of the formal wear. And everything else.

He sprawled on top of her and buried his face in the curve of her shoulder, inhaling her light, tantalizing perfume. If it came down to a blind test, he was positive he could locate her in a dark room.

Between them, his erection pressed painfully.

He sighed. It was time for honesty. She deserved that. "Daley," he said.

"Hmm?" She played with his ear.

"When you told me you had a date for the party tonight, it nearly killed me. I wanted to punch somebody. For the first time, I realized I had feelings for you. Something different than anything I've had with anybody else. I'm sorry I didn't tell you that."

She shoved his shoulder, urging him off her so she could see his face as he rolled onto his side. Her gaze searched his eyes. "Tristan?"

"Yes, my sweet?"

"What if I wanted more from you than sex?"

His gut clenched. The snippet of alarm was a reflex, quickly gone. "Like what?"

"Companionship. Dating. A chance to see if we have anything beyond being great in bed. I like you a lot. At least I do when you're not tormenting me and deliberately driving me crazy. I'm not saying you're *the one*. But I've never wanted to explore the possibility with another guy. Not really. I'm putting you on the spot. I get that."

He put a hand over her mouth. "You're babbling, darlin'. The answer is yes."

When she bit his finger playfully, he jerked back. Her eyes widened with pleasant surprise. "It's that easy? I thought you'd point out our reservations about upsetting the people we love and the fact that we're now working together and that neither of us has any experience with commitment."

He shrugged. "All those things are true. I can't deny it. Plus, I can't predict the future. So we may be making the biggest mistake of our lives."

She reached to smooth his eyebrow with her thumb. "Yes. We might. But I have a feeling if that happens, you'll go down in history as my very favorite mistake."

"I think I'm insulted." He tried to look mad, but it was difficult with her hands all over his chest and her lips on his throat.

Daley climbed on top of him, bracing herself with her hands on his shoulders. "Make love to me, Tristan. I've waited all night for this."

He scowled. "Even when you were dancing with another man?"

"Especially then."

It was too much trouble to be mad at her. He couldn't do it. How could he be anything but exhilarated when he was about to push inside her and feel her body welcome his?

"I care about you, Daley," he said gruffly. The words didn't express the whole of what he felt, but he wanted to give her something. Something to bind them.

Her eyes warmed. "Ditto."

She wiggled her bottom until he was forced to take action. "Easy, woman." He entered her slowly.

"I think about this all the time," he admitted. "It's disconcerting. You did something to me at that wedding."

"All I did was ask for ice," she said, her expression innocent.

"You didn't ask. I offered. So *I* get credit."

"But *I* was the one who invited you into my room."

"Let's agree we had the same agenda." The conversation distracted him enough to draw out the pleasure. He pulled the pins from her hair and watched it tumble around her shoulders. She was sensuality personified. Reckless abandon. Glorious femininity.

And she was his…

The territorial thought came out of nowhere. He'd never wanted to claim a woman before. To take her off the market.

It didn't sound like him at all.

He should be worried. Scared.

But right now, all he could see was the look in her eyes when he surged deep. He experienced utter certainty that he had done the right thing.

Soon, the position made him want more. He rolled them over, putting her beneath him.

Daley wrapped her arms around his neck, gasping when he thrust hard.

He reared back, alarmed. "Too much?"

Her gaze was dreamy. "Not at all. I love your caveman moves."

Tristan gave her a fake scowl. "You're calling me a Neanderthal?" Frankly, she could call him anything she liked as long as she stayed in his bed.

"Nooo," she drawled, extending the syllable and toying with his nape.

Goose bumps erupted all over his body, though he wasn't cold in the slightest.

"Then what?" he demanded.

"You're two different men, I think. A cosmopolitan, suave businessman in public and a…"

"A what?"

Her cheeks turned pink. "A down and dirty guy in bed. You take what you want, but you make me like it."

Though they were as close as two people could be, her description bothered him. "I didn't realize I was *making* you do anything." His pride stung.

"I'm describing it wrong. What I'm trying to say is that I've never been very adventurous in the bedroom, but you make me want to be a bold woman. A femme fatale. You're so confident, I feel comfortable exploring my limits."

Suddenly, he wanted to come so badly his eyes crossed. "Your limits?" The two words came out barely audible.

"Yes," she said, sinking her fingernails into his shoulders. "Teach me, Obi-Wan."

That was it. He was gone. He crashed over the proverbial cliff, groaned and whispered her name as he came.

When he could breathe, he rolled to his hip, slid a hand between her legs and gave Daley the last little bit she needed to join him. She cried out and arched her back as she climaxed, her soft moan telling him everything he needed to know.

Exhaustion claimed him. He dragged her close, spooned her and fell asleep.

Daley had consumed too much late-in-the-evening champagne without food. Her stomach rumbled even as her heart sang. She'd broached a future with Tristan, and he hadn't freaked out. That was progress. Right?

She wanted to close her eyes and fade out. Having him hold her like this was blissful. But she needed to pee, and she wanted a snack.

Tristan was deeply asleep. His arm was a dead-weight around her waist.

Even so, inch by careful inch, she extricated herself without waking him. She used the bathroom, freshened up and found a terry robe on the back of a door.

The navy robe smelled liked Tristan. She bundled up in it, feeling the chill of the AC as she tiptoed out of the bedroom. Fortunately, she knew her way to the kitchen.

She didn't bother turning on a light. When she opened the refrigerator and peered inside, she found half a carton of fresh blueberries and a slab of cheddar cheese with a gourmet shop label. That would do.

On the counter, there was a loaf of homemade wheat bread. She paused a moment to wonder who supplied Tristan with such a treat. But then Daley reminded herself he had taken *her* home. There was no point being jealous of a man like Tristan Hamilton.

Either she believed he wanted her, or she didn't.

Judging by the last hour, he did.

She shivered, remembering all the ways he touched her. As if he couldn't get enough. And he'd admitted to having *feelings* for her. She suspected that was huge. Hearing him speak those words had been astonishing.

Her heart burst with hope and anticipation even as her brain told her to be cautious. This thing with Tristan was tenuous. Fragile. Maybe something would come of it and maybe not. She needed to protect herself.

When she opened a cabinet to find a plastic tumbler for water, a voice behind her startled her badly.

"Daley…"

She whirled around, her hand at her chest. "Don't do that," she cried. "You nearly gave me a heart attack."

"Sorry, love." He put his arms around her waist and slanted his mouth over hers for a long, thorough kiss. "I woke up and you were gone."

He wore nothing but snug black nylon briefs—which served the purpose of thoroughly distracting her. But she gathered her composure, barely. "I was hungry," she said. "Dinner was a long time ago."

Tristan glanced past her to the blueberries and cheese. "I think we can do better than that. How do bacon and eggs sound?"

"You cook?"

He pinched her cheek, grinning. "I do a lot of things you haven't seen yet. Why don't you have a seat at the bar and talk to me while I get everything ready."

"You don't want me to help?"

"I can't concentrate if you're too close."

The words were funny and sweet, but she debated their sincerity. Was there a standard script that men like Tristan used for romantic evenings? Had he cooked for a long line of women in his life?

Her own thoughts bothered her. If she didn't have confidence in this relationship, even on a superficial level, she was going to destroy things before they even got started.

She perched on a barstool and leaned her elbows on the counter, chin on her hands. It was fun watching her lover range around his own kitchen with purpose. He was clearly comfortable. His body flexed and moved with masculine grace. He was at the peak of his physical prowess. Sleek muscles. A taut frame. Not an ounce of excess weight anywhere. She knew he worked out.

Oddly, though, it wasn't his striking body that had won her over. Not that she hadn't noticed. But she was drawn to the way he cared about his brother and his uncle and now Tabby. Tristan Hamilton had a big heart and a generous nature.

Soon, Tristan's techie, modern kitchen was filled with the mouthwatering aroma of bacon. When there were a dozen crispy strips draining on a paper towel, Tristan whisked eggs in a bowl and added his own special touches. He dumped the lot into the same iron skillet and tended the mixture.

"You want coffee?" he asked.

"Not at this hour." It was after one o'clock. "I'll take juice or milk or both if you have them."

He nodded. "If you want to get butter and jelly out of the fridge, I'll slice some bread for toast. This is almost ready."

When they sat down together at the cozy table in his kitchen nook, Daley's stomach growled. She had been too nervous at dinner to eat everything. Then, with the dancing and the drama and, later, great sex, she was ravenous.

Tristan didn't tease her when she cleared her plate and reached for seconds.

They ate in companionable silence. She watched his hands. Long fingers lifting a knife. Buttering toast. Holding a glass.

She was in way over her head already, but she couldn't regret it. Being with Tristan made her happy. For the last few years, she'd poured her energy into her work.

Now, she wanted to concentrate on her personal life. Tabby's radiant joy was hard to miss. Daley wanted that same certainty, that same bliss.

A huge yawn caught up to her.

Tristan smiled. "We'd better get some sleep."

"Okay."

They stood and cleared the table together. Tristan wiped out the iron skillet with paper towels. "The rest of this can wait till the morning," he said.

He held her hand as they walked down the hall. When they were huddled together under the covers, he pulled her close. "So how do we go forward, Daley? I want to do what makes you happy."

She tried to clear the lump in her throat. "Maybe we should start small. I'll leave a few things here, and you feel free to do the same at my place. We can be together more, but not in each other's way."

He turned on his side and smoothed the hair from her cheek. "You don't think this is going to work, do you? Not in the long haul?"

Now, her throat was tight. "I want it to," she said honestly. "But I don't know. I think it's best if we take things slowly. Maybe a week at a time. If either of us changes our mind, we can go back to where we started."

"Sex with nothing else?"

"Um, no. I meant nothing at all."

"So you're saying we have great sex now, but if we suck at the relationship stuff, we lose the sex all together."

"Something like that."

"Whew. You're tough."

"Don't tease me. I'm trying to be sensible."

"And what about the public part of us as a couple?"

"Maybe we keep that on the down-low. You know. Because of work."

"If that's what you want."

He sounded resigned or grim or something. They had turned out the lights, so she couldn't be sure.

"I want to be with you," she said, rubbing her hand along his bare flank. Despite the hour, she felt a buzz of excitement. "In every way."

"Does that mean now?" he asked, the words husky with a volatile mix of fatigue and arousal.

She consigned her doubts to a dark compartment deep in her mind. "Yes," she said. "Definitely yes."

Twelve

Daley was mortified when she stirred Sunday morning and realized they had slept until almost eleven. In fact, Tristan was still out cold.

They had fooled around again just before dawn. Tristan had been focused and hungry, but so very sweet. His lavish compliments and genuine pleasure began to convince her that maybe he wanted this chance as much as she did.

While she was in the shower, Tabby and John texted, separately of course, to invite them out for an afternoon on the boat.

Tristan shared the news, buck naked and beautiful, as he stretched his arms toward the ceiling. His gorgeous eyes were hooded, his hair a mess. "What do you think? Are you up for a few hours on the lake?"

"Sounds like fun," she said, trying not to stare at his semi-erect sex. The man was a machine.

He caught her watching him and smirked. "See something you like, Daley? All you need to do is ask."

She lifted her chin. "I'm all clean now. You missed your window."

He tackled her to the bed, chuckling when she screeched and threw her arms around his neck. "To hell with windows, my sweet. You're mine. I thought we agreed to those parameters last night."

She inhaled sharply as her world turned crystal clear for one shining moment. "Yes," she said. "But don't forget—that works both ways. If I text you for a booty call, I'll expect your full cooperation."

Tristan blinked. A flush rode high on his cheekbones. "What if I'm busy at work? What if I'm not in the mood?"

"Priorities, Tristan. Priorities."

They were almost late meeting Tabby and John. After finally getting dressed and out the door, they had to stop by Daley's apartment so she could change into shorts, a bikini top and sandals, and grab plenty of sunscreen.

Then they hit the road.

They had debated riding in John's car, but at the last minute decided to meet the other two at the lake.

While the men prepped the boat, Tabby, wearing a large sun hat, quizzed her sister. "You and Tristan look awful cozy. I take it last night went well?"

Daley tried not to blush. "You could say that."

She paused, having a hard time putting words together. Fortunately, her sister was patient. "Tristan and I have decided to give this relationship a chance," Daley said quietly, glancing across the dock to make sure they weren't being overheard.

"That's awesome!" Tabby did a little jig in her white Keds. "I've never seen him take things so far with a woman. At least not since I've known him. He really likes you, Daley. And why the heck not? You're amazing."

"Thanks for the cheerleading." Daley grinned wryly. "But to be honest, days like today are why I was reluctant to do this. What happens to our social life if Tristan and I fizzle? Or, even worse, blow up in a nuclear-level meltdown?"

"Don't be such a pessimist. Sit back. Enjoy yourself. You don't have to have all the answers right now."

Daley did her best to take her sister's advice. There was a lot to be said for a lazy afternoon on the water. Though the boat wasn't huge, there was room for two deck chairs. The women commandeered those and let the men recline on the bench seats with ball caps over their faces.

It was a perfect day to doze and enjoy the best of a Georgia summer.

Though they had plenty of snacks and drinks, by six o'clock, everyone was getting hungry for a real meal. Back at the dock, they unloaded and agreed to meet at a small local restaurant not far away.

The menu was limited, but the burgers and fries were legendary.

Tabby brought up the subject no one had addressed all day. "So tell me, Tristan. Are you going to buy the company? John said you're not sure."

Daley froze inwardly, uncertain whether she should be present for this family conversation. Tabby was a Hamilton now. Daley was not.

Tristan grimaced. "I'm *not* entirely sure. I've thought about it a lot since Harold talked to me. I'd be an ass to say no because he's essentially *giving* L&D to me. That's a hugely generous gesture on his part. He trusts me to do the right thing."

John frowned. "But you could sell it after he's gone, right?"

"Maybe." Tristan shrugged, his expression guarded. "Or maybe Daley and I could rebuild the brand from the ground up." He shot her a glance. "That's exciting to think about. All these years I've been content to let the old man call the shots. He's been good to me, and I haven't wanted to rock the boat. But if Lieberman and Dunn were truly mine, I would feel free to make changes without guilt. What do you think, Daley?"

She felt three pairs of eyes on her. "Um, well, I've barely gotten my feet wet, Tristan. I don't know that I'm qualified to help you make those kinds of decisions."

John clearly picked up on her unease. "You both have plenty of time to work through the details. It will take Harold several weeks at least to deal with the legal hoops. Besides, this is the weekend. Work can wait. Who wants ice cream?"

* * *

Tristan knew his impulsive comments about changing the agency had spooked Daley, but he wasn't sure why. She was mostly silent on the ride back to Atlanta.

They were almost back to the city when he broached the subject of her spending the night again.

She shook her head. "I'd love to," she said, "but tomorrow is Monday. I need at least a couple of hours with my laptop tonight to be ready for an important meeting. And if I stay at your place…well, you know what would happen."

"I do." He sighed, battling disappointment on multiple levels.

She reached across the console and touched his arm. "This weekend has been wonderful, Tristan. I'd love to play hooky, but my team is still getting settled. I need to be a hundred percent. People are counting on me. You understand that."

"I do," he said. "But I don't have to like it."

At her apartment, he walked her upstairs and kissed her at the door.

She gave him a small smile. "Good night, Tristan."

He felt a strong urge to close the deal. As if something important were slipping out of his grasp. "We have an agreement, Daley. No huge decisions. One week at a time. Or one day at a time if that works better for you. We're on the same team now."

Her lips quirked in a bigger smile. "And what team is that?"

"Team Boyfriend-Girlfriend. We can get this right if we try."

She snickered. "Aren't we a little old for those titles?"

"Team Significant Other?"

"That's better."

He leaned in and nipped her earlobe with his teeth. "That's so you don't forget about me, my sweet."

"As if I could." She cupped his face in her hands and gave him a quick kiss. "I'll see you around."

For Daley, the week that followed was a crash course in how to separate her emotions from her daily schedule. On Monday, Tuesday *and* Wednesday, Harold came by her office bringing new clients in tow. He made introductions, demonstrated his people skills and set things in motion. At this rate, she would have to hire more staff.

Tristan had gone into hiding again. She didn't know if that was because he juggled big decisions or if he was trying to respect her boundaries.

Either way, she missed him.

Thursday, Daley took the afternoon off to meet Tabby at her elementary classroom and begin setting up for the new school year. The teachers had been required to box up all their things in May because the building was painted from top to bottom as soon as the kids left for the summer.

Her sister looked frazzled when Daley found her. "You okay, Tabby?"

"I suppose." She threw up her hands. "They've moved all my stuff around. This is going to take forever."

"Not with me here to help. Where can I change clothes?"

Tabby pointed. "That's a girls' bathroom over there. You do *not* want to go in the boys' side." She shuddered.

Daley came back out moments later, laughing. "The toilets are so little. It's like being in Munchkinland."

"I could have sent you to the teacher's lounge, but I was afraid you'd get lost and not come back."

"I'm here for you, Mrs. Hamilton. By the way, you do know you need a new name plate for out in the hall, right?"

Suddenly, Tabby burst into tears.

Daley grabbed her up and hugged her, alarmed. "Hey. Easy. Sorry I said anything. The name plaque isn't important. We'll get this stuff done. No problem. Why don't I start moving the desks where you want them?"

"It's not that," Tabby wailed.

"Then what is it, sweetheart?"

Tabby was pale as milk. She glanced around the open classroom configuration to make sure no one was close by. "I think I'm pregnant. But it's too soon."

Daley beamed. "That's incredible, sweetheart. Congratulations."

"It's not incredible," Tabby insisted, looking defiant and scared. "Teachers are supposed to get pregnant in late June so they can go on maternity leave after state testing in the spring. But I think we slipped up the first night we got home from our honeymoon. We were so excited to be in our own bed that we—"

Daley covered her sister's mouth with her hand. "TMI, love. And besides, do you know how crazy you sound? No one can legislate due dates."

"It's not a law," Tabby said sulkily. "But it might as well be."

"What does John think?"

The tears flowed again, Tabby's expression several notches beyond distressed. "He doesn't know yet. I'm afraid to tell him. He's been trying to make changes at work so that his schedule is more conducive to fatherhood."

"You're not having a baby tomorrow. There's time." She hugged her sister again, marveling that little Tabby had taken a huge step beyond Daley. "Congratulations, hon. I think it's probably the hormones making you upset, right? Everything is going to be okay, I swear. We'll get this classroom whipped into shape, and then you can go home and tell your sweet husband the good news."

Finally, Tabby quit crying and found a roll of paper towels to wash her face. When she was calm, the two of them came up with a system.

Daley insisted on moving all the furniture. "You put names on workbooks and label cubbies. I don't want you getting all tired and sweaty."

"Yes, ma'am." Tabby's smile was tremulous, but at least it was a smile.

They worked in tandem for two and a half hours. When it was almost time for the custodial staff to lock up the building, Tabby's room wasn't finished, but it was a lot closer than it had been that morning.

Daley straightened a poster on the wall and glanced at her sister, who was filling the drawers of her teacher desk with supplies. "Tabby?"

"Hmm?"

"May I ask you a personal question?"

Her sister's head snapped up. "Of course."

"Was it easy falling in love with John? Did you see it coming, I mean? From early on? Or was it a struggle?" Daley knew they had been set up on a blind date by mutual friends and that there had been a considerable gap between the first date and the next.

Tabby was no fool. She had to know the context of Daley's query. But she didn't pry. Instead, she answered, "Oh, no. It wasn't easy at all. He and I had almost nothing in common. I work with children all day, and he manages huge portfolios worth millions of dollars. At first, I was sure we wouldn't have a thing to talk about."

"What were your biggest struggles?"

Tabby shrugged. "Time. He stood me up once, early on, and that was almost it for me. I'm not a diva. I don't demand slavish loyalty. But I certainly wanted a man who cared enough to be with me and to respect me."

"What happened after that night?"

"I made it clear his behavior was unacceptable. But the truth is, Daley, I had to do some changing, too. John's work requires a lot of social functions.

I tried to bow out of those for months. I was sure his clients would see me as a boring public school teacher. I had a chip on my shoulder. And you remember how shy I was for a long time. John insisted on making me admit there was more to me than my job. He wouldn't let me fade into the background. We argued a lot. But the making up was fun."

"And then?"

Her sister's smile was wistful. "There came a day I just knew. I saw him walking up the driveway to pick me up one evening, and it hit me hard. I was head over heels in love with him. Those feelings scared me so badly."

"But everything turned out the way it was supposed to in the end."

"It's true. I'm a very lucky woman."

Daley didn't press any more. She had a lot to think about. John and Tabby were proof of the old maxim "opposites attract." But if that were the case, then maybe Daley and Tristan's similarities made them a bad bet.

Her head ached from trying to logically analyze her love life. Maybe that was the bigger problem. Love defied logic.

Daley and Tabby were gathering their things—preparing to leave—when a surprise awaited them. John showed up carrying a fancy new swivel chair with a red bow. "I brought my bride a back-to-school-gift," he said.

Almost predictably, Tabby burst into tears again. The panic on John's face was painful to see. He shot Daley a stunned, questioning glance. "What's going on?"

"I'll step into the hall," Daley said quietly. She squeezed her sister's arm. "No worries, Tabby. This is a good day, I promise."

Half an hour later, all three of them walked out into the sunshine. John insisted on carrying his small wife's voluminous purse and had one arm tucked solicitously around Tabby's waist.

Daley opened her car door and smiled. "I'm happy for you guys. This is exciting."

Tabby still seemed unsure, but Daley had a hunch John would be able to change her mood.

He grinned hugely. "Thanks, Daley. And thanks for helping with the classroom. I know Tabby appreciates it."

Tabby yawned, looking dead on her feet. "I do," she said. "Bye, love."

Friday morning, Tristan waltzed into Daley's office as if it were the most natural thing in the world. She didn't close the door. That would look suspicious. But she lowered her voice, her eyes wide with shock. "What are you doing here?" she said. "Didn't we agree to keep things under the radar at work?"

He grinned, perching on the corner of her desk. "I thought we should take the kids out to dinner tonight to celebrate their big news."

"Oh." She sighed with relief. "So not a date. Just a platonic family celebration. I get it. Yes. That sounds perfect. Have you asked them?"

"I called a little while ago. They're both on board. What do you think about Rélajate over on Ponce? It's a new place. Upscale. Linen tablecloths."

"Sounds good. But what if I'd had plans?"

He cocked his head, his smile fading. "It's Friday. I assumed my *significant other* might want to spend the weekend with me."

"That's fair." She tapped a pencil on her desk. Her blotter pad was covered in doodles. "May I ask you a work-related question, Mr. Hamilton?"

"Knock yourself out."

"Last Sunday when we went out on the boat with Tabby and John, why did you say that stuff about me helping steer the company in a new direction with you?"

He stood and shoved his hands in his pockets. The door was open. They were still speaking in hushed tones. Anyone walking by would assume the conversation was general and not confidential. But Daley was keenly aware this exchange encompassed many layers of personal.

Tristan's expression had turned grim. "Because I meant it. It makes perfect sense. We each have areas of expertise that complement the other."

"But you're assuming a lot."

"Such as?" One masculine eyebrow went up. She saw a hint of the arrogant Tristan Hamilton who was accustomed to ruling his domain.

"You know what I mean. I think you're deliberately sugarcoating this. We can work together in a meaningful way, or we can have a personal relationship. I don't think both are a possibility."

His shook his head slowly. "You have a lot of rules in your life, don't you, Daley? Little boxes and columns and categories? I was thinking big picture. Imagining a future where we both get emotionally invested in Lieberman and Dunn. Silly me, I thought you'd be pleased. But apparently you only have room in your life for a single version of you and me."

He was irritated. That much was clear.

Her hands fisted in her lap as her stomach clenched. "I'm not saying it *couldn't* happen, but what about taking things slowly?"

Now his blue eyes flashed with frustration. "I sincerely doubt any relationship between us can work if you're always going to be standing on the sidelines so you can have a clear shot at the exit doors."

"That's not fair," she said. The knot in her throat was a grapefruit now.

"Isn't it?" He glared. "You've doubted me from the beginning, and yes, I get it. For good reason. I'm not a poster boy for commitment. But how can you expect that from me when you're barely willing to dip a toe in the water?" He ran his hands through his hair, ruffling perfection. "At some point, we have to trust each other."

The pent-up annoyance in his voice and the escalation in volume told her all she needed to know about his mood.

She'd been hiding behind her desk. Now, she stood and closed the door. "I'm sorry," she said quietly. "You're right. I've been holding back because I don't want you to hurt me." She shrugged. "Maybe that makes me a coward. I don't know."

He crossed his arms over his chest. Some of the tension left his body when she apologized. But his stance was still braced and wary. He grimaced. "Was this our first official fight?"

"Haven't we been fighting in some way or another ever since we met?" Her words were rueful.

"Have you ever wondered if we clash because we're both a lot alike?"

"How so?"

Tristan shook his head slowly. "We're ambitious. We're focused when it come to our careers. We love and respect family. But we both think we're better off alone—though we're trying hard to believe otherwise."

She stared at him. "That's very insightful, Tristan. Not necessarily flattering, but insightful."

He held out his hand. "Truce?"

Daley went to him and laid her head on his shoulder. "More than a truce," she said. "A promise. I choose you. No exit doors. No sidelines."

He exhaled sharply, his arms coming around her to hold her tight. "I want to kiss you, but I can't. Not here."

She stepped away from him, though it was the last thing she wanted to do. "We have the weekend," she said.

He stared at her, his gaze hot. "Will you spend the night with me, Daley? Or can I come to your place?"

"I like your house a lot. I'll pack a bag and leave it in your trunk. What time will you pick me up?"

"How about six? I made a reservation for six thirty. John and Tabby are going to meet us there."

The conversation was suddenly pedestrian, though undercurrents still swirled.

Daley wanted him badly, and she sensed he felt the same. But that was the problem they faced. Boundaries at work.

"You should go," she said softly. "Before one of us cracks. I'm not feeling very adult and responsible right now."

He heaved a sigh. "Me either." He paused. "What did you think when Tabby told you she's pregnant?"

"I was thrilled. But she's not there yet, emotionwise. Apparently, this was an accident. An accelerated timetable. She's feeling unsteady on her feet in more ways than one."

"John will settle her. He's over the moon."

"I guess this aunt and uncle gig is going to be sooner than we thought."

Tristan nodded. "It's a little surreal right now. The whole pregnancy thing is scary. I feel for my brother. He's going to need nerves of steel. So many things can go wrong."

"They won't. Surely. Tabby is healthy and strong."

"Life can change in a heartbeat."

"Are you thinking about your mother?"

He seemed shocked that she would bring it up. "I thought she was going to die, Daley. I was a kid.

And I thought my mom was going to die. I can still remember what that felt like. Sheer, abject terror."

"But she's fine now."

"Yeah."

"Bad things happen," she said, "in everybody's family. But that's the exception. We're going to support John and Tabby through this pregnancy, and it's going to be great."

He pulled her close and kissed her hard. "Everything is going to be great, Daley. Everything."

Thirteen

Daley thought about her conversation with Tristan a long time that afternoon while juggling her to-do list. He seemed truly worried about Tabby.

Too worried? That was hard to say. Childhood traumas could be long-lasting and life-altering. He'd wanted to be a doctor because of his mother's illness. Now, he was afraid for his sister-in-law.

Hopefully, when things settled down, he would see that uneventful pregnancies were the norm. Miscarriages happened. Yes. But there was no reason for alarm.

Still, something about Tristan's unease kept Daley unsettled.

Did this mean he would never want kids?

And there she was again. Back at the beginning.

Wondering if she should even be part of this relationship.

But now, she *had* committed. She'd said very clearly that she chose him. No more keeping the exits in view.

As she drove home that afternoon, she acknowledged her biggest fault. She *sucked* at living in the moment. No couple ever figured out everything in the beginning. It was dumb for Daley to feel like she had to have all the answers before giving her heart away.

That wasn't going to happen.

Either she trusted Tristan, or she didn't. If they came to a place where they both wanted different things in life, maybe they could part as friends.

When he showed up at her door at six and swooped in for a deep, wonderful kiss, she knew the friend thing was a nonstarter. Tristan was hers. She adored him. He had stolen her heart when she wasn't looking.

If they ever parted over irreconcilable differences, she would be a mess.

Because the evening was a celebration, she knew she needed to focus on Tabby and John and keep her romantic uncertainties in the background. That was hard with Tristan constantly touching her. Nothing overt or embarrassing. Just subtle, affectionate caresses that made her squirm with longing to be alone with him.

But first, the reason for the evening.

Tabby looked better than she had yesterday, more

at peace certainly. But nausea was giving her fits. She managed half her dinner as John hovered.

Daley lifted her glass. "Let's toast to this baby." Three of them had pinot. Tabby's goblet was filled with plain tap water and ice.

Tristan smiled. "Or better yet, a toast to the new mom and dad. May you always be as happy as you are now. And may this little baby bring endless joy to your home."

John chuckled when his wife's eyes leaked tears. "I should buy stock in tissues," he said ruefully.

Tabby nodded. "I'm an emotional mess. Please tell me this part will get better soon. I used to cry at sappy movies. Now I'm a wreck when I see a boring car commercial. This is not how I thought I would feel."

"You'll be fine," Daley said, laughing sympathetically. Then she shot Tristan a questioning look. He nodded. "We're so excited for you guys," she said. "Tristan and I want to buy your nursery furniture when you're ready. As a way of saying thank-you for all the happiness you two have brought to our lives."

Now Tabby really lost it. Daley mouthed, *I'm sorry*, to her brother-in-law. "Let me take her to the ladies' room and get her dried up. We'll be back."

Tristan watched Daley walk away and realized he was in so deep there was no way out—even if he wanted to find one. He could hardly wait to have her alone tonight. He was in love with her.

The knowledge should have been calm and peaceful. Satisfying. And maybe it was all those things. But it also scared the shit out of him.

John touched his arm. "Have you told her how you feel?" he asked quietly, his expression sympathetic.

"Not in so many words." Tristan grimaced. "She knows I care."

"Why are you holding back?"

Tristan didn't have a good answer for that question, so he took another tack. "How are you going to bear it?" he asked in all seriousness. "Having Tabby pregnant and knowing all the things that could go wrong. Isn't it terrifying?"

John's gaze held a maturity that Tristan might not be able to match. "It's terrifying every day," John said. "Being married to her. Responsible for her. Loving her. Knowing the world is not always a safe place. But I don't have another choice. She's part of me now. My breath. My heart. She's made everything better, Tris. I can't even describe it. Honestly, I don't know what I did to deserve such happiness."

"And if life isn't always happy?"

"We'll face it together." John leaned back in his chair and stared at his brother with a gaze that saw too much. "Is this about Mom?"

Was Tristan really so transparent to everyone around him? "I suppose it might be," he said, feeling sulky and ridiculous. He was a grown-ass man. This wasn't a very macho conversation to be having with his brother, or any guy for that matter. He felt like he was losing control. Of his life. Of the situation at work. Of everything.

John finished his wine and poked at what was left of his cinnamon donut dessert. "We both went through hell with Mom. Dad did, too. But in some ways, you took the brunt of it. I was too little to understand it all. Dad was too wrapped up in helping her get through treatment. But you, Tristan, you carried the emotional weight. She used to ask you to sing to her. Do you remember that?"

"Of course I do. It was the only way she could fall asleep in the afternoons when she needed rest so badly. I watched her slipping away, and I hated it. I didn't want to love her anymore because it hurt so much."

"And that made you feel guilty and helpless."

"Yeah."

John sat up and leaned forward, his expression urgent. "You've got to get a handle on this. Before it interferes between you and Daley. You've shut yourself off from the deepest part of life because you think having surface relationships with women will protect you. But Daley has made it past your defenses. I can see it. You know it's true."

"So you're insinuating I need to see a shrink."

"It's not a bad idea. But no. Not necessarily. I do think you need to ask yourself if it's better to be alone and not deal with *any* emotions or to take a chance and go all in with how you feel about her."

"I'm being ridiculous, aren't I?" Tristan said, looking at John helplessly.

"Our feelings are our feelings. We're stuck with them. But look at the facts. Mom is still with us.

Tabby is going to have a good pregnancy. Daley seems to care about you despite all the odds."

"Very funny."

Before John could throw any more verbal punches, the women returned to the table.

The men stood.

John kissed her cheek. "Better, my love?"

"Yes. But I'm flat-out tired. This has been great. Thank you both for dinner."

Daley kissed Tabby's cheek. "Go to your nice bed and get some rest, little mama. We'll have lots more time for partying."

John rolled his eyes. "At least until this kid gets here."

Tristan noticed that his brother didn't look at all upset about the prospect of a curtailed social life.

In the parking lot, they said their goodbyes.

When John and Tabby pulled away, Tristan looked over the hood of the car at Daley. "You ready to go home?"

Her smile hit him in the gut. "I am," she said. "I've looked forward to it all day. My *significant other* has been on my mind."

"I'm gonna be on more than your mind," he muttered. "A week is too long, Daley. And I guess you're going to sputter and wring your hands if I suggest moving in together."

Her jaw dropped. Her cheeks turned pink. "How much have you had to drink?"

"One glass of wine. Not even all of it. I'm dead sober. I don't like having to be apart for days at a time."

"Wow. Okay. Maybe we can talk about this later."

"After sex?"

She smiled. "Sure."

He tucked her in the car, leaning in to kiss the side of her neck beneath her ear. "I'm going to make us both very, very happy," he whispered.

It was interesting that Daley didn't have a thing to say on the ride home. He knew he had shocked her. Hell, he had shocked himself.

By the time they made it into his driveway, he had a painful erection.

He grabbed her suitcase out of the trunk and unlocked the front door. "Do you need to freshen up?" he asked, trying to be accommodating.

Daley stared at him, her brown-eyed gaze searching his face. "No."

"Good." He dropped the suitcase in the foyer, took Daley's hand and dragged her down the hall. "I don't think I remembered to make my bed this morning."

"I don't care."

"Let's get you out of this," he said, untying the little straps at her shoulders.

She was wearing a pink sundress and gold sandals. He had her naked in no time and decided he was too revved to wait for her to return the honors. When he stripped down and faced her, Daley licked her lips.

"Somebody is in a hurry," she teased.

"I'll slow down when we get to the good parts." The promise was ragged but heartfelt.

Daley came closer and wrapped her arms around

his neck. Now they were pressed together, delightfully so. "It's all good parts," she said.

When he kissed her, it was like sliding into a dream. The kind of dream a man had when he'd been on his own too long. Daley was everything he wanted. She smelled good, she tasted good, and the feel of her in his arms was like Christmas morning.

He flipped back the covers and eased her onto the bed, coming down beside her, trying not to break the connection even for a moment.

Her body was warm and curvy and welcoming. When he touched her intimately, she arched her back. "Don't tease," she begged. "Do it now."

Though he tried to breathe, his words came out on a wheeze. "What about foreplay?"

"Later," she said, wrapping her fingers around his sex and using her thumb to torment him.

A better man would have resisted temptation. Tristan never claimed to be a saint. When he entered her, they both murmured each other's name. He smiled down at her. "You're so damn cute it ought to be against the law. Luring fine, upstanding men to their doom."

Daley squeezed him with inner muscles. "You don't seem to be complaining."

"Not with you here like this. No complaints ever."

He moved in her slowly, pleasing them both. Trying to let her know how he felt. At the back of his mind, uncomfortable questions lingered. He shoved them away. Tonight was not the moment for introspection. He had Daley in his house. In his arms. In his bed.

She came first this time. He followed.

His chest tightened when he heard her whisper, "I love you." It was easy to feign unconsciousness and pretend he didn't owe her an answer.

They slept for an hour, then started all over again.

Daley woke up Saturday morning feeling sore in all sorts of random places. She had never participated in a night quite like the one before.

Tristan had been insatiable. His need for her had made her hope—for perhaps the first time—that he was serious about their relationship. If it was true, she was a happy woman.

The reference to moving in together might have been an impulsive comment. Did they know each other well enough for a step like that?

She wasn't going to worry about it now.

Things were going well. She didn't want to rock the boat. For now, she was content to spend time with him and see what unfolded.

By the time Tristan stumbled into the kitchen at ten, she had figured out his coffee maker. He mumbled something and grabbed a cup, filled it and then added sugar and cream. How did the man stay in such great shape?

She waited for the caffeine to kick in. As did he.

Eventually, his gaze cleared. "Good morning," he said.

She shook her head, bemused at his aura of debauchery and sexual satiation. "Good morning to you, too. You didn't have to get up."

"I didn't want to waste a minute of our day."

"Our day?" She frowned, confused. "I thought you were taking me home. I have lunch with my friends at noon."

"Cancel," he said, cajoling her. "Please."

She was very tempted. But something told her she needed to preserve her independence or risk being swallowed up by his forceful personality. "I'd love to stay all day," she said quietly, holding her cup to her lips and inhaling the aroma of expensive coffee. "But these are old friends, and we haven't been able to get together for a long time. I don't want to blow them off. Especially on such short notice."

"Fine," he grumbled. "But you'll come back later, right?"

"You and John are playing in a golf tournament at four."

She saw the moment it registered. He muttered a not-so-polite word and poured more coffee, gulping it down. "I can get out of it."

"It's for charity," she said. "The children's hospital. Remember? Plus, it's going to be great weather to be outside."

"Screw that," he said, looking grumpy and disgusted and way too frustrated considering how many times they had made love.

Deeming that he had consumed enough coffee to be reasonable, she crossed the kitchen and wrapped her arms around his waist. When she pressed her cheek to the spot just over his heart, his T-shirt smelled like laundry detergent.

"We have all the time in the world, Tristan. I'm not going anywhere."

"Except home to your apartment," he said, looking fierce. "How about tonight and tomorrow?"

"I'll make a deal with you. Let me contemplate your surprising offer. Assuming you were serious."

"I'm serious," he said.

"If we're going to cohabitate for any length of time, I want to think about stuff I'll need over here. And whether I should bounce back and forth. What schedule might work. Those kinds of things."

"Do you ever throw caution to the wind?"

"Not often," she said, shrugging with the admission. Tabby's wedding had been a particularly memorable exception.

He kissed the top of her head and then palmed her breast. "Monday night, Daley. What do you think?"

"I thought you were giving me time to think about it."

"Forty-eight hours seems fair. Tell me that works for you."

"Maybe. Probably. I suppose I could have a couple of boxes ready."

He cupped her ass and dragged her closer still, letting her feel his arousal. "We'll make it work. This arrangement will give us more time together."

"I can't argue with that."

"Good," he said. "Then it's settled."

* * *

Tristan was worthless for the rest of the weekend. He played golf with John. Had dinner with buddies afterward. Spent much of the day Sunday emptying drawers and freeing up closet space.

Once he had left college and the collection of roommates he'd shared rooms with over four years, he had never again lived with another adult. Male *or* female.

He had always enjoyed his privacy.

If he chose to watch four straight hours of baseball or blast music from his expensive speakers, there had been no one to protest. Carryout was acceptable. Every night if he wanted. His once-a-month-housekeeper wasn't intrusive. In between times, he wasn't a slob. His domain had for years been comfortable, solitary and perfect.

Until Daley.

Now he could think of nothing else but coming home *to* her or *with* her at the end of a busy day and screwing their brains out.

He knew that was a fantasy. They both had friends and family and professional commitments. She wasn't his exclusively. But she was going to be under his roof. That was a start.

Monday, he got to the office early and dove into work. For three hours he plowed through phone messages, dealt with a mountain of emails and finally managed to get his inbox under control.

He and Daley hadn't spoken since she left Saturday morning. That was okay. She had asked for time and space to think about his offer. He didn't want to spook her. If he read the situation correctly, she wanted what he wanted.

They had texted back and forth at odd hours. Nothing important. Mostly at night. He had found himself lying in bed with an urgent need to connect with her. Even via something as impersonal and un-satisfying as a text.

At eleven thirty, he started to get hungry. Skip-ping breakfast hadn't been a good idea. Maybe Har-old would like to grab lunch.

Their offices were only a few yards apart in a wood-paneled, carpeted hallway. Perhaps the decor was something Tristan would change sooner than later. Appearances mattered. If he was going to mod-ernize L&D, he might start with remodeling the two floors they rented. Install light hardwood. Change everything to brighter colors.

He was only steps away from his uncle's door when he heard Mildred, Harold's executive assis-tant, cry out.

Tristan broke into a run, knowing instinctively something was wrong.

When he burst through the door, Mildred was kneeling beside his godfather. She shot him a pan-icked glance. "He keeled over," she said. "No warn-ing."

Tristan dropped to his knees as well. "Call 911."

He shook Harold, trying to rouse him. The old man's skin was ashen, his face sweaty. Try as he might, Tristan couldn't tell if he was breathing. And no detectable pulse. Tristan shoved back the nerves and the fear and began CPR. He'd been recertified only three months ago.

The next minutes passed in an agonizingly slow blur. He did compressions over and over and over until his arms and his back ached. Every few minutes he paused to check for any change. But there was none.

Random fractured prayers bounced inside his head.

At some level, he recognized that people were in the room with him. Their presence didn't matter until other people with uniforms began to arrive.

As the professionals used oximeters and oxygen masks and injections, Tristan continued his dogged drive to sustain life. He couldn't stop. Harold couldn't die. Not like this.

Eventually, a grizzled EMT knelt beside him. The man put a hand on Tristan's shoulder. "That's enough, son. He's gone. I'm sorry. You did everything right."

Tristan couldn't stop. If he did, the world would fall apart.

Two men physically restrained him. Lifted him to his feet.

While Tristan watched, woozy from shock and exertion, the team of medics loaded the body onto a gurney.

Time stood still. A medical examiner showed up. Pronounced time of death.

And then the body was taken away.

L&D's chief operating officer was a woman in her

fifties. Her eyes were red-rimmed as she stared at Tristan.

He cleared his throat. "Shut the offices, please. Tell everyone to go home. I'll communicate via email about arrangements."

Tristan was Harold's power of attorney. He knew Harold had a DNR, though it wouldn't have mattered today. It was over.

Slowly, the room emptied.

The only person left was Daley. When she came to hug him, he eluded her. "I have to deal with things," he said. "Excuse me."

He saw the startled surprise on her face. But he couldn't bear to have her touch him. Not now.

Daley stepped back, giving him physical space. But she didn't leave. "Let me get you a bottle of water," she said quietly. "You're in shock, Tristan."

"I'm fine." The two words were audibly impatient. He shouldn't use that tone with her. She was only trying to help.

"You're not fine. I've called John. He should be here shortly. And he's letting your father know. Please come to your office and sit down. Just for a moment."

"I don't need a babysitter," he snarled.

To her credit, Daley didn't react. She didn't even flinch.

Again, she came to him. This time he didn't step away.

Her arms tightened around his waist. She hugged him tightly. "I am so very sorry," she whispered.

Tristan was horrified to feel his eyes sting and burn

as tears welled from a place deep inside his soul. "He was like another grandfather to me," he croaked. "More than that, really. A dear friend. A mentor. He taught me everything. Gave me confidence. Opportunity. A solid career."

"He was very proud of you," she whispered.

Daley's comfort and support were an indulgence he couldn't afford. "I can't do this," he said curtly, shoving her away. "The offices are closing, Daley. Go home."

Fourteen

Tristan was not in a good place. He had carried out his duties. Made all the funeral arrangements. Dealt with immediate work crises. But his grief was overwhelming. He'd never lost anyone close to him to death.

The time with his mother's illness had given him a taste of what it might be like. Now he knew the full extent. The what-ifs and the if-only feelings.

Tuesday evening, he and John had dinner together. John gazed at him with concern. "Clearly, Harold was closer to the end than he let on," John said. "Maybe he was never going to have chemo at all. Maybe the talk about selling the company was his way of telling us he was dying."

"Well, he picked a piss-poor way to communicate it," Tristan snapped. "He owed us the truth. He owed *me* the truth."

"And what if he didn't know?" John asked quietly. "What if his heart just stopped? It happens, Tristan."

Tristan put his head in his hands, feeling empty and wrecked. "Sonofabitch."

"Why don't you call Daley? Let her come over. You need someone."

"I don't need anybody," Tristan replied, though without heat. Things were all jumbled up in his head, but this much he knew. He and Daley were through. Maybe he loved her. Maybe he didn't. But he was never going to court this agonizing feeling of loss.

Harold was an old man who lived a great life. Losing him was still a blow.

What if Tristan kept Daley in his life and then lost *her*? It would destroy him.

It was better to be alone.

He'd known that instinctively for years and lived his life that way.

But Daley's sweet personality and sexy body had made him believe some things were worth the risk.

And yet, no. No risk was worth this pain.

They weren't a couple. That was for the best.

Daley thought she knew Tristan Hamilton very well. But she'd been wrong. Never had she expected this complete icing out from him. He'd made her invisible.

Tabby and John had tried to make excuses for

him. He was grief-stricken and feeling guilty that he couldn't save his honorary uncle.

But Daley saw it as more than that. It was at moments like this when people in love held on to each other, held each other up. Tristan had made it painfully clear he didn't love her or want her during this most emotionally draining time of his life.

He was coping on his own.

For the first two days, she told herself it was just his way. He would come around.

But then Tabby had to be the one to tell Daley she wasn't being seated with family at the funeral on Thursday. Daley took the hit stoically. Inside, she was crushed, but Tabby was emotionally and physically fragile right now. She didn't need to add Daley's heartbreak to her plate.

When Daley was alone, she cracked. Hours of crying did no good. The L&D offices were closed all week. She had nowhere to go, nothing to do.

Except wonder why she had let herself believe Tristan could ever care about a woman.

She attended the funeral. It would have been unbelievably rude not to. Despite Tristan's shortcomings, John and Tabby deserved her support.

Because she sat several rows behind and to the right, all she could see of Tristan was the back of his head. When he stood to deliver the eulogy, her chest ached so badly she thought she might be sick.

He looked terrible. Gaunt. Pale. Thinner.

His words were beautiful and came from the

heart. Clearly, he was capable of deep emotion. But not for a romantic partner. Not for her.

The burial in the churchyard was brief. John and Tabby had invited her back to their house for a small reception. She declined.

For twenty-four hours, she tried to be furious and indignant. She had let herself fall in love with a broken man. That was on her. Not him.

Yet no matter how much she wanted to hate Tristan and be angry and righteously indignant—all those things were true—she couldn't erase the image of his face in the church.

It was so clear to her now they had no future. She couldn't be with someone who would treat her with callous indifference. But love wasn't easily banished even when the other person had been cruel.

She had to try one more time to reach him. Not because she thought he might love her in return or that they might reconcile, but because despite everything, she cared about him.

After a run to the grocery store Friday afternoon, she put together a homemade lasagna, a crisp fresh salad and bakery rolls. She packaged it all in disposable containers and loaded it in the trunk before she changed her mind.

Tristan's car was in his driveway. She had thought it probably would be.

When she rang the bell, he answered immediately, though he didn't invite her in.

"Why are you here?" he asked, the words emotionless.

"I brought you dinner."

"Thank you."

"Can we talk a minute?" She hadn't meant to say that. Was she a self-destructive optimist?

He took the containers, set them inside the door but still didn't move out of the way. "I don't think so. There's not anything to say. I made a mistake. You're a very nice woman, but you and I don't have a future."

She agreed with him. Mostly. It was that pesky sliver of yearning that kept her feet where they were.

"Yet you asked me to move in," she reminded him tartly.

He winced. "That was my dick talking. I'm sorry, Daley."

"Sorry? That's it? Nothing else? I love you, Tristan. I think you know that."

He shrugged. "You'll get over it. I'm not a very nice person. You deserve better."

She was filled with trembling rage and fear and a suffocating certainty that she had no way at all to break through his deliberate wall of indifference.

"Do *you* love *me*?" she asked. Her throat was painful.

Blue eyes met hers. In them she finally saw unbelievable suffering. "It doesn't matter if I do or not," he muttered. "Goodbye, Daley."

Then he shut the door in her face.

Monday morning, the Lieberman and Dunn offices reopened. Clients had been understanding, but certain projects were time sensitive. Tristan had no choice but to take the helm.

The one thing he wanted more than anything else was to go to Daley's office and wrap his arms around her. Find comfort. Swallow the terrible knot of pain and regret in his throat.

Instead, he held on to his icy control and did what he had to do.

Harold's assistant was at her desk even before Tristan arrived at eight. He said a brief word to her and then went to his own office. This transition was going to be tricky. He didn't need two assistants. Perhaps Mildred would be amenable to an early retirement offer. She had worked with Harold Dunn for three decades. It was doubtful she'd be happy in any other capacity.

He sent that thought to the back burner and went on to more pressing matters, all the while wishing Daley might extend another olive branch. Why? Because he wanted her forgiveness even if they were done.

He knew that possibility was as likely as finding dinosaurs on Mars, so he kept his head down, and he worked.

Midmorning, he realized it wasn't enough to juggle his own projects. L&D was a big company. Obviously, there would be things Harold's death had left hanging.

Reluctantly, Tristan walked down the hall. He didn't want to go inside that office. He didn't want to see the spot where his friend and mentor had taken his last breath. But if Mildred had the balls to do it, surely Tristan owed her his support.

He crossed the threshold, paused and inhaled sharply. "How are you holding up, Mildred?"

Her eyes got teary, but she held it together. "I'm okay, Mr. Hamilton. He was a sweet man. I'm glad he didn't suffer."

"Yeah. Me too. Did you know he had advanced cancer?"

She grimaced. "I suspected as much. There were the occasional phone calls and voice mails. I didn't pry."

Tristan shook his head slowly, remembering that awful day. It had only been a week, but it seemed like longer. "I thought we had more time," he said.

Mildred's smile was wry and sympathetic. "Don't all of us think that? It's so hard to contemplate death. We gloss over it and assume the people we love will be with us forever. That's a natural human reaction, I think. You don't need to have any regrets. I'm old enough to be your mother, so I think I can say that. He loved you, and you honored him by taking the role he had for you at Lieberman and Dunn."

"Thank you," Tristan said. He cleared his throat. "Are there any of his matters that need my attention right away?"

"Just one," she said briskly, picking up a single sheet of paper from a stack. "Ms. Martin would like to exercise the escape clause. She mentioned that she signed a contract with Harold, and she doesn't feel comfortable continuing now that he's gone. All

I need you to do is initial this agreement, and I'll send it over to legal."

Tristan froze. He took the paper, but his vision was wonky. A scary haze hit, leaving him shaky and and confused. "Please ask her to come to my office right away," he said. "I'll take care of it."

He returned to his suite—asked his admin not to be disturbed once Daley Martin arrived. Then he took a seat behind his desk and waited.

When Daley burst through his door twenty minutes later, he could have sworn her hair was on fire. She was livid. "How dare you summon me here like a misbehaving child?" she hissed.

"Shut the door."

"Shut it yourself."

He had always thought of her brown eyes as beautiful pools of warm chocolate. Today they flayed him.

Because she refused to do his bidding, he rolled to his feet, calmly closed the door—despite his inner turmoil—and then had to pass by her a second time to reclaim his desk.

"Have a seat," he said, waving a hand at the small armchair near him.

"I'll stand." Her gaze was bitter. "This won't take long."

Suddenly, he saw himself through her eyes, and he was ashamed. Daley had more courage in her body than he had accumulated in a lifetime. Even though he had treated her badly, she'd brought him dinner Friday night.

But he had kept her standing outside. Refused to

accept her care and concern. Pretended what he felt for her was unimportant.

All his callous stupidity crashed down on him at once. He was an idiot and a fool.

There was more than one way to lose a person. Had he truly believed having her in the building would be enough for him? The occasional glimpse? A casual hello once a week? How was that supposed to make up for his lonely bed? His barren life?

The ice that had encased him for seven days began to melt, leaving him aching and raw. Finally, he was clear about what he had lost and what he stood to lose even now.

Harold was gone. No way to change that ending. But Daley was here with him still. Could he erase what he had done to her? Make up for his failings?

He had to try.

Because she wouldn't sit, he stood. "I'm sorry," he said. "I went a little crazy when Harold collapsed. At some level, his death meant I could lose you, too. I couldn't bear it."

Her mood didn't soften one iota. "So you thought it was better to suffer alone? You're an ass, Tristan Hamilton. Normal people *turn* to loved ones in a crisis." Her mask of anger flickered for a moment, allowing him to see how much he had hurt her. "But I forgot," she said. "You don't love me. You never did."

"You know I love you," he muttered, shoving his hands in his pockets.

Daley's gaze reflected heartbreak and resignation. "Actually, I know no such thing."

"It's true." He said it calmly. No amount of bluster would fix this. "I fell in love with you during Tabby and John's wedding weekend. But I didn't know what it was at first. I wrote off the way I felt to good sex and chemistry."

She stared at him in silence. "If that's the argument for your defense, then your college fiancée had it all wrong. Not a head of lettuce. You have the emotional awareness of a turnip, Tristan Hamilton. Don't try to sweet-talk me after the hell you've put me through. I'm not stupid. You're a flight risk. A bad bet. A hundred-to-one long shot."

He walked around the desk and faced her but at a careful distance. She was wearing a light summer dress today with a tiny pink cardigan. She stood in front of him as the image of hopes and dreams when he had lost all his. "You are the only woman I've ever loved," he said, forcing the words from a throat aching with pain and uncertainty. "It's why I was terrified, Daley. I don't know how to deal with that."

"Oh, Tristan." She collapsed in the chair and put her face in her hands. "I can't help you. I can't fix or protect the future. If that's the way you feel, we can't do this. Relationships mean vulnerability."

She was crying quietly. He reached a new low. Crouching beside her, he touched her knee. "I don't need you to fix anything. The truth is, this morning when Mildred said you were leaving, I had a blinding revelation. Losing you now would be unbearable. Even more dreadful than worrying about what might happen down the road. Don't leave me, my love. I swear I'll be the man you deserve."

They were eye to eye when she raised her head. With an unsteady hand, she ran her fingers through his hair. Her gaze searched his, looking for the truth. "Tristan…"

He grimaced. "I know it may require time for you to believe me, to forgive me. But I'll wait as long as it takes. I can't lose you."

An odd expression crossed her face. "You're the big boss now. I doubt you'll have time for soul-searching."

"Work comes second," he said firmly. "You're first. I swear." He kissed the back of her hand. "You changed my world, Daley. In every way. Forgive me for hurting you. This last week would have been so much easier with you by my side. I screwed up. Badly. Please give me another chance."

Her silence was so long, he began to sweat.

She shook her head slowly, her expression grave. "I want so much more from you than sex, Tristan," she said. "I want cuddling and shared secrets and watching TV together. I want to be your support here at work and your refuge at home. I need those same things from you. Plus babies, too. That's a big list. You have to be sure."

Fear dogged him, but he shoved it aside. He could do this. "You are everything I have ever wanted, Daley. Christmas and birthdays and all the celebrations wrapped up in one. I adore you. I'll spend my life proving to you that we're the perfect match. I am so sorry, sweetheart. For everything. Please tell me you'll find it in your heart to forgive me."

A giant sigh escaped her. She slipped to the rug and wrapped her arms around him. "I don't have much choice," she whispered. "I don't think I can live without you. I was a very happy single woman, but you've invaded every corner of my life."

"Is that entirely bad?" he asked, completely serious.

Daley lifted her lips to his. "Kiss me so I know this is real."

He held her tightly. The kiss started out reverently, thankfully. But the fire that burned so hotly between them sparked and flamed and soon they were both barely able to breathe. The wanting and the needing were searing and bright and perfect.

"I adore you, Daley," he said. "Marry me. Make babies with me. Grow old with me."

She pulled back, saw the certainty on his face and cried another tear or two. "Yes," she said. "I believe I will…"

* * * * *

Look for these other steamy romances from USA TODAY *bestselling author Janice Maynard!*

Return of the Rancher
The Comeback Heir
Staking a Claim

ONE STEAMY NIGHT & AN OFF-LIMITS MERGER
ONE STEAMY NIGHT
The Westmoreland Legacy • by Brenda Jackson
Nadia Novak thinks successful businessman Jaxon Ravnell is in town to pursue a business location. What she doesn't know is that he's also there to pursue *her*. Will Jaxon's plan to seduce the innocent beauty end with a proposal?

AN OFF-LIMITS MERGER
by Naima Simone
Socialite Tatum Haas is strictly off-limits. She's the daughter of the man Bran Holleran needs for his latest deal. But the passion between them can't be denied—even if it burns everything in its wake...

WORKING WITH HER CRUSH & A BET BETWEEN FRIENDS
WORKING WITH HER CRUSH
Dynasties: Willowvale • by Reese Ryan
Tech guru Kahlil Anderson plans to sell the horse farm he's just inherited. Not that he's confessing that to manager Andraya Walker. He has other plans for the sexy, determined beauty. But when Andraya learns the truth, will forgiveness be in *her* plan?

A BET BETWEEN FRIENDS
Dynasties: Willowvale • by Jules Bennett
When baseball star Mason Clark retreats to a dude ranch in Wyoming, he comes face-to-face with the best friend he left behind. Darcy Stephens has her own ambitions, which don't include an affair with Mason. Until one fiery kiss changes everything...

SECRET HEIR FOR CHRISTMAS & TEMPTED BY THE BOLLYWOOD STAR
SECRET HEIR FOR CHRISTMAS
Devereaux Inc. • by LaQuette
Actor Carter Jiménez lost his world to celebrity and now avoids it at all costs, protecting his daughter and his still-broken heart. Can billionaire Stephan Deveraux-Smith mend it? Or will the truth about his wealth and his family's public scandals be too much?

TEMPTED BY THE BOLLYWOOD STAR
by Sophia Singh Sasson
Bollywood star Saira Sethi has fame and fortune, but what she really wants is Mia Strome. Yet no matter how much explosive chemistry sizzles between them, will Mia risk her career for the woman who once broke her heart?

You can find more information on upcoming Harlequin titles,
free excerpts and more at Harlequin.com.

HARLEQUIN
PLUS

Try the best multimedia
subscription service for romance
readers like you!

Read, Watch and Play.

Experience the easiest way to get
the romance content you crave.

Start your **FREE TRIAL** at
www.harlequinplus.com/freetrial.